# THE DETECTIVE UP LATE

# BOOKS BY ADRIAN McKINTY

THE SEAN DUFFY SERIES

*The Cold Cold Ground*

*I Hear the Sirens in the Street*

*In the Morning I'll Be Gone*

*Gun Street Girl*

*Rain Dogs*

*Police at the Station and They Don't Look Friendly*

*The Detective Up Late*

THE MICHAEL FORSYTHE SERIES

*Dead I Well May Be*

*The Dead Yard*

*The Bloomsday Dead*

THE LIGHTHOUSE TRILOGY

*The Lighthouse Land*

*The Lighthouse War*

*The Lighthouse Keepers*

STANDALONE NOVELS

*Orange Rhymes with Everything*

*Hidden River*

*Fifty Grand*

*Deviant*

*Falling Glass*

*The Sun Is God*

*The Chain*

*The Island*

# ADRIAN McKINTY

## THE DETECTIVE UP LATE

**BLACK STONE**
PUBLISHING

Printed in the United States of America

First edition: 2023
ISBN 979-8-212-01900-2
Fiction / Mystery & Detective / General

Version 1

Blackstone Publishing
31 Mistletoe Rd.
Ashland, OR 97520

www.BlackstonePublishing.com

I offer you lean streets, desperate sunsets, the moon of
the jagged suburbs . . . I am trying to bribe you with
uncertainty, with danger, with defeat.
  —Jorge Luis Borges, "Two English Poems" (1934)

I'm the detective up late.
                    —Tom Waits, "Bad as Me" (2011)

# CONTENTS

# PRELUDE IN E-FLAT MAJOR: SEAN DUFFY, YEAR ZERO

Night coils above the eastern skyline.

An occult sun sinks into an alien sea.

The fog smells of rust and rot like an old bicycle.

The boat glides over the unseen water, its 25 cc engine barely turning the prop. "Belfast" in Irish means *river mouth*, and we are in the city's throat, where the river Lagan is smothered by the lough.

*Put, put, put* goes the little outboard. The constable at the prow is waving a xenon arc lamp back and forth as I steer the skiff through the grey twilight. Dusk is falling and it's not yet three in the afternoon.

We are on a body hunt. The girl was last seen loitering by the Queen's Bridge and is now nowhere to be found.

We glide over the opaque water, the surface hidden by a thin line of oil and a scum of weed. The yellow light of the lamp oscillates through the gloom, revealing nothing.

Constable Cathcart is a solemn, nervous young man and is not in the mood for conversation, which suits me fine.

From out here Belfast looks abandoned—land and water merging over the estuary. The city has a diluvian feel. It is a city of Doggerland or Heraklion or Atlantis. A flock of scolding herring gulls flies away from us and skids onto the greasy deck of HMS *Caroline*, a light cruiser dating from World War I that has been attached to its dock for so long that it's now the second-oldest commissioned vessel in the entire Royal Navy. (The oldest, of course, is HMS *Victory* in Portsmouth.)

The stillness deepens. The odour of decomposing wood floats across from the crumbling *Titanic* wharf. Belfast lurks there in the night, swathed in black silence, as taciturn and broody and gruff as its populace. Even the Gazelle helicopter that hovers continually over the Falls Road seems muted, tired and far away.

Calm the water is. Calm the heavens are. Calm the city is.

But underneath the surface of the discernible world is another world of kin struggle and blood feud and death. An older order of ancient laws and obligations, customs that go back to the footfall of the first men through the grasslands of the Great Rift Valley in Africa.

I steer the boat along the piers and jetties, everywhere I think a body might have washed up. Chip papers, newspapers, Coke cans, beer cans but nothing pertinent.

"I'm cold," Constable Cathcart finally says. "Can we go home now?"

He's asking me because although we are the same titular rank, I am the senior constable. And realistically all of this—the boat, the spotlight, the search—is only for form's sake. The tide's been ebbing for the last three hours, a body would be miles out to sea by now.

Still, returning so soon seems irreverent and unprofessional. "If you're cold, put the hood up on your parka," I tell him.

He obeys and the funnel hood restricts his field of vision to about thirty degrees in front of him.

I steer the nameless RUC dinghy into the deep-water channel.

An emerald sandpiper emerges from the murk with a crab wriggling in its mouth. It flies directly through the spotlight beam giving Cathcart a start. But the deep-water channel turns out to be far too choppy for the little boat and water starts coming over the gunwales. We're out here in our uniforms, sans lifejacket, and with our body armour on we'd sink like a stone if we went over the side.

I turn us around and head back into the harbour towards the Harland and Wolff shipyard where the tide and current might have carried a body onto one of the slipways. Lights are coming on and a mile south across the channel are the chalky outlines of towers and steeples.

We punt under the cranes, derricks and gantries. The ship looming in the dry dock is the SS *Ravenscraig*, a 950-foot long bulk carrier being built for British Steel. It'll be one of the last vessels H&W will make for anyone. Not anticipating the cruise ship boom of the nineties, the Tory government will let the shipyards in Belfast and the Clyde wither on the vine. Once a third of all the ships in the world were built here but within a decade that venerable tradition will be all but extinguished.

But the Duffy of that night doesn't know that yet. The Duffy of that era knows hardly anything.

The Duffy of that night starts whistling. It will take his girlfriend Beth to tell him that it's unlucky to whistle in an open boat. The tune he is whistling is "Lament of the Lagan Valley" whose last two lines are "Forgive us, oh, Lord, the sins of the past / and may you in our mercy be kind to Belfast," which, when you think about it, is a little obvious, a little too on the nose to underscore this scene.

Even the Duffy of that time can see that, and his mind starts playing a different aquatic melody: the Vorspiel in E-flat Major of *Das Rheingold*, the culmination of Wagner's work in Romantic drone music.

"Over there along the wharves," I direct Cathcart while I play in my head the unhurried Von Karajan version that so captures the tension within the counterpoint, as Wagner tries to hide his love/hate relationship with Heine. Love because how can you not love the poems, hate because Heine is a Jew.

The police boat moves slowly back through the calm as the music swirls to a climax. The whiteness darkens into the shapes of buildings. Ruined buildings. Buildings that evoke despair. This town has been broken by ten years of bombings and murder and sectarian civil war. A town from the aphotic zone. A city of the apoca—

"We've been out here nearly an hour, how much longer? I've a party to go to," Cathcart mutters.

Party? What party? What's he talking about?

"An hour's not enough. The sergeant will accuse us of not fulfilling our due diligence."

"The sergeant doesn't give a damn about some wee doll who might or might not have thrown herself in the tide. We've bigger fish to fry now we're on the Butchers case."

The hood falls, and I look at the back of Cathcart's neck, white and young, quivering like a goose gizzard. He's right, of course. This whole thing reeks of pro forma. A going-through-the-motions.

Our entire section has been seconded to the team under Detective Chief Inspector Jimmy Nesbitt, head of the CID Murder Squad in Tennent Street RUC. Nesbitt is investigating the Shankill Butchers—a Loyalist death cult who have slaughtered at least twenty people in random attacks over the last three years. Almost all the victims have been Catholics, dragged off the street and hacked to death with butcher knives and meat cleavers.

The Shankill Butchers have become a cause célèbre, folk heroes to some of the more warped denizens of Protestant West Belfast and bogey men to everyone else in the city. DCI Nesbitt has been given carte blanche to try to bring the bastards in. And in fact, the ring leaders are well known but no one is brave enough to testify against them; so its catch them in the act or get forensic residue—neither of which is a very promising prospect. In the end they'll probably have to fit them up to get them off the streets.

I look at my watch. We've been at this over an hour now and there's nothing out of the ordinary. I turn the tiller to the right and head back up the Lagan.

An elderly cop waiting at the jetty throws me a rope.

"Anything?" he asks.

"Nope."

We tie the boat and get out.

The jarring suddenness of the land. The air shivering with the smell of rain.

Cathcart and I walk sullenly to the station. The pavements are slippery. The Vorspiel in my head circles continuously around the E-flat major chord before it crescendos, resonates and gutters into silence.

We show our faces to the security camera, go in the station and report to O'Neill, the big ruddy Incident Room sergeant.

"What's the story, Duffy?"

"No sign of her, sir."

"Waste of my bloody time. Waste of my officers' time. Remember that, Duffy. Police work is about priorities. No, no, don't take your armour off, we're heading straight out."

"Right now?"

"Aye, right now. No rest for the wicked. We're first responders. Nesbitt and the bloody TV news are gonna be right behind us. I hope for your sake you didn't have a fry for lunch."

We drive to Montague Street where the body of a trainee nurse has been found with nineteen stab wounds in her chest and back.

"Raped first, a new low for the Butchers," O'Neill says. Her clothes have been torn off and she's been disemboweled.

She has ginger hair and delicate features. A kind face. Would have made a wonderful nurse.

We set up a perimeter and began canvassing for witnesses.

When Jimmy Nesbitt arrives with the BBC, ITN and hacks from the English press, we've already done all the grunt work.

"She was a Catholic, of course," O'Neill whispers conspiratorially to me as we take a smoke break.

"How can you tell?" I ask him.

"Rosary in her left hand. She'd have been better to have had a bloody hammer."

I nod and say nothing.

"Did you hear me, Duffy?"

"Yes, sergeant."

He looks at me. "Christ you're exhausted. Get on back to the station, the boss wants a word with you and when he has that word you go on to your bed. You hear me, son?"

"Yes, sergeant."

Back to the station through the devastated streets. Past bomb sites turned into parking lots and derelict buildings and huge craters

brimming with rainwater. I'm being watched by men in doors and al-
leyways. A peeler on his own. A tempting target. Death is close here.

The blue retreats.

The stars slink out.

Darkness.

Go back an hour, see what the angels saw. See what the angels saw
and did nothing to prevent. The trainee nurse on her way to work. The
intoxicated men pouring out of the car and dragging her away. Witnesses
quickening their step, seeing nothing, hearing nothing.

Go back four hours to the runaway girl sitting on the edge of the
Queen's Bridge. Driven there by what demons? Drunkenness, domestic
violence, sexual violence?

Any civilization that fails to appreciate its women is lost.

Deserves to be lost.

Rosemary Street. High Street. The station. Half a dozen cops around
the telly watching Olivia de Havilland watching Errol Flynn showing
off his archery prowess. Upstairs to the gaffer's office. His hand out-
stretched. "Congratulations, Sean."

I shake the hand. "Congratulations for what?"

"Obviously the higher-ups like what you've being doing here. I pride
myself on being a mentor."

"I'm still not clear what—"

"No more foot patrols for you my lad. You're off the bloody streets
for good. You're the new breed, I suppose, Duffy. University men."

"I'm being transferred, is that it?"

"Transferred? What? No. You've been promoted. You're not an acting
detective constable anymore. In fact, you're not even a detective constable! You've been promoted to detective sergeant. Jesus, you're really being
fast-tracked. In a year you'll probably be bumped up to DI. Some quiet,
out-of-the-way station with your own team. They're grooming you, Sean.
They like the cut out of your jib. Be a good boy and keep your nose clean
and don't get bloody shot and you'll end up a Chief Superintendent or
an Assistant Chief Constable or maybe even the big prize itself with the
knighthood and the house in Bangor and the six-figure pension."

"Yes, sir. Thank you, sir."

Downstairs again.

Rain battering against the bulletproof glass of the locker room. A detective sergeant? My own team? Maybe now I can really make a difference.

I change out of my uniform into my street clothes. White jeans, black T-shirt, black parka.

"Where are you going in this weather? Home, I hope," the desk sergeant asks.

"Just one more thing to do. I'm going to let Mrs Keeley know we didn't find anything."

The desk sergeant guffaws. "You're going to let her know you didn't find her daughter's body? She won't thank you for that."

"Letting her know we're still on the case."

"We're *not* still on the case. We've got dead nurses now. No one gives a shite about another teenage runaway."

Nevertheless, I walk to Mrs Keeley's house in a ruined terrace in the Markets.

Knock on the door.

A big man answers. Big man in a white shirt, brown braces, brown slacks. "Who are you?"

"The police. Acting Detective Const—*Detective Sergeant* Sean Duffy. Is Mrs Keeley home?"

"She's making the tea. What is it?"

"Well it's just that we had a look for Louise and so far nothing has—"

"If you do find her you can tell that wee hoor from me that when she gets home she's getting a pounding."

"Who is it?" Mrs Keeley asks, appearing in the hall with a fresh black eye.

"Mrs Keeley, just wanted to let you know that there's no sign of Louise yet."

"The harbour?" she asks, clutching her throat.

"We took a boat out and there was no sign of anything untoward. The eyewitnesses said she just sat there for a bit on the bridge. No one actually saw her jump."

"That's a relief," Mrs Keeley says before her husband turns and glares at her and she goes back to the kitchen.

"Calling the police for the likes of this," he mutters to her and then turning to me he adds, "you can run along now."

And maybe it's the exhaustion, maybe it's the promotion and the knowledge that I'll be moving to a new parish, or maybe it's the Chief Inspector telling me to *be a good boy and keep my nose clean* . . . Because instead of running along I step into the house and close the front door behind me. "You like Wagner?" I ask him.

"What?"

"Wagner."

"What are you on about?"

"Big influence on Wagner was the poet Heine but he could never admit it because Heine was Jewish. You know any Heine? Schubert liked him too. Both were inspired by Heine's poem 'The Lorelei': '*Ich weiß nicht was soll es bedeuten. Daß ich so traurig bin,*' which translates as 'I do not know what this can mean. I am so very sad.' The English doesn't really do it justice though, trust me."

"Are you off your rocker, sunshine?"

"No. I'm just sad. Sad about the Troubles, sad about the way this city treats its womenfolk, sad that an evil bastard who beats his wife and beats his daughter always seems to get away with it because no one will ever testify against him. And you know what I think?"

"What do you think?" he growls, his face turning purple with rage.

I take the service revolver out of its holster and point it at his head. "I think they'd all be better off without you," I whisper. "I think the world would be better off with you. I think no one would miss you. What do *you* think?"

He looks at me in horror and falls to his knees. He starts to cry. Like many bullies, the merest hint of a pushback is enough . . .

I put the revolver back in the holster, a little shocked to see that it got taken out in the first place.

I open the front door. "I'll be keeping tabs on you Keeley, any more bruises on Mrs Keeley or any of the little Keeleys and there will be a knock at your door. Do you hear me?"

"I hear you," he sobs.

Outside the house I catch a look at my reflection in a car window. Jesus, Duffy, is this the kind of detective you are going to be? Power corrupts, of course, but does it have to corrupt this quickly?

I walk back to the station through the drizzle. When I get into the Incident Room, everyone is wearing party hats and blowing kazoos. Someone's birthday? Surprise promotion party for me?

Sergeant O'Neill spots me. "Christ, Duffy, you look terrible. I've seen better-looking corpses down the morgue. Thought I told you to go home. When did you come on duty?"

"Noon."

"What day?"

"Friday."

"It's midnight Saturday. You've been on duty for thirty-six hours straight!"

"What's with the pointy hats?"

"It's the new year, lad. It's January 1, 1980."

"Happy new year, Sean," WPC Porter says, kissing me on the cheek with motherly affection.

"Happy new year to you, Liz," I say, kissing her back.

"Ach, thanks Sean, and let's hope the eighties are better than the seventies, eh?"

Sergeant O'Neill laughs bitterly. "Well, Liz love, they certainly can't—"

Don't say it! Don't jinx it!

"—be any worse, can they?"

# 1
# PERDIDO STREET STATION

Cold hand on arm. "Sean . . . Sean . . ."

Wha . . . ?

"Sean!"

"What?"

"You were a million miles away. I thought you were having a stroke."

A thousand miles and ten years away.

"Uhm, I'm fine. I was just . . . thinking."

Thinking, forcing time forward through the hourglass . . .

"What time is it?"

"Midnight in one minute," Beth said.

Sixty seconds. That's all we had to get through now.

You could hold your breath for sixty seconds.

The crow flew. The sands ran. And then, midnight. A few church bells followed by nothing. Silence all across this ancient holy city.

Silence but for ". . . Sussudio / I just say the word / Oh, Su-Su-Sussudio / Oh, Su-Su-Sussudio, oh, oh, oh / Just say the word . . ."

After a moment or two there was a kind of discontented muttering from around the room.

12.01, my watch said now. The 1980s, at least in this time zone, were definitively over. There had been twelve hundred Troubles-related murders in Northern Ireland over the decade, and for every murder there had been a dozen shooting or bombing victims who had lived but who were horribly injured.

But the 1980s, at last, were over.

I breathed out a sigh of relief and swallowed the last of my brandy.

Somewhat surprisingly, Beth and myself were not in Belfast celebrating this significant temporal event, but were in a restaurant on Jericho Street halfway up the Mount of Olives with an excellent view over the entire eastern portion of the city of Jerusalem. Behind us was the grove of the Garden of Gethsemane and in front of us the Dome of the Rock and beyond that the rest of the Old City which was lit up by spotlights.

Outside the restaurant it was eerily quiet: secular Israelis looking to party had all gone to Tel Aviv for the New Year's Eve concert and fireworks display, religious Israelis were asleep, most of the Palestinians were also all abed effectively leaving this part of Jerusalem to the tourists and the odd party of religious nutcases.

Case in point, Beth's father and his party. "It's that bloody racket. That would put anybody off."

There are a lot of reasons to hate Phil Collins but blaming him because the world hadn't come to an end yet seemed to be a bit of a stretch. Nevertheless, it was after midnight, Jesus had not yet appeared and nowhere in the Bible is the Prince of Peace recorded as being tardy. Using only sundials and perhaps the odd water clock, Jesus had managed to keep all of his Judean appointments in timely fashion.

"Sussudio" continued to reverberate through the speakers for what seemed to be the third time this evening. It was not good Judgement Day music, but I imagined that it was high up in the rotation on the radio station that the damned listened to in hell.

Why was my (de facto but not de jure) father-in-law disappointed? Well, everybody knows that the date of Jesus' birth was wrongly calculated by Dionysius Exiguus when he was setting up the whole Anno Domini system, but exactly how wrong was he? Should the year AD 1 have been put where 4 BC is now or at the 6 BC mark as some claim? Apparently only the Elders of the Free Presbyterian Church of Ireland had been able to compute the correct hour and time of Our Lord's nativity: 3.15 in the morning, December 25, 10 BC, exactly four thousand years after (according to Bishop Ussher, the Archbishop of Armagh) the creation of the universe.

Armed with this information, it had been further deduced that the double millennium spoken of in the book of Revelation would come to an end at the stroke of midnight on December 31, 1989. This would be the real year 2000, and, of course, the end of the double millennium would bring with it the Second Coming and the end of the world.

Hence this trip to the Holy Land for my father-in-law (a high-up muckety muck in said church) and his party and hence the invitation to Beth and myself to witness firsthand Jesus' triumphant return. All of that was definitely a must-miss but for three factors which had changed my mind: (1) Hector was paying, (2) we didn't actually have to travel with the church group and (3) I had ten days of vacation time from the police that I had to take before December 31, 1989, otherwise I would lose it.

Belfast to Ben Gurion then where Beth and I said our goodbyes to the Presbyterians, rented a car and carved out our own itinerary through Israel and the Palestinian territories, only joining up with them for this, the final night.

12.04 now. No Jesus on a donkey or white horse (opinions differed), no opening of the heavens, no blaring trumpets, no dead rising from the grave. Only stray cats, the occasional passer-by and Phil Collins.

"Sussudio" came to a close and "You Know and I Know" began. Synthesiser, drum machine, sax and horns combining together in a horrifyingly up-tempo number. Great songs, like great books, illustrated the ineffable, and this was a song, I felt, that was emblematic of the failure of the whole of the 1980s corporate Brit pop project.

This was the third time the restaurant had played this CD. No sane human could possibly bear *No Jacket Required* three times in a row and I wondered if, like Zacharias, father of John the Baptist, I too could get the Lord to strike me deaf.

I helped Beth to her feet.

"Well, Hector, thanks for the meal, but I think we'll be getting back to the hotel now," I said, shaking the big old eejit's hand.

Hector was obviously disappointed. He'd been expecting gnashing of teeth and the Angels Michael, Gabriel and Raphael carrying swords, kicking arse and taking names. The only people on the planet who would, apparently, be spared the harrowing were the members of the Free Presbyterian Church of Ireland and, just possibly, congregants of the Free Presbyterian Church of Scotland. Definitely not yours truly: a Papist policeman who drank alcohol, conducted idol worship at the Marian shrine of Knock and supported Celtic FC.

12.05 now.

We called a taxi and went to wait for it on the street. The Presbyterians at the outside tables were undergoing a curious synthesis of expressions: fearful anticipation that was slowly transmuting into disappointment with maybe just a smidgen of relief.

Suddenly a spectacular burst of brilliant white light appeared in the East Jerusalem skies in front of us. Beth gripped my arm. "Fireworks. A little late," I said, but perhaps the dazzling light and its suddenness would—

Yes, it surely would.

Comedy lives in the reaction shot. And for a delicious couple of seconds there was a confused screaming and yelling from the Irish Presbyterians behind us.

"It's the end!"

"Oh my God!"

"The redeemer cometh!"

The redeemer did not, of course, cometh but the taxi did. Fifteen minutes later we were in our quaint but well-proportioned hotel room in a very quiet part of West Jerusalem near Sacher Park.

Beth got ready for bed while I opened the mini fridge and popped the cap on a Heineken. I looked out the window at the city. Devotees of many faiths were making their way home from midnight masses and celebrations, cats were leaping across the narrow alleys, the odd drunk was staggering up Eilat Street looking for a falafel stand.

"It's really been a nice break this," I said as Beth sat on my lap and took a swig of the beer. I squeezed her bum and she kissed me.

"You deserve a break, Sean. And from here on in you can take it easy in the part-timers."

"Yeah," I said, not completely convinced.

Beth mind-read me.

"You're not abandoning anyone moving to Scotland. You've done your bit, you know?" she said with such conviction I almost bought it.

"Yeah, I *have* done my bloody bit. More than my bloody bit and it hasn't made a damn bit of difference. Four years as a beat cop. Two as an acting detective. Ten years as a detective. And what have I achieved?"

This was the rather obvious cue for Beth to leap in here with a list of my achievements, but she didn't pick up on it or perhaps was just too dog-tired to say anything. I took another sip of beer.

"What's that light over there by the phone?" Beth asked.

"What light? Oh, that light. Dunno."

"I think that means we have a message! What if it's about Emma?" Beth said with alarm.

While we had gallivanted around the Holy Land, Emma, our precocious three-and-a-bit-year-old, was hopefully being spoiled rotten by my parents back in Belfast.

I played the message, but it was nothing to do with Emma. It was a call from John McCrabban at the station. "Sean, I hope your holiday's going well. Listen, I know you were hoping for an empty ledger to complete the handover to young Lawson tomorrow but there's an MPC that you'll have to put to bed first. I'm very sorry, Sean, but it's on our watch and you'll have to sign off on it. Action/no action. Give me a call if you get the chance. Cheerio. Best to Beth, of course."

Beth looked at me. "What's an MPC?"

"Missing Persons Case. Won't be a big deal," I said as I dialled the number for Carrick RUC.

Crabbie picked up. "Carrick RUC. This is Detective Sergeant Mc-Crabban."

"It's Sean."

"Sean! My goodness. How's the Holy Land?"

"Interesting trip mate and I'm calling from the future, which would normally set me off on a tangent, but international phones rates being what they are we better get down to business. What's the case?"

"MPC. This afternoon. A Traveller girl called Kat McAtamney. I talked to the Chief Inspector and he said that it was a waste of police time running after an MPC on New Year's Eve. He said that tinker girls went missing all the time and nobody gave a crap. Except, uhm, he didn't say crap."

"So what does the Chief Inspector think we should do?"

"Nothing. File the paperwork on the robbery, log it in the computer and then both of us gracefully bow out and turn the department over to Sergeant Lawson."

"Cos no one gives a shite about a missing tinker?"

"That was the gist of his remarks."

"I give a shite, Crabbie."

"I thought you might which is why I've left the case file open and asked Lawson to look into it."

"All right. I'll come in first thing. I'm still hoping this is going to be a straightforward handover."

"Me too. I promised Helen I was done with all this palaver."

"After this one we will be. You and me both, mate."

Crabbie cleared his throat. "Do you think this has sufficient, uhm . . . what's the word . . . *gravitas* to be Sean Duffy's last case?"

"They can't all be homicides, can they?"

"I'd be happy never to be part of another murder investigation in my born days."

"Me too. See you tomorrow, buddy."

I hung up the phone and looked at Beth.

"I heard," she said. "Don't worry. It'll be a good excuse for getting you out of my hair on packing day."

"I'll never hear the end of it. You'll say I didn't help with the move."

"Oh, my God, is that what your previous girlfriends would do? Cos that is so not one of my moves."

"'Previous girlfriend' is it? We've a kid. We're practically—"

"Don't you say it, Sean Duffy."

"I won't then."

She yawned, and I kissed her.

"I'm off to bed," she said, and in five minutes she was sound asleep between the sheets.

I couldn't sleep.

Never could. Never will. Worrying about a case. Worrying about the family. Just general every day worrying. You're always being chastised by time's whips. You've read Schopenhauer haven't you? No? Lucky you. Take my advice: don't.

Beer to the balcony.

Quiet now on Gezer Street, Eilat Street and on Nisim Bachar, quiet save for the jackals calling to one another in the Judean hills.

Amazing, really, to be here.

Belfast is Jerusalem's twin.

Both holy cities.

Both at the crisscross of evil lay lines that demand blood and sacrifice.

Both blessed, cursed.

Ciudad Perdida. Cahill Chathair. הדובא ריע.

I took another sip of beer and put the bottle against my forehead.

Eyes closed.

To have survived the 1980s when dozens of my colleagues did not. To have cheated death so many times. Aye, Crabbie, it's fine to finish up my career in the peelers with a bog standard missing persons case.

Eyes open.

Light from dead stars. Uncoiling of bat wings. Jackal calls.

The night mild and beautiful and the starfield rich and deep.

Part of my brain began thinking about the missing girl, but the other part was thinking about John Strong. Strong was an Assistant Chief Constable in the RUC but who had been for the last decade or so a double agent working for the IRA. I had turned John Strong a year ago and now he was working for us as a triple agent. He was a flighty, highly strung, nervous agent and it took me and three other guys in MI5 to handle him. I had agreed to continue to help baby him even after he got a permanent full time set of case officers. Even after I moved to Scotland, I'd still have to be involved as he was an important asset. It had been ten days since I'd heard anything about Strong or even thought about him, but his big orange beardy face was nagging me.

I stretched the phone cable all the way to the balcony and called the duty office in Cultra.

"Wilson Foods, this is Siobhan," said a woman with a voice so posh she was never going to convince anybody she was a "Siobhan" in a million frigging years.

"I have a case number, Siobhan," I said.

"What is your four-digit case number?"

"4556."

"And the reference number?"

"Tango 887."

"Is this an emergency Tango 887?"

"No. I just need to speak to the duty office."

"I'm putting you through."

A pause. Then, "Duty office."

"This is Duffy. Case number 4556."

"Duffy, good to hear from you! A little bird told me you were in bloody Israel of all places," Oliver said. This was young, lanky, good looking Oliver Carson, twenty-two, from Manchester. He had a BA in Russian and Slavic languages which is why MI5 with its typically twisted logic had put him in their Belfast station.

"The little bird was well informed."

"Where are you exactly?"

"Jerusalem."

"Only you, Duffy, would take a holiday from Belfast and go to an even more religiously riven and dangerous city."

"I was thinking that myself just now. Father-in-law's idea. And he was paying for it, so why not? How's our boy, Oliver?"

"Oh, he's a mess as usual. He keeps thinking they're onto him."

"Are they onto him?" I asked with some concern.

"No! Of course not. He's paranoid."

"So everything's all right?"

"Everything's fine."

"Good. This is my last week in the full-timers remember."

"Jesus, that's right, you're moving to Scotland aren't you?"

"Yup. Just one last case to put to bed and then that's it."

"Strong will be upset. He trusts you, Duffy."

"You'll have to get him to trust you too. As soon as I'm done with my case you'll be seeing a lot less of me."

"What's the case? Something juicy?"

"Nope. A missing girl. A Traveller girl."

"Jesus, who can keep track of them lasses? I see them all the time in Lavery's. Sixteen, tarted up to look like they're thirty. Little sluts."

"Charming as always, Oliver. Talk to you later."

I hung up, listened to the jackals for a bit longer and went to bed. *Who gives a shite about a lost tinker girl?*

"Carrick CID does," I muttered and slid between the sheets.

I slept for a couple of hours and woke suddenly. The clock said 5.00 a.m. What time was that in the UK? I counted back the time zones. Two in the morning, which meant, aye, the 80s were finally over there too. The grim, greasy, seedy seventies had bled into the violent, neon, awful 80s.

"The 90s can't be worse," was something I would not only never say but something I wouldn't even allow myself to think.

I climbed out of bed and opened the shutters. It was quiet and an early morning golden light was spilling spectacularly onto Jerusalem's white limestone buildings. Maybe this was a good place to meet the new decade, the last decade of the second millennium. Maybe a prayer for better times? The air above of Jerusalem was already thick with prayers but one more couldn't hurt. I checked to see that Beth wasn't looking and got down on my knees. "*Salve Regina, mater misericordiae,*" I whispered. "Two decades the Troubles have been going. Let this be the last one. There are other lands. Other feuds lying dormant under the ice. Let peace come to Ireland. Let the fools in London be more circumspect. Let the fools in America close their wallets. Let the fools in Belfast think of the soft brows of their children and fight no more forever. Please."

# 2
# DUFFY'S LAST CASE

We flew out of Ben Gurion at 8.00 a.m. Everyone made the flight on time. Dour Presbyterian farmer types from the County Antrim hill country could be called many things but "late" was not one of those things.

You had to wonder, though, why they'd even bothered booking the return leg of the trip if they were so confident that the end of the world was nigh . . . I kept these thoughts to myself and managed to kip a bit on the journey back to Ulster, God's other promised land.

It was a five-hour flight to Belfast but since the UK was three hours behind Israel, the direct charter actually landed at 10.00 a.m.

I picked up the Beemer from the medium-term car park. It was the brand-new 1991 525i sport. This was the first all-wheel drive I'd gotten in the 5 Series. It was powered by the M50 engine and—(if you hate car talk you should skip ahead) the centre differential normally would divide 36% torque to the front axle and 64% to the rear axle, but crucially it could adjust the ratio according to the driving conditions. Perfect for Ireland's cattle tracks, single lane roads and motorways and perfect too for those Irish days when it would be snowing in the morning, sleeting in the afternoon, sunny in the evening and belting with rain at night.

The top speed was 143 mph but the car itself was computer restricted in the UK and Ireland to a top speed of 110 mph. As a policeman I had been able to get the computer restrictions removed and at 1.00 a.m. on the motorway I'd had her up to a ton and a quarter.

But with Beth in the vehicle I kept to a sensible speed back to Carrickfergus. I put on the radio and killed it after a few seconds. Radio 1 was still playing the dystopian 80s music that was dominating the top of the singles chart: Phil Collins, Cher, Kylie—but on other stations hints of a musical revolution were starting to appear from Manchester and Seattle. You didn't want to jinx anything, but it seemed probable that in terms of music, at least, the 90s could be a turning point for the better.

We pulled into Carrickfergus along the top road, down North Road to the road formerly known as Kennedy Drive, past the leisure centre and home to Coronation Road.

Feelings of nostalgia as I weaved the Beemer between groups of kids playing kerby and soccer and 1-2-3 kick-a-tin. This would be our last full day on the street. We were finishing our packing this evening and moving tomorrow. Of course I'd still live here while I was doing my seven-days-a-month part-time service but eventually we'd sell the house and I'd buy a one-bedroom flat down near the Marina which would be more appropriate for my needs.

I pulled the Beemer into my spot outside #113.

Dad and Mum were outside waiting for us. Mum was affectionately holding Emma and Dad was much more reluctantly holding Jet the cat.

As the car stopped, Beth bolted out of the front seat and hugged Emma.

"Never again. I'm never leaving you again. Ten days was too long. Never again. You're coming with us next time!" she wailed and began to cry. I had missed Emma too, but this display surprised me a little. Beth was normally pretty reserved. These Protestants were full of surprises. I hugged Emma too, hugged my mum, man-hugged my father and patted the cat on the head. We gave Emma her gifts: chocolates and a cuddly camel.

"Daddy! You're all red!" she said.

"You have got a bit of the sun," my mother said scoldingly. "You know you don't do well in the sun, Sean. Like Bromeliads."

"It was winter sun, I'm fine," I said.

We went inside the house which smelled of my mum's powerful home-made dish soap. All the surfaces had been scrubbed and the pictures dusted. I hoped to God they hadn't scrubbed or dusted my records. I quickly checked a few LPs at random, but they were unscathed.

"I wouldn't let her near them," my father whispered.

"Emma safe, cat safe, records safe," I said to dad, "Pretty successful bit of babysitting there."

"What were you expecting? The house burned down, the cat run off and the kid in the hospital?" Dad replied a bit huffily.

I had, in fact, feared all of those things. "No, I knew you'd handle it," I said.

"Your father tried to put a leash on the cat so he wouldn't go after the starlings but Jet was having none of it," Mum added.

"Sean, here's one I've been saving for you: there once was a kid from Peru / whose limericks stopped at line two," Dad said.

"Very good. Listen, I can only stay for five minutes, folks, work calls," I explained.

We retired to the living room. There were boxes everywhere and we still had more packing to do. The movers were due tomorrow morning first thing. We'd already furnished the house across the water but we had to bring cutlery, books, bed linen and most of my records.

"So where did youse travel to?" Mum asked.

"Jerusalem, Tel Aviv, the Dead Sea, Eilat and then we drove up to the north," I said while Beth cooed with Emma and Emma played with the camel.

"Did you see the Sea of Galilee?" Dad asked.

"Saw, swam in it, sunbathed by it. In fact we brought you some holy water from Beit Yerah where the Jordan flows south of out of the lake."

"Oh yes!" Beth said and rummaged in the suitcases for the bottles of holy water.

My father looked sceptically at the bottle. "It's not just water from the sink in your hotel room is it? I know you only too well."

"I wouldn't let him get away with that Mr Duffy!" Beth said. "We filled this up by the riverside."

"Did you see any birds?" he asked.

"Millions of them."

"And?"

"I didn't sit down and write the names of the birds in a big bird book for you, dad. I was on me bloody holidays. My first holiday in about five years, actually."

"Stop torturing him, Sean," Beth said and dived into the suitcases again. She passed him the notebook I'd made with observations on black vultures, grebes, pygmy cormorants, squacco heron and a wall-creeper. Beth had even done some drawings, so naturally, the old man was in raptures.

"Did you really see a wallcreeper?"

"Yes, Dad."

"Oh! What a find! It is the only member of the genus tichodrome, Emma."

Emma nodded solemnly and recalled something to mind. "Are you going to tell Daddy and Mummy about Mary Poppins, grandpa?"

My mum shook her head. "No, we don't want to get your grandfather all worked up again."

"Grandpa was upset about the robin," Emma explained.

"The robin?" Beth asked missing my throat cutting gesture. Whatever this was about it was clearly one of dad's hobbyhorses and the smart thing would be not to engage it.

"Oh, yes, the robin," Emma said, with a sarcastic tone I wasn't convinced I liked in a three year-old. "It lands on Mary's finger," Emma said.

"That? It was obviously a bad special effect, dad, you have to remember this was 1964 or something—"

"It wasn't about the special effect. The mechanical or stop motion nature of the robin is neither here nor there. They could never have trained a real robin to alight on Mary's finger, so that doesn't bother me at all," Dad said.

"So what was the problem?" Beth asked.

"The problem was that the robin that landed on Mary's finger was a North American robin. A songbird of the thrush family. It is named after the European robin because of its reddish-orange breast, although, as everybody knows, the two species are not remotely related! The European robin belongs to the Old World flycatcher family and that is what should have landed on Mary's finger as she is supposed to be in London."

"Your father got quite upset," Mum whispered in that stage whisper of hers. "He stopped the video and he wanted to write to Walt Disney until I told him that Mr Disney had passed on. I'll make everyone a cup of tea."

Mum went to put the kettle on. Jet went outside to chase the starlings. A silence descended on the living room. Beth and Emma were looking at me to fix things.

"Uhm, the North American robin is a migratory bird, is it not, dad? *Turdus migratorius.* Could not one have been blown off course and ended up in London by accident? The prevailing winds are from west to east and in a hurricane force gale?"

"The wind was strong enough to carry away all the other nannies, grandpa," Emma said.

My father cleared his throat. "Well, I suppose it's not impossible," he admitted.

"Whew, that's one crisis dealt with! And now if you'll excuse me, folks, I have to head into the station to deal with what everyone's been calling Sean Duffy's last case."

I slipped outside and made a mental note never to let dad see David Lynch's *Blue Velvet*—the robin at the end of that would probably give him a heart attack.

I looked underneath the Beemer for bombs and finding none drove to the station at a cool 50 mph down Victoria Road and 60 on the Marine Highway.

Not quite a handbrake turn into the cop shop but a certain élan in my stop and ID flash.

A few nods and hellos from the downstairs crew and I went up the steps to CID. Crabbie wasn't in yet and Lawson apparently was in the bog or somewhere, so I retreated to my office. The desk calendar said December 20, 1989. I flipped it forward to January 1, 1990.

This day had been a long time coming. Crabbie and I were both re-signing our posts as full-time detectives to move into the RUC's part-time reserve. Crabbie was doing it so that he could spend more time on his expanded dairy farm. I was doing it for more complicated reasons. First and foremost, of course, was Beth and Emma. The attack on our home at Coronation Road just over a year ago had been the last straw for Beth. She didn't want to raise Emma in a country where soldiers patrolled the streets and bombs and riots happened every night. She'd completed her degree as an out student at Glasgow University and with a masters degree in English and a masters in education it had been no problem for her to get any secondary school teaching gig she'd wanted in Scotland. She'd gotten a job at Stranraer Girls Grammar School and she started there next week at the beginning of the new term. We'd bought a big old house overlooking the Irish Sea in Portpatrick and spent the autumn and summer fixing it up. Moving to Scotland would keep Beth happy but obviously I could no longer remain the full-time head of CID in Carrickfergus. In fact, I couldn't be a detective anymore as detectives had to be on call twenty-four hours a day. But I could remain in the police as a part-time reservist working only seven days a month. Those seven days were vital because if I logged seven working days a month for the next three-and-a-half years, I could retire with a full twenty-year pension from the RUC. Thus, I could live in Scotland in relative safety with Beth and still make my twenty.

The seven days would mostly be admin, but I'd also be handling our IRA double agent John Strong when the occasion arose. Strong was high maintenance, but he was worth it. The IRA still thought he was their mole in the police and had no idea we'd turned him. Over the last year he had given the IRA significant disinformation and he had gleaned valuable operational intelligence about the IRA's command structure both north and south of the border. Strong trusted me more than his other handlers, which is why I was able to get this little deal for Crabbie and me—working in the part-time reserve but still collecting our full pension at the end of our twenty.

January 1, 1990 was supposed to be the start of the new arrangement and all I had to do was finish out my caseload and give the keys to the store to Lawson.

He wasn't a bad copper, Lawson. His chief attributes were his youth, intelligence and enthusiasm, but he lacked experience and sometimes he had the lean and hungry look of an ambitious man. Lawson could probably see himself as a Chief Superintendent by the time he hit my age and maybe he'd be head-hunted by the Metropolitan Police and end up a Commander over the water. Ambitious men were always a bit dangerous to have around and you worried sometimes that he'd crush a butterfly on a wheel to keep his arrest statistics high.

We'd see, I suppose.

I rummaged through the correspondence on what was soon to be someone else's desk. There was an internal memo on top of the in tray that was stamped important.

I opened the envelope and a sheet fell out. It was a series of bullshit complaints from admin about our allowances and down at the bottom in a Man-Walks-on-the-Moon sized font Dalziel had hastily added: "See me in my office before you leave, please, Inspector Duffy, you are way over budget."

CID always went over our overtime allowance for the simple reason that we worked harder than everybody else in the station. And if my men were going to work hard they were going to be paid appropriately. Inspector Dalziel was not going to bully Sergeant Lawson and any new detective constables into taking less money than they were due. I was about to call him up on the internal line and give him a bollocking when the door opened and the arse himself came in without knocking.

To me he was a sallow, yellow, unctuous little chap, but some of the ladies around the office thought he looked like Leslie Howard which would not have pleased the late Mr Howard.

"Ever hear of knocking, Dalziel? Is this about the overtime?"

"This is about the overtime and the expenses and the travel allowances. Your department draws deep from the company well doesn't it?" Dalziel said.

"That's your problem, Kenny. You think we're a company. We're not a company—we're a fucking police force."

"I wouldn't be grinning if I were you, Duffy. I've gotten payroll investigators interested. This has gone beyond simple overtime fiddling. I think it's fraud we're talking about here," he said with satisfaction.

"Well that's a big bowl of wank and piss, as my dear old gran used to say."

"Your gran, eh? I can see where you got your filthy mouth from then."

"I met your mum and dad at the police club, Kenny, they were nice people, so I have no idea where you got your *being a cunt all the time* from."

He sat down opposite me and shook his head. "This is serious, Duffy. Just because you're heading into the part-timers, don't think they won't go after you."

"Sit down, make yourself at home."

"I'm letting you know formally that I'm involving Special Branch's Internal Affairs Task Force. I'm going to do a thorough accounting of your division going back at least five years and Sergeant Lawson is going to have to cooperate."

"If I get word that you've bullied my sergeant you're fucked mate."

"Is that a threat?"

"A promise, Dalziel, a fucking promise."

"You forget your position, Duffy."

Dalziel had been promoted to Inspector and there was some talk that he was going to be given the station. He was an influential sod was Dalziel with relatives in the higher echelons of the plod and other relatives prominent fuckfaces in the Democratic Unionist Party. Oh, and did I mention he was a freemason? The old tickle my cock and get me off this speeding ticket. The old wink twice and raise an eyebrow and get promoted to Chief Constable. But not on my bloody watch. Not while they needed me to run John Strong as an agent for them. I shake my head and Kenny Dalziel's ascent up the promotion ladder is stopped on the second rung by unknown forces and he is told to sit in a corner wearing a pointy hat.

"What position is that, Kenny? Reverse cow girl?"

"We're the same rank now, Duffy."

"But I have the seniority. Ten years seniority, mate."

"That doesn't mean anything. All that means is that for ten years nobody has thought you were worth promoting."

He got to his feet and brushed back his partial and very un–Leslie Howard–like comb-over.

"I wouldn't worry about the Payroll Investigation Team or the Internal Affairs Task Force if I were you, Kenny. I have a funny feeling that your request to have me investigated is going to vanish into thin air. Puff! Just like that."

"You have a fairy godmother, do you?"

Yup, as long as John Strong was alive I certainly did. Three fairy godmothers in three sparkly tiaras: the head of Special Branch Intel, the head of MI5 Belfast Station and the RUC Chief Constable himself.

"Do me a favour, Kenny, send in your report this morning. I want to see your face at 5.00 p.m. when you've had a phone call from the mountain top telling you in no uncertain terms to leave Sean Duffy the fuck alone."

"We'll see," he said and walked out of the office.

"Close the door, you shite!" I yelled after him, but he didn't.

Thirty seconds later here was an awkward little knock at the still-ajar door.

"Come in, Lawson!" I boomed.

Lawson came in looking embarrassed. He'd clearly heard the whole encounter with Dalziel and he was probably worried about it. He didn't want a Special Branch investigation to be part of the nonsense he had to deal with on his first week in charge.

"Have a seat, son, and wipe that troubled look from your brow. As the Bible says, the evil bastards shall be smote and humbled before the Lord."

"What verse is that sir?"

"I'm paraphrasing Lawson. Paraphrasing the entire Old Testament."

Lawson seemed thinner and paler than usual. God, was the stress getting to him and he hadn't even taken over yet? Or was it only the fact that I wasn't used to this pale pasty Mick after ten days spent in the company of people who ate vegetables, took the occasional walk and got a bit of sun?

"What are you thinking about, sir?" Lawson asked, his bright blue eyes shining innocently.

"I was thinking that it's good to see you my lad. How have you been?"

"Good, sir. How was Israel?"

"Lovely. Have you been?"

"No. Like to go, though, some day. I have an aunt and uncle in Haifa."

"I've a present for you," I said, giving him the standard giant Toblerone one bought at the airport.

"Thank you, sir."

"I brought some holy water as well. You fancy some? McCrabban will say no."

"Uhm, not really my cup of—"

"Forget it then. Everything all right around here?"

"Oh, yes, sir. Quiet. That Post Office robbery case and those vandals that we lifted and the MPC that came in yesterday."

"Action on the robbery?"

"No leads, sir, I'm afraid. Put out the usual feelers but no one has been spending an inordinate amount of money or showing off down the pub."

"Not yet, they haven't, but they will. They always bloody do, the poor stupid fools. Action on the vandals?"

"Put the fear of God into them. Said we could charge them with breaking and entering or attempted burglary. That's five years up the Kesh, I said."

"And what was their reaction?"

"Well, if pissing your pants is cool, they were Miles Davis and Duke bloody Ellington."

"Nice jazz reference, appreciate that. What was your action report?"

"The Chief Inspector wanted a prosecution in the books, but I explained to him the *de minimis non curat lex* rule."

"Very good, Lawson! The law does not concern itself with trifles . . . or pavlovas or other desserts your granny might make."

Lawson tried not to roll his eyes, but he couldn't help himself. He cleared his throat. "Anyway, uhm, sir, Sergeant McCrabban and I felt a prosecution was over the top."

"I've got one for you, son. Me dad has put me in a Limerick mood. Let me see if I can remember it? Oh, yes, here goes: There once was a lawyer called Rex / Who had very small organs of sex / When charged with exposure / he said with composure: / *De minimis non curat lex*!"

Lawson did not react. Not even a courtesy guffaw. Clearly my shtick was wearing thin. Another reason to get out. I took a puff of my asthma inhaler. My first such inhalation in a week. Cutting way down on the smokes and getting some fresh air was definitely good for me.

"So let them go with a warning then, did you?" I asked.

"Exactly, sir. I think the message went home."

"Action on the MPC?"

"Usual alerts to the airports and borders and other police forces. Logged it into the computer for Interpol."

"Aye, well, I'll need to take a look at the file on that one I think."

"Of course, sir."

Lawson went off and came back with a very thin-looking file. Indeed, when I opened it, it was only the mother's statement and the printout from the computer log-in. Two pages for a missing child. If she hadn't been a tinker, there would be a team on this, and if the mother had had the sense to involve any of our local politicians or the BBC, there would be dossier an inch thick by now. But she wasn't related to anyone and she hadn't called the Beeb. She was a Traveller who lived at the Kilroot Caravan Park—hence, two pages.

Lawson could sense my disapproval.

"Sir, is something amiss?"

"I haven't quite fulfilled my pedagogical duties with you, Lawson, my lad. And don't be doing that eye rolling thing you think I don't notice."

"Oh sir, I would never roll—"

"You would too. You think me and Sergeant McCrabban have

nothing left to teach you. You're a numbers man and I can dig that. And you've read bloody Aristotle and I can dig that too, but it's not just about the numbers, is it? It's about knowing when to go deep into something and when to hold back. And this is one we're going to go deep on."

You could tell that he wanted to ask why. And the answer would have to be because of that other New Year's Eve case a decade ago and the half dozen teenage runaway cases I'd been involved with since joining the police, none of which had ever been taken seriously.

"Much as we would like to, we're not going to hurry through this case. You'll get to take over the store, Lawson, and I'll get to go gently into semiretirement across the sheugh and Crabbie will get to spend more time with his cows all in due course."

"Sir, I wasn't—"

"I know what you're thinking; you're thinking: it's an unjust world, and virtue is triumphant only in theatrical performances. Well you're not the Mikado and I'm not Mr Gilbert."

He had no idea what I was talking about, which was fine—good to occasionally remind the young 'uns that they didn't know fucking everything.

I took a triangle off the end of his Toblerone and read the mother's statement about her missing bairn:

STATEMENT EILEEN MCATAMNEY, CARRICK RUC,
SCOTCH QUARTER, CARRICKFERGUS
31/12/89
4:12 PM

Q: When did you notice that your daughter hadn't come home?
A: Yesterday afternoon she wasn't around.
Q: Has she run away before?
A: Only the once mind. Went down to Dublin by herself.
Q: How long was she away that time?
A: Four days.

Q: It's only been a little over one day. Why so worried now?

A: Ach, she's hanging around with a bad crowd now.

Q: Did she take any money with her?

A: I don't know.

Q: Does she have relations in the south or over the water?

A: Oh, aye, lots of them. Millions of them.

Q: Do you think you could maybe call them for us and let us know if she's staying with any of them?

A: Aye, I could do that.

Q: Was she wearing anything distinctive? Bright wee jacket or anything or distinctive jewellery?

A: A bright wee jacket? Aye, she does have one of those. A red shiny one, I think . . .

I got up and put my coat on over my shoulder holster. I was still in my aeroplane clothes: black polo shirt, blue jeans, black Adidas sneakers—but I'd thrown on a brown tweed sports coat to look at bit more fusty and professional. It'd do for meeting the general public.

"Follow," I said to Lawson as I walked out into the Incident Room.

"Where?"

"Who took this statement?" I said handing the file back to him.

"WPC Rice."

"Is she a detective?"

"No. But she's a woman. I thought a sympathetic ear might—"

"It's full of leading questions, there's a shocking lack of detail, there's no photograph in the file and there appears to have been no follow-up apart from logging the case in the computer. I'm surprised at you, Lawson."

"It was New Year's Eve sir, and the woman didn't seem particularly alarmed. She said the girl had run before," Lawson explained.

"'Does she have a bright wee jacket? Aye, she might have something like that.' I mean, really, Lawson . . ."

Lawson's eyes got damp.

Damp? Jesus, he had led a charmed life so far in the RUC. I was his

THE DETECTIVE UP LATE

gaffer and I was a pretty easy going guy. And Chief Inspector McArthur was his station chief and he was a mellow sort too on the whole. Lawson had been shot at and missed, which encouraged you to think that the angels were looking out for you and you could do no wrong. But this little report was not good police work.

"It's ok, son, no need for the waterworks, but better effort next time, ok?"

"Yes, sir," he replied, chastened.

"It's been twenty hours since this witness statement and Carrick CID has taken no action."

"I'm really sorry, sir, it didn't seem like a big deal. I hope you haven't lost confidence in my ability to—"

"Everything has to change so everything can remain the same, you'll do fine in the job, I know it and Crabbie knows it and that's why we're completely ok with letting you take over."

"Thank you, sir."

But I hope to God this doesn't become a murder case or we might have to explain the twenty wasted hours to a bloody inquiry, I thought but didn't say.

# 3
# TWENTY WASTED HOURS

Coat. Stairs. BMW.

We drove out of the station and along the seafront in the direction of Kilroot. The Traveller population of Carrickfergus had swelled in recent years as a result of a number of acts of Parliament aimed at curbing illegal Gypsy and Traveller camp grounds. Councils could evict Gypsies and Travellers but only if they had designated camp grounds where Travellers and Gypsies were supposed to go. Carrickfergus Council had set aside no such campgrounds, which paradoxically meant that its Traveller population had boomed. No campgrounds meant that an eviction order could be successfully challenged in court by any lawyer who knew what they were doing. After the fourth successful challenge, we—the police—had stopped even bothering with the eviction notices. There were now half a dozen technically illegal Traveller campgrounds on half a dozen sites in and around the town, mostly on waste ground or on the edgelands next to fields and forests. Land that no one had ever claimed, until the gypsies came, of course, which was when the neighbouring residents would all start protesting to the peelers.

This campsite looked harmless. On wasteland between Kilroot Power Station and the railway lines were a dozen small white metal caravans, a couple of horses and a few beat-up old 70s motors. Half a dozen kids of assorted ages were playing football with an old leather ball that had been patched and sewn so much you wondered if it was a relic of the nineteenth century.

I parked the Beemer and found the biggest, scariest-looking kid of the bunch.

"I need someone to watch my car," I said.

"Ten pound an hour," he replied immediately.

"Five."

"Done."

He examined the car. "Nice wheels."

"Thanks. What's your name, son?"

"Danny. Hey mister, you ever get that thing over a ton, speed-wise?"

"Yup."

"Nice car, but you should get yourself a steering wheel lock. The remoteless key system on the new Beemers uses infra-red instead of radio waves. My Uncle Cecil has a device to get into any infrared keyless car."

"Good to know. Which caravan is Eileen McAtamney's?"

"That one over there."

"Is she home?"

"Aye."

"Listen Danny, have you seen Katrina McAtamney around here lately?"

"Not for days."

"When was the last time?"

"I saw her in the Tourist Inn on Thursday."

"Doing what?"

"Drinking."

"Alone or with someone?"

"Alone."

"'Member what was she wearing?"

"Probably her big white jumper and her black jeans."

"Ok. Thanks. Don't let anyone touch—and I mean touch—my car."

We walked through the muddy caravan park being trailed by half a dozen dogs and an overfriendly donkey.

Mrs McAtamney's caravan was an ancient one, probably dating from the fifties. An aluminium frame and aluminium cladding. There was no tensile strength in the structure and over the years movement, water and temperature changes had weakened all the joints, causing breakage between the metal panels. In other words, unless you lived in the South of France it would be cold, damp and miserable all year round.

It was no place for anyone to live or bring up a kid.

I knocked on the door.

No answer.

I knocked louder.

"Who is it?" Mrs McAtamney asked.

"DI Duffy, DS Lawson, Carrick CID," I said.

She opened the door. She was late thirties or early forties, brown haired, attractive in a cadaverous, weather-beaten sort of way. She was wearing an old black polo neck sweater, flared jeans and clogs, a look that had been fashionable in about 1972. Behind her in the caravan, three children aged from four to nine were playing a board game of some kind.

"What do you want?" she asked.

"You reported your daughter Katrina McAtamney missing yesterday?"

"Aye, I did. Did you find her?"

"No. Not yet."

"Well she's definitely not at Jordy Hardcastle's. I went there last night and he told me to fuck off. And he had one of his lads rough me up. He's lucky I didn't press assault charges."

I got my notebook out. "Jordy who?"

"Jordy Hardcastle."

"An address?"

"Number three Water Street in Carrick, there."

"And what happened exactly?"

"I went 'round there to see if Katrina was there, and he said he hadn't seen her, and I demanded to be let in and he sent some big lad out to me."

"And the lad hit you?"

"Shoved me. Shoved me hard."

It began to rain. "Can we come in?" I asked.

"Aye, you might as well. Suppose you'll be wanting some tea?"

"Not if it's any trouble."

"No trouble. Harry, make the peelers some tea!"

The oldest boy got up from the game and put the kettle on. While I talked to Mrs McAtamney I watched him fish two used tea bags out of the sink and drop them in a couple filthy-looking mugs. In Ireland you could not under any circumstances refuse a cup of tea without giving offense, so I'd have to at least take a sip.

"Kat's your oldest?" I asked, looking at the kids.

"Nope," she replied.

"How many children do you have, Mrs McAtamney?"

She sighed. "There's the four wee ones living here with me. Them three and John outside playing football. The two middle girls live with Daniel, their da and their stepmother in Manchester. My oldest, Roy, he's in the army. He's in Belize. Kenneth is in America. Sandra, well she's took off with a black man and lives with him in Kilburn. And then there's Kat."

"So that's ten kids all together?" I said counting them up.

"And Mary, who died of diphtheria."

"All with the same father?" I asked.

"What do you think?"

"I have no idea."

"Different fathers, none of whom are about here anymore. Two of them are dead and one of them is in prison in Holland."

"Kat's father?"

"One of the dead ones. Patrick. Lovely man he was. Struck by lightning he was once. Survived that. Hit by a car in Glasgow. That done for him so it did. Drunk driver."

"We're going to need the addresses and phone numbers of Daniel, Kenneth and Sandra. I'm guessing Kat's not going to make it to Belize."

"Do you want sugar?" the tea-making boy asked.

"Yeah, milk two sugar," I said.

"Same," Lawson said.

I got the names and addresses of Kat's older siblings and wrote them down at a little table Mrs McAtamney unfolded for us.

"Now it says in my notes that you told WPC Rice that you would give your relatives a call to see if Kat had shown up. Has she?"

"No one's seen hide nor hair of her."

"Well, we'll call again and give them our number and if she does show we'll be sure to let you know. Any of Kat's stepfathers that she was close to?"

"Roy. She got on great with Roy."

"Couldn't she have run off to stay with him?"

"Nope."

"Are you sure?"

"Very sure. He's been dead two years. Kicked by a horse at Appleby."

The kid making the tea plonked the two mugs and a plate of Jammie Dodgers down in front of us.

"Thank you, sonny," I said and made a big show of dipping the Jammie Dodger in the tea and pretending to eat it while really palming it so I could slip it into a tissue under the table when no one was looking.

"What's Appleby?" Lawson asked, looking up from his notebook.

"The biggest Gypsy horse fair in the British Isles, I believe," I said, and Eileen McAtamney nodded.

"We were separated then, of course, but he used to send money for Kat and always a present on her birthday. He was her favourite. Shame. *Ar dheis Dé go raibh a anam.*"

"*Go ndeana Dia grasta ar a anam dílis,*" I replied in the proper form, which impressed her and, I think, made her trust me a bit more.

"When did you notice Kat had gone missing?" I asked.

"Yesterday. I went over to her caravan to see if she was done with my washing. Went in. She wasn't there. Hadn't been in all night."

"She has her own caravan?"

"After her uncle Norman died I decided to give her his caravan, and she's been living there for about a year."

"We'll need the keys to that caravan."

"Why? She's not in there. It's not as if she's hiding under the bed."

"No, but maybe she left a note or a diary or something."

"Her old suitcase is still in there. If she run it was spur of the moment, but I don't think she run. I think something's happened to her. That Jordy Hardcastle . . . wee bastard that he is. I'll get you that key."

She got the key and I circled Hardcastle's name in my notebook. I took another Jammie Dodger and ate that without doing any tea dipping and nodded at Lawson to ask some questions. He'd be doing this on his own in a couple of weeks.

"When was the last time you did see her?" Lawson asked.

"She had dinner with us on Saturday evening."

"What time on Saturday?" Lawson followed up.

"Early dinner. About five."

"And after that?" I asked.

"She went out I think. It was a Saturday night."

"What time did you see her last?"

"About half five."

I did the ticktock in my head. It was Monday, coming up to 2.00 p.m. That was almost forty-eight hours she'd been gone. If she'd run she could be anywhere in Europe by now. If she was dead that was plenty of time to clean off the forensic traces of her murder.

"She seem nervous or in any way different on Saturday night?"

"Normal. As far as I could tell."

"What was she wearing?"

"I don't remember."

"Was she dressed up for a night out?"

"Nope, just jeans, I think, and her coat."

"Coat colour?"

"Black. Just ordinary black. And her big white jumper, I think."

"Shoes?"

"I don't remember. Kids, any of you remember what shoes Kat was wearing on Saturday?"

A general shaking of heads.

"Trainers, boots or dress shoes, those seem to be the options," I said, but no one remembered.

"Does she have a boyfriend or a friend that she confides in?" I asked and flipped open the notebook.

"No boyfriend I know of. Jordy certainly isn't her boyfriend. And she was the oldest girl around here. Everyone else has gone. Robert she liked. Robert Patterson. Mary Patterson was the last girl sort of 'round her age too, she was good friends with Kat, but the Pattersons went off just at the end of November there."

"Where are they now?"

"Ach, who knows? Glen's a smith. There's call for that line of work these days."

"Who's Glen?"

"That's Mary's father. I think he might have heard about some work down south and they moved down there. Glen, Robert, Mary and Coral. Coral is Mary's stepmum."

"How old is this Robert?"

"Sixteen. There's half a dozen older brothers, but they're all scattered to the winds years ago."

"Forwarding address for the Pattersons' post?"

"There is none."

"So how would you get in contact with them if you needed to?" I asked.

"They'll be at the Ballycastle Horse Fair," she said.

"And that's in August?" I asked.

"At Lammas, yes."

"And there's no way to get in contact with them before that?"

"None that I can think of."

We tried to nail down the timeline a bit more but there was nothing to add. I asked the kids if they had any details to contribute but they had nowt pertinent.

"So who is this Jordy Hardcastle?"

"She got money from him. Checks and cash."

"For what?"

"He took pictures of her."

"I see," I said. I didn't like the sound of that.

"And once she came back from his place stinking of drugs."

"What drugs?"

"I don't know. Grass, I think. I don't touch the stuff."

"I see, Kat bought drugs from him?"

"I don't know if he's a drug dealer. Them are pretty scarce 'round here on account of how the IRA or the UVF would kill him like your man over a year ago in Sunnylands. Remember that one? They arrowed him to death. What a way to go."

"That was actually my case, Mrs McAtamney. It was a crossbow bolt in the back, but I take your point. Right, we'll go check her caravan then, and if you think of anything at all or she gets in contact with us or any of your relatives please don't hesitate to give me a call," I said handing her my card. "Oh, and before I go, I'll need a recent photograph if you can rustle one up while we're across the way."

"I'll see what I've got."

On the way across the muddy site to Kat's caravan I asked Lawson if he'd had cards of his own made up.

"Cards? No, no one told me to—"

"You gotta have hundreds of these printed up. Your name, the CID phone number, the station phone number and if you're really keen your home phone number. Don't believe what they tell you in the manuals. It's isn't forensic. It isn't confessions. Ninety percent of this business is tips and cooperation from Joe Public."

Lawson made a note of that in his notebook too.

The drizzle had increased and the football game had ceased but the kid watching my car was still there without a coat or an umbrella.

"You can wait inside as long as you don't touch anything," I said unlocking the Beemer.

"Can I smoke?"

"No, you can't," I replied almost hysterically. I didn't even smoke in the car. In fact, I was such a good boy, I was down to seven cigarettes a week and never in the car.

The door to Kat's caravan turned out to be unlocked. We put on latex gloves and went inside.

Small, neat caravan with a partially buckled roof. The bed was made and her clothes were put away in drawers. There were a few books in a breeze block-and-timber bookshelf, which was always an encouraging sign. I flipped through them: *The Silver Chair, The Hobbit*, the Earthsea Trilogy, not my cup of tea but encouraging. Some Traveller children never learned to read at all.

I showed the books to Lawson.

"She was a reader," I said, before correcting myself: "She *is* a reader, I mean."

There weren't many clothes, and those that there were had been recycled from several generations of cousins, aunts and the like. There was a tape player and a few tapes. A swim cap, a faux silk dressing gown, a few nice new dresses. The new dresses might possibly be significant. Recent money.

Her musical taste was fairly typical of the times, I imagined. Bands and singers I had never heard of.

We searched the place for a good thirty minutes but unfortunately there was no diary or notebook or journal. There were two phone numbers on sticky notes. I took the sticky notes and put them in evidence bags. The suitcase was still here right enough and there was thirty quid and rings in a jewellery box.

"She left her suitcase," I said.

"And if I was running away I would have taken the money," Lawson said.

"Yeah, me too," I agreed.

"Unless I didn't want me mum or the cops to think I was running away," Lawson added.

"That would be crafty, but maybe it's overthinking things a bit. In Ulster, Occam's razor is usually pretty sharp."

We went to Mrs McAtamney's caravan.

"Find anything useful?" she asked.

"No. Couple of phone numbers on some yellow sticky notes but that was it," I said. "There's money and jewellery over there you might want to look after until she gets back."

"I will."

"She have a bank account or anything like that?"

"No! Nobody 'round here has a bank account."

"Seems like a bright girl. A reader. How was Kat doing in school?"

"School?"

"Yeah, how was she doing? Good student, bad student? Popular?"

"She didn't go to school. The last time she was in school when she was eleven or twelve and we were living Nantes."

"Nantes in France?"

"Aye. Big Traveller community there but the authorities made sure all the kids went to school. If they didn't you ended up in court."

"How long was she in school there for?

"About two and a half years until we left."

"So she speaks French?"

"Oh, aye, fluent so she is."

"So she could maybe be in France?" Lawson asked.

Mrs McAtamney shook her head. "If she's bolted, I doubt she would have gone back there. The food didn't agree with her. Fish all the time for school dinner, and all that bloody garlic."

"If she's got connections in France we'll need to alert Interpol," I mused to myself.

"I already put her in the database," Lawson said.

"What other languages does she speak?"

"Shelta, of course, and she's fluent in the Irish. And French. Wee bit of Spanish from when we lived in the Basque country."

"You lived in Spain as well?"

"When she was wee like. Just for a year. Lovely down there so it was. We got burned out, so we had to go."

"She's only fifteen, why didn't you send her to school here?" Lawson asked, annoyed by Mrs McAtamney's lapses in parenting.

"She wouldn't go. She was awful bullied, so she was. She was better out than in."

"You said she ran away before, once?" I asked looking at my notes.

"Oh, that? A year and a half ago she 'found' a wallet, took herself off to Dublin and checked into the Gresham Hotel. Had a fine old time until the money ran out. She called me from a phone box. I had to send someone down to get her."

I made a note in my book to call the Gresham Hotel and see if any waifs or waifs with new boyfriends had checked in.

"If you were going to look for her where would you look first?" I asked.

"The Tourist Inn 'round the corner and Jordy's. She was always hanging at the Tourist and your man's. But I checked both them places and she's not there."

"We'll check again," I said.

"Do you have that photograph I was after?" I asked.

"Yes, I do, this was Robert's sixteenth birthday," she said handing me a Polaroid. I couldn't really get a good look at in the dimly lit caravan but if it was of sufficient quality we could photocopy it and put it up on missing posters. We'd certainly send it across the wires to the British and Irish and now the French police too. Spain as well maybe—I mean, why not?

"Would you be willing to appear at a press conference?" I asked.

"On the TV?"

"Yes."

"Do I have to?"

"We've often found that they are effective in missing persons cases."

"Can I think it over?"

"Time might be a factor here, Mrs McAtamney," I said sternly.

"Can I let you know tomorrow?"

"What's your concern about appearing on TV, if I might ask?"

"I'd rather not say."

I stared at her and then at Lawson and then at the kids. I could think of a number of reasons why she wouldn't want to be on TV but surely the safe return of her daughter was paramount. Maybe now wasn't the time to push it.

"Well I'll talk to you about this anon. And we'll be in touch to keep you abreast of developments."

I put the photograph in an evidence bag and went outside.

I was curious about Mrs McAtamney's camera shyness so I made a quick radio call to the cop shop and, of course, she had a rap sheet as long as your arm. Robbery, receiving stolen goods, pickpocketing, insurance fraud. No violent crimes, no social services stuff either, but a lot of petty theft. No doubt she was worried that someone would see her face and remember her as the person who took off with a car on a test drive or nicked their wallet or something of the kind. But without the tearful mother at the press conference it would make finding the missing girl all the harder.

Not impossible though.

Not for the likes of the brilliant detective Sean Duffy. Right?

Yeah, right.

Still it was a missing persons case.

A missing Traveller girl, it was the sort of thing that was going to put me and my team in physical jeopardy was it?

Yeah, right—again.

In Ulster everything always went deeper than you could ever imagine.

# 4
# THIS IS A BAD TOWN FOR SUCH A PRETTY FACE

We headed to Eden Village's only pub, the Tourist Inn, which was, literally, just around the corner from the caravan site.

I took out the picture of Kat McAtamney and examined it in the light. She was a strikingly attractive girl. All Traveller children looked older than their years and Katrina could easily be taken to be nineteen or twenty. Five foot seven, sophisticated looking, leggy. She had brown hair cut in a bob, high cheek bones, very pale skin, oddly Asiatic grey-blue eyes.

"Oh, dear," Lawson said, looking at the picture.

"I know," I agreed.

Neither of us needed to say the word "jailbait," but that's what we both were thinking. Crabbie, thank God, wouldn't have had those thoughts, but Lawson and I were not cut from the same sturdy cloth as Sergeant McCrabban.

In the photo her look was incredibly well put together too; she was wearing jeans and half boots and a tight red sweater. She wasn't smiling, which you had to think was odd if this was taken at a birthday party. She wasn't exactly frowning either, but the eyes did not look like the eyes of a happy person.

I shared this last observation with Lawson.

"Druggie?" he suggested.

"I don't know. If so not for long. Heroin addicts don't look as healthy as she does; she's thin but she's not frail."

"And there was no drug paraphernalia back at the caravan."

"No."

I sighed. "All right then, let's try the local watering hole."

Across the muddy caravan site and 'round the corner.

We went inside the grim cinder block Tourist Inn to be confronted by half a dozen ruddy-faced denim-clad members of the Eden UVF hugging pints of Harp Lager and smoking Rothmans Longs while ABBA's "Ring Ring" played over the jukebox. It was a meeting of the local brain trust and our presence was not appreciated—any minute now they were expecting Carl Sagan and Garry Kasparov to come marching in.

"Quite the hive of scum and villainy," Lawson muttered, no doubt the reference to some TV show I hadn't watched, because otherwise it was a bloody odd thing to say.

I sat at the bar. "Sorry gents, private function, today," the barman said. "You'll have to go elsewhere."

He was a youngish bloke with a likeable mop of curly brown hair. And really it wasn't his fault he worked in a scumbag paramilitary pub.

I took out my warrant card and put it on the bar. "We're the Old Bill, son. Carrick CID. We need to ask you a few questions," I said quietly.

But before he could reply one of the denim-clad skinhead UVF men was coming over and then physically tapping me on the shoulder.

"Oi, pal, we're having a meeting, you'll have to fuck off," he said.

"No, I'm terribly sorry but you'll have to fuck off," I said, waiting a good five seconds before picking up the warrant card and showing it to him.

Those five seconds a delicious ellipse during which the UVF man wondered if he could beat me to death then and there and I wondered if I could take the big bastard without having to draw my sidearm. I don't know about you but the badness in me lives for moments like that. It's an affectation and a sign of immaturity but what can you do?

He looked at the warrant card and then at me and Lawson, shook his head and went back to his table. The denim clad UVF men grabbed their pints and their cigarettes and carried them to the lounge bar next door muttering "fucking peelers" and "black bastards" as they went.

"Drink gents?" the barman asked.

I was actually pretty thirsty, and I was desperate to get the taste of that horrific tea out of my mouth, but in a place like this the beer and spirits were most likely watered down.

"Do you have any kind of lime juice back there?"

"Yeah. Should do. Wee bottle."

"Do me a favour then, mate: lime juice, vodka, ice in a pint glass and top it up with some soda water."

The barman did as he was asked and put the concoction down in front of me. "Is there a name for that?" he asked.

"Yeah. It's a vodka gimlet."

"Oh, is that right? Bogart?"

"Marlowe anyway."

"And you, sir?" he asked Lawson.

"I'll just have a Coke and any crisps if you got some."

When we'd gotten our drinks, I showed the barman Kat's photograph.

"Seen her?" I asked.

"Oh aye, she's been in here from time to time. Kat, is that right?"

"That's right. Who was she in with?" I asked, taking a big refreshing drink from the vodka gimlet .

"Her, uhm, boyfriends," the barman said, looking uncomfortable.

"Boyfriends?"

"Yeah, if that's what they were."

"What are you hinting at here, son?" I asked, a sinking feeling beginning to descend upon me.

"I don't want to cast aspersions on anyone, but I think she might have been, an, uhm, a what do you call it? An escort."

"A prostitute?"

"I didn't say that. All I know is that she would come here a couple of times a week, order a Jack and Coke and wait and usually within fifteen minutes a gentleman would meet her and they'd go off together.

She always come in here by herself when it was raining. But if it was a clear day like she was probably picked up outside."

"You know she's only fifteen," I said.

The barman looked upset. "I didn't know that! Shite. I wouldn't have served her if I thought she wasn't eighteen. This is my uncle's place and I wouldn't want him to lose his licence."

"What did these gentlemen look like?"

"Older, obviously."

"Suits, jeans, what?"

"'Well heeled' you would have said. Suits."

"How many different men in total?"

"I don't know. Three or four?"

"Some more than once?"

"Yup."

"And when did this start?"

"When did she start coming in here or when did she start meeting men here?"

"Both."

"She's been coming in for about a year and I suppose since last summer meeting with the, uhm, gentlemen callers."

I looked at Lawson. He was scribbling furiously in his notebook.

The alarm bells were ringing now.

Ringing for both of us.

We knew how these things went most of the time. A teenage girl goes missing. One day, two days, no trace of her anywhere and then on that third day she shows up. She's at a friend's house, she's at a boyfriend's, she's with her estranged father. This was a surprisingly common narrative. Maybe got three or four of those a month. A million reasons for it: domestic abuse, kid growing out the nest, a row with her mum, a row with a sibling, a row with her dad, guilt over some minor infraction of the social norms, a boy at the back of it . . . Like I say, three or four of those a month.

But a prostitute going missing? A teen prostitute?

That was another kettle of fish.

That was never good.

That was front page of *The News of the World* stuff.

Alarm bloody bells.

"You didn't demand a piece of the action or anything since she was using your space to meet clients? Bright lad like you, wee fiddle on the side," I asked the bartender.

"God no. It was none of my business!"

"And those denim-clad gentlemen?"

"You'll have to ask them."

"I will ask them."

I went next door to the lounge bar but the UVF men indignantly denied ever shaking Kat down for a piece of the action, denied, in fact, knowing that she was a prostitute. They were a particularly stupid bunch and I wouldn't put it past them not to have realised she was meeting clients here on rainy days. In any case if she was meeting clients here on rainy days it was her pimp's job to pay off the local goons, not hers. Because a girl like Kat would surely have a pimp, wouldn't she? It seemed unlikely that a kid got into the business as an independent operator, not at her age. Waste of time talking to these characters though, anyway—they could never be seen to be cooperating with the police even on a missing persons case. The bastards.

I went back into the public bar.

"What's your name, son?" I asked the barman.

"Michael Reed."

"Did she have a pimp, Michael? Someone who was looking out for her?"

"I don't know anything about that. Nobody I saw. It was always just her and her, uhm, boyfriends."

"Is it possible that they really were boyfriends and she was just seeing three men at the same time?" Lawson asked.

Michael Reed thought about that. "I suppose it's possible."

"Might not be what we're thinking, sir," Lawson said to me. "Popular girl, pretty girl, likes to have men take her out for the occasional meal or whatever. No harm in that."

"Hmmm," I thought dubiously.

"Have you got a telephone in here?" I asked Michael.

"Yeah."

Time to start ringing some of those bloody alarm bells to be on the safe side. I called the station and asked Eva to page Sergeant McCrabban. We would need the big lad for this one. I asked Eva to up the alerts on one Katrina McAtamney and I told her that I'd be in soon with a photograph. I hung up and dug out the phone numbers scrawled on Katrina's Post-it notes. I thought I almost recognised the first one, a Carrick number, but I couldn't place it. The second one was a Belfast number.

Dialled the first one.

"Carrick Clinic. This is Heather."

"Heather McGowan? It's Inspector Sean Duffy."

"Hello Sean, how are you?"

"I'm good, Heather."

"I heard you were away in the sun."

"Jesus, word gets around doesn't it? Listen, Heather, I need you to look something up for me. Was one of your patients a Katrina McAtamney?"

"You know I can't tell you that, Inspector Duffy. Our patients' confidentiality is protected under the Data Protection Act."

"It's a missing persons case, Heather. You know I wouldn't ask unless it was something important."

"I'm sorry to hear that but I can't discuss patients' files with the police or anyone else for that matter. Data Protection Act 1984. It's a privacy thing."

"Can you at least tell me what prescriptions she was getting? Was she on the pill?"

"I can't tell you that either. You know I can't and I won't," she said icily.

"All right. Thanks," I said and hung up. I turned to Lawson. "The first number was Carrick Clinic but Heather McGowan over there wouldn't tell me if Kat was a patient or not. Says the files are protected under the DPA. We won't get those records until we show them a bloody death certificate."

Lawson nodded. "Oh, yes, they're very strict about that these days. Easy enough though to get a court order, if, uhm, you know, God forbid, this becomes a murder inquiry."

I dialled the second number, but it just rang and rang. Directory assistance told us that it was a phone box near City Hall in Belfast. That was bloody useless.

I called the Gresham Hotel to see if Kat or anyone resembling Kat had checked in but no dice there. I left my number and made them promise me to call if she did check in. Finally, I called the list of Kat's relatives in England and Ireland. Again no Kat, again I left my number.

I took a big final sip of my vodka gimlet and looked at Michael. "Sorry mate, you're going to have get a replacement or close up for the night."

"Why?"

"We're going to have to take you down the station and draw sketches of those boyfriends of hers. Unless there's a CCTV camera in here—which it doesn't look like there is."

"There's no security camera."

"Right then, come along with us."

"I don't think I remember what any of them looked like, except for the guy with the moustache. And he'd shaved that off the next time he was in."

"That's fine, draw the guy with the moustache then."

"Does it have to be now?"

"Yeah, it does. Katrina's gone missing and it's been nearly forty-eight hours. About time we got a bead on these Johns."

"If I call Danny, he can be over in ten or fifteen minutes to mind the bar."

"Yeah, ok, but we're on the clock. You call your mate Danny and get yourself down to the station as soon as he arrives. Ask the desk sergeant to send you up to the CID Incident Room with Roddy Cullen, he's our sketch artist. You give him a description as best you can of all the clients you remember, ok?"

"Ok."

"Make sure you get yourself down there. I don't want to have to come looking for you cos I'll be pissed off if I do."

"I'll come."

"Good. Right, Lawson, time for us to hit the bricks."

As I walked out of the pub into the drizzle, Lawson was staring at me.

"What?" I said.

"Nothing."

"No, what?"

"Well . . . teenage girl who has run before, no hint of foul play, no evidence of any crime and you're . . ."

"I'm what?"

"You're going in all guns blazing. You're acting like we have a body."

"Yeah, look, just to be clear, this isn't me doing the old man thing and trying to put off my retirement, I promise you it's not that. There's something about this case . . . something about it doesn't feel right."

I looked into those blue, trusting and rather intelligent eyes. "You can feel it too, I know you can."

He thought about it, bit his lip and nodded.

"Aye, I thought so," I said.

I put Kat's photo in my pocket and walked back to the car.

"Where to now, boss?" he asked.

"Station to get everything properly in motion, run down these leads and connections and then we go to see the grass-smoking photographer. Hopefully he's a photographer not a pornographer cos they don't like kiddie pornographers in prison and I'm in an arresting sort of mood for a fucker like that today."

"This is this Jordy Hardcastle fella?"

"Aye. I don't even like his name."

"No, me neither," Lawson agreed.

# 5

# S = K LOG W

New Year's Day, 1990, in Carrickfergus by the sea. Beemer along sea front. Black coal boats. Black sky. The greasy borderlands of the rain's titanic empire.

1990. Believe it, pal.

Forget the rain. Forget the weather cos the future's coming. The future was a silver light. The smell in the air was change. Before year's end Thatcher will be gone, the Soviet Union will be on its last legs, Germany will be one country, not two. Iraq's about to invade our consciousnesses and a rich kid called Osama bin Laden is going to start a jihad to rid Saudi Arabia of the infidel.

Silver light my arse.

I drove the Beemer into the station to check on the alerts on Kat McAtamney. Everything in hand. I scanned her photo into the Interpol database and then photocopied it onto handouts. I got coppers with nothing to do to go out and do some leg work.

"Stick these flyers up, lads, earn your pay this week. The walk will be good for you."

I dialled the BBC and UTV and tried to get the TV interested but it was no go. A missing tinker girl? Where was the news story in that?

What's the angle? There in fact was an angle, but I was not willing to discuss the prostitution thing yet until I checked it out.

"I'll call you again when we know more."

I called my contacts at the local radio station and at least got promised a space on the bulletins.

I put Jordy Hardcastle's name into the database and a Jordan Hardcastle popped up who lived down at Carrick Marina. Driving licence with no points on it and no convictions of any kind. A little disappointing if I'm honest, cos it meant nothing to threaten him with. His date of birth was August 6, 1970, in Osnabrück, West Germany. His father must have been a squaddie in the British Army because Germans did not emigrate from prosperous engine-of-the-European-Community Deutschland to rainy, edge-of-the-world-endemic-unemployment Ulster.

"Sean!" Crabbie yelled, spotting me across the open floor plan of the office. He was a little greyer 'round the temples but the big, dour Raymond Massey–like visage never changed. He was wearing a sober suit, black rain coat and dark green tie. He was a presence was the Crabman. A presence from an older world. You could imagine Crabbie in a production of *The Crucible*, lurking there at the side of the stage, ominous and silent. Except you couldn't because Crabbie would have been far too sensible to put up with all that witchy stuff in the first place. Pretty boring play it would have turned out which would have suited him just fine.

And speaking of plays, even as I conducted this case, I knew I couldn't forget John Strong, my fucking agent, my Chekovian loaded revolver sitting there on the table ready to go off in all of our faces at any time. I made a mental note to call MI5 at some point today or tomorrow.

I stopped dead, and when Crabbie came over I gave him a hug, partially because I knew he'd hate it, and partially because I missed the big ganch.

"What's afoot?" he asked. "Where are you going so sharpish?"

"Didn't like the smell of that missing persons case. She was apparently working as an escort to some well-to-do men in nice suits. It might have ended nasty."

"Nasty?" Crabbie asked. "Murder?"

"You never know."

"What's the motive?" Crabbie wondered.

"She started blackmailing them? One of them was a psycho? She met a Ripper? One of those satanic paedophile conspiracies of the great and good you read about in the Sunday papers," Lawson said eagerly.

"Well, that's certainly covering your bases," I replied.

"An, escort? Are you sure, Sean? The report said she was fifteen, if I remember rightly," Crabbie muttered.

"I'm afraid that's what it looks like, buddy."

He frowned and shook his head. His eyes told the story. The world was going to hell and there was nothing he could do about it. I nodded. Nothing any of us could do about it really. Big picture. Long view. In geological time we were all dead and forgotten. The letters they had carved onto Boltzmann's grave as a permanent tribute, "S = k log W," were already decomposing into the stone.

"What are you thinking, Sean?" Crabbie asked.

"Heat death of the universe, entropy, decay, the utter pointlessness of police work."

"The usual then?"

"Aye."

"You went out to the caravan site already?" he asked.

"Yup. Interviewed the mother. Decent sort, I thought. Not a hitter. Not a drunk. Thief, of course, but who isn't? Kids seemed nice. They were in the background playing bloody Monopoly, not swigging cider and throwing things at the telly."

Crabbie nodded. "So what makes you think Katrina was a working girl?"

"She used to hang out in the Tourist Inn, met various men there. It's possible this bloke Jordy Hardcastle might be her pimp. Need to interview him."

"Is that where you're heading?"

"Yup. Wanna come? I'll give you your present when we get back. Big Toblerone each for you, Helen and the boys."

"Sean, that wasn't necessary. I—"

"You're not into holy water are you? I filled up half a dozen bottles at the Jordan. The friggin River Jordan itself, mind, but I can't get rid of them. I gave one to me da and he took it reluctantly. Beth's parents said no, Lawson said no . . ."

Crabbie looked embarrassed. "It's not something I would normally like to have in the house, Helen—"

"Jesus! Forget it then! Let's go."

Down the stairs we went.

"Everything all right on the home front? Everything ready for the big move? If you need any help on that, let me know," Crabbie asked as we got to the car park, and unlike those other lying bastards who offer to help you move the Crabman actually meant it.

"Nah, we'll be fine. Moving company coming tomorrow," I said.

"How's Emma?"

"She's good. Missed us but she was spoiled rotten by her grandparents."

"Oh, that's good."

"Bit of an incident with *Mary Poppins* but let's not get into that."

"*Mary Poppins*? Did the chimney sweeps upset her?"

"No, nothing like that, my dad got annoyed about the robin during the 'Spoonful of Sugar' song. Wrong type of robin apparently. Set him right off. You know what he's like."

"Don't let him see *Blue Velvet*, sir," Lawson piped up.

"Great minds, son, great minds."

We went out to the Beemer. No need to check underneath for bombs here in the safety of the police station car park, which was a good job because it was lashing now.

Lawson moved from the front to the back seat, remembering that Crabbie was the senior sergeant. He had a look on his face I couldn't interpret. "Are you ok back there, Alex?"

"Yeah. Hey boss, do you think it's ok that only one company is allowed to make Monopoly?" he asked. So the funny look had been a wisecrack he'd been brewing. He wasn't chaffing against me and the

Crabman still running the show and keeping him in his place behind us. Good.

"Oh, you're very droll, Lawson. He's droll isn't he, Crabbie?"

"A laugh riot, as the kids say," Crabbie said.

"He'll need that sense of humour over the coming months dealing with Kenny Dalziel. He was on to me again about our expenses this morning," I said.

Crabbie sighed. "He would test the patience of Job that one. Free Presbyterian, of course."

"Free Presbyterian, eh? Hard to keep track of all your heretical dissenting sects. In general the Presbyterians are the dour, hard-working sensible ones and the Free Presbyterians are the shouty, evangelical unreasonable ones? Is that right?" I asked.

"That's about right," Crabbie said.

Well shouty Kenny Dalziel was going to get a phone call later today to leave me the fuck alone. At least while my agent Johnny Strong lived and breathed.

Beemer out the station gates and along the sea front.

Jordy Hardcastle's place was in a new development near the Model School in Carrickfergus. I parked the Beemer in the school car park and got out.

The rain had increased, so I grabbed a flat cap from the glove compartment and put it on. Crabbie turned up the collar on his raincoat.

"Did I ever tell youse about this Ray Bradbury story about these astronauts who go to this planet where it rains all the time?" young Lawson said.

"No, I don't think so," Crabbie replied, heroically trying to fill his pipe in the wet.

"They all eventually go mad cos of the endless rain pounding on their heads. I think that's what's been happening to Ireland for the last three thousand years," Lawson said.

"I think I told you that story and now you're stealing my theory and passing it off as your own," I said.

"Oh, sir, that's outrageous. I've been reading Ray Bradbury since I was eleven!" Lawson protested.

"It's worse up my way. Up in the high bog we have rain and midges and those big clegs that follow the cows around. That's worse by far," Crabbie said and then hastily added: "Not that I'm complaining, mind."

Jordy Hardcastle lived in a shiny new town house overlooking the water, next to the brick wall of the Model School itself which was covered with graffiti. Good for a copper to scope graffiti. Gives you a clue to what kind of area you were in. This was all UDA and UVF sloganeering with the odd Glasgow Rangers or Linfield football club. In amongst all the paramilitary hatred there were two good ones that elicited a chuckle:

"I can't spell Armmageddon but hey it's not the end of the world."

"They used to call it a jumpoline before your mum got on it."

But these of course, were drowned out by terrible things people were saying about the Mother of God and the Holy Father. I said a silent prayer against all the bad voodoo and again thanked my lucky stars that I was getting out.

"Neighbourhood's changed 'round here," McCrabban said.

"Aye. Curious mix of old-school graffiti and brand-new apartments and town houses, " I agreed and looked around with my cop-vision specs on.

This bit of Carrick reflected the times well. They had built a Kentucky Fried Chicken over the site of the old ship repair yard and this was now the preferred hangout for delinquents too young for the pub but too old to vandalise the kiddies' playground. Chilly Ballardian vibe, with its psychiatrists living in the marina flats and gangs of preteens hanging about in track suits mocking your sartorial choices, shoes and haircut.

Only half a dozen twelve-year-old girls today but with our sensible shoes, boring jackets and peeler haircuts we braved their dirty looks as we tried to find Hardcastle's place. Unfortunately, all the flats looked the same and it was evidently uncool to have numbers on your apartment door.

"We're going to have to ask the locals," Lawson said.

"I'm not doing it," Crabbie said quickly.

"You're closer to the age demo, Lawson. Go on, then," I insisted.

Lawson approached the girls who were dressed in late-80s Lauper-Madonna-Bangles layers, head bands and scarfs.

"Girls, excuse me, I was wondering if you could help me," he began. The barrage came back at him all at once:

"Aye looks like you need fucking help, pal, help getting it up!"

"He needs a fucking mirror that's what he needs, look at yon shirt!"

"He's beyond help. Ever hear of the gym, skinny malink? Lift some fucking weights why don't ya?"

"He's gelled his hair up, not down, what is this 1982, you dumb fuck?"

Terrified, Crabbie and I immediately backed away lest we get collateral. Lawson finally returned to us a minute later looking shaken.

"It's that apartment over there at the end," he said. "Jesus, that was rough."

"Part of the job, son. Builds character," I told him as we walked over.

"That's what happens when people stop going to church," Crabbie said definitively. He was wrong though, Kentucky Fried Chicken was their bloody church. Probably had Colonel Sanders nailed to the crucifixes on their necks.

I killed the nihilism, got in character, rang Jordy's doorbell. An intercom crackled.

"Who is it?" a voice asked with a bit of an English accent. East London crossed with Belfast—not that unusual a combo 'round here what with British soldiers marrying local girls.

"The peelers."

"I haven't done nothing. Piss off."

"We need to ask you some questions about a missing girl."

"What girl?"

"Katrina McAtamney."

"Who says she's missing?"

"Her mum. Are you going to let us in or I am going to have to come back here with the HMSU and break your bloody door down?"

"You can't break my door down. I haven't done nothing wrong and you'll need a warrant to get into my place. And you can't get a warrant without probable cause," Jordy said with a sneer.

"Warrant will take two seconds, sunshine. I suspect you of abducting a minor for immoral purposes and I think I smell marijuana, do you smell it too, Sergeant Lawson?"

"I think so, sir."

A long pause. "You're all the fucking same, you lot," Jordy said, and the door buzzed open.

We pushed the heavy wooden door open and went into a shiny futuristic-looking townhouse. A long marbly corridor led to a big living room overlooking Carrick Marina and Belfast Lough. Leather sofas, glass coffee table, big screen TV embedded in the wall, tons of windows, lot of light. Balcony in the living room and stairs to a couple of bedrooms. Black and white photos and original art on the wall: sort of place I wouldn't mind after I sold Coronation Road.

Hardcastle was a lanky fellow with prematurely balding ginger hair, a figure-eight sort of face that Edvard Munch would have enjoyed sketching in charcoals. He was wearing a red Adidas tracksuit over a white shirt and a gold chain. Drug dealer/minor gangster uniform but you couldn't prejudge the issue. Maybe he was an athlete.

I introduced the team and we sat down on the sofa. Hardcastle did not get up or even turn the TV off which was showing live football. Crystal Palace versus someone by the look of it. He did not offer us tea either which was quite the rarity around these parts. There was someone else in the flat—you could hear them moving around upstairs in the rooms behind the interior balcony—but they didn't make an appearance. Mrs McAtamney claimed that she'd been assaulted, maybe it was by one of Hardcastle's goons? It had to be said though that this didn't quite seem like the pad of a drug dealer. No drug dealer I'd ever gone to anyway. This clown had money and he knew how to spend it. Still, he vibed dirty. And confident dirty. The fuzz shows up at your door and you keep sitting there watching the telly?

Nobody did that.

"We'd like to ask you a few questions about a Katrina McAtamney," I began.

"Ask away," he said.

"Could you turn the TV off?" McCrabban said.

"I'll mute it. I've got a bet on this one," he said and muted the game.

"What *do* you do for a living, Mr Hardcastle?" I asked.

"Photos."

"You develop them?"

"Photographer. Some detectives you are. Didn't you notice the work on the walls?"

I looked again. Photographs of the Troubles. Photographs of attractive girls on beaches and forests. Moody landscape shots. The city in the rain. Van Morrison singing with Bob Dylan at the Ulster Hall. A football player scoring a goal.

"Very nice," I said.

"I've won awards," he said absently, as Crystal Palace got a free kick on the edge of the box.

"So, Katrina McAtamney, how do you know her?"

"Took her picture, got her some catalogue work."

"Modelling work?"

"Yeah, couple of catalogues. They're always looking for new faces."

"How did you find her?"

"She saw my ad in the *Tele*. She called me up. I told her to come down the shop on West Street. Wouldn't have bothered if I'd known about all the fucking baggage she come with."

"What baggage?"

"Her fucking mum for a start. She come 'round here the other night. Put a brick through my balcony door. Steve had to restrain her. Should have called you lot."

"Who's Steve?"

"Well this is going to shock you inspector, but Steve is my boyfriend. I know you'd love to bloody arrest me for that but you can't. Legal now, mate, even here."

"So what happened the other night?" I asked, flipping open my notebook.

"Her mum comes to see me looking for her. Drunk out of her mind. I don't know where she's gone. And her mum starts screaming and yelling. Pissed as a newt. All the neighbours coming out. And then she chucks a half brick through me French door. Fucking lunatic. Steve goes out and tells her to piss off and eventually she fucks off."

"How well did you know Katrina?"

He shook his head and his green eyes narrowed but that appeared to be because Crystal Palace was bollicksing up its chance.

"Not very well. She wasn't on my books, not really. She come to see me to get into the business. I took some snaps of her and got her a couple of gigs in the C&A catalogue and the Argos catalogue. Oh, fucking hell, how could you miss that? Useless wankers!"

"So she's one of your models?"

"Nah, it didn't work out."

"Why didn't it work out?"

"Like I say, baggage. She come late to both shoots. And she was giving me the old lip both times. I don't need that."

"She was pretty," Lawson said.

"She was pretty, yes, but pretty girls are a dime a dozen even in fucking Belfast. And the brutal fact is that she just wasn't quite tall enough to make it in the business. She was five seven or something like that. That's just a bit too short these days. That would have been ok four or five years ago but the trend now is for super tall, super thin and flat chested. I did send her pictures to an agency in London. They liked her face but they told me that if she didn't suddenly shoot up in the next six months or so they couldn't use her."

"So what happened then?"

"That was it. She had no future in the business. Not at the moment. Trends change, of course, but, well, that was that. Try to grow four inches is what I told her when I last saw her."

"When was that?"

"About two months ago."

"Why does her mother think you've been in contact with her more recently?"

"Cos she's fucking crazy? Who knows? Cos I sent Katrina a residual check for three hundred quid a couple of weeks back to her mother's address and she thinks she can squeeze a few bob more out of me?"

"She thinks you supplied her with marijuana," I said.

"Bollocks."

"We're not the drug squad, you know. We're not interested in your personal use. We're looking for Katrina."

"I'm saying nothing about that. Not incriminating myself," Jordy said and winced as Palace's opponents made a break towards the goal. Crabbie got up, walked to the TV and turned it off.

"Fuck do that for? I was watching that. All right. The lot of you, piss off!"

"For heaven's sake, Mr Hardcastle. It doesn't have to be this way. If you want I'll come back with the K9 team and we'll rip this place apart looking for your stash and when we find it, I'll charge you with dealing," I said.

He glared at me. "What exactly is it that you want to know?"

"Did you give Katrina drugs?"

"No, I bloody didn't. Hard enough to get puff 'round here without me giving it to some tinker bint who was always bloody late and underprepared to begin with. Last thing she needs is grass. Speed would have been more her ticket."

"Did you take any glamour pictures of her?" I asked.

"What do you mean by that?"

"Nudes?"

"Do me a favour, mate. She was fifteen."

"So you're saying you didn't give her drugs and you didn't take nudes of her?"

"That's exactly what I'm saying," Jordy insisted.

"And if we find any nudes?"

"You won't."

"Her mother says she came back from your house stinking of marijuana."

"She didn't bloody get it from me. She was bad news, that girl."

"When *exactly* did you last see her?" I asked opening my notebook.

"Told ya, a couple of months back. I gave her a lift back to her caravan after the Argos gig."

"What was her state of mind, then?"

"She was excited. She thought the photo shoot had gone well."

"Hadn't it?"

"No. It hadn't. Clients were furious that she was late and that she was lippy and chain smoking the whole time."

"Did you tell her that the clients were unhappy?"

"I decided to let her down gently. I gave her the up-front money and told her if anything else come up I'd be in touch. And then I gave her the old spiel about it being a tough business and her being too short and maybe she should think about doing something else."

"And how did she take that?"

"She wasn't so bright. I don't think she could read between the lines of what I was saying. But there was no way I was going to use her again."

"So you never called her back?"

"No."

"Did she call you?"

"She left a couple of messages on my machine but I didn't return them."

"And her mother?"

"Is fucking nuts as you probably know already after meeting her."

"She seemed perfectly fine to me," I said.

He shrugged. "She comes over banging on about her daughter running off. Nothing to do with me, I told her. And she gives me the old yaketty yak. Yelling her head off. Upsetting the bloody neighbours. That's pretty fucking bonkers if you ask me."

"Did you know she was working as an escort?" I asked.

"A what?"

"An escort, a prostitute."

"No! Is that what she was doing? Jesus Christ!" he said and shook his head.

"You wouldn't have encouraged her down that route?"

"Why would I?" he asked incredulously.

I didn't have an answer to that one. Crabbie and Lawson said nothing. They could see I was only fishing.

"Do you have any headshots we could use in a missing poster? Her mother only has a family snap," I asked in a less confrontational manner.

"Yeah. Lots, got a whole contact sheet. Steve!"

No response.

"Steve!" Jordy yelled louder.

A tall, blonde-haired young man in an Aran sweater poked his head over the balcony railing. He took off a set of headphones.

"Yeah?" he asked.

"Can you find the headshots of Katrina McAtamney? The brunette. The young one we used for the Argos catalogue."

"Oh, yeah, no problem. Who's that you're with?"

"The police."

Steve looked at us with concern. "I never touched her. If anything, I should be pressing charges."

"Never touched whom?" I asked.

"Her mother," Steve said. "Wasted, she was, threw a brick through the bloody window."

"We're not here about that, we're looking for the daughter."

After a few minutes, Steve brought us down a headshot that would look perfect over the wires. We thanked both men and drove back to the station.

"That was disappointing. I had a feeling he would be the break in the case we needed. Me and my spidey sense," I said ruefully.

"Just a dead end, really," Lawson said.

"We got a good picture at least," Crabbie said.

"Your man seemed not to know about her escort work," I mused.

"If indeed that was what she was doing. Perhaps we're being a bit too uh, what's the word, *cynical*, here?" Crabbie asked, hopefully.

"How so?"

"We don't actually know she was working as a prostitute, for one thing."

"She met several older men that she didn't know in the Tourist Inn and then went off with them. I'm trying to think what an innocent explanation of that could be?" I asked him.

"We shouldn't assume the worst," he said.

When we got back to the Incident Room, Lawson photocopied and sent out the better headshot of Katrina across the wires. We checked for any developments in the case but there was nothing from the ports, nothing from Dublin hotels, nothing from England, nothing from France. Nothing from the Confidential Telephone, the CID tip line, Interpol of the general public.

"How does a girl just vanish off the face of the Earth?" Crabbie asked us mournfully.

None of us knew.

But we knew.

It happened all the time. If Mrs McAtamney hadn't reported it, we wouldn't even have known about Kat's existence in the first place. She didn't go to school, she wasn't on the electoral roll, she didn't even have a criminal record.

I went down to see how Mr Reed was doing with Roddy, our sketch artist. Not good. The sketches were virtually worthless. Three vague looking blokes who looked like everyone and no one.

"These are shite," I said.

Roddy shrugged. "Not my fault. Only following directions."

"I really don't remember what they look like," the kid said.

"Didn't you say one of them had a moustache?" I asked.

"I think so. But then he shaved it off, I think."

"At least give one of these guys a moustache and maybe the rest of it will come to you."

I took the preliminary sketches up to the lads. Neither Lawson nor Crabbie were impressed. "There's no point in even circulating these," Crabbie said. "Make us look ridiculous."

"If they'd been better we could have shown them around the Tourist Inn or the caravan site," I agreed.

"So what *do* we do?" Lawson asked.

"Leg work."

I called BT to get Jordy Hardcastle's phone records. When I went through his incoming and outgoing calls nothing jumped out at me. Neither Katrina nor her mother had a phone in the caravan so how this was supposed to help exactly I didn't really know.

Clutching at straws, really.

Lawson looked knackered so I sent him home. He asked to take the case files with him, but I wouldn't let him.

"Don't forget to live your life, son. Make friends, go down the pub, get a hobby. Don't let the job get you down. Before I met Beth, before I had Emma, Jesus every Saturday night it was the old Hunter Thompson: fill the bath, drink a pint of Vodka, put on 'White Rabbit,' and think about dropping the hair dryer in the tub."

"What's 'White Rabbit'?" he asked.

"You're missing the point, the point is . . . oh, forget it, go on home."

"The point is a wife and kids grounds a man," Crabbie said.

"Sounds ghastly," Lawson muttered as he exited the office.

"The lip on that one," I said to Crabbie.

"Better get used to it, Sean. He's gonna be the gaffer as soon as we're done with this."

"Ach, he's a good lad, Lawson, probably just overcompensating from those girls taking the piss out of him, earlier . . . All right, I'm going to head out."

"Where to?"

"Eagle's Nest."

"I don't think I'll come with you."

"Fine."

I took Katrina's headshot and drove up to the Eagle's Nest brothel at the Knockagh. It was a high-class establishment that didn't employ anyone under the age of eighteen, but nevertheless, Kat might have gone there looking for work.

I asked to see Mrs Dunwoody in her office. She remembered me.

"Inspector Duffy, it's been a while," she said affectionately.

"Indeed, it has, Mrs D. And it will be a while. I'm settled down. Lovely daughter. Young wife. I've even got a dog. A very bad dog. A dog so bad it's actually a cat."

Mrs Dunwoody laughed.

"So, it's all good on the home front is what I'm saying," I said.

"Well we're always here if things on the home front become more strained," she said. She'd never met Beth but she knew *of* her and she almost certainly had sussed out my more exotic tastes and proclivities.

I showed her Kat's photo and diplomatically explained the situation. Mrs Dunwoody was a touchy woman and I stressed that I in no way was implying that she would have hired someone of Kat's age, but was it possible that Kat came here looking for work?

Mrs Dunwoody passed the photograph to an assistant to investigate this possibility while tea and shortbread was served. I sipped the tea, nibbled the shortbread and exchanged pleasantries until the reply came back that Kat had not come to the Eagle's Nest looking for work.

Another dead end. But that was the life of a detective—the elimination of possibilities on the probability tree until you were left with what had probably happened.

Back to Carrick RUC. I sent Crabbie home and drove out to the caravan park.

I knocked on Mrs McAtamney's door and asked her if she could get the kids to play outside for a bit. It was drizzling, but when wasn't it drizzling? Black and white, Dutch camera angle, low cloud ceiling, drizzle was Carrick's default cinematic condition. The wee kids looked at me and I nodded outside. They put on coats and grabbed a football and went out.

"Have you got news?" Mrs McAtamney asked.

There was no polite way of broaching the question, so I just jumped in. "Do you know if Kat was working as a prostitute?"

"How dare you!" Mrs McAtamney seethed.

"There were older men she—"

"She might have had boyfriends. Ever think of that? Dirty-minded peeler. She's always been a looker. A whore? I didn't raise a whore!"

Five full minutes of talking her down from the indignation ledge. Sometimes all this righteous anger is an act, but not this time I felt.

This time I felt she didn't know.

And there was nothing more she could add.

I Q&A'ed her about these "boyfriends" but Kat had her own caravan and her own life, and Mrs Mac was in the dark.

I thanked her, apologised and went out to the Beemer.

I sat in the car in the muddy caravan park and watched the day end in drizzle and sleet and dirty black clouds rolling down from Knockagh Mountain. It had been a long day. I had begun the day in another continent for crying out loud. Another continent and another decade.

And I didn't like this case.

It had already uncovered a network of middle-aged pervs.

Hopefully she'd just taken her money and run.

Hopefully no one had topped her.

I sat in the car and looked at the rain pouring down the windscreen. I put on some Radio 3.

Displacement activity. Nothing more I could do on this case. Should go home now and help ma, da and Beth pack up the house.

Still the Radio 3 was having a rare foray into contemporary classical music by playing Wim Mertens.

I listened for a while and rested my head against the window.

"Ah, fuck it," I said at last and drove back to Coronation Road for the last time ever to our family home. Sentimental vibe coming down the street. Oh, Sean, you'll have to sell this place eventually. And then who knows who'll be living here.

Fast forward to the future, me checking out the old neighbourhood with me bad knees and grey hair and walking past #113 Coronation Road and finding a Union Jack, an Ulster Flag and a UVF flag proudly flying from flagpoles in the front garden. Don't know what you heard, Fenian cop lived here? Don't think so. Not 'round these parts. No way.

Down the path. Commotion inside.

"What's going on?"

"Jet's a UB40 fan," Beth said, winking, while my mother screamed.

It took me a few beats to catch her drift. Slow today, pal, slow.

"He dragged a rat into the kitchen?"

"You got it, mister."

I disposed of said rat and gave the cat tuna as a poor substitute.

Dinner with my mum, dad, Emma and Beth surrounded by boxes in the bare-bones dining room.

"So how's this case of yours going, Sean?" my mum asked.

"Not so good, no leads."

"You didn't find the girl?" Dad asked.

"No."

"Do you know where to look?"

"No."

"You'll find her; you always do," my mum said inaccurately.

Tea in the living room while we packed boxes. "Oh, I forgot to tell you! The Assistant Chief Constable called for you!" Beth said, impressed.

"Fancy," my mum simpered, "Maybe you're getting a promotion."

"Better take that one in the shed," I said.

I dragged the phone on its cable out to the shed. I poured myself a glass of poteen and rolled a gentle spliff.

I dialled John Strong's number.

"Hello?" he said warily.

"It's me."

"Duffy, where the hell have you been?" he asked.

"I told you I was going on my holidays."

"You should have left me a number! Why didn't you leave me a number? I had to deal with that bastard Olly in Cultra. I don't trust him."

I sighed. "What's the matter, John?"

"They're on to me, aren't they? They're fucking on to me. They're going to kill me. At the next meeting they're going to shoot me dead and chalk up their most senior copper kill of the war."

"You think they're going to shoot you without a meeting of the Army Council? Really?"

"Something's wrong, Duffy."

"What makes you think that? Has anybody said anything or done anything to make you suspicious?"

"It's just a feeling. You can't ignore these instincts, can you?"

"No, I suppose you can't, John."

"Jesus it's good to talk to you, Duffy. Where have you been? You understand. You get it. You're a copper. That Olly bastard and his crew, I think they want me to get shot. I think they'd enjoy it."

Part of me would enjoy it too. All the crimes you've done, Strong, all those lives you've destroyed with glib indifference . . .

"Everything's fine, John. I'll talk to Olly this week. As far as I know there haven't been specific threats and everything is floating close to normal. It's all fine. You just have to keep a cool head. Ok? Will you do that for me?"

"Where were you, Duffy? Olly says you were in fucking Israel! You can't leave the country. Leave me in the lurch like that! And now you're moving to Scotland!"

"I'm keeping my house here, John. I'll be here all the time. It's all going to be dandy, I'm promise . . ."

You get the picture.

Talking him down.

Talking him down.

Talking him D O W N.

When I hung up, I was up exhausted. I killed the spliff, hid the resin and the poteen and went back into the house.

Dad was trying to sort out which records I would need as the bare bones of a collection.

"What about your Wagner, Sean? Scotland or here?"

"Scotland. Oh, maybe except for the Rheingold. I like the Vorspiel on that one. In fact, I'm in the mood for it right now."

Vorspiel in E-flat Major.

"This is nice, for once," Beth said.

"Oh, it's a lovely piece," Dad explained. "Of course, Wagner got most of his ideas on this one from Heine. But he could never admit it because Heine was a Jew. Did you know that, Sean?"

"Uhm . . ."

"See? Hang out with your old man and you'll learn something."

"Yes, dad."

When everyone was abed and the cat was asleep and the melancholy house was filled with cardboard boxes, I couldn't help but mutter that line of "The Lorelei" to myself in the back garden. It was what I was feeling, so why not?

*"Ich weiß nicht was soll es bedeuten. Daß ich so traurig bin."*

*I do not know what this can mean. I am so very sad.* You know what I'm talking about. You've felt the same bloody thing.

# 6
# MOVING DAY ON CORONATION ROAD

Moving truck, moving men, getting-in-the-way parents, happy girl-friend, happy daughter, terrified and freaked-out cat.

Moving was not the total existential nightmare it could have been because I was keeping a single bed, most of the furniture and about a third of my records in Coronation Road. I'd be living here until I sold the house and bought myself a flat down by the seafront and there was no way I was living in a house without a record player.

A third of my records represented about fifteen hundred albums. Just the essentials in blues, jazz, classical, R & B and rock 'n' roll. To get my pension I'd be working at Carrick RUC and staying here seven days a month for the next three and a bit years, which came to just over three hundred days. If I played just four or five albums a day, I'd never have to repeat a record in all that time which gave me a tremendous sense of comfort.

I called Crabbie and Lawson at the station and told them to work on the McAtamney case all day and keep me informed of developments. I just might be able to get in tonight.

"Sean, don't even think about it. Get your family settled," Crabbie insisted. But duty called.

"It's Duffy's Last Case, you said so yourself, mate. If I can make it in, I will."

The movers finished loading the lorry and Beth said goodbye to all the neighbours who had, of course, filtered out onto the pavement with offers of tea and cake, sympathy and the occasional strong back. Beth hugged and said cheerio to Mrs Campbell, Mrs Doherty, Mr House and, across the street, the McCaghans and the Stewarts. She kissed Bobby Cameron on the cheek because he had saved our lives a year ago in an unsanctioned IRA ambush. I shook everyone's hands and assured them that I wasn't leaving quite yet.

It was quite the contrast to that rainy day ten years earlier when I'd moved in. I was five significant things they were not, and it had not initially sat well with any of them. I was a Catholic, a policeman, middle class, something of a Bohemian and I was from Derry. I had a different accent, religion, world view and education and the icing on the cake was my job.

It had taken ten frigging years, but we were all used to each other now and I knew that these working-class Prods from the North Belfast suburbs were all friends of mine. If someone came to kill me or my family they would intervene to stop it, had in fact, intervened to stop them. And they knew in turn that if one of them had a parking ticket or a neighbour who was beating up his wife and kids I, in turn, would sort the bastard out.

Tears.

Hankies.

"Bye!"

"Bye!"

"Bye!"

I had Deep Mapped this little stretch of Coronation Road from my house to the McCombs' and then to Victoria Road. I knew every crack in pavement, every hedge, every parked car, every weird shape in the asphalt.

But Duffy's going. This isn't a feint. I have to go—my family just isn't safe here. Retreat, sure, but I'm not the only one—thousands of us are getting out.

Little Samantha McComb was the last to wave us off at the end of the street. We turned right on Vic Road and then left on the A2 Larne Road.

Cold day but a glimpse of sun.

We had an uneventful drive to Larne where we caught the large drive-on drive-off ferry to Stranraer. I drove on.

Sea air.

Diesel.

Only a little bit of chop near Ailsa Craig.

All in all, a fairly pleasant two-hour chug across the North Channel and a nice drive south of Stranraer to our new house in Portpatrick.

We'd already furnished the house over the previous few weeks and it didn't take the movers more than a couple of hours to unload the things we wanted from Carrick.

Emma sat with Jet the cat in her bed and after a couple of hours of initial panic he began to investigate his new surroundings.

By nightfall we were all set. We had dinner in the surprisingly chilly dining room overlooking the Irish Sea.

Everyone was so cold you could see their breaths.

"That heater's not going to cut it," I said glaring at the portable electric job we'd set near the old fireplace. "We'll need to get a big paraffin heater like we had in Coronation Road."

"You and those paraffin heaters of yours. We were all high as kites every time we lit those things. The fumes. What we need to do is get the fireplaces cleaned, the chimneys swept and get some good fires lit."

"I should have come over on a recce mission, stayed a night. I would have realised how cold it was going to get. Obvious, really, I screwed up."

Beth took my hand and patted it. "Lot on your plate, Sean Duffy. Don't worry about it. It's a lovely old house and we can sleep with a lot of blankets on the bed. We'll be fine. And tomorrow I'll look for a chimney sweep in the phone book."

Emma had listened to this conversation with no comment but at the repeated mentioning of chimney sweeps you could tell she was thinking about Mary Poppins again and this made her smile.

At seven o'clock I took her upstairs up to her bed. A proper bed, with safety bars on the side, but not a crib. This was her first proper bed, which also excited her.

"So how do you feel about the move?" I asked her when she was snuggled in in her pyjamas.

"I feel ok," she said but she was still too young to really understand it. Four at her next birthday. Would she remember any of this? Would she remember Ireland at all? Would she grow up with a Scottish accent?

"Book!" she said.

I picked *The Runaway Bunny* from off the shelf.

"No!" she said. "One of your books."

"You won't like them. They're grown-up books."

"One of yours!" she demanded.

"Honey, they're not even unpacked, we only unpacked yours because we knew you'd want to read something."

"One of yours!" she demanded, and Beth saved the day by coming upstairs with *20,000 Leagues under the Sea*.

"Will this do?" Beth asked.

"Yes, fine, I think."

"What's it about?" Emma asked.

"You might be able to cope with this one. It's about a man in a submarine and all his adventures."

"What's a submarine?"

"It's like a car that goes underwater. You want to hear it?"

"Yes!"

"*Twenty Thousand Leagues under the Sea* by Jules Verne," I said and stopped.

"Go on!" Emma and Beth both said.

"Well, I was going to read you the opening, but the title is a bit confusing."

"Why is it confusing?" Beth asked.

"Well if I was to say to you, 'twenty thousand leagues under the sea,' and you are vaguely aware that the book is about a submarine, you would probably think of that as a measurement of depth. But that doesn't make any sense, does it?"

Beth and Emma both stared at me uncomprehendingly. Beth sixth-sensed I was about to climb one of my hobby horses so she smiled and slipped out to put the kettle on.

"It's confusing because you think it's a measurement of depth, but it isn't. Because a league is about three miles, so twenty thousand leagues under the sea would be sixty thousand miles under the sea which would be so far under the sea you'd be out the other side of the Earth wouldn't you? I mean to say the Earth's diameter is only about eight thousand miles so you'd be right through the Earth and fifty thousand miles into space. You'd be a fifth of the way to the moon and this is a novel about a submarine! So the thing is, it's not a measure of depth it's a measure of distance and the French title lets you know that it's a measure of distance. *Vingt Mille Lieues Sous les Mers. Sous les mers*, plural. You see? It's been mistranslated into English for the last hundred years as *Twenty Thousand Leagues Under the Sea*, but in fact it should be *Twenty Thousand Leagues Under the Seas*, plural, and the reason they've gotten away with it for so long is because nobody really knows what a league is. Ask a hundred people to define a league and nobody knows. They probably think it's the same as a fathom, which it isn't!"

I turned to the first line on the first page, but Emma was sound asleep under her duvet and cotton blanket and wool blanket and comforter.

I closed the book and kissed her on the forehead.

"Jesus, I'm becoming more like my father every day," I muttered to myself. Is this what semiretirement was going to do to me?

I closed the nursery door and turned off the light.

"Did you read her the book?" Beth asked, when I came downstairs again.

"Yeah I just started it and she fell asleep. She seemed to like it though."

"Jules Verne, eh? You gotta admit that's impressive at her age."

"Absolutely. She's got a brain, that one. Let's steer her away from the cops, eh?"

"And from teaching—if she ever wants to make any money."

"Teaching's an honourable profession."

"And the police?"

"Semihonourable."

When you weren't fitting people up or bashing them during a riot or getting them to grass up their nearest and dearest to save their skins.

Beth was shattered, and she too went up to bed in the big master bedroom that also looked out on the Irish Sea and from which, on clear nights, I imagined you could see all the way over to the very edge of Carrickfergus.

I poured myself a whisky and huddled on the sofa in front of the malfunctioning fireplace. I hadn't plugged in the new record player I'd bought for this place or the TV or the radio.

Just me and my thoughts and my Jura whisky on a cold leather sofa under a wool blanket.

Not a good combo that. Bored. I rummaged among the boxes of books and grabbed a volume at random and opened at random:

You will reply that reality has not the slightest obligation to be interesting. I will reply in turn that reality may get along without that obligation, but hypotheses may not.

The phone started ringing in the hall. I rushed to get it so it didn't wake the rest of the house.

"Hello?"

"Hello, Sean, are you settled in?"

It was my ma. I told her that we were completely settled in and there was no buyer's remorse and I was quite chipper about the move. All lies but that's what mothers want to hear.

Back to the living room and the cold sofa.

It was too foggy to see Ireland tonight.

The cat was staring at me phlegmatically.

"You wanna go for a walk?" I asked it.

I took its silence for a tacit acceptance.

I pulled on a sweater, lopped the cat over my left shoulder and went out into the street.

Nice quiet street. One side facing the water, other side facing the hill, a through road, yeah, but a quiet through road.

The guy directly opposite was out tinkering with his car. Brand new Audi.

Big guy, didn't mind the cold, appeared to have a big set of metric spanners, seemed nice enough. Hard to tell with these Jocks. Still, Jocks/Micks—two sides of the same coin. Scotland means "land of the Irish" after all.

I walked to the bend in the road and back again.

Cat was impressed and went straight to the electric heater and curled up in front of it. I poured another whisky and called the station and asked if there was anyone up in CID.

"Sergeant Lawson's in," Dora said.

"Put me through, will ya please?"

"Lawson, CID."

"It's me, Sean."

"Oh, hello, sir. This was moving day for you, wasn't it?"

"It was indeed, and I moved."

"You're calling from Scotland?" Lawson said, as impressed as if I were calling from the Moon.

"Yes. So what's the story on the McAtamney case?"

"She's still missing if that's what you mean," Lawson said.

"Any developments at all?"

"Uhm, no, not really. I checked in with Interpol this afternoon and our colleagues down south and across the water but there haven't been any sightings. Nothing on the ports and nothing from the flyers you sent out yesterday. I didn't circulate the artists impressions because they were so bad."

"So there's nothing to report at all?"

"That's what I was saying, sir. No developments."

"She can't have just vanished."

"No . . . but there it is."

"What about the press? Have they taken it up?"

"Not really, no, sir, if I'm honest."

"Fifteen-year-old girl has vanished for three days and that's not a story? Christ, if this was England, the *Sun* and the *Daily Mail* would be all over it."

"Well, like I say, sir, I haven't been able to drum up a lot of interest, I'm afraid. I don't know if it's because she's a Traveller or that she's run before or what."

"Anything else?"

"No. Oh, Sergeant Dalziel came in to tell me about the cuts."

"What cuts?"

"Five percent. Every department."

"Yeah, he would wait until he knew I was away. Yesterday he was all for throwing the book at me for bloody fraud, but he bottled it as I knew he would. Now he sneaks in and tells you about a five percent budget cut. Don't believe him. We're the most important department in the station. No one's cutting our budget."

"It would be fairly easy to cut five percent, if we just—"

"We're not doing it!"

I opened the sliding door to the wet Caledonian night. Still too foggy to see Ireland but it was over there right enough.

Everything was going to hell in my absence.

I was maybe going to take two days over here to get everything sorted, but clearly I was going to have to come back earlier if the world was to keep on spinning in its ellipse around the sun.

"Don't worry about it, lad, I'll be in first thing in the morning."

"Oh," he said, sounding disappointed. "Fine, sir, I'll see you then."

"See you."

I hung up the phone and went back inside.

The job of the detective was to restore balance to the world. To impose order on a chaotic state. The detective was the vehicle for uncovering uncomfortable truths. By discovering truth and imposing a narrative on events, he or she was reversing entropy for a moment or two until a great tsunami of disorder swept everything away again.

It was a holy task.

Uncovering truth.

Holding a middle finger up to the void.

Witnessing against the beast.

I remembered Crabbie's words: You know what they're calling this around the station? They're calling it Sean Duffy's last case.

"Better not bugger it up, then," I said to myself.

# 7

# THE RETURN OF ULYSSES

I woke at five in the morning to a quiet house and a quiet world. Blue horizon, greensward, milk float in empty street. Whistling milkman picking up empties and leaving yellow butter and gold top. Postman will come in an hour or two. Maybe bread man after that. This was a world from before the Fall. 1950s world. War over, antibiotics invented, good jobs for all. Every family a house, every family a car, and the kids? The kids will be off to university to do even better than us. Lawyer, doctor, journo.

Northern Ireland was a purple line on the horizon to the west. That big grey Stalinist chimney at Kilroot visible from here. Visible from space probably. Northern Ireland was the other world. The nightmare world where men in hoods put Semtex explosives under your car because they hated you. They didn't even know you, but they hated you. A Catholic copper—you were the lowest of the low, worse even than an informer.

Over there.

Not here.

Why go back? Why ever go back?

Go back because of John Strong. Go back because of a pension. Go back because of a missing girl . . .

I sat up in the bed.

It was cold. All those glass windows overlooking the water allowed much of the heat to leave in the wee hours. The small heaters in our rooms we had turned on the night before just weren't up to snuff.

I went downstairs and took a look at the chimney. I rummaged around in the shed at the back of the house and the crawl space under the stairs and found some old painter sheets and a chimney sweeping brush.

I spread the blankets around the fireplace, opened the flue and swept the chimney.

The cat made a run for it as ash and black filth poured down, but it wasn't an unreasonable amount and the sheets caught most of it. I mopped the living room floor to get rid of the rest. I found some newspapers and kindling and chucked a couple of turf logs on top of them in the hearth. I lit a match under the newspaper, got the kindling going, got the peat going and surrounded the fire with the fireguard.

A warm fire started to eat at some of the buyer's remorse.

Not that we could have stayed. What can you do if your partner and mother of your child wants to move house. And move for a bloody good reason: we had, after all, been machine-gunned at the other house.

Machine-gunned.

Not much you can argue about there.

I put the kettle on and wrapped my hand in a plastic bag and scooped out the cat's litter box. Jet was an outdoorsy cat who seldom used the litter box, but the vet had told us to keep him inside the new house for a few weeks lest he bolt. Inside apart from the odd walk on shoulder. Jet wasn't a panicker, but I could see him doing one of those *Incredible Journey* type things to get back to Ireland. That would just be the sort of him. The kettle boiled in the kitchen and I poured the hot water onto the grains in the French press and waited for it to steep.

I pushed the French press and transferred the coffee to a Thermos flask. Coffee on the ferry at this hour would be shite. Only drinkable if you ask for whisky, cream and sugar and you don't want to go down that road at this hour of the day.

I opened a packet of cat food for the cat but yesterday's trip in the cat container had pissed it off and it huffed at the food and at me.

"Suit yourself," I said, "We're here to stay. Nothing you can do about it."

Jet gave me a look of chilly disdain and walked away from the food dish. "You don't realise it, but this is Britain, this is you back on your native heath," I said to it in Irish.

More chilly disdain.

I left a note for Beth and Emma on the kitchen table: "Off to work, catching the 6.30 fast ferry. I'll call you later. Love you."

I went outside to the Beemer and looked underneath it for explosive devices. This was another country across the sea, but the terrorists had a long arm—they had killed Mrs Thatcher's PPS in the House of Commons car park with a mercury tilt switch bomb, so it would be easy enough to kill me.

I turned on the radio.

Our main story: American military forces have entered the country of Panama. The whereabouts of President Noriega are unknown at this time, but a spokesman has called this a blatant violation of national sover—

Yeah, yeah.

I caught the fast ferry, the SeaCat, which got into the port of Belfast at 8.00. Since I was in town anyway I drove to the offices of the *Belfast Telegraph* and found the city desk.

I showed them Kat's picture. Missing for two days now. Fifteen-year-old girl. You need to cover this. If you cover it, the BBC and UTV might cover it too. It will really help us.

The city editor was a complacent young blonde-haired man called Hilditch. He was wearing a blue shirt with a white collar, red braces and a paisley tie—yeah that's right, the full eighties megillah.

I stopped speaking. He handed me the photograph back.

"What'll you do for me?" Hilditch asked.

"What'll I do for you? I've already done for you. This is a major news story. A missing fifteen-year-old girl. Christ Almighty."

He shook his head. "No. She has scarpered before more than once, it sounds like. No evidence of foul play. This isn't a front-page story for anybody."

I was seething but what else could I say? You couldn't force the bloody papers to run your story. I tried to think if there was any way I could pressure them, but they held all the cards. The press needed us more than we needed them.

"Nice picture though," Hilditch said, holding her photograph. "Good-looking lass and that helps. I'll tell you what, if we can't find anything for page five today, I'll see if Harry wants to run it. Tell me the details."

The details and then along the motorway and the Shore Road back to Carrickfergus.

A left turn up Victoria Road.

Quick check on the old house in Coronation Road.

"For sale" sign in front yard. A third of my records still in the living room where I also kept a sleeping bag and a camp bed.

This house felt even colder and lonelier.

Outside. Garden shed.

Mrs Campbell hanging her washing.

"Oh! Morning, Mr D. Thought I heard a noise next door. Thought it was burglars. Or squatters. You hear about them squatters don't ya? I was thinking: poor Mr Duffy's only out one day and the glue sniffers have moved in. Terrible thing to waste your young mind like that. I heard one wee lad thought he could fly and went out the second-floor window. Fell on his grandmother in her lawn chair otherwise he'd 'ave died. That happened just there on Victoria Crescent."

"Morning Mrs Campbell," I replied.

"And there's me out checking the mouse traps. Suppose you have mouses too. Maybe not. You'll get them now you've taken your wee cat across the sheugh with you. Your wee cat and your baby and your music I suppose. Sad. Many's the time I'd hear you blasting away some of that jungle music. All gone now though. You're standing there but you're not really there are you? You're gone. You're like a banshee."

"Actually, I've left about a third of—

"And you won't have heard the big news?"

"What big—

"Carrick cinema reopened last night. First time since it was fire-bombed in 1972. We all went to see *Hook*. Have you seen it?"

"No. 'Fraid not. Anyway, I must get on down to the station. I was just checking the house."

"Life all right in your new place?"

"It's good. Yeah."

"Aye, I was there once. Scotland. I heard you can't drink the water. Gives you the runs."

"I don't think that's tru—"

"Well, I must get on myself. Them mouses aren't going to murder themselves, are they? Well they are, I suppose, but you have to bait the trap, don't you? Bye, Mr Duffy."

And she went in with her washing.

Down the station the talk was of the new cinema too. A new cinema. In Carrick. It was a thing of wonder. Almost every cinema in Northern Ireland had been firebombed out of the existence from 1972–1982 and the only ones that had been repaired were in high-traffic areas like South Belfast. A new cinema in Carrick in the new decade of the 1990s. Could that possibly be a sign of hope?

Were the men of violence finally wearying of this twenty-two-year-long death fugue?

Hmmm. Puff of asthma inhaler instead of smoke. Another cup of coffee.

Up to my office.

My office until this case was closed.

Then no office for yours truly.

But if this case took a while?

No.

Not going to be the kind of arsehole who makes the closure of this case last a year. Not keep Lawson and Crabbie waiting like that. Time to move on. I'd be forty in a little over a year and forty in Northern Ireland years was fifty everywhere else, and forty in Northern Irish–policeman years was sixty. And I was a *Catholic* policeman, so you can do that arithmetic yourself.

A knock at the door. Lawson with two cups of coffee.

"Thought I saw you come in, sir. The move went well?"

"Everything went ok. As well as can be expected."

"And the house is ok?"

"It's a bit colder than I imagined it, but apart from that, fine."

"All the windows, I suppose," Lawson said handing me the cuppa.

I looked in the mug. Black, no sugar. The way to take coffee. The way to take tea, of course, was, as they say in the Army, Julie Andrews fashion (milk, two sugars).

"All quiet here? You manage to survive one day without me?"

"Yes, sir."

"My spies tell me the cinema opened."

"Yes. You are well informed. My father and I went to see *Hook*."

"I actually heard a joke the other day about an alternate ending to the movie *Hook*."

"Oh, yes?"

"Yeah, where Captain Hook wins the final duel and sends Peter back to London in a body bag. It's a good joke, but a wee bit dark and it does require a *dead Pan* delivery."

Lawson shook his head and looked out of the window with a pained expression.

"Come on, I've been working on that for fifteen minutes," I said.

"When you go part-time, sir, I urge you not to take up stand-up, not if you want your child to eat," Lawson said with barely a twinkle in his eye. He was a good kid, Lawson.

"Ok, so Richard Pryor I am not, but I might be Columbo. Anything new cooking on our case?"

"Well," Lawson said with a cat-who-got-the-cream smile, "I may have turned up something."

"I bloody knew it. You little minx. You've found her, haven't you?"

"No, I haven't found her, but just on the off chance I looked her up in the DVA computer last night and—"

"She's too young to have a licence, surely!"

"Well she is, of course, too young to have a licence, but if she lied about her age, which she did, she could have been given a provisional licence—which she was," he said, holding the computer printout.

"What's the address on it?"

"Her mum's address."

"So how does this help us, Lawson?"

Another shit-eating grin from blondie. "Well, sir, if you search the police traffic records for a—"

It suddenly all fit into place. Like all Traveller children, Kat could ride a horse before she could walk and could drive a car before her feet could really reach the pedals. She'd either bought a car or got one of her friends to nick one for her. But there was no way someone of her age and inexperience in a hot or junky second-hand car could not have been stopped by traffic branch at some point. And of course she had. Lawson handed me a second printout.

"Speeding on the A27 between Portadown and Newry, doing sixty-five on a fifty-five-mile-an-hour road. The car she was driving was a white Ford Escort, registration: FJB 111C. English reg which should be pretty distinctive in these parts.

"And the white Ford Escort Estate?"

"Unfortunately, they're pretty common. Few thousand in Ireland, but, like I say, not that many with English plates."

"So even the doziest of traffic cops shouldn't miss it."

"Nope."

"Have you put the word out?"

"I have. Nothing yet. But I think we'll get a bite on this."

"I agree. A dark-haired fifteen-year-old girl can hide anywhere but she can't hide her car forever if she's run."

"Or if someone's done her a mischief and stolen her motor."

"This is good police work, Lawson, I'm proud of you. This will help. I went in the *Belfast Telegraph* this morning and browbeat them into doing a story, but I should have been doing this; this is much better. It's good thinking. And while you're on a roll, see if you can track down the previous owner of this Ford Escort. I'll go out to the caravan site and have a look around for it."

I drank my coffee, went down to the Beemer and out the A2 to the caravan site at Kilroot. Asked the wee muckers if they'd ever seen Katrina driving a white car and a couple of them said yeah, course, that was her car. Where'd she keep it parked? Over there at the power station fence. Not there now. How long has it been missing? Since Katrina went missing. If it shows up, give us a call. Here's a quid for each of you. Fiver if you spot the car.

Back to the station. Crabbie was in now, wearing a funereal black suit, white shirt, black tie, another Ballymena speciality from his neo-Lutheran colour palate.

"How do, Sean. Life over the water treating you all right?"

"Peachy, so far. How are you?"

"Not too bad."

"Well, listen, me old china plate, you've probably spotted young Lawson here quivering with excitement and there's a reason for that quivering. We've got a break in the case."

"Has she shown up?"

"Not quite. But Lawson here has discovered she had a car and we've got traffic branch looking for it. All right, I know what you're thinking, that's not exactly a break, but it's more than we had, isn't it?"

Crabbie nodded and was about to say something when Peggy O'Reilly handed me a fax from the DVLA in Swansea. The white Ford Escort had been bought in York in 1986 by one Arthur Connolly who had sold it to an Anne Grant of Stranraer in 1988 who had sold it to one Cecil McCullough of Ballintoy, County Antrim, in January 1989 who had sold it to our Kat McAtamney in September 1989.

"Wasn't stolen. Legitimately bought and paid for. So how does that fit in with your racist stereotypes of Travellers," I said to Lawson.

"I don't have any rac—"

"Save it for the judge. Fancy a wee run up to Ballintoy, lads?"

They weren't that fussed, but they came anyway, the sports. I told Peggy we were heading to the coast but if all went well we'd be back later.

The Beemer loved the A2 Coast Road up past Larne and Glenoe. One of the great roads of Europe really. Radio 3 was playing Edmund

Rubbra, a big favourite of my father's. Rubbra had one foot in and another out of the twentieth century and he attacked symphonies in entirely his own quixotic, very English way. It wasn't my cup of tea at all and the lads hated it, but it went with the landscape and if I called dad tonight and told him I'd listened to Rubbra's Fourth (Op. 53) he would be pleased.

Cecil McCullough was a Pavee who lived in a caravan in a field with a spectacular view over the Atlantic near the lovely whitewashed Ballintoy Harbour.

"A horse and car dealer by the looks of it," Crabbie said, for indeed the field was full of horses and cars. A remarkable variety of both. Foals and twenty-year-old mares juxtaposed with Morris Oxfords, Jensen Healeys and 1991 Toyota Celicas. No way *all* of these were bought and paid for. You don't leave classic cars you've bought with hard earned cash to rust out here in the sea mist and the rain.

We marched through the menagerie and knocked on the aluminium door of McCullough's caravan.

"What is it?" he asked.

"It's the peelers," I said.

"Who says it's the peelers?"

"The peelers do."

The door opened and a grizzled, bearded, raggedy old geezer stuck his head out.

"What do you want?" he asked looking up at us under bushy white eyebrows with a set of dishonest but likeable blue eyes.

"Do you even need to ask?" Crabbie said. "It would be easier for you to tell us which of these vehicles isn't stolen property."

McCullough's watery blue peepers blinked. "Can't prove anything about the horses," he said slyly.

"And the cars?" I asked.

"I have title for all of them," he said and coughed.

"Oh, yeah?" I said giving my *the-truth-will-set-you-free* look.

"For most of them. Ok, some of them," he admitted.

"Well, luckily for you, Mr McCullough, we're not interested in any of that. We're Carrickfergus CID. We're interested in this girl," I said and showed him Kat's photograph.

"First of all, call me Cecil," he said.

"OK, Cecil, tell me about the girl."

"Aye, I know her," he said immediately. "You couldn't forget a face like that. What's she done?"

"She's gone missing," I said.

"Is that so," Cecil said. "Well you better come in then, please don't sit on any of the cushions, they're not cushions, they're cats."

Inside.

Random bits of car engines, rattan furniture, a small electric fire in front of which were half a dozen moggies.

The obligatory tea and biscuits and finally down to business.

"Yeah, she come up here looking for a car, five or six months back," Cecil said. "She only had about seven hundred quid to spend, but I let her have a 1986 Escort Estate with a book value of a thousand quid. Good car. Manual transmission, of course, with an overdrive, but she knew how to work the gears. I made her practice on it before I let her out on the roads. She was a good wee driver."

"Did you know she was fifteen?" Crabbie asked.

"That's not what her licence said," Cecil replied.

"Why did you let her get the car cheaper than the book value?" I asked.

"I know the family a wee bit. Her grandfather was Louie the Fist McKenna," Cecil said and paused to let that sink in.

I looked at Crabbie and Lawson who were none the wiser.

"Louie the Fist! The fighter!" Cecil said.

"Fighter?"

"Bare-knuckle heavyweight champ '62 and '63!"

"Where's this Louie McKenna now?" I asked.

"Oh, gone now. Massive heart attack in '81. He was only forty-five. Strong as a bloody ox too. So what's going on with young Kat?"

"She's been missing for almost three days now."

"Three days is a long time," Cecil said with a whistle.

"And we didn't know she had a car until this morning. She could be anywhere," Lawson said.

"If she's run," Crabbie said.

"You wouldn't have any clue where she might have gone, would you?" I asked.

He shook his head and then rubbed his chin reflectively. He coughed, picked up one of the cats and put it down again.

"What? Do you know where she might have gone?"

"No. But, uh, when she bought the vehicle, she did ask if the car would get her to France without any problems and I told her it would," Cecil admitted.

"She's run back to bloody Nantes!" Lawson said. "She must have met some boy and been pining for him this whole time."

"While I was away, did we hear anything from the French peelers?" I asked him.

"Nope. Nothing. Nothing from the Nantes police or from Interpol, but the car's plates have only been on the wires for less than a day."

"She was fluent in French, did you know that?" Cecil asked me.

"Yeah, so we heard," I said. "You've heard nothing since you sold her the car?"

"Why would I? She's not coming back here complaining about the warranty!" he said with a chuckle that descended into another cough. He coughed so hard Lawson had to slap him on the back.

"Gimme that wee bottle over there," Cecil said, and Lawson passed him a little souvenir bottle of holy water from Lourdes which he took a sip of.

"I've got holy water from the Jordan if you're ever down in Carrick. Nobody else seems to want it."

Cecil looked sceptical.

I turned to Lawson. "Do you have any questions for Mr McCullough?" I asked.

Lawson couldn't think of anything more and neither could I. It was madness to think of a fifteen-year-old driving down to Rosslare and getting the car ferry to Cherbourg and then driving down to bloody Nantes, but that seemed to be the direction the case was pointing.

I put down my tea cup and offered Cecil my hand. "Well, thank you, Mr Cecil, you've been very helpful. Here's my card if you can think of anything else. Lawson, you give him your number too."

Lawson gave him his number and we said our goodbyes and exited the caravan.

We drove back along the coast road and when we got to the station we checked the logs a final time before calling it a day.

I parked the car on Coronation Road, called the wife and fam and nipped down the chip shop for a fish supper.

Fish supper and while it was cooking, I went to the offy and got a bottle of vodka and a few limes.

Home again in the rain, up the hill to the graveyard.

We're all heading up that hill to Victoria Cemetery.

But not yet.

Inside #113. Out to the coal shed where I grabbed a bag of pine cones. I threw some newspapers in the bottom of the fire and chucked the pine cones on top. I got the fire lit, transferred the fish supper to a plate, made myself a vodka gimlet in a pint glass.

No TV, no radio either but I still had a third of my albums and my emergency turntable. Of course, the ones you wanted in that particular moment were never going to be there. I looked at the empty slots of all the albums that were across the sea. What did you do when you were in the mood for Shostakovich's Symphony no. 13 and you didn't bloody have it? One of the others? I flipped out Symphony no. 10 and put it on. I listened, looked at the fire, drank my vodka and ate my fish.

Aye, clearly old Dmitry S. had written this after binge-listening to Mussorgsky, but it lacked Mussorgsky's drunken cheerfulness. The tonal repetition and all those declamations were definitely Modest Mussorgsky, but this was much darker material. It was a choral symphony, of course, and I was supremely grateful that I couldn't understand any Russian, otherwise I'd probably have been deeply depressed. I glanced at the liner notes. Apparently the first movement was all about the Baba Yar massacre.

Jesus Christ.

I took the record off and hunted about for something more cheerful. Mozart Symphony no. 13? Yes, that would do nicely. F major, K. 112 (1771) that Wolfgang had written when he was fifteen years old.

The fire burned to a glow and became less interesting to stare at. There was nothing going on the street. My books were over the water. There was, however, one picture left in the house. A print that I'd got when I lived in Belfast. Giorgio de Chirico's *The Return of Ulysses* (1968). It's a painting of a man, Odysseus, in a Greek himation rowing across his living room rug. The painting is full of what Robert Hughes calls the uncomfortable electric blue silence of dusk and the chilly weirdness of de Chirico, but the absurdity of the scene delights the eye and makes it less uncomfortable. Makes it funny. At least to me. Beth never liked the picture. No one who has ever come to the house has liked it, which, of course, has endeared the bloody thing to me.

I closed my eyes and lay down on the rug.

Why did you run, Katrina?

*You know why I run. Why does everybody run? You're going to run too someday.*

No, I'm not. Not everybody runs. My dad didn't run.

*No, but his father did. To America? Isn't that right?*

I've only got a quarter of that DNA. I won't run. I'm not like him. I'm like my mother's father. The Foxrock solicitor. Steady.

*Everybody runs.*

They don't.

*You're the protagonist, Duffy, not me. The punters want to see you run.*

It ain't gonna happen.

I sat up and looked at the picture.

There was a sense in the painting too, that something was on the verge of happening.

The painting and life existed in the imminence of the now.

Waiting.

Waiting.

The phone rang.

"I'm bloody psychic, I am," I said to myself. I finished the vodka gimlet and went into the hall.

"Hello?"

"Sir, it's me. I hope I wasn't disturbing you."

"No. Not at all, Lawson. I was staring at that painting in my dining room. You know the one. The guy in the boat."

"Oh, yes, is that one of yours, sir? I didn't know you, uh, dabbled in the visual arts."

"No. God, no. It's Giorgio de Chirico."

"Sounds expensive."

"It's a reproduction. I couldn't afford—Look, what did you call me about?"

"It might be big news."

"Go on."

"Two boys found a car in the River Bann, sir. The local police read that story about Kat in this afternoon's *Belfast Telegraph*. The story mentions the missing car and they put two and two together."

"Do the plates match?"

"Yes."

"It's Kat's car?"

"Apparently so."

A shudder went through me. "Is she in the car?"

"We don't know, sir. It's still under the water, just the boot partially poking above the surface. The local police have secured the car with a heavy chain, so it's not drifting away. I hope it won't anyway. Too late to send divers and forensics and a tow truck out tonight, but they're all going out there first thing in the morning. I assume we'll want to join them?"

"You assume correctly. Whereabouts on the River Bann is it?"

I could hear Lawson flip back the pages in his notebook. "A place called Bendooragh? I've never heard of it."

"I have. It's near Ballymoney. Not a million away. Forty-five minutes up the road, thirty with me driving. We'll want to beat forensics there though. Meet you at six at the station. Let Crabbie know, will you?"

"Six? I'm on until midnight!" Lawson protested.

"A policeman's lot is not a happy one, Lawson," I said and hung up on the poor sod.

I made another vodka gimlet and went back to the painting. More people should check out de Chirico. The low sunlight, the deep shadows, the empty walkways are reminiscent of Edward Hopper who reminds us all about being alone even in the presence of others.

I lay back down on the rug.

You lied to me, Kat, you didn't run, someone killed you, didn't they?

*What makes you think it was murder?*

You don't accidentally drive your car off the road in an out-of-the-way place like Bendooragh. Me da's been fly fishing there. The road's nowhere near the river.

*I didn't say it was an accident. I just said that it might not be murder. I'd had enough of grubbing about for money, dirty old men pawing me . . . you can understand that.*

No, Kat, you didn't top yourself either. Someone killed you and I'll bloody find out who and bring them in for it.

# 8
# WET DAYLIGHT

As a boy in short trousers, Seamus Heaney was obsessed by the rich clay soil of the Bann Valley. That rust-red clay he thought of as being like *wet daylight* or *viscous satin under the felt and frieze of humus layers.*

On this particular crisp, frosty morning on the high bog, the wet daylight was two clear parallel lines through the grass leading directly into the river. The car had gone in, but it hadn't completely sunk beneath the surface, at least not now at low tide. The rear bumper was sticking up an inch or two out of the water and you could read the number plate quite clearly. This was definitely her car.

A diver from the RUC Forensics unit had taken some underwater photography and had assured the tow truck driver that there were no obstructions preventing the vehicle from being dragged out onto the bank.

The local peelers from Ballymoney RUC were very impressed by the diver and the dozen Forensics officers who were getting changed into their white boilersuit outfits. Forensics had also brought a charlady with them who had set up a little refreshment tent serving tea or coffee and biscuits or Danish. An unpleasant woman who had refused me a cup of coffee, saying that it was "FO only."

"FO yourself," I muttered and went to examine the possible crime scene with Crabbie and Lawson. Blue sky with white puff clouds.

THE DETECTIVE UP LATE

Another freezing January morning with a bitter wind coming express from Greenland.

I looked at the tyre tracks leading into the river. "What do you make of those Lawson?"

"Well, I'm, uhm, not an expert on car tyres, sir," he said hesitantly. He was wearing a light-grey suit, with a striking paisley tie and a white raincoat. Not the ensemble I would have chosen for a visit to a muddy riverbank, but he could do what he wanted and in a week or two he would be setting the sartorial standard for Carrick CID. It would probably be an improvement. I was in my bog standard black leather jacket, black jumper, blue jeans, black DM's. Crabbie his usual funeral suit and thick overcoat.

Lawson was staring at me.

"Sorry, what did you say, son? I was miles away."

"I'm no expert on car tyres, sir," he reiterated.

"I don't care about the make. We'll confirm the make of the tracks and the car in five minutes when they tow it out. Look closely at the tracks. What do you see? Stream of consciousness. Just tell me what you're looking at."

Lawson bent down to examine the tracks.

"Uhm, I think I see what you're getting at, sir. These are old, I'd say, there seems to be foot tracks on top of these tracks."

I nodded. "Yes, indeed. The tyre marks are at least a couple of days old. There are half a dozen sets of tracks on top of the tyre marks. Look over there, you can see where someone wearing boots walked his or her dog. And here's another dog walker. And here there's another dog walking by itself off the leash. This one appears to be a rabbit."

"A hare," Crabbie corrected.

"Anyway, point is, the vehicle has been in the river for about two days. How come none of these people reported it?"

"Afraid of the police? Don't want to get involved?" Lawson suggested.

"Tell him, Crabbie," I said.

"It's because of the tides. We're just off the spring tide on New Year's Eve. The water's only gotten low enough to show the car under there at this tide in the last twelve hours or so."

"And even then, you might not have noticed it if it was dark," I said. "Which is very unfortunate because I'd say that this car entered the river forty-eight hours ago, which, if this is a murder investigation, has given the killer plenty of time to compose an alibi and get rid of forensic linkages between them and the victim. But there's something else about these markings. Take a look at those boots at the point where the tyre tracks began."

Crabbie and Lawson walked to the beginning of the tyre tracks and looked at the Wellington boot prints. Unfortunately, the heel wasn't imprinted in the turf so you couldn't really estimate the size of the boot, but the two forefeet were perfectly visible.

"Crabbie?"

He examined them, stood, nodded. "It's murder then," he said.

Lawson hadn't caught on yet. "Sirs?" he asked puzzled.

"We're going to need you to be sharper than this, son. You're going to be the big bossman soon. We'll need you to be on top of your game."

Lawson bent down and examined the boot prints again just as a light snow began to fall.

"What am I missing here, sir?"

Socratic method probably best here, I thought.

"What were the boots doing pointing that direction?" I asked. "Was he standing there birdwatching, looking at the river, casting a line, what? They start here and move forward."

"Oh, I get it. The prints are deep and moving."

"Which means?"

"He was shoving the car," Lawson said.

"He was shoving the car into the river," I agreed. "When we pull it out I bet we find that the clutch is in neutral and the handbrake is off."

Realisation dawned fully on Lawson and his blue eyes lit up. "She didn't drive the car into the river. It wasn't a suicide or an accident. Someone drove her car here, rendered her unconsciousness and pushed the car into the river, hoping it would sink to the bottom."

"But it didn't sink because the bank is not as steep as it looks. Killer got unlucky. A wee bit further up the meander the car would have gone into the water and might have stayed vanished until the next drought."

"And unless the killer had an accomplice, he walked home from here," Crabbie said.

"Or he walked to the nearest taxi rank and got a lift. He sloppily left these boot prints, so why couldn't he have sloppily got a taxi in Bal- lymoney? Maybe even a taxi straight to his house?" I looked at Lawson. "Now you're probably thinking: oh, if only it'll be that simple, but in fact most cases around here are that simple. Your drunken killer could well have gotten a taxi straight to his own house. It's happened before. Do me a favour, Lawson, and ring every taxi company in the area and ask if there were any suspicious clients on December thirtieth or De- cember thirty-first."

"Busy nights for a taxi company."

"I know, I know, but we can still ask, can't we? Any customers cov- ered with mud or sopping wet from having fallen over . . ."

Lawson went off to make the calls.

"Now Crabbie, let's get these forensic boys over here to take pho- tographs and casts of these boot prints."

The FO in charge was Chief Inspector Frank Payne with whom I worked a number of times. When he himself was running the show, he was competent and thorough, but Frank was getting lazy in his old age and often let his younger officers run entire investigations while he sat in his car, smoked Embassy Superkings and listened to BBC Radio 2.

He was a big man, going on sixty, with jam jar glasses and a brown comb-over. Six two and seventeen stone and a full Chief Inspector, he could be an intimidating presence to some, but we went back and I wasn't afraid to tell him the score.

"I know it's freezing Frank, but I want your close attention on this one," I said.

"What's that supposed to mean, Duffy?" he said, annoyed.

"Don't want a repeat of what happened at Carrick Castle," I ex- plained. What had happened at Carrick Castle was one of Frank's men giving us the wrong time of death because he'd been too shy to fully insert a thermometer in a victim's anus. Our wrong time of death had subsequently been ridiculed in a report from the pathologist and we'd both been embarrassed.

Frank nodded glumly. That had indeed been a professional low point. To have the patho tell us practically to our faces that we were idiots.

"Just keep out of our way Duffy, and keep those local plodders away too," he said gruffly and got out of the car.

The little jibe worked, and Frank closely supervised everyone. His boys photographed and took casts of the boot prints and when they had finished I let the RUC frogmen unit go into the river to do a final recce on the car and attach a tow line. When they were done one of them gave me the thumbs up and the tow truck reversed slowly backwards and dragged the car out of the river. The windscreen was intact but all four car doors were open and the body was long gone.

Water and fish came gushing out of the sides of the car. Silver trout, perch and salmon flopping on the river bank and writhing their way back into the water. I could tell the Ballymoney cops wanted to grab the fish and brain them but we townies just stood there and let them escape.

Forensics went to work examining the interior of the car. Definitely a 1986 white Ford Escort Estate and the licence plate matched. This was Kat's car without question.

"Who found the car?" I asked one of the Ballymoney coppers.

"Couple of kids fishing."

"Where are these kids?"

"Over there in the back of the Forensics Land Rover."

"Are they locals?"

"Aye."

"Crabbie, can you come over and help me with the translation in case I don't get the Ballymena gist, hey," I said doing my best unfiltered Liam Neeson.

The kids were both about ten. Little boys with fishing poles and big sweaters and big coats straight out of a Van Morrison song.

They were called Monty and Norman. Norman had hooked his line on what he thought was reeds. He'd jumped into the river to rescue his fly and the float and then he'd noticed the car.

"Is there a reward or anything?" Norman asked.

"Not that I've seen, but you did the right thing calling this in. Your reward will be in heaven," I explained.

Norman's freckled face contorted into a look of disgust.

"Do you boys fish here often?" I wondered.

"Every day when we're off school," Monty said.

"Every day. So you know this part of the river quite well do you?"

"Aye. As good as anybody else."

"Let me ask you something, do you think the car was here yesterday?" I asked.

The boys shrugged. "Who's to say?" Monty said. "We're always on a new part of the bank wherever the midges aren't and the fish are biting."

"This is the lowest tide in a few days. Could the car have been in the water since New Year's Eve?"

Both boys acknowledged that it could have been. I gave them a fiver each and my card. "If anything unusual shows up along the bank in the next few days, call me at once, ok?"

"What's unusual?"

"Anything. A piece of clothing, a bag, anything," I said.

"There won't be a body if that's what you're thinking," Norman said.

"Why's that?"

"The flood yesterday was roaring past us, anything that can float would have been carried miles away, so it would," Monty said.

I thanked the boys, walked gingerly to the river bank and hallooed one of the divers who was still looking for the body or anything else that might have spilled from the vehicle. "Did you open the car doors or were they like that?" I asked him.

"They were like that, Inspector Duffy. All four doors were open. It's a pretty strong current down here."

"How far could the current take a body?" I asked.

"Round here?" the diver asked. "Round here it could take a body all the way to Coleraine. Maybe even all the way to the Atlantic."

"The Atlantic?"

"Sure, the coast is only about ten miles that way," the diver said, pointing north.

"How fast did you think the current is moving?"

"The tide's running at about three or four miles per hour at the moment. Faster yesterday."

"Christ. So she really could have been taken out to sea."

"Oh, yes."

I thanked the diver and moved away from the water's edge.

"Might never find her," I said to Crabbie.

"What do you do in a circumstance like that, sir?" one of the Ballymoney coppers asked me.

"I've never had a circumstance like this before. What about you Crabbie?"

He shook his head. "No."

I sighed and shook my head. "It's our duty to find the body. Especially if this is a murder case. I'll call Coleraine RUC and see if they can lend us some officers. We'll search down river and alert the Coast Guard. Alert the police in the Irish Republic and in Scotland too. If it did get carried out to sea, I suppose a body could wash up on a beach in Donegal or Scotland."

"More likely it'll never show up," Crabbie said. "And that won't help with a prosecution."

"No," I agreed. "But we'll do all we can."

We retired to the car to let the forensic officers finish. Lawson came back shaking his head from his taxi investigation.

"Nothing suspicious so far. Quite the night for drunks apparently, but none of the drivers reported anything resembling what we're after. Some of the drivers are on their holidays though and won't be in for a few more days."

"Did you give them your number?"

"I did."

"Good."

Fifteen minutes later Frank Payne came over to give us the sitrep.

THE DETECTIVE UP LATE

He lit a ciggie and shook his head. "Don't think we're getting much forensically out of this mess," he said. "It's been wiped clean by the river, so it has."

"Clothing, DNA, anything like that?"

"No blood stains, skin, none of the usual stuff from a car crash. If she'd gone into a lake it would have been better but a river like this with the doors open, it's a bloody vacuum cleaner. We'll put it on a trailer and take the car to a lab, but the initial inspection is not promising."

"So what did you find?"

"A few dead fish, the vehicle registration book, one personal item."

"What was the personal item?"

"A purse. Do you want to take a look at it?"

He showed me the purse inside a plastic evidence bag. It was just a little red leather purse with a brass clasp.

"Money in it?"

"Nothing."

I gave the purse to McCrabban. "We'll show this to the mother and see if she recognises it."

I offered Frank my hand and he shook it. "Good job, mate. Are your men done?"

"More or less, for now, aye. We'll be taking a closer look in the warehouse."

"Ok if we take a look?"

"Be my guest."

Crabbie and Lawson and myself walked over to the car. We put on latex gloves and Crabbie produced a torch, which wasn't really necessary because, despite the rain, there was plenty of light.

"What sort of things are we looking for here, Lawson?" I asked.

"Windows, obviously, sir."

"What about them?"

"Well they're all wound up and none of them are broken, so I imagine she didn't try to get out of the car through the windows. And the doors would have been impossible to open until the water pressure equalised."

"So?"

"I don't think she made it out alive."

"And why are all the doors open now?"

"As you can see, the locks are pretty rusty and the battering the current did on them would have opened them."

"If she couldn't open the door and she didn't try to open the windows, what does that mean?"

"She must have been unconscious or otherwise incapacitated. If she was inside the car at all."

"Why wouldn't she be in the car?" I asked.

"She could have faked her own death for insurance or other reasons," Lawson said.

"And the boot prints?"

"Are her boots. She drove here and pushed the car in herself," Lawson said.

"Very good, Lawson. Let's take a look at these door locks."

We examined the door locks on the Ford. They were simple push-down-to-lock jobs. All four locks were in the "up" position, but when I toggled them they moved up and down easily. It wouldn't have taken much for the current to toggle them up if they had been locked and for the doors to have swung open.

But as Lawson pointed out, she probably wouldn't have been able to open the door against the water pressure on the sides of the vehicle and if she had managed to open the door the Ford would have immediately flooded with water.

The smart thing, indeed the only thing to do if you are in car that plunges into a lake or a river is to get out through the windows. None of the windows in this car had, however, been lowered.

"If she was in the car and she was murdered, she wasn't wearing her seatbelt, otherwise she'd still be in here," Crabbie said.

"Yes," I agreed.

We examined the inside of the vehicle with the torch but there was nothing that Forensics had missed. Red dirt, weeds, caramel-coloured river pebbles. I carefully examined the inside of the driver's-side and front passenger's–side doors. If someone had knocked me in the head, put me in my car and shoved my car in the river, the freezing cold water might have woken me up, and if that had happened I would have attempted to batter my way out. But there were no obvious dents or cracks in any of the windows or the windshield.

"What do you think, gents?" I asked them.

Crabbie shook his head. "I think this is a murder investigation," he said. "Those boot prints. Someone pushed this car into the water."

"And the body?"

"Carried out to sea on the flood."

"Lawson?"

"A Traveller girl who we know is looking to make a few quid? Why not fake her own death and split the insurance with her mother or who-ever else holds the policy?"

I sighed. "Let's not jump to any conclusions just yet. I think we can deal with the insurance ang—"

Frank Payne tapped me on the shoulder. He'd had something to eat and a ciggie and from the sly cast to his eyes I could see that he was in a more combative mood now.

"What's the story on this one, Duffy?"

I filled him on Kat's disappearance. He looked at Lawson and felt a pedagogical urge coming on: "There are generally four reasons why fifteen-year-old girls go missing in these parts. One, they've gotten them-selves pregnant and have gone off to Liverpool to have an abortion. Two, they've gotten themselves pregnant and have gone off to Liverpool to have the baby and avoid the shame. Three, they've gotten themselves pregnant and they've gone off somewhere to kill themselves. Or four, they've gone to tell the father that they're pregnant and he's killed them."

"That's some gloomy world view, Francis," I said.

"That about covers it don't you think, Duffy? I mean there's the odd girl who runs off to join the circus but there aren't many of those are there?"

"No," I said, but I didn't agree with his interpretation at all.

We thanked the FO team and finished up our work on the scene and drove back to Carrick. On the way to the station, we pulled into the caravan park at Kilroot.

I told Mrs McAtamney what we had discovered. It was Kat's car and it went into the river.

"There's no proof she was in the car, no one saw her go into the Bann, but we're treating the circumstances as suspicious and we'll certainly keep you informed of any progress we make in the investigation," I said.

She took it well and she was an intelligent woman; she could read between the lines.

"Do you recognise this?" I asked, handing her the purse inside the evidence bag.

"Aye, that's hers, all right. She loved that wee purse. Got it in Wales somewhere. She wouldn't leave it," Mrs McAtamney said, turning it over in her big, gnarled hands.

"Can I keep it?" she asked.

I shook my head. "I'm afraid not, it's official evidence, if there's an inquest the coroner will demand to see it. Of course you'll get it back eventually but not until all the uhm, legal, uhm, avenues . . ." I said, and my voice guttered into silence.

It was pathetic. I wasn't going to let her have this one thing that tied her to daughter.

"Well, those are the rules," she said, handing me the purse back.

"Did you know she had a car?" I asked.

"I saw her driving a car, didn't know she owned it," Mrs McAtamney said.

"Did she have insurance?"

"I have no idea."

Once we were back at the station, I sat down at the computer to type up the report so far.

Yes, there's the riot duty, the truth telling, the holding-back-entropy part of being a peeler but so much of police work is typing bloody reports . . .

Consider yourself lucky you don't get to see the way it really operates in a cop shop. Endless tedium punctuated by random excitement.

"While I finish this up, you two call every insurance company in Northern Ireland, Scotland and England and see if Kat or her mother is on their books."

The boys came back with negatives. No insurance policy from a company we knew about. No sign of Kat.

I went to the Incident Room and put her name and photograph on the whiteboard. I underlined her name in blue. Suspicious circumstances was exactly right. It was a murder inquiry now.

A knock at the door. The Chief Inspector came in. I gave him a seat and offered him a drink, which he declined.

"Progress?" he asked.

"Just finishing typing the report, actually. Lawson will tell you the details."

The Chief Inspector looked at Lawson's bright, eager young face. "So what's the verdict?"

"We're thinking homicide," he said and told him about the car in the Bann.

"Why not suicide?"

"No reason for suicide: no note, no sign of depression and the boot prints behind the car. Pretty hard for her to shove her own car in the river and then run and get in that car."

"Maybe she was never in the car at all," the Chief Inspector said, thinking like a detective, which pleased me, and I gave him an encouraging nod of the head.

"We can't think of a reason why she would have faked her own death. There doesn't appear to be a fiduciary reason anyway, although we're ruling nothing out."

The Chief Inspector got up from the chair. "Well, it seems you have everything in hand," he said and then fired a warning shot across my bows: "Don't let it get complicated, Duffy, you know? Don't leave us a shitstorm on your way out the door."

"No, sir. Oh, before you go, you don't want some holy water from the River Jordan, do you? I brought it all the way from Israel and nobody seems to want it."

Chief Inspector McArthur shook his head. "My wife wouldn't approve," he said and slipped out of the office.

The light on my office phone was flashing.

"Hello?"

"Sean, it's Peggy from the switchboard. I have a phone call from a Sergeant Michael Burke of what he's calling the task force homicide command of Ballymoney RUC. Never heard of that."

"I think they just made that up."

"Anyway, he said that he's got an update for you on a body in the Bann?"

"Put him through immediately, Peggy, this is important. I'll stick him on the speaker phone."

"Is this Sean Duffy?" Sergeant Burke asked.

"Yeah, it's Duffy," I said.

"I knew your father, Sean. Do you remember me? I took youse both birding on Lough Beg, must have been '68 or '69."

"Of course, I remember," I said, and I did remember. I remembered his daughter anyway. Who could forget Bridget? Three years older than me. Long legs, curly brown hair. "You had your pretty daughter with you. Bridget."

"Bridget. Yes. Married. Twelve children. Lives in Cork now."

Twelve kids out of that slip of a girl? Jesus.

"So Michael, what's this about a body?"

"Oh, yes, me and your father birding on Lough Beg. Fine time we had of it there, didn't we? Four pages in me book. Lapwing, gannets, whooper swan, a tawny owl."

"You have a fine memory, Michael, now I believe you were calling about the—"

"Tufted duck, pochard, coot. Wigeon, teal, mallard, shoveler—"

The coveys, colonies and companies of birds might have gone on all night had not Lawson put an end to it.

"Sergeant Burke, I'm sorry to interrupt, this is Sergeant Lawson of Carrick RUC here. It looks like we're in the midst of a murder inquiry now and we're sort of pressed a wee bit for time. Have you had any luck finding a body or anything from the car?"

Sergeant Burke was recalled to his duty and reported that no sign of any body had shown up along the Bann between the crash site and the sea. The coast guard and the RNLI had been notified and they hadn't found anything either.

"I talked to Glen McPherson here who fishes the rip and he said that anything going into the water on New Year's Eve would definitely have been taken to the Atlantic."

"That is bad news, Michael."

"She might never show up . . ."

"Well, keep me in the know, Michael, and don't be a stranger, eh? We birdmen, *ní mór dúinn a bata le chéile*. And say hey to Bridget."

"I will Sean, take care now."

No body.

No chance of a body it seemed.

The Gulf Stream and the North Atlantic Drift might take a corpse up the west coast of Scotland . . .

Lawson shook his head. "This is going to be a tough nut to crack."

"Indeed."

The clock marched its way to 5.00 p.m., stealing our lives from right under our very noses. Crabbie went home, Lawson went out with a couple of the younger officers to get some dinner and I poured myself two fingers of Islay and awaited developments.

Night on the lough.

Water clanking through the station's ancient heating system that had never, Peggy said, worked properly since the Luftwaffe had seen fit to drop a bomb on it in the 1940s.

Still the drink was ok. As the man said: twelve-year-old Islay— good stuff if you liked peat, smoke, earth, rain, despair, and the Atlantic Ocean, and who doesn't like that?

Another two fingers of Islay and another.

I stared out across the water. From this angle you could see all the way to Portpatrick. One of those twinkling lights were the lights of my house.

The ringing phone.

"Duffy."

"Thank God."

"No, not God, just Duffy, easy mistake to make, though."

"Blasphemer! Duffy, it's me, Olly."

"What do you want, Oliver?"

"Your boy is nervous. He's going to pieces. He wants you on site for the next meet. He insists upon having you. He accuses you of fear-lessness and competence."

"Is that what he said? That's nice. When is this meet?"

"Thursday."

"Oh, I think I can handle that. Where?"

"Donegal."

"Who's he meeting with?"

"No names over this line, but it's people known to us."

"Ok. I'm in. If he needs me I'm in."

"You're a good egg, Duffy. We'll pay you, you know. You get an al-lowance."

"How much?"

"A petrol voucher and two pounds an hour hardship money."

"How long is this meet suppose to take?"

"About half an hour."

"Whoopee, the drinks are on me, then."

"See you, Sean."

"Later, mate."

Hung up phone stared across lough and Irish Sea.

This was getting us nowhere.

Outside to the Beemer.

Victoria chippie again. The newsagent was still open so I bought *The Times* and *The Guardian*. Another fish supper in front of the fire-place but this time I could at least do the crosswords.

I put on Mahler Symphony #2 and attacked the crossword. Tele-phone in hall.

"Yes?"

"Lawson, sir."

"What's cooking, Alex? Please, don't hit with me any bad news, I've just done *The Times* cryptic in six minutes."

"It is bad news. Those boot prints we were so excited about . . ."

"Yes?"

"What about them?"

"Forensic report came through from CI Payne. He says there's no way to say definitively one way or the other that they were made at the same time as the car going into the water."

"What does that mean?"

"It could have been a bird watcher or a dog walker or someone who came long just after the car was under the water."

"Why do you have to complicate my life, Lawson? We just told the gaffer this is a murder inquiry. And now you're telling me the fact that the boot prints are exactly where a murderer might have begun pushing Katrina's car into the river has no probative value?"

"'Fraid not, sir. Geographically they're in the right place but temporally they're not probative. They could have been made at any time twelve hours before or after the vehicle went into the water."

"Bugger me. Well don't write that down anywhere. If we ever do catch who did this, a defence lawyer will use that line to get them off the hook."

"Sir, I *have* to write it down. We're officers of the court. And there's more anyway."

I took a sip of Bass and sighed. "Go on."

"They did find a hair sample. But it was a longish, probably female hair, so it was probably Katrina's and not the hair of a potential murderer. They sent it off for DNA analysis anyway."

"Ok, that's not bad or good news. That's just news. Doesn't upset the murder theory. We never expected DNA evidence, did we?"

"Yeah well here's the other bit that chaffs against the idea of a homicide: Payne had the tech guys analyse the gear box on the Ford and it looks like the thing was so worn down that it constantly slipped in and out of gear. Inspector Dunluce says that its entirely conceivable that she drove into the river and the impact knocked it back into neutral."

"The impact knocked it into neutral?"

"Uh-huh."

"So that means—"

"It wouldn't be a murder it could just be an accident."

"My gut says foul play on this one, laddie."

"Let's look at the evidence, sir," Lawson began with that slight air of condescension I often took with senior colleagues who weren't detectives.

"Go on, then," I said.

"Sir, she's fifteen. She's going to pubs, she's drinking, she's driving, she's meeting strange men, she doesn't know what she's doing. Drinking and driving on an unfamiliar bit of road up near the Bann. Probably had a few beers, goes off the road and into the river. Impact with the water knocks her out and knocks the engine into neutral. The car fills up with water and she drowns. The current rocks the car back and forth until the rusty old doors open and gradually she's rocked out of her seat and into the water. The current carries her downstream into the Atlantic where we never hear from her again."

It sounded about right, and it was typically tragic. I wondered if Lawson was aware that it was tragic? That old peeler balance: you care enough to do your job well but not care so much that the tragedy cripples you.

"As you always say, Occam's razor, sir," Lawson said into the increasingly uncomfortable silence.

"Maybe you're right. We'll discuss it on the morrow."

"And if there are no further developments in the case, sir?" Lawson asked eagerly.

"If there are no further developments, we can yellow the file, you can wave to us from the porch and Crabbie and I will ride off into the sunset together. Sound ok?"

"Sounds fine, sir."

"All right, good evening Lawson."

"Good evening, sir."

"Would he steal my grave as quick," I muttered after I'd hung up.

I looked at mirror Duffy. He wants it to be an accident, you want it to be a murder. Forget it, mate. Let this one go, give in to the new blood. Time to leave all this behind.

I slunk upstairs and started running the bath. I thought of my first day in this house when I'd almost scalded myself after I'd discovered that the hot and cold taps had been playfully reversed. I thought of the drunken bath I'd taken, with Kate from MI5 sitting outside the door. Poor, smart, pretty, wise, dead Kate. I thought of the time I smashed the bathroom window and climbed onto the washhouse roof with my girlfriend and my daughter to escape a hit team.

So many memories in this bloody place.

Too many.

I turned the water off and went back downstairs. It wasn't that late. Was it even eight? I could bathe later if I wanted.

The mood needed a different frame. Jazz not classical.

Miles led inevitably to Charlie Parker and Dizzy Gillespie.

People didn't really listen to Dizzy anymore. They should, if only for the baroque fading curve of the high notes on his trumpet. No one could hold a note like Gillespie. I looked at the liner notes on the album cover, a thank you to Cab Calloway, which was possibly sarcastic, for as far as I knew the two men hadn't spoken since they'd attacked each other with knives in 1941. Perhaps with age they had—

The phone rang.

"That'll be that wife," I said as I picked up.

It was the wife. She was crying, and I knew immediately and guiltily that there was trouble at mill.

# 9

# I AM THE ONE WHO KNOCKS

A big intake of breath.

"Beth is that you?"

"Sean, you know I'm not a very good parker. I'm not. I'm a good driver but I'm just not very good at parking," she said between sobs.

"Are you ok? Has there been an accident?"

"I'm ok. We're ok now."

"Is Emma ok?"

"She's fine now. I'm going to put her to bed in a bit."

"And you?"

"I'm making a cup of tea."

"Good. I was going to suggest that. So what's happened?"

"I was parking the car and I was listening to the radio and it was a good song and Emma was singing along and before I knew what had happened I had hit the back bumper of that man who lives over the road."

"Ok."

"Anyway, it didn't look too bad, just a little dent, and I was going to ignore it and I thought better not. So I went down his path and rang his bell and told him . . . And he comes out onto the porch furious. And storms down the path to look at the car and starts screaming and yelling at me . . . And he's a big man and I got so scared, Sean. And Emma started crying and I tried to go and he said I owed him the money for a new bumper and how his car was a classic and that it would cost a fortune to fix it. And he was screaming the whole time. And I agreed to everything and finally he let me go . . . and I came in here and told you."

"Did he touch you or Emma? If he touched you, that's 'actual bodily harm.'"

"No. No, but he sorted of blocked us from leaving. I was so scared, Sean. I'm still trembling. I know you have a case but—"

"I'll be home shortly."

"Oh, you don't have to, it's not—"

"I'll be home tonight, honey. It'll be ok. Does he know what I do for a living, this neighbour of yours?"

"I don't know. I may have said, I don't know."

"Are you sitting down? Are you ok?"

"Yes."

"Good. Sit down, have your tea and biscuits and I'll be home soon, ok? I'll get the fire going. Warm you all up."

"Oh, Sean, I'm so sorry for calling you when you're so busy. I can handle stuff like this, you know?"

"I know you can."

We talked a little more and when she was completely chilled I opened my notebook and got her to retell the incident while I jotted down the facts. She said it all again and this time added that she thought that maybe the neighbour had had a few drinks, but she wasn't sure.

"It'll be all right. Look after Emma. I'll be home soon. Call that friend of yours who teaches at the school and just lives in Stranraer."

"Jane?"

"Yeah, Jane. Call her. Drink tea, have a few biscuits, talk to Jane. Don't worry about a thing. I'll be back on the first ferry. Love you, sweetie."

I looked at the clock. It was five minutes to nine. There was an HSS high-speed hydrofoil crossing from Belfast to Stranraer at 9.25.

I packed my Glock and took a knuckleduster from the desk drawer under the phone table. This would be a job for the latter not the former.

I went out to the BMW, looked underneath it for bombs and got inside. We were never supposed to use the portable siren. In fact the portable sirens were being phased out for CID and all police divisions except for traffic branch.

Nevertheless, I put the portable siren on the roof and gunned it down Coronation Road and onto Victoria Road.

Lights.

Speed.

Cars moving out of the way.

Victoria Road to the Marine Highway to the Shore Road to the M5.

I hit 110 as the motorway came into Belfast. I was at the ferry terminal in the docks nine minutes later.

I flashed my badge and drove through security straight to the HSS loading ramp.

I was stopped at the boat itself by the loading deck officer.

"Oi! How did you get through here? We're full. Go back."

"I need to get on this ferry," I said.

"You can't. It's fully booked. The gates have been closed. We're leaving in six minutes."

I showed him my warrant card. "This is police business. If necessary, I'll stop the ship leaving tonight all together."

"You can't do that!"

"I can and I fucking will."

He saw the look in my eyes.

"All right, take it easy, we'll bloody make room," he said.

Five minutes of shunting cars later, the gates reopened and I squeezed the Beemer on board.

The HSS departed, gingerly making its way out of Belfast harbour and down Belfast Lough before accelerating on its hydrofoil fins across the Irish Sea.

We reached Stranraer in Scotland at 10.55.

Stranraer is only up the road a little bit from Portpatrick, and since I was first off the ferry I was in Portpatrick by 11:10 pm.

I parked the Beemer outside our house and went in to see Beth and Emma, but they had both gone to bed. Emma sleeping, Beth on the verge.

"I'm back, it's ok," I whispered.

"Oh, Sean," she said and wiped the tears from her cheeks and hugged me.

I reassured her that everything was fine, kissed Emma on the cheek and went back outside.

It was a cold, clear night on Britannia.

I was getting messages from my amygdala that I was attempting to quieten. Men quietening messages from their amygdalas was what Ireland needed more of. My deep engine wanted the shit to go down, but man is not a slave to his emotions or his evolution or his lizard brain. David Hume was wrong: reason could and perhaps should enslave the passions.

Maybe this gentlemen could be talked to.

I opened the BMW and took the brass knuckleduster out of the glove compartment and slipped it into the right-hand pocket of my leather jacket.

I walked over to the neighbour's house and knocked on his front door. Red front door, sloppy paint job that had left bubbles in the lower part of the frame. He had left the door to dry in the south facing sun. The door made me think he was an impatient, hot-tempered man.

On the second round of knocking, he opened said door. He was very tall—maybe six five—muscly, rangy with jet black hair done in a mullet like the guy from REO Speedwagon. He was wearing a red plaid shirt, baggy blue jeans and Docksider shoes. He had a little goatee that was also jet black. I supposed he was thirty, maybe a bit younger.

There were two little dogs behind him. Highland terriers. One of them white, the other reddy brown. Good doggies, not barking like mad at the sight of a stranger as is the wont of some of their ilk.

"Aye? What de you want at this time of night?" he asked in an Aberdonian accent. Wouldn't have been able to tell it was an Aberdonian accent before I started coming back and forth to Scotland but now I recognised it. A very pleasant accent actually, under normal circumstances. Sort of accent you wanted your surgeon to have.

"I bet I can tell what your dogs are called," I said.

"Who are ye?"

"Whisky and Soda. I'll bet you, they're called Whisky and Soda," I said.

"They're no' called Whisky and Soda. They're called Angus and Andy. What the fuck do you think you're doing coming around here at this time of night talking about ma wee dogs. Are you off your fucking heed?"

"I'm your next-door neighbour, Sean Duffy. I live just across the street. We moved in day before yesterday. I'm afraid my wife bumped your car."

"Aye, she did."

"Your name is?"

"Ryan McCallan, if it's any of your business.

"Can you come outside with me for a minute, please, Ryan?"

"Why?"

"I want you to show me the damage."

"All right, I fucking will at that. Angus, Andy, you fucking stay here!"

We went outside to the street and he showed me the car. There was barely a dent in the bumper of his Audi.

"A hundred quid will fix that," I said.

"And what about ma insurance premiums?"

"You don't tell the insurance about it. You just get it fixed and it won't affect your no-claims bonus. You know the garage on the hill there?"

"Aye."

"Good lads. I think it's a guy called Dunhill who runs it. I'll bet he'll knock that out for you for a hundred quid."

"And who's goanta pay this hundred quid?"

"I am," I said, taking my wallet from my jeans and counting out five twenties.

He took the money in his big fist without a thank you or a by your leave.

"That's your car fixed," I said. "And now I fix you," I said.

"What do you mean?"

"I mean, now I fix you for scaring my wife and baby girl."

"Oh, I get the picture! Big tough guy, now are you?" Ryan said.

"And aye, I know you're poliss, but I called my mate in Glasga and he told me all about it. You have no jurisdiction on this side of the water. You're no poliss over here. You're nothing over here, pal!"

He had eight inches on me and his hands were enormous. If he'd been a bit more lithe he would have made an excellent goalkeeper. Powerful shoulders too. If he connected with those shoulders he'd knock your lights out. But he'd be slow, wouldn't he? Big and slow.

"You think youse cops can do what you like, do ye? Well ye cannae. Ye fucking cannae," Ryan was saying.

I sighed. I mean, it's the weak man that resorts to violence isn't it? Violence, aggression, war is always the failure of policy. It means you've done something wrong. War, as Clausewitz says, dreams of itself.

You have to resist getting sucked into these dreams.

When we moved in I should have seen what sort of a person this man was. I should have taken action that first day. Shown him what sort of a person I was with nuance, subtlety and intelligence. I take full responsibility for that mistake.

"I suppose you think you're a hard man, no speakin like. You're no' a hard man, pal. You're no' anything."

He didn't know that I was armed. I'd forgotten that I was armed too. But any eejit can stick a gun in your face and talk tough.

Better to reset it.

"Hold on a minute," I said. I put my knuckleduster back into my jeans pocket. I held up my hand to stop him coming forward, reached into my jacket and took out the Glock and walked it over and placed it on the boot of my car. Then I took my jacket off and put it next to the gun. Then I took off my shoulder holster.

"Oh, ho, he's serious, he means business. What do you think you're going to do, pal?"

"I'm going to knock the living shite out of you."

"You, wee man?"

"Aye. Me."

The certainty of my statement perhaps alarmed him a little. "I never laid a finger on your lassie."

"No, you didn't touch her. Lucky you, if you'd hurt her physically . . . well, I'd probably be looking at a manslaughter charge."

"Big talk again. Ho, ho. Coming from you. It's all talk. You know you cannae do fucking anything about it. I've kenned ye out, pal. Poliss in a fight with his neighbour, they'd have ye out on your ear, so go inside before I give ye a hiding and ye get the fucking sack."

I shook my head and laughed. "You misunderstand completely. I'm not the sort of policeman you're used to dealing with. I'm not your friendly neighbourhood copper giving you the time of day and chatting to you about Kilmarnock versus Partick Thistle. No, mate, I'm RUC. We're a different beast completely."

"What's the difference?" he asked, still not afraid.

"You're about to find out, pal. Now, listen, I'm going to need you to throw the first punch so what I do in response to that will all be self-defence."

"What?"

"If you throw the first punch then what I do subsequently is covered by self-defence as long as it's reasonably proportional. What I need to do is to get you to throw that punch. What's the best way of that happening? Should I insult you?"

"Insult away I'm no' going to lay a finger on you," he said, crossing his arms triumphantly. So he wasn't a complete idiot then.

I slipped my fist into the knuckleduster.

Look away now if you think Sean Duffy is the decent man who fights fair. He doesn't fight fair. He fights very fucking unfair.

"I'll tell you what. Let's just assume you threw the first punch, eh? I came in to tell you about your bumper and you'd had a few drinks and I self-defended."

"You fucking micks are all the fucking same. You're all big fucking swagger. Showboat. Maybe your bird would like a real man after all, eh?" And then he did swing at me. And he was faster than I'd been expecting. But, you know, big man fast, which is to say, not fast enough.

I ducked the blow and punched him in his gut with my left and then my right. The right fist had the knuckleduster in it and the blow knocked the wind out of him. I punched him on the nose with a left jab and then another big gut punch with my right. His knees buckled. Another jab at his face. I easily avoided his attempt at a haymaker, but he slapped me with his left hand and I wasn't expecting that. I staggered backwards, face stinging. One of his nails had sliced open my cheek. I had to recover and react immediately. I couldn't allow him to clobber me again. I hit him with another jab in his face. This one burst the capillaries in his nose and he started to bleed. I punched him in the face twice more and he swiped at me and managed to connect with my shoulder. It was like getting hit by an anvil, lucky I'd avoided that first blow and the haymaker.

I punched him hard in the gut and he collapsed onto his haunches. He was gasping for air, bleeding from both nostrils and a cut under his left eye. I pushed him over backwards with the flat of my hand and when he was on the ground I kicked him in the balls. He winced in pain and curled into a protective comma shape.

I took a step back. "Have you had enough, Ryan?"

"Cunt!"

I kicked him in the back.

"Fucking stop it! I've had enough," he gasped.

I leaned down next to him. "Now, Ryan McCallan of the Cliff Road, Portpatrick, I need to know that you're properly afeared."

"Afeared of what?"

I grabbed him 'round his throat and fucking squeezed. Squeezed so hard his face went red and then white.

"Afeared of getting in my bad books ever again," I whispered in his ear.

I let go of his throat and he gasped for breath.

"Well?" I asked.

"Aye," he said.

"Good. Get your bumper fixed. And the next time you see my wife outside the house you fucking apologise. You apologise like your life depends on it. I don't want her thinking the street she lives on isn't safe. Hear me?"

"I hear ya."

"If there's any more trouble you won't fucking hear anything, sunshine, I promise you that."

I left him there, grabbed my side arm, shoulder holster and jacket and went back to the house.

I examined my arm and shoulder in the mirror. There was a bruise, but it wasn't bleeding. There were several lateral cuts on my fingers. A smack mark on my cheek and a thin scrape there too. I ran the cuts under the tap and dabbed them with cotton wool and iodine.

I turned the water off and listened.

All was quiet.

Just the hum of a fan in Beth's room and the sea beyond that. I petted the cat, kissed my daughter again and slipped into the bed.

"Are you really back? I thought I was dreaming it. I can't believe it," Beth muttered half in and half out of sleep.

"Believe it. It's the one and the only Sean Duffy," I said.

"Do you see the neighbour?"

"Yeah. We had a friendly chat about the bumper. He's really sorry for scaring you. He said he just lost the plot a bit. Won't happen again."

"Good. I'm glad you didn't fly off the handle. Dialogue. That's the way to solve things."

"It is."

"How long are you staying here?"

"I have to get back to the coalface tomorrow."

"Well let's enjoy tonight then," she said, turning towards me and kissing me on the lips. I was shattered but a man who has driven 110 mph on a two-lane motorway and stopped a ferry and punched out another much-bigger man has enough memory of the adrenaline to stir the blood. And who can resist a redhead between the sheets on a cold, misty, moonless night?

# 10
# THE THREE SUSPECTS

Emma was surprised to see me in bed with her mother.

"Daddy, I thought you weren't going to be home until the weekend," she said stringing together a full sentence in that uncanny Damien-like way she'd been doing since she was fourteen months old.

I hoisted her up into the bed between us. "Are you sad to see me?"

"Happy!" she said and immediately launched into a question about why there was always two disgusting flavours in a packet of Revels, wondering if it was a mistake or not. I explained that no it wasn't a mistake and that in fact that was the reason Revels continued to be popular amongst school children: in every packet at random there were always a couple of disgusting ones. It added a certain frisson of adventure to the chocolaty treat.

Emma asked what a frisson was, and I explained that it was a word meaning *a quick thrill* and came from the French word for *to shiver*, which itself had a Latin root, also meaning *to shiver*. "Apart from fear, why else do you shiver?" I asked her.

"Because you're cold!" she said.

"Which is why *frisson* and *fridge* sound the same at the beginning," I said.

We went down to breakfast which was toast, marmalade, three bowls of Crunchy Nut Cornflakes and coffee. The radio was on in the background.

"A summary of the latest headlines: American special forces continue to hunt for General Noriega in Panama. Thousands of people have stormed the former Stasi HQ in East Berlin seeking their Stasi files. Russian soldiers have massed on the borders of Azerbaijan in what has been called an attempt to intimidate a secessionist government from declaring independence. In Yugoslavia the autonomous republic of Slovenia has given notice of its intention of declaring independence. The weather will be overcast and rainy for most of Britain and Ireland today with highs in the south approaching eight degrees Celsius."

I examined the *Times* crossword while Emma surreptitiously ripped pieces of paper from the sport section and ate them.

"Don't eat Simon Barnes' column, that's the only bit of the paper I like apart from the crossword," I muttered dryly.

Beth was not so sanguine. "Don't eat the newspaper, darling, they put bleach in the pulp and it's bad for you."

I had been a determined newspaper eater as a child and youth and I still occasionally enjoyed a nibble, but Beth was probably right on this one, so I gave Emma a little shake of the head.

I grabbed a pencil and did the *Times* crossword.

I got stuck on the clue "Greek Character eats in. Good food will make the keratin grow and please Chinese wives (5)."

It took me a full minute to realise that the Greek character was RHO and that you added "in" to the RHO to make RHINO. My finishing time was a disappointing eight minutes for the cryptic. Another reason you shouldn't go around getting in fights with people.

I made Emma's lunch while Beth made her own sandwiches. As a teacher she was entitled to free school lunches, but she'd tried them once and declared them not fit for man or beast.

"You might want to consider teaching when you hit your twenty. That thing about fridge and frisson. You'd enjoy teaching, I think," she said.

"When I hit my twenty, I'm taking a couple of years off to do nothing but listen to music. Maybe write about it."

"You'll be bored out of your mind."

I shook my head. "I'll love it. I've had enough excitement in this life."

I walked Emma to school and caught the 9.30 a.m. SeaCat to Belfast. I was back in the station just before lunchtime. No one suspected that I'd even been out of the country. I could have killed that fuck next door and had a perfect alibi for it. Me? No. I was in Carrickfergus conducting a murder investigation, mate.

Although they probably had video of the cars driving onto the boat and it was some poor sod's job to log the number plates. If I'd been going home to murder Ryan it would be better for me to go on as an anonymous foot passenger. In disguise. Maybe bring a bicycle. Bicycle down to Portpatrick, kill the fucker, bike back, get the ferry to Belfast, ditch the bike, pick up the car from a car park and drive home.

"Yeah, that's how to do it, Duffy," I said to myself. Maybe my last case, like Poirot's would be the one where the bloody detective did it.

A knock at the door and Crabbie came in.

"You seem happy," he said.

"Do I?"

"You had a big grin on your face."

"I snuck home yesterday and saw Emma and Beth."

Crabbie nodded. "I'm glad you did that, Sean. Can't neglect your family. Did you give them my best?"

"I forgot."

Crabbie looked down and started filling his pipe. I knew he'd sulk all day unless I did something about this immediately. I called the office at Stranraer Grammar and they put me through to the staff room.

"What is it, Sean?" Beth asked. "You can't call me here! I'm the new teacher!"

"Just to let you know that I'm home safely, and Crabbie here was miffed that I didn't give you his best."

"Is he standing there looking at you with his arms folded?"

"Uh-huh."

"Tell him his best has been delivered and deliver mine right back."

"She thanks you and delivers her best back."

I hung up and Crabbie was satisfied.

"Any breaks in our case while I was away?"

"Nope, I'm afraid not."

"Well, a new day, a new hope. That's my motto."

"You seem to have a lot of mottos, Sean, not all of them that chipper or that unsweary."

"Whisky with some holy water in it?" I said, opening the drawer to those four bottles of the stuff that I had lugged from Israel.

"No thanks. Bit early in the day."

"All right. Let's get to work."

More like pretending to work really.

Waiting on the DNA, waiting on feedback from the Confidential Telephone, waiting for anything . . .

And in fact, there was nothing.

Lawson came in. He also shuffled the papers and followed the leads and came up with zilch.

No body, no clues, no tips, no forensic.

Coffee at the coffee machine.

Lunch down the pub.

The front room in Ownies. Roaring peat fire, three pints of Guinness, three bowls of Irish stew. Convo about the football.

"Sad display from Liverpool at Swansea."

"Oh, it'll be a different story at Anfield. It's always a different story at Anfield."

Back to the barracks.

A note from the switchboard. A Sergeant from Ballymoney RUC wanted a word.

"Christ, I hope it's not about bloody birds again," I muttered as I dialled the number.

It wasn't about the bloody birds.

After the phone call I went and got the lads.

"We have to drive up to Ballymoney RUC, those two kids we literally sent on a fishing expedition . . ."

"They found the body!" Lawson said, hand to mouth.

"No, but they found a girl's coat, and in that coat there was a diary, a waterlogged diary, yes, but an entry at the end was still legible and that entry contained names and phone numbers. The cops gave it to their resident FO, but I told them not to bloody touch it until we got there."

Outside to the Beemer. Up the A2 and along the coast road and down the Dark Hedges to Ballymoney.

Never been to Ballymoney?

Don't sweat it, you're missing nothing. North Antrim country town in the heart of Paisley country. Lots of tractors, shops selling wool and "Repent While Ye Still Have Time" billboards. Go to the Dark Hedges, yes, but you have my permission to skip B'money.

Ballymoney RUC was behind the usual concrete walls and bomb-proof fence.

Sergeant Michael Burke was now a heavy, ruddy-faced man with white hair and a gleaming set of false choppers. He looked to be about sixty-five and how he hadn't been involuntarily retired by now was beyond me. Maybe he knew where all the bodies were buried, and they didn't want him to retire to write his memoirs.

He'd made us tea and we had to do the necessary small talk, tea and fairy cake before he took us to the diary waiting for us in a plastic bag on an empty desk in the Incident Room. The coat was next to it in a larger plastic bag. Also in there were the two wee muckers, Norman and Monty, to whom I'd promised a reward.

"Where did you find this coat?" I asked.

"About two miles downstream from the car on a tree branch dipping into the water," Norman said.

"It was me that fished it out," Monty said.

"Well you did good finding this. Here's a tenner each and keep your eyes peeled for anything else out of the ordinary along this stretch of river."

"We will," Norman said.

"You think you could show me where exactly you found the coat after we're done here?"

"Easy," Monty added.

"Good, wait outside until we're finished in here."

When they'd gone I put on latex gloves and examined the coat. A sodden red Anorak with the stitching all torn up the back. It was from Marks and Spencer and it was the very coat that Kat had been wearing in the photograph Mrs McAtamney had given us. Just to be sure I examined the photograph and the coat. I held them up for Crabbie and Lawson to do the mental comparison too.

"Beyond question, now, I think," Crabbie said. "Katrina went into the river with the car."

"Yeah," agreed Lawson.

"The question is, did she make it out of the river?"

"If she did, where is she?" Crabbie asked.

"I don't know," I said. "Banged her head? Memory loss? Is now living with kindly farmers, falling in love with their only son."

"It would be nice to have a happy ending for once," Crabbie said with a sigh.

I put down the coat and picked up the diary. It was more of a journal than the little pocket datebook I'd been expecting, and it could have been very useful indeed except for the fact that water damage had utterly destroyed it. Almost all the pages had fallen out except for a few at the end which appeared to be blank.

"Is it all like this?" I asked Sergeant Burke.

"All like what?" Lawson asked.

"Completely illegible," I said and handed it to him.

Burke shook his head. "Two pages from the end," he said.

I looked over Lawson's shoulder while he carefully turned the diary back two pages from the end.

There were four telephone numbers written in ballpoint pen. She'd drawn a box around the bottom three numbers which meant they were somehow significant.

The first number was Carrick hospital. The other three?

"Have you tried these numbers?" I asked Burke.

He nodded, smiled, and handed me a sheet of paper. "BT gave us the names and addresses of all three of them. All three live in the Belfast/ Carrick area and are within easy driving distance of your victim's house."

The first phone number was registered to a man called Johnny Dunbar who lived at Fourteen Pasture Drive, Carrickfergus. The second phone number was registered to a Charles McCawley who lived at somewhere called Hobbs Hall, County Antrim. The third phone number was registered to a Terry Jones who lived on New Line Drive in Carrickfergus. Next to McCawley's and Dunbar's numbers Kat had written: "Don't call them at home." Those two were married then.

"That's the only salvageable evidence in the book, but I think it's something that will be worth your while following up on," Burke said with a look of quiet satisfaction.

I give him a nod of the head. Yeah, I had you pegged as a useless old codger too, but you did good, mate.

"Next step, boss?" Lawson asked.

"Standard stuff. We'll run some records checks and interview these fellows about their whereabouts when Kat went missing," I said.

"Pity this didn't show up sooner, it's given them a few days to get their story straight," Crabbie said.

"Aye," I agreed.

By the time we made it back to Carrickfergus Police Station, the RUC, Great Britain, Irish Republic and Interpol criminal records checks came back on our three men. There was absolutely nothing in the files for Charles McCawley or Terry Jones, but Johnny Dunbar made up in spades for the other two.

Born in Belfast in 1950, he'd been arrested for arson at the age of twelve, arrested for arson again in 1964, B&E in 1966, B&E again in 1967—and this time they'd put him away for it. Three years in the Kesh. Out in 1971, he apparently joined the UVF and was arrested in 1973 for attempted murder of a Catholic taxi driver in a heist and shooting that left the victim partially paralysed. He'd been identified because he hadn't been wearing the customary balaclava as they "bring me out in a rash something chronic," he told an arresting officer. In 1980 he was released from prison and in 1982 he was arrested for the attempted murder of two men at a private airstrip in Fermanagh. He was acquitted of that murder but only because the victims had dramatically recanted their testimony before the trial. Since 1982 Johnny had managed somehow to keep his nose clean.

"Let's see if we can get more details on that attempted double murder," I said to Lawson.

"'We' being me?" he asked.

"'We' being you," I agreed.

"Don't worry, I'll make the tea."

Three teas, a half a packet of McVities Dark Chocolate Digestives later.

A sour look from Crabbie.

"Yeah, I know," I said. "Dark chocolate digestives? This isn't why I put five quid into the kitty every week. Someone around here has unconventional tastes."

"And I found skimmed milk in the fridge," Crabbie said, making this discovery sound as grim as if he had discovered an artefact of the Antichrist.

Lawson came back twenty minutes later with a copy of the Dunbar 1982 incident case file which he'd had faxed from Enniskillen RUC. Interesting that the file wasn't on the central computer log. Not all the cases were computerised, but I had thought the techs had worked everything back to 1981 or so.

I handed Crabbie a copy of the file and we read it together. Apparently a plane carrying guns for the Protestant paramilitary UDA had landed at an old USAAF strip near Enniskillen. After the weapons had been unloaded into a lorry it had been hijacked by Dunbar and two other men.

A gun battle had ensued, and the two drivers had fled with multiple gunshot wounds as Dunbar successfully drove off with the lorry full of weapons. The smugglers had been arrested in the hospital and agreed to turn Queen's evidence. Dunbar had not, again, been wearing a balaclava and was easily picked out of the perp book.

But then one of the witnesses had "disappeared from the safe house" just before the trial was due to begin. He had, amazingly, turned up alive, but his story had changed and now he said he couldn't remember who had attacked his lorry. And his mate couldn't remember shit either, and with both eyewitnesses recanting, the trial collapsed.

"Disappeared from a safe house," Crabbie said with a low whistle.

"What does that mean?" Lawson said.

"That little phrase covers up any number of iniquities: incompetence, collusion, indolence . . . who knows . . . but it makes Johnny sound like a scary fucking lad. Let's put him at the top of our list."

The scary fucking lad lived out of town on Pasture Drive up the Acreback Road between the woods and the freshwater lake Lough Mourne. Cattle county up here. Fourteen Pasture Drive was a whitewashed heavy stone farmhouse with a 360-degree view all around. A sign on the gate at the front of the farmhouse said BEWARE OF DOG, and sure enough there were a couple of snarling Mastiffs and a slavering Alsatian prowling about the farm yard. Also on the gate post there was a large poster of a smiling man under a Union Jack with the phrase VOTE DUNBAR FOR A BETTER TOMORROW.

I rang the doorbell on the gatepost.

"Yeah?" a woman's voice said.

"It's the police. Here to talk to Johnny."

"Have youse got a warrant?"

"It's not at the warrant stage. It's just a friendly chat."

There was a long pause before the gate buzzed. I opened it an inch and pressed the intercom again.

"What about these dogs?"

"What about them?"

"Can you get them in the house, please."

"Are you frightened of a couple of puppies?"

"Can you get them back in the house."

"All right."

I was expecting the owner of that voice to be about sixty but when the front door opened, a pale, ginger-haired woman about twenty-two years old opened the door and yelled: "Toby, Zen, Arthur!"

The three dogs immediately ceased snarling at us and ran back into the house.

"Youse can come over now," the woman said.

"Well-trained brutes," I said as I approached the woman

"Aye," she agreed. "They can smell peeler from a mile off."

She had a cigarette hanging out the left-hand side of her mouth and her skin had a bluey-white transparent quality which made you think a little too much of the Jamesian skull beneath the skin.

"Detective Inspector Sean Duffy, Carrick CID; these are my colleagues Detective Sergeant McCrabban and Detective Sergeant Lawson," I announced.

"Are you Catholic?" the woman asked, squinting at me as if the horns were showing.

"Yes, actually," I said.

"Thought so, you can always tell," she said.

"How?" I wondered out loud.

"Something about your eyes, your sleekit, Fenian, peeler eyes," she said.

Crabbie winced and Lawson coloured.

"Are you Mrs Dunbar?" I asked.

"I am," she said.

"Can we come in? I want to ask your husband a few questions."

"Nope," she said defiantly.

"We need to talk to your husband," I insisted.

"What about?"

"About his whereabouts on December thirtieth."

"What about his whereabouts on December thirtieth? What's he supposed to have done?"

"That's a private matter between the police and Mr Dunbar," I said.

"What's her name and how old is she?" Mrs Dunbar asked. She was a hell of an intuitive guesser. If you could have rubbed the prejudice out of her she might have made a good cop.

"We just want to talk to your husband," I insisted.

"Johnny's not well," she said.

"What's the matter with him?"

"Late night."

"Maybe you can tell us where he was on December thirtieth?"

"We were both in the whole night. We were supposed to go to Brooks' Bar for the dance but Johnny had the feeling . . ." she began and trailed off into silence.

"Johnny had the feeling?" I offered.

She threw away her cigarette end, lit another and said nothing.

"Johnny had the feeling?" I tried again.

"That he was being surrounded by horses?" Lawson couldn't help but whisper.

I gave him a look. There was a time and a place for quoting Patti Smith lyrics and this was not that time or place.

"Mrs Dunbar, Johnny didn't want to go to Brooks' Bar because . . ."

"He heard a rumour that someone was going to firebomb that place because they weren't keeping up with their payments. He thought it best we shouldn't go. Had a quiet night in instead."

"He was here the whole night?"

"He was too."

"What was he doing?"

"Well, if I tell you *The Great Escape* was on the telly . . ."

"So he stayed in and watched *The Great Escape*?"

"He watched it. There's only so many times you can watch fucking Gordon Jackson fucking up with the fucking Gestapo."

"What did you do?"

"I read a book."

"What book?"

"*Remains of the Day*. It's about a butler. Bit slow. I was in the same room with him, so he didn't sneak out, believe me."

"Where is this Brooks' Bar?"

"We didn't bloody go, I told you!"

"I'm curious if it was actually firebombed."

"Oh, aye, it was. Burned to the ground. Everybody ordered out and they fucking torched it. Up the Shankill Road if you wanna go, but you'll have to wait a year till the insurance comes through. Now, I think I've been very cooperative, so I have. Turn about is fair play. What's her name and what's Johnny got to do with her?"

"I'm afraid I can't discuss the particulars of the case with you, only with Mr Dunbar."

"He's not well, like I say. You'll have to fucking come back. I'm closing the door now. I'll be letting the dogs out the back. That'll give you thirty seconds to get to the front gate."

"Thank you for—" I began but she slammed the door in my face.

We walked hurriedly across the yard and only just made it to the front gate before the slavering dogs came bounding towards us.

"Bloody hell!" Lawson said closing the gate behind us. Two seconds later and the mastiff would have had a piece of him.

"Thoughts, gentlemen?" I asked.

"I saw him peeking at us through the living room window. There was nothing wrong with him," Lawson said.

"We will definitely have to interview him again, but if I'd murdered a girl, driven her car to Ballymoney and come back in the wee hours with a missus as suspicious as that one, I'd 'ave prepped her in advance for a visit from the cops," I said.

"Me too," agreed Lawson.

"But then again Johnny might not be the sharpest chisel in the shed," Crabbie said.

"He might not at that. And he likes the young girls apparently. His wife wasn't twenty-five was she?"

"No. And I don't think she'll be surprised when she finds out he was a name in Kat's notebook."

"And he's still a connected man. That tale about the firebombing had the ring of truth about it," I said. "All right, boyos. One name in the book, one pretty terrible alibi, who's next on our list?"

"Terry Jones should be just down the road here, maybe ten minutes?" Lawson suggested, showing me the map. I nodded. "Mr Jones it is," I agreed. "Let's see if he's been able to come up with a good story about December thirtieth."

"If he's innocent, he doesn't need a story," Lawson said.

"We all need a story, son."

Seven minutes and thirty seconds later we were at Mr Jones' rather large and really rather impressive house on the Lough shore. It was a leafy three-story affair with a Mansard roof. Georgian, you would have said if it had been Dublin or Bath, but did they build Georgian houses out in the wilds of the County Antrim shore in the late-eighteenth century? The house had a drive off the shore road that was gravelled and lined with pear and apple trees and the gravel extended to a semi-circular parking area in front of the house where a lime green Jaguar XJ6 was parked at a rakish angle.

"Nice wheels," Lawson said as we got out of the Beemer.

"Yeah it does look nice, all that chrome, but have a wee gander under the front and I'll bet you there's a nice little pool of oil dripping from the engine. Alas, that's the Brummie calling card these days. Trust me, I've been rebuilding a Bonneville on and off for the last five years."

"Don't listen to him. I've a Land Rover Defender that was built in 1967, never had a moment's problem with it in twenty—"

The front door of the house opened and a man in a black sweater and grey slacks opened it. A handsome man, although a little on the thin side; hair thinning too and greying (blonde hair though so you didn't notice it as much). He seemed to be about fifty or thereabouts, although with a few hearty meals in him and a touch of the sun he could have passed for thirty-five.

He was not, a little disappointingly, the Terry Jones of Monty Python fame.

He had a moustache, which was interesting because one of the men Kat had met in the Tourist Inn had had a moustache. How many men these days had moustaches, I wondered. Five percent perhaps? Maybe twenty percent in the cops and the army?

"I say, what are you doing here? You can't park here! This is a private residence!" he demanded in what, possibly, was a Northern Irish accent, although clearly he'd lived in England and overseas for most of his life.

"Mr Jones?" I inquired.

"Yes?"

"I'm Detective Inspector Sean Duffy of Carrick CID; these are my colleagues, Detective Sergeant McCrabban and Detective Sergeant Lawson. Do you mind if we have a word?"

"What's this about?" he demanded. "Something to do with my car?"

"No, sir, it's a murder inquiry and we'd like you to account for your whereabouts on December thirtieth. Do you mind if we come in?"

He shook his head and then nodded. "Yes, I mean, no, uhm, come in."

The house was fussy and ornate. Large and overstuffed with furniture, bookcases and knickknacks in the Edwardian style. There were big windows, but the light was blocked by heavy russet-coloured curtains and thick lead panes that looked as if they hadn't been cleaned since the sooty 1950s. He showed us into a living room dominated by a gorgeous red leather sofa. I sat at the end, Crabbie took the other end and Lawson ended up in the middle. Our boy sat opposite in a matching leather arm chair.

"Interesting house," I said.

"Oh? Yes, uhm, my mother lived here until two years ago when I moved her to a nursing home. She couldn't really look after herself. I haven't really put my stamp on the place yet."

"What do you do for a living, Mr Jones?"

"I'm a civil servant," he said.

"What department if I might ask?"

"Uhm, well, I work for the Northern Ireland office, now . . . I was abroad for many years and, well, I just got a bit sick of it all, actually, and asked to come back home."

"What do you do?"

"Oh, nothing terribly important. I'm sort of involved in infrastructure at the moment. Roads, railways that kind of thing. Planning. Cross border stuff. Dull work, I'm afraid."

"So you work in the transportation department?"

"Well yes and no, I'm more sort of a planner really, actually."

"Who do you work for?"

"I'm under the Senior Civil Servant, Sir Arthur Bryant."

"Do you have access to the Secretary of State?" I asked, wondering if they even bothered to do security clearance on civil servants these days.

"Very rarely."

"How rarely is very rarely?"

"Perhaps once a week I prepare a brief for him when we're in a meeting together," he said.

Once a week sounded like a lot to me.

"You say you've moved here recently from overseas?" I asked.

"Yes."

"May one inquire where?"

"Look, what's all this about? December thirtieth? A murder investigation?"

"Do you know this girl?" I asked, showing him Kat's photograph.

"No, I don't think so," he said with the slightest little twitch you ever did see. In fact if the three of us hadn't been looking for it we probably would never even have noticed it. Only lovers, cops, make-up artists and professional poker players ever looked so closely at someone's face.

"You've never seen her in your life?" I asked.

"No, I don't think so."

"You don't *think* so?"

"No."

"Then perhaps you can tell me why your phone number was in her address book?"

He had two ways to go here: brazen it out and say that he had no idea why his phone number was in her address book or admit it and get on the high horse and accuse us of being the morality police. Nota bene: always better to deny, deny, deny.

Actually, always better to say nothing at all.

"Oh, God, all right, all bloody right. So I was a bit lonely and I went out with her a few times!" he exclaimed.

"You paid her for her company," I said as a statement of fact.

"Do we have to go into that?"

"Yes."

"I'm sure we'll be able to trace the cash you paid her, so you might as well admit it," Lawson said.

"Yes, yes," he said shaking his head. "I mean, I'm sorry, I know what I did was technically against the law but it's a victimless crime isn't it?"

Time to hit him and hit him hard.

"Were you aware that Katrina was fifteen years old?"

His face fell. "Oh, sweet Jesus! She said was eighteen!" he said, getting to his feet.

"She told you she was older?"

"Of course! She said she was eighteen!"

"How old are you, Mr Jones?"

"Forty-seven. Christ, I need a drink," he said and went over to the drinks cabinet. As he poured himself a stiff whisky from a crystal decanter he remembered his manners. "Would any of you care for something?"

"I'm all right," I said.

Crabbie and Lawson shook their heads.

He carried his whisky back to the chair and sat down again. "I really had no idea! Fifteen!"

"Where were you on the evening of December thirtieth?"

"The night before New Year's? Uhm, I was here," he said mournfully.

"In this house?"

"Yes."

"Alone?"

"Yes."

"Doing what?"

"It's going to sound ridiculous."

"Try us."

"Reading poetry."

"Generic poetry?"

"Catullus."

"Until when?"

"Until I went to bed."

"And what time was that at?"

"I don't know. Midnight?"

I flipped open the notebook and wrote "reading Catullus alone in house, no alibi."

"What happened on the thirtieth?" he asked, with a widening of the eyes that might possibly have indicated alarm, or, perhaps a guilty man attempting to simulate alarm.

"We're trying to determine that. It looks like someone may have driven Katrina's car to the River Bann, locked her inside, perhaps having first incapacitated her, and then put the car in neutral and pushed the vehicle into the water."

"Oh, my God! That's horrible! Poor Kat!" he said and hid his face in his hands.

It was quite the theatrical gesture, but people did do it in real life. I'd seen them do it in the interview room.

He made a little squeaking noise behind his hands and muttered something to himself which might have been the words "n . . . again."

Not again? Never again?

"Mr Jones?" I inquired.

He looked at up me. "Yes?"

"Mr Jones, so you can see why we want to know where you were on the evening of the thirtieth."

"But why would I want to do something like that?"

"A million reasons. You had a fight with her? She threatened to blackmail you about the relationship? She was, in fact, blackmailing you about the relationship and you decided to put an end to it?"

"Nothing like that happened! Katrina was a lovely girl. She wouldn't do anything like that."

"Was?"

"Christ, she *is* a lovely girl . . . have you found a b . . ."

"No, we haven't. Not yet. If she was in the car the body may have been carried out to sea, in which case it's unlikely that we'll ever find it."

Jones put his head in his hands again. Now he appeared to be sobbing. He took a drink of whisky and then, red-eyed, looked at us.

"You've got to believe me. This has nothing to do with me. Nothing.

I wouldn't harm a fly. I have trouble meeting . . . I'm a shy person, I don't meet a lot of . . . I wouldn't harm her. I wouldn't!"

"There are places to go where you can meet girls of legal age."

"I know. But those girls . . . I wanted someone that I could, well, this is also going to sound silly . . ."

"Try us again."

"I wanted someone that I could take to a restaurant or to the cinema. It wasn't about, uhm. You could talk to her. She listened. She was listener and she wanted to know things. She wanted to know about . . ."

"About what?"

"About everything. She wanted to know about history, and travel, and even bloody Catullus. Look, I promise you, I didn't know she was fifteen! I had no idea. She spoke French. Fifteen-year-olds don't speak French. You need to have done A levels for that."

"Not if you've lived in France."

"Yes, she mentioned that. Oh, God. Poor Kat."

"I take it wasn't all just conversations about Latin poetry? You did have sexual intercourse with her?"

Again, best thing here was to deny, deny, deny.

He nodded and groaned. "Oh, my God. Could I be charged with that?"

"Statutory rape."

Another groan.

"And if you killed her, kidnapping and murder," Lawson added a little too jauntily for my taste.

"No, I didn't do that! I had nothing to do with that. I was here by myself."

"So, what *exactly* could he be charged with, then, Sergeant Mc-Crabban?"

Crabbie frowned. "Certainly statutory rape under Section 6 of the Sexual Offences Act 1956. Gross indecency? Procuring a minor for the purposes of prostitution? Transporting a minor for the purposes of committing an immoral act?" Crabbie mused.

"That's quite the list, Sergeant McCrabban. How long would he get for all of that?"

THE DETECTIVE UP LATE

"Oh, it depends," Crabbie said.

"Five to ten years, depending upon the judge," Lawson said, firmly. "Minimum five under the current sentencing guidelines."

"But you've no proof!" Jones said.

I sighed and shook my head. "Mr Jones, you've just confessed to having had a sexual relationship with a minor in the presence of three police officers."

"Oh, shit! Yes, I did. Oh, God, I'm sorry. I'm so very sorry."

"For yourself?"

"For her, for whatever has happened to her," he said and began to sob again.

Crabbie got to his feet. "Maybe I should make a cup of tea," he suggested. I nodded. This was gold. We wanted to keep Mr Jones blabbing as long as possible. If he asked us to leave the house we'd have to leave and if we arrested him and brought him down the station, he'd almost certainly bring a solicitor with him, so drain him now, for everything he had . . .

"Tea, Mr Jones?" Crabbie asked.

"What? Oh, yes. Kitchen's over there."

Crabbie went off to make the tea. I pulled a chair next to Mr Jones.

"Look, Terry, if we find out later that you've lied to us, things are going to go very badly for you I'm afraid, but if you tell us now what happened that night . . . An accident perhaps? You were driving along the Bann and—"

"No! No, no, no. I wasn't there. Whoever killed her, it wasn't me. I was here. Look I can't have been her only, uhm . . . It wasn't exclusive, and I knew that. There were times when I wanted to see her, and she said she was busy. So I know there must have been other men."

"How did you get in contact with her? She didn't have a home phone," Lawson asked.

"I left messages for her and she would call me back," he said.

"Where did you leave messages for her?"

"Once or twice I left a note for her at her caravan. She lived in a caravan at that site out near Kilroot Power Station. I used to meet her out there sometimes. At a pub nearby there. The Tourist Inn, I think it was called. Although you'd never get a tourist near the place. This was all before she got the car. Wait a minute, she had to be at least seventeen before she could get a driving licence! Right? You must have made a mistake. She's been driving for a year, she must be eighteen."

"No mistake. We've seen her birth certificate. She would have been sixteen in March," I said.

"Shit! But then how did she get a driving licence?"

"She lied to get a provisional licence. As far as we know she didn't have insurance, an MOT certificate or a road tax stamp," Crabbie said bringing a tea pot, milk and cups.

"How did you meet her in the first place?" I asked.

"I, I don't know."

"Sure, you do," I said.

"I don't remember," he said.

I shook my head and put my hand on his shoulder. "You were doing so well. You were telling us truth and we were starting to get a bit of sympathy for you, but now? Now you start lying? To homicide detectives? Bad move. Very bad move."

Crabbie distributed the tea and I took a sip.

"I—I—there was this chap. He said that there was this girl, a nice-looking girl. Well, for shy men like me, uhm . . ."

"Tell us more about this underground network of perverts."

"Oh, God, it's nothing like that. It was just this chap who did a lot of work for the department. He came in as a freelance."

"Freelance what?"

"Photographer. He photographed all the visiting dignitaries and things like that, but he had connections in the modelling world and he knew a girl who was looking to meet, uhm . . . well you know how it is."

"This man wasn't a certain Mr Hardcastle, was it?" I asked, with a sinking feeling.

"Yes. That was his name!"

"He gave you Kat's name and address?"

"Yes. And when I couldn't reach her, he passed on the occasional message or two."

"That lying fuck!" I wrote in my notebook.

"Right, we'll need a photograph of you, Mr Jones," I said.

"Why?"

"To see if your story checks out," I told him.

"Don't you need a warrant or something to take one of my photographs?"

"Just get me a bloody snap, Mr Jones," I said.

He scurried off to another room and came back with a picture that looked like an official headshot for a civil service ID.

I enveloped the photo, nodded and looked at Crabbie and Lawson. Crabbie nodded. That about covered it for today.

I stood up. "Don't leave town, Mr Jones. We'll be back to interview you in due course and we may need you to come to the station to make a formal statement."

"I really hope you find her," he said.

"Yes, I hope so too."

He saw us to the door.

When Crabbie and Lawson were on the porch I did my parting Columbo move: "One more thing, Mr Jones. What did you mean by 'not again'?"

"Sorry?"

"When I told you about Kat you put your head in your hands and said, 'not again.' What did you mean by that, exactly?"

He shook his head. "God, I don't know. I was just muttering. This is all a bit of a shock isn't it?"

"Yes, it's a bit of a shock, sure, but has something like this happened to you before?"

"No! Nothing."

"If we look you up in our criminal records check we're not going to find your name connected to a missing persons case? Because if we do and we find out that you haven't told us the complete truth, we won't be best pleased."

"Do your records checks. I've never done anything wrong in my entire life. I'm a civil servant. I work with sensitive matters. I wouldn't risk all that."

I shook my head. "Mr Jones, you *have* risked all that by having a relationship with a fifteen-year-old, which is why, if I were you, I'd co-operate with us as fully and completely as possible."

He nodded dolefully. "I have been. I will," he said.

Back outside.

Under the BMW for bombs.

No bombs.

On the drive over to Jordy Hardcastle's flat, we unpacked the conversation.

"Your take, Crabbie?"

"Seems like he was telling the truth. He's a civil servant though so he's used to dissimulating."

"Your take, Lawson?"

"I'm with Sergeant McCrabban. Don't think he was lying. He doesn't have an alibi but that doesn't mean he did it."

I looked at Lawson in the rear-view. "No, it doesn't," I agreed, "but we'll look him up again in all the databases." If he really was saying "not again" or something like that, that was the bloody tell of the year.

We drove into town and the BMW took us to Jordy Hardcastle's apartment by the harbour.

Doorbell. Jordy's angry face. Police ID in that angry face.

"Oh, yeah you lot, what do you want now?" Jordy asked.

"A wee chat," I said. "Inside. Tell your boyfriend to put the kettle on."

"No, no wee chats. I've developing to do this afternoon. You're not coming in. I've been very cooperative so I—"

"You lied to us, Mr Hardcastle. You gave Terry Jones Kat's name and address. You took messages for her. You gave other men her name and address. You knew how old she was. You know what that's called? That's called being a ponce. That's called living off immoral earnings. That's called procuring a minor for the purposes of prostitution."

"That's bollocks! I never took a penny off her. I never took a bloody penny."

Two doors down a woman opened her door and looked right to see what all the racket was.

"It's all right Mrs Anderson, these gentlemen are coming inside," Jordy said. We entered the house and sat on the sofa. This time Jordy did turn the football off the telly because now he saw that he was in deep shit.

"Look, what do you want to know?" he asked.

"Why don't you attempt to get on our good side now and tell us the bloody truth, eh?"

"I haven't broken any laws I'll tell you that for nothing," he began.

"I'll be the judge of that," I said.

"My solicitor will be the judge of that," he snapped.

Patience—that's what a good copper needs. Patience in following up all the leads, patience in running through the hoards of data, patience in talking to the general public when most of them are eejits or wankers.

But then maybe I just wasn't cut out for police work, you know?

"Solicitor? Is that what you just said?" I snarled at him.

"Yeah, my solicitor. I mean, I know I haven't broken any—"

I got up, stomped across the white shag rug, grabbed him by the scruff of the neck and lifted him off the ground. While Crabbie and Lawson shrieked behind me I shook him, dumped him on the floor and picked him back up again.

"Now you listen to me, you sleekit wee shite! A girl's gone missing, presumed dead, possibly murdered by one of the men *you* put her in contact with. If you don't start singing like Kiri Te fucking Kanawa, I'm going to fucking crucify you to this fucking wall. And when you're off the fucking wall, I'll be charging you with accessory to murder as well as everything else!"

"Accessory to—"

"Yeah, that's right. And they fucking do not like child killers inside, believe you me. That's the one that brings the Protestant inmates and the Catholic inmates together, both of them unite and do their bloody best to castrate the child killers. Seen it happen more than once."

I let go of him and he crumpled to the floor.

"I, I didn't do anything—"

"Talk you little shit. How did Kat get into this business?"

"She wanted money, and I told you she didn't have the look to make it in the modelling world, she just didn't have the look. And she asks me if there's any other way she could make any money and I said I had no fucking idea. And she said was there any men that I knew who wanted a bit of female companionship. It was her idea! Not mine! I would never have—"

"And what did you say?"

"Well I gave her the name of a couple of blokes I'd done some work for who might possibly want to take a pretty girl out to a restaurant. That's all! That's all I did."

"You were also a conduit for these men, weren't you?"

"Oh, my God. Once or twice I got a couple of messages for her. That's all. That's all, I promise!"

"Names and addresses of these men, now. And if I find out later you've been holding out on me . . ."

We'll cut it there shall we?

We'll cut back to the Beemer heading out along the Shore Road.

You can imagine Crabbie's annoyance at the way I'd handled a witness. You can imagine Lawson's terror at the way I'd handled a witness. *You* can imagine that, why do I have to do all the work around here?

Fifteen minutes later.

Leaden silence.

Four tyres on the asphalt.

Light rain falling.

Crabbie thinking: yup, this is one of the reasons I'm getting out, glad I'm getting out. Lawson thinking: I hope this old tosser doesn't fuck it all up for me, drag me down into an internal inquiry or something . . .

Hardcastle hadn't actually given us any new information.

The two lonely men he had told Kat about were Charles McCawley and Terry Jones. How Johnny Dunbar had found about her was a mystery still to be unpacked, but for now, Mr McCawley needed a visit.

# 11
# MRS McCAWLEY

McCawley had an unusual address: The Lodge, Castle Hobbs, County Antrim, and we found out the reason for this unusual address pretty quickly when we went to the wrong house.

Castle Hobbs, a butler or perhaps a footman told us, was the ancestral home of the Hobbs family. The current owner, Major Arthur Hobbs, was the Lord Lieutenant of County Antrim, the Queen's representative in the county.

Castle Hobbs was a big, old, red sandstone seventeenth-century pile that had been expanded in the eighteenth century to accommodate stables and bigger servants' quarters. It lay on a gentle river valley between Carrickfergus and Whitehead. I didn't know a lot about country houses, but this seemed to be a pleasant one. Maybe a bit chilly this time of year.

"You're looking for Mr Charles McCawley?" the butler said when I told him why I'd come.

"Yes."

"You'll have to go back down the drive and turn left for the lodge. I'm not sure that Mr McCawley is in the country at the moment, but Carol is here."

"Who's Carol?"

"The Major's younger daughter, Mr McCawley's wife."

"All right. Back down the drive. Thank you."

Back down the gravelly drive between fig trees.

The Lodge was also done in red sandstone, a handsome home but, of course, a considerably smaller residence.

When we parked the Beemer and rang the doorbell, no butler or footman answered but instead Mrs McCawley herself. She had an attractive Pre-Raphaelite look about her with her long chestnut hair put back in an Alice band. Intelligent grey eyes and a brisk, no-nonsense figure. She was wearing a dark green jumper, an ankle-length skirt and knee-length rubber riding boots.

I made the introductions and came to the point.

"Good afternoon, Mrs McCawley. We'd like to speak to your husband," I said.

"I'm afraid my husband is not at home," she said in a soft, old-fashioned, Irish gentry accent. "May one ask the nature of your inquiries?"

"I'm afraid not, madam," I said.

"Why not?"

"It's a delicate inquiry at this stage and concerns only your husband," I said. "Do you mind if we come in?"

"May one ask what department of the RUC you are a member of?"

"I'm a detective in Carrick CID."

"What type of detective? Homicide? Fraud squad? Traffic? What?"

"We are such a small department that we do a bit of everything," I said. "Can we come in? It's a little nippy out here on the doorstep."

"Not much point you coming in, is there? My husband is not at home."

"Where is your husband?"

"He's been sent to Coventry," she said with a thin smile. "Literally, I mean. He's in Coventry."

"Is he likely to be there long?"

"Yes, he is. He's at a conference," she said. "What's the nature of your investigation? May one ask that, at least?"

"I'm afraid not. When did your husband go to Coventry?"

"New Year's Day."

"So he was here on December thirty-first and presumably December thirtieth?" I asked.

"Yes. Why? What happened then? Was there an accident?"

"Why do you say that? Did something happen to his car?"

"No, his car is fine. It's in the garage. You can look yourself. What's happened?"

"I really think we would all be more comfortable inside the house," I said.

"I don't think our family solicitors would want me to invite police officers into the house without one of them being present. Not if something has happened to Charles."

"Why do you think something may have happened to Charles?" I asked.

Her lips thinned. "Because policemen have come asking about his whereabouts on December thirtieth and December thirty-first."

"Where exactly was he on those nights, do you know?"

"Yes, I do. On December thirtieth he was here working on a speech. On New Year's Eve we were at the Lord Mayor's Banquet in Belfast."

"What speech?"

"He's at this conference in Coventry giving a series of speeches."

"Are you able to vouch for him being here the whole night?"

"What a strange thing to say. I went to bed early, but I heard him pacing about all over the house rehearsing his lines. He does that when he's writing. That went on for hours. The wee hours."

"So you're quite certain he was here all night?"

"Perfectly certain."

"I'm going to need his address and phone number in England."

"And you're not going to tell me what this is about?"

"No."

She looked at me and Lawson and McCrabban, shook her head and went inside leaving the door slightly ajar. She came with a piece of card with an address and phone number.

"He's staying at the residence hotel of the University of Warwick.

The phone number is on the back of the card. I hope you find the answers to your questions, gentlemen. This is certainly very mysterious. You have piqued my curiosity and my alarm."

"Nothing to be alarmed about, Mrs McCawley. We'll sort everything out with your husband, and I'm sure he'll explain everything to you," I said.

"Some hope," Lawson said a minute later in the car back down the drive.

# 12

# DUNBAR, JONES AND MRS McCAWLEY

Back to the station. We tried Mr McCawley's number in England, but it just rang and rang and rang. Home to Coronation Road. Mrs Campbell looking at me over the fence. "I saw your 'For Sale' sign go up yesterday. You're selling the house? I thought you were staying here a few days a month?"

"No, Mrs C. I just really need a flat over here. Not a big house. Looking at one of those new flats down by the marina."

She thought about that for a second and bit her lip. "Ach, we'll all miss you on Coronation Road."

"Will you really?"

"You know we will. Some of us have grown very fond of you and the rest have gotten used to your ways. Won't be the same having someone else in the house."

I was touched by this. It had been hard graft winning over these crazy Protestants, but it had been worth it. A little bit of détente had improved understanding on both sides. Détente and getting them off their speeding tickets.

"I saw you've been eating fish and chips the last couple of nights."

"Well, I—"

"Our Janette has made lasagne. Doing domestic science at the tech. You can't say no."

I couldn't say no.

I brought over a bottle of wine and some flowers. Mrs Campbell's boyfriend was nowhere to be found and was not spoken off. It was an all-female affair at the table apart from me and a baby of sex undetermined.

The lasagne, it had to be said, was amazing.

"This is amazing, Janette."

"Glad somebody appreciates it. Tired of catching them dirty looks at the bottom of the table from the weans. Wouldn't know good food if it hit them in the back, which it will do if they don't start eating."

The meal was good craic. I listened to gossip about the neighbours, and Mrs Campbell told the kids an old joke which cracked them up: "A Guinness brewery worker travels to the home of his co-worker with bad news. 'I'm sorry, Mary, but Keith died at the brewery today. He drowned in a vat of Guinness.' 'Oh, my god!' replied Mary, 'That's terrible! Was it a quick death, at least?' 'I'm afraid not,' the worker replied, 'He got out twice to take a piss.'"

Like I say, a very old joke but guffaws from the kids. I told a couple of benign cop stories.

"I want to be just like you when I grow up, Mr Duffy," one of the non-eating little kids announced.

"A crusader for justice, you mean?"

"No, somebody who has a cat, you still have your cat?"

"Yes."

The wine flowed. Beer flowed. Dinner was followed by several of Mrs C's famous cakes. The girls' tongues loosened, and more gossip flowed.

Convo snippets:

"She is married. But not here. Her husband's over the water."

"Sure, I seen him out there stamping on them roses."

"Nope, the milkman says they won't be continuing service. It's the supermarkets. Cheap plastic milk has driven them out."

"Ach, he's mad, so he is. You can't lose a homing pigeon. If your homing pigeon don't come home, he's just a pigeon, isn't he?"

Home, bed, sleep.

Miss this place. You think everything is going to last forever, but it isn't. Heraclitus was quite right. You cannot step into the same river twice. All is flux.

The milkman, postman, bread man, coalman and rag-and-bone man used to come out every day. Not anymore. All is change. Gonna miss Carrick when this case is over. It's not all rough men, sweaty pubs, violence, itchy wool sweaters, missing girls, grieving parents, tea, endless tea. There's also the craic. The craic out here in the estates.

I called the family in Scotland and they were fine. Didn't tell Beth about my feelings for Coronation Road. She was two notches above lace-curtain Irish—she hated it here.

Morning.

Shave. Shower. T-shirt. Jeans. Black polo neck. Look under Beemer. *Keine Bomben.*

Lawson meeting me in the police station car park with a mug of coffee.

"Oh, shit, what are you doing out here? It's a visit by the Chief Constable is it?" I said, taking a puff of my asthma inhaler and wondering if I had a shirt and tie stashed away anywhere.

"No, nothing so dramatic, it's just Johnny Dunbar who's come to see you. He's in the Interview Room. Wants to make a statement."

"Lawyers with him?"

"No, just him."

"A confession? Nice way to start the day."

"Don't think it's a confession. Just a statement."

I swallowed the coffee. "Right, let's get on with it, then."

Johnny Dunbar in Interview Room 2. Squat little guy, dyed-blonde hair that screamed wig or comb over. Denim jacket, diamond earring. Some sort of animal-skin boots. Handsome though. Roguish face. He'd have to be a rogue to hijack a lorry full of guns being unloaded from a plane. He was a twitchy eejit through the glass. But not crazy twitchy, just bored twitchy. I went inside and introduced myself, Lawson and the Crabman. I gave the spiel about the Police and Criminal Evidence Act and started rolling the tape recorder.

"So," I said. "Katrina McAtamney."

"What about her?"

"Your name was in her appointment book."

He looked at the tape recorder. "How confidential is this?" he asked.

"As long as you didn't kill her, your girlfriend won't get to hear this tape," I said.

"I didn't kill her. Didn't even know she was dead."

"How did you know her?"

"Met her in the Tourist Inn out in Eden. Took her out a few times, but I stopped all that when Andrea got pregnant. Four months along now. Can't be dicking around when your girlfriend's four months along."

"Higher-ups don't like that, do they?"

"What higher ups?"

"Higher ups in the UVF."

"Oh, I don't run with those boys anymore. Not anymore."

"What do you do for a living, Mr Dunbar?"

"I'm a financial planner."

"Financial planner?" I said incredulously.

"I take people's money and invest it, so I do."

"That I believe. Do they know you've taken the money?"

"I didn't come here to be insulted."

"Where do you usually go?"

"That's an old gag."

"But still a good one."

"Look, I've done nothing wrong here. I come in of my own free will. I've done no crimes."

"Did you know Kat was fifteen?"

"I found out. That's another reason I stopped seeing her. I did a wee bit of research on her."

"And what did you discover?"

"Her ma is the worst fucking shoplifter in Ireland, her grandpa was a bareknuckle boxing champion, her dead da was also a boxer, her great uncle is a forger and car thief and she's bloody fifteen. That was enough for me, I tell you. Dropped her like a hot potato. Like I say, no laws broken."

"Statutory rape?" I suggested.

"We never had sex," Dunbar said.

"You never had sex?"

"Nope. And if we had, which we didn't, I'd love to see you try to prove it."

"Where did you take her?"

"Status Quo concert at the Royal Dublin Society. Motorhead at the King's Hall. The Kinks at the RDS. Andrea's not a music fan. Katrina is. Or was, if you're saying she's dead."

"We haven't found a body," I said.

"No body? Well, don't rule out some kind of fucking life insurance scam. She comes from some family."

"You're not exactly the Golden Boy of Purity. A few sins of commission in your CV."

He lit a Benson and Hedges cigarette. "I'm not a bad lad, not really. My cousin Marty burned a boy's dick off with acid. That's bad. The other day I had to stop a teenage hood called Scotchy Finn from blinding some guy. He says to me about this third party: 'If we top him they'll have the funeral and then everyone will forget that we done it. What's one less joyrider between friends, eh? Whereas if we blind him, he'll always be around with his stick or his dog and everyone will be whispering, "see him, that maniac Scotchy Finn fucking blinded him so he did, look at him, gouged out his fucking eyes."' That's the sort of thing I have to deal with and I do deal with it, you know? I stop bad things from happening and becoming a problem for you lot."

"We're very grateful, I'm sure," Lawson said sarcastically.

"I thought you were a financial planner?" I asked.

"I've got a finger in a few pies."

"A few UVF pies."

"You said that, not me. I deny it. I just do wee odd jobs for people. No O levels."

"Not a one? How did you manage that? Everybody has one," Lawson said.

"Not me. No skills. Look, I want an easy life. I want to die like my grandfather, peacefully in his sleep . . . not screaming like all the passengers in his car."

"Now who's doing the old jokes?" I said.

"Bottom line, Inspector Duffy, is this: we both know I'm a dodgy guy, right? We both know I went out with Katrina. But I never slept with her and I never killed her. I was home on December thirtieth. The whole night. It's the truth."

"What were you doing?" Crabbie asked.

"Watched a film. *The Great Escape*. Ok? That's it. Six pack of Harp and a wee flick. And then Andrea goes to bed and I listen to Phil Collins."

"Phil Collins?"

"Aye."

"The new album?" I said. Crabbie and Lawson could see I was starting to get worked up. Track two, which got a lot of radio play, was about the Northern Ireland conflict and was so trite that it—No, they were right, don't get side-tracked, don't get worked up.

"So you'd prefer it if we didn't mention any of this to Andrea," I said.

"That's right. I come in here of me own free will. Good citizen. Good relations with the cops. I didn't sleep with that wee doll and I didn't kill her either."

"For your sake, I'm very glad to hear that."

Few more rounds of this. Tag team. Duffy out. Lawson lead. Lawson out Crabbie lead.

Didn't matter. He stuck to his story. He didn't kill her, he was home watching a film and we couldn't even threaten him with the statutory because he was too smart to admit that.

We let him go at lunchtime, thanked him for his cooperation and retired to the pub.

Three pints of Guinness and three Ulster fries.

"Thoughts gentlemen?"

"Hard to say," Crabbie said. "You want to believe him but he's a professional criminal."

"He is a crim," I agreed. "Don't know what exactly he does for the UVF, but he's no financial advisor or whatever it was he said. Still, he was pretty convincing."

"He didn't do it. I don't think so, anyway," Lawson said, simply.

Crabbie took a sip of Guinness. "So what do we do now?"

"Mr Jones again, I think. Down the station, tonight."

"Do you want me to call him at work?" Lawson asked.

"Aye, do that."

Tick, tock, went the afternoon in my office.

Rain on the windows, case notes, paperclip chain now five hundred clips long.

Radio 2 was playing "Ebony and Ivory" out in the Incident Room. I sat up and paid attention. I liked to hate that song. It was the perfect song to hate. It was more perfect to hate than "My Gang" by Gary Glitter. Everything about it: the weak singing, the clunky lyrics, the tinny melody. I enjoyed listening to it and hating it.

Lawson broke my concentration with a knock on the door.

"Yes?"

"Personnel report on Jones from the Civil Service. Confidential HR report but they had to give it to us because it's a murder investigation." Aye, you can't piss around with the cops even if you are a close-mouthed civil servant in the upper echelons.

I read the report.

Jones was born in Belfast in 1942 of a Welsh father and an Irish mother. Dad worked for Harland and Wolff as an accountant. Mum was the daughter of Charles Grigg, MP, for Lagan Valley. Good schools, good uni: Royal Belfast Academical Institution and then Balliol Oxford, where he read classics and managed to bring home a first.

Joined the diplomatic service after uni. Cape Town for five years followed by Cairo for two years; Warsaw for two years; Washington, DC, for two years; Moscow for four years; Prague for one year; then appears to have got homesick. Back to Northern Ireland in '81 and joins the Northern Ireland Civil Service at a high rank. Been working in the Northern Ireland Office planning division ever since.

I passed the report over to the lads and we were all up to speed on Mr Jones' background.

He also did not bring a solicitor when he appeared at six o'clock.

There's a perception amongst members of the public that if you bring a lawyer it makes the cops think you're guilty of the crime with which you're being questioned. It doesn't. All it makes us cops think is that you've possibly got something to hide, something that might be and in many cases is tangential to the case. Not bringing legal counsel doesn't make us go easier on you, in fact quite often the reverse happens . . . So, you know, another tip from Sean Duffy here: bring a lawyer with you when you're down the cop shop talking to the peelers.

He was wearing a dark blue suit with a red tie and nice black brogues. He was trim, and his wavy hair was brushed. He looked every inch the competent civil servant. He had a briefcase with him too, so he might have just come from work.

Crabbie had to dash home to the dairy farm, so it was just Lawson and me to do the interview. We could handle this joker.

We probed his past history, his interesting diplomatic service career, his return to Northern Ireland and then we got to the nitty gritty.

"Were you ever married Mr Jones?"

"Never. Not yet."

"Girlfriends? Boyfriends."

"One or two. The former."

"Here in the UK?"

"No, actually. I went out with a woman in DC for a year. We were engaged but that didn't, in the end, work out."

"Was she your age?"

"Yes. A little younger. Two years younger."

"And anyone else?"

"A girl in Russia, briefly. And actually, in Cairo I had a girlfriend in the embassy."

"Around your age, Mr Jones?"

"Yes, what are you getting at inspector?"

"I'm trying to ascertain if you're a paedophile or not. If we were to get a warrant and go to your house, would we find child pornography?"

"Certainly not! That's an outrageous thing to say."

"Are you quite sure about that?"

"Come back with me. Search it from top to bottom. You won't need a warrant, I give you my permission!"

"So you're back in Belfast, you sort of inherit your mother's lovely house by the water, you've an excellent job, an excellent degree and you can't find someone your own age to go out with?" I asked.

"It's not as if I didn't try. I did. But it didn't work out."

"Why didn't it work out?"

"I don't know. I wasn't relaxed. I was set up a few times, but the women never wanted to see me again. I suppose I wasn't . . . With Kat I felt very relaxed. We hit it off right from the get-go. She came to my house, she spent hours looking at my books. Asked to borrow some of them. Always returned them, read. She didn't *pretend* to read them. She read them. She read *Une Page D'amour*, have you read that?"

"I didn't catch that one, I'm afraid," I said.

Lawson shook his head.

"It's the eighth novel in the Rougon-Macquart series. The central character of the novel is Hélène Grandjean first introduced in *La Fortune des Rougon* and—"

"Mr Jones."

"Look the point is, she read it in French. Very intelligent girl. Charming. And like I say, I thought she was eighteen. I had no idea!"

"If you had learned that she was fifteen would you have kept going out with her? Sleeping with her? It sounds like you were quite besotted," Lawson said.

"Of course not! I'm not a complete idiot, you know. I'm a civil servant with access to the Secretary of State for Northern Ireland. I've been in the room with him when he's been giving briefings to the Prime Minister. I've been in Downing Street on two occasions! Do you seriously think I would jeopardise all of that with a scandal, with a minor? That's why I'm here today. I'm trying my damndest to keep this quiet. I've messed up horribly and I'm throwing myself at the mercy of the RUC to keep this as quiet as possible. You both seem like reasonable men."

"How often did you see her?"

"Once or twice a week. She was often busy."

"And did you pay her?"

"I—I paid for her company. As an escort. We didn't always have a sexual, uhm, encounter."

"But you did have sex with her?"

"Yes. I'm not proud of that. I didn't know."

"When was the last time you saw her?"

"It was before Christmas. We went to the *Nutcracker* at the Opera House. We met there and went out for a meal. She drove home in her car. I drove home in mine. It was a lovely evening."

"No sex that time."

"No! It wasn't like that. Why won't you understand?"

"Let's go back to the night of the thirtieth. You were home reading Catullus, if I recall. Why weren't you with Kat that night?"

"She couldn't go out that night."

"She was going out with a different client?"

"I didn't ask. I never asked. If she said she couldn't come on a particular evening, I didn't press it."

"So you were home the whole evening, reading poetry?"

"Yes."

"The love poems, no doubt."

"No. Not really, I was trying to come up with a better translation of the poem to his friend Caecilius. The one where he urges him to come see him in Verona."

"I forgive you, my girl, who art more learned than Sappho's muse," I said.

Jones smiled at me, but Lawson headed off the Latin wankfest by bringing us back to the matter at hand:

"Did she ever talk about her other clients?" he asked.

"Never."

"Did you ever meet any of them?"

"Of course not."

"So you've no idea who she was meeting on the thirtieth?"

"I don't know that she was meeting anyone. She might have been doing her Christmas shopping. She merely said that she was busy."

"And you have no alibi for that night at all? You didn't order a pizza or phone an old friend or anything like that?"

"I'm afraid not."

I looked at Lawson. He shook his head. He had nothing else f or now.

"Well, Mr Jones, I think that does it for today."

He stood up and offered his hand. I didn't shake it, neither did Lawson. We were not old chums now. He was a suspect in a murder investigation who had had sexual intercourse with a minor and who bloody should have known better anyway because he had such a sensitive job.

"Will we be able to keep this quiet, do you think? If the Civil Service finds out about this, I'm finished. If the papers find out . . ."

"I'll be honest with you, Mr Jones. I don't know if we can keep this quiet or not. Obviously Kat isn't around to testify against you, but this is a very serious matter indeed."

He put his hands flat on the table and looked at me pleadingly. His eyes were watery again. But this time it was clear that he was feeling sorry for himself not the poor lost missing girl. He brushed back his thatch of wavy hair and loosened his tie.

"I understand that, but you, I think, have considerable discretion, don't you? I didn't kill her. If you find the real killer I might not have to come to court? I'm a good citizen. I'm good at my job. The Secretary of State trusts me."

"Maybe he shouldn't trust you," I said coldly.

"But it's your call, isn't it?"

"My call over what?"

"Over whether my testimony will have to come out."

"Yes, it's my call, Mr Jones, and at this stage it looks to me like you're a very important witness indeed."

Lawson looked at me. He didn't want Mr Jones killing himself or anything. But he didn't seem like the killing-himself type to me and there was no sense in giving him false hope.

"You should prepare yourself for public exposure, Mr Jones. I will certainly do my best to keep this discreet but if I need you to testify at the coroner's inquest, then I'm afraid you will have to testify."

"If there's no body will there really be an inquest?"

"Oh, yes, even without a body, there will still be an inquest. I can assure you of that."

He left the station fifteen minutes later in a state of some distress. It couldn't be helped. I couldn't lie to the man. It was true that a different detective might have invoked the old boys' club or seen what a decent chap he was and assured him that he could be kept out of the papers. But I could make no such assurance or promise, and why would I? He was unlucky, but he had broken the law, and the law on statutory rape was very clear. And the law on murder was even clearer.

"What now?" Lawson said as we stared out at the grey lough water and hugged a glass of whisky each.

"I think we have to pay another visit to the Lord Lieutenant's daughter. That phone number she gave us is bloody rubbish."

Back along the A2 to the Lodge of Castle Hobbs.

Gravel drive under wheels making a very pleasant sound.

Doorbell.

Mrs McCawley wearing a painter's smock and Wellington boots.

"Yes?" she said curtly.

"Sean Duffy, Carrick RUC," I said.

"I remember you. Why are you back here? I'm very busy."

"Doing what if I may inquire?"

"No, you may not. An impertinent question for an impertinent young man," she said.

It was a comical and weird thing to say. She was clearly younger than me. Thirty? Thirty-five maybe? An attractive woman with a shock of black hair and that imperious hawk nose of the gentry over here. And those eyes were pretty imperious too. Smart and sexy.

"I'm not going to guess your age, Mrs McCawley, but I'm pretty sure I'm your senior," I said with a grin.

She couldn't help but smile. She had a sense of the ridiculous and she saw then that the role she was playing was ridiculous.

"What can I do for you officers?"

"That phone number you gave us for your husband was rubbish."

She nodded. "Was it? Well, he gave me a whole contact list, let me see if I can find it. Come in."

We followed her through a Spartan, cold living room with a tiny old-fashioned TV and a rather empty bookcase to a well-lit art studio at the back of the house. There were a dozen portraits stacked up on the floor and one on an easel of a handsome grey-haired guy in his forties.

"Is this what you do for a living, Mrs McCawley?"

She laughed and blushed rather adorably. "Oh, God no!"

"So I can see, these are very good," I said looking at the canvasses on the floor.

"No! Don't look at the ones at the back! Don't touch them. They are so embarrassing. I'm going to paint over those."

"You only do portraits?"

"Yes, the human face is so expressive and interesting, don't you think? Your face for example, Inspector Duffy. I'll bet not many people realise you were in a fight a few days ago."

Lawson looked at me. He hadn't seen that.

"A fight?" I said, trying to sound sceptical.

"Yes, someone slapped or punched you, you can see the bruises. If you look at faces as much as I've been doing lately you really see faces. Trouble on the home front?"

"No," I said hastily. "Slight difference of opinion with a neighbour about parking."

"You should see the other chap, I suppose, eh?"

"Yes," I said with a smile.

"So what do you do for a living if you don't mind me asking?"

"Oh . . . nothing. I'm rich. See that big house down the road? My dad's."

"And you'll inherit it?"

"Oh, no. It's entailed through the male line, but I have a trust fund. I'll be all right when the old man pops his clogs. The family has a third share in a diamond mine in South Africa, if you can believe it," she said lowering her voice to a comic whisper to suggest the depravity of such a confession.

"A diamond mine?" I said, thinking of Big Jim and the Jack of Hearts and that Bob Dylan song with the easy chord progression.

"Old man says he'll sell it as soon as they release Mandela because the whole country will go Zimbabwe belly up," Mrs McCawley said.

"What does a Lord Lieutenant do exactly?"

"Ceremonial buff when her Maj is over."

She was being a lot chattier now. I supposed the chilly sexy stuff was just the wall you had to get through to get to the real woman. Pity though, I was kind of digging on the former more than the looser, nicer latter. But that's just me.

"Have you met the Queen?" Lawson asked.

"Met her, curtsied to her, and she asked me where I got my hat."

"And what did you say?"

"I told her I made it myself, which wasn't true at all. I don't know why I said that. I got it on Regent's Street!" she said with a little laugh. "Right. Contacts in Coventry for my better half. Where did I leave it? Aha, here it is," she said, handing me a sheet of paper with several phone numbers and addresses.

"Thank you. When will he be back?"

"The weekend or possibly Monday."

"Hmmm, we may want to talk to him before that."

"You're still not going to tell me what this is about?"

"No. I'm afraid we can't do that."

"Can't or won't?"

"It's a privacy issue."

She thought about that for a moment and bit her lip. "It has to be drugs or another woman then, doesn't it? Anything else you would have told me about, a traffic offense or something, but you can't go around destroying marriages willy nilly can you?"

"I'm afraid I can't say," I said.

She glared at me for a moment.

"Well whatever it was he's done. It wasn't on the thirtieth. He was here with me. I heard him pacing around half the bloomin' night," she said and picked up a paint brush. Paint dripped from the end of it down onto her smock and onto her Wellington boots.

"Now look what you've made me do! Mr Smith says that only house painters and Jackson bloody Pollock get paint on the bloody floor," she said.

"Before we go, what does your husband do again?"

"He's a lecturer at Queens. Architecture. More of a critic, really, nowadays. He wrote a book on Coventry. That's why he's over there. Telling them everything they did wrong. Damn it, look at that paint. Right through the cracks of the floor. Never get that out. Charles predicted it. Said I should paint out in the greenhouse. He was right. Mr Smith was wrong. It's because you distracted me."

"Well, again, sorry, I think we have what we—"

"Yes, yes, you do. You can see yourselves out."

Outside to the Beemer.

Car ride back to the station.

"What do you make of her, Lawson?"

"Bit old for me," he said.

"Not her looks. What she was saying."

"She wasn't really saying anything was she?"

"There's something her husband has been doing to make her suspicious. And a bit annoyed, it seems. She thinks he's done *something*. Something bad."

"Affairs are one thing, sir, murders are quite another. And whatever he was doing, it wasn't on the thirtieth she says."

"Aye, so she says. It would be her instinct to cover it up until she has it out with him, don't you think?"

"I don't know."

I drove and thought.

"We have to have it out with him first. I haven't seen Dalziel around for a couple of days. I can't get through a week unless I have a good old blow up with him," I said reflectively.

"So how will you accomplish that?"

"Book us three flights to Coventry leaving first thing in the morning. Try to get them business, that will really explode his head."

# 13
# SENT TO COVENTRY

Shed. Morning toke. Phone ringing in the hall. Run down the path, trip, slip, bang my head. This path will be the death of me.

"Yes?"

"Sir, where are you? We're here, but they say you haven't checked in."

"You're where, Lawson?"

"The harbour airport, sir. The flight leaves in fifty-five minutes."

"Christ, lost track of . . . Can you send someone from the station to pick me up? I'm in no fit state to drive. Kearney from traffic. He won't mind burning rubber."

"Yes, sir."

Bill Kearney from traffic did not mind burning rubber, but nobody ever wanted to drive with him because of the way he threw the car around changing lanes and cornering. And then there was the fact that all those traffic guys were chatty bastards who could never button it even though it was obvious that you'd had a rough night. Why were they all like that? Long periods in the car with nothing to do but watch the motorway sliproads? Who could say, but it was bloody annoying.

"Scotland, eh, Duffy? Rather you than me. Scots are grumpy bastards, aren't they? What was it they said on that Stephen Fry programme? It's always easy, no, that wasn't it, it's never difficult, yeah, it's never difficult to tell the difference between a Scotsman and a ray of sunshine. Never go independent. This is the way they like it, always able to blame everything bad that happens on the English . . ."

100 mph up the A2 and 90 mph on the M5.

"I mean, England's going to the dogs. But that's the nature of England; it's always going to the dogs. When England isn't going to the dogs, that's when we'll all be in trouble. At least that's what the wife's father says. Bit of a wag, he is. From Nuneaton. We've been over a few times, I wouldn't recommend it. Went to George Eliot's house. That's a lass' name, by the way."

Ten more minutes of this, but at least I made the airport.

Crabbie and Lawson waiting for me.

"Oh, my God, Sean, you look terrible. Your scalp. Is that mud or blood?" Crabbie said when I arrived at the gate.

"Don't ask, Crabman," I said. "And don't you give me dirty looks, Lawson. I can feel your look. I'll shave and get a tie at Birmingham airport."

"And maybe, if I can be so bold, a shirt too, sir. You're wearing what looks to be a Frank Zappa T-shirt under your jacket."

Belfast Harbour Airport to Birmingham International.

I found a razor and a shirt and a tie and while Lawson and Crabbie rented a car, I got myself half respectable.

They rented a Toyota and I sat in the front passenger's seat.

Forehead against the leaden coolness of the window. It was a drizzly damp day and if I'd bothered to check the forecast, I would have packed my raincoat, but I didn't. We chugged east out the airport through woods and rapeseed fields. It was pleasant enough until we hit Cov which was grey and concrete, rain-worn and weary. Like me. How could you not be weary?

Crabbie was driving and as soon as we got into the city, we got lost. Lawson was navigating, but he couldn't figure out the one-way systems and none of us, of course, had ever been here before.

We had to stop and ask directions three times before we got to Warwick University, which turned out not to be in Coventry or, indeed, Warwick.

Dr Charles McCawley was at something called the Future City Symposium. In fact, by the time we tracked him down, he was giving a lecture. We slipped in the back while he was in midspiel. He was a tall, stooped, handsome man with a little bit of a stutter, but as he warmed to his theme, his confidence grew and both his posture and speech improved.

"Luftflotte 3 dropped hundreds of b-bombs and incendiary devices on the city. Black bombs t-tumbling out of the November sky on Leofric's double-headed eagle and the C-Coventry Ordnance Works and the Cathedral of Saint Michael. This was Operation Mondscheinsonate— the wiping of the city of Coventry from the map. But, my f-friends, it wasn't the Luftwaffe which destroyed Coventry. It was Donald Gibson, the city's chief postwar architect, who wiped out the medieval lanes, squares and markets and replaced the lot of them with ring roads, pedestrian precincts and mugger-friendly underpasses . . ."

As fascinating as this was, my head was spinning and I felt like I was going to be sick. "I'm going to have to find a bathroom, mate," I whispered to McCrabban. "Nab the Prof as soon as he finishes and keep him here. He's an elusive cat and he's not getting away this time."

I exited the lecture theatre and went down a set of steps where I found the gents. I picked the end stall, locked it, raised the toilet seat and vomited the aeroplane breakfast of beans, bacon, sausage and oily coffee. I vomited again and this time nothing came up.

Dry heave after dry heave until I was shivering.

Bloody hell. Getting weak.

No bombs under car, no one had shot at me, I'd just slipped and fell on the path from house to the shed. A younger man would have laughed that off. But a man hitting forty after dog years coppering in Ulster . . . I wiped my mouth and flushed the toilet and exited the stall. The bathroom had a big brightly lit mirror and standing in front of it was an old tramp. Vomit on tie, vomit on face, bags under eyes, creases on forehead, greying hair, thinning hair, dishevelled suit, a bad shaving job. I looked fifty-five or older. A poorly maintained fifty-five. It was the job. That was the job during the Troubles. If it didn't actually kill you, it aged you at double the speed of coppers over the water, the lucky bastards.

"Yeah, no regrets, Duffy, no regrets. You're right to get out. Save yourself, mate," mirror Duffy said.

I splashed water on my face and binned the tie. I gargled away the vomit and washed my hands. I went outside into a quad and sat for a while by a duck pond. The University of Warwick was all around me. At first glance it looked as if an alien spaceship had crashed into the English countryside, but under the pointy shiny-glass buildings there was a dreary 1950s/Le Corbusier/dishwater/Milton Keynes vibe too. All this, however, was improved by the hundreds—thousands actually—of really pretty, fresh-faced, brightly dressed girls from all over the UK, Ireland, northern Europe and South Asia. Belfast had its fair share of beautiful women, but they all came from the same mould. Variety cheered the soul.

Buoyed by all this youthful beauty, I bought a coffee and some Polo mints and slid in the back of the lecture hall again where Charles McCawley was finishing up.

"We need a bold reimagining of Coventry and Belfast, the other city I am working on. Gibson culverted over the River Sherbourne and demolished the little shops and lanes in the cathedral precinct, to build department stores and multi-storey car parks. At the time it had seemed like a good idea: Europe's first real attempt to separate people from the automobile by means of a pedestrianized CBD. A bold experiment in post-war living that hasn't worked. Coventry is a dreary concrete city during the day and a rather scary Brutalist wasteland after dark. But we can fix that. Our plan is to unculvert the river, zone the central CBD for housing instead of shops, demolish the high rises and give people gardens and shared spaces . . ."

McCawley ended the lecture with a bold vision of a community at one with the environment. Banishing cars was the answer to Coventry's, Belfast's, Glasgow's and indeed every blighted British city's woes.

Crowd lapped it up.

Post talk: lots of enthusiastic applause, handshakes, questions and answers.

We made our way to the front.

"Dr McCawley, I wonder if we might have a word," I said.

"I know what you're going to say. You're going to say where's the money going to come from?" he said affably while he took more handshakes and even a couple of requests for autographs. Could architectural lecturers be celebrities? I guess they could. He signed copies of his book as if he'd done it more than once.

Close up, he was about forty, blue of eye, ruddy of cheek and with a mop of curly red hair that made him seem a good bit younger. His was a likeable face, and if he wasn't a statutory rapist and a potential child murderer I would have liked the face too. But he was almost certainly the former and possibly the latter so fuck that for a game of soldiers.

"That's not what we're going to say, sir. I'm going to say do you mind if I ask you a few questions about Katrina McAtamney?"

"Who?"

"Katrina McAtamney. She's gone missing and we'd like to ask you a few questions about her."

"Are you the p-police?" he said, his confidence evaporating completely.

"Indeed, we are. Is there somewhere we can go talk?"

"Oh, God! Oh, my God," he said, quite visibly disturbed.

"Sir, is there somewhere private where we could talk?"

"What? Oh, yes, they've given me a temporary office, w-would that be all right?" he asked plaintively.

"That'll do fine, I'm sure," I said.

We walked back across the campus through the throngs of optimistic young people to a shiny steel office building that a plaque announced had been OPENED BY THE PRIME MINISTER ON AUGUST 3, 1989. Smart move that, when all the Bolshie students were off for their holidays. Dr McCawley's office was a bare rectangular room on the fifth floor facing west into the rapeseed fields.

While Crabbie followed Dr McCawley inside, Lawson stopped me at the door.

"Sir, I may be wrong, but it looks like he's going to spill. He almost fainted on the spot when you told him you were a policeman," Lawson whispered.

"That's what I was thinking," I said.

"Could be some legal issues if he confesses here, sir. Rules of evidence, that kind of stuff. We'd be safer taking him to a local police station and having him interviewed there under caution."

"But then the West Midlands Constabulary get the collar and we get nothing. And once his lawyer gets involved, there's going to have to be an extradition request at the bloody high court. A good silk might even argue he can't get a fair trial in Northern Ireland on account of his bloody father-in-law or some other bullshit . . . No, Lawson, let's get him talking and if he admits to the murder we'll quietly get him to come with us to the airport—no question of formally arresting him—then when we're back in Belfast we'll stick the cuffs on, ok?"

"If you say so, sir."

"Well I'm not sure, actually. I'm tired and I took a spill this morning. What do you think?"

"I don't know."

"I defer to you, lad."

"We'll play it by ear. If it looks like a confession is on the cards, we'll have a quick case conference?"

"Right. Good. Now let's go in there and break the bastard."

# 14
# THE TOTAL GIRLFRIEND EXPERIENCE

Crabbie and Lawson took seats by the door, and I sat opposite him at his desk by the window. He eyed me with fear and suspicion. Frowny face or smiley face? Try smiley first, as he already appeared to be scared shitless.

"That was a most interesting talk. And it solved one thing that had been puzzling me all day. Why is the University of Warwick neither in Coventry nor in Warwick? Took us ages to find this place but it all makes sense now. If you're going to build a new university in Coventry, of course, you'd go out to a greenfield site rather than the miserable city centre?"

He smiled thinly. "Yes, that's right. N-nobody wanted to be in the Cov. Poor old Cov. If your twin towns are Dresden and Stalingrad, it's a pretty big clue that you're well and truly screwed."

I held up a copy of his book, which was an attractive hardback with a bleak derelict building on the cover. "Why the interest in this place?"

"I'm actually from Coventry. No one but a n-native would ever write a book about here," he said with a little laugh.

"And how long have you been at Queens?"

"Since I finished my PhD."

"And when and where was that?"

"UCL. University College London. Uhm, 1974, I finished it. And I moved to Belfast in '75"

"What took you there?"

"A job. They offered me a junior lectureship, so I moved."

"But moving to Belfast in what, 1975? Who does that?"

"Someone who wants to earn a c-crust. I'd been unemployed for the two years before that. Not much call for a PhD in geography, then or now, I'm afraid. Should have done architecture, it's my passion. Too late now."

"I was in Belfast in '75; people were fleeing the city in droves," I said, still surprised by this.

"I needed the job, I was broke. Still am."

"We've seen your home, Dr McCawley," Crabbie said.

"What h-home?"

"More of a castle, really," I said.

"Oh, you mean my father-in-law's place? That's not our house. We don't actually have a house. We live in the lodge of my father-in-law's house, and doesn't he let us know it."

"Ah, I see."

"And he makes us pay rent. My wife doesn't work so we live entirely on my university salary which isn't much, I promise you."

Yeah, I'd buy that. I suppose it would have been too easy for the villain of the piece to be a rich aristocrat, but then again, what about the bloody diamond mine?

"But what about the diamond mine?" I asked.

"She told you about that?"

"She did."

"Well, yes, there is the theoretical diamond mine. I don't know if any of that's true, really. Certainly we're not getting any money f-from it at the moment."

"You do know Katrina McAtamney, don't you?"

"Yes."

"How do you know her?"

"I had to have an author photograph taken for my b-book."

"And?"

"The photographer chappie and I got on quite well."

"And?"

"We got to talking. Funny how you'll open up to a p-perfect stranger sometimes, isn't it?"

"And?"

"Well, I w-was there for the whole afternoon. The university was paying for it so I w-wanted a really good one. Awkward to be in a room for a whole afternoon while someone is t-taking your photograph."

"Go on," I said.

"I told him about my m-marital difficulties. You've been in our house, I take it?"

"Yes . . ." I said looking at Lawson and Crabbie. What had we missed?

"Your marital difficulties?" Lawson attempted.

"As I'm sure you saw, my wife and I live entirely s-separate lives in the lodge. The lodge isn't the castle but it's still an ample residence."

"Separate lives in the same house? How does that work?"

"Different bedrooms, different bathrooms. I have my upstairs study. She's taken up art downstairs."

"That can't possibly work, can it?"

"It can. It's a charade, really, of course. But Carol is terrified that if we divorce, Arthur will cut her out of the will. She's already been married twice."

"Arthur's your father-in-law?" Lawson asked.

"Yes."

"Hence separate lives in the same house," I said, writing it down in my notebook.

"Yes. Separate lives, but so far amicable separate lives."

"It sounds like a nightmare."

"Oh, it's not really. You're getting the wrong idea. C-Carol and I both still love each other very much. We just don't want to be married to one another."

"You're her third marriage?" I asked.

"Yes, and she pays maintenance to the other two chaps, one of whom was a real rotter. Absolute fortune hunter. Married her when she was just a girl really, just out of school. Bit of trouble there. She's still quite a vulnerable person, really."

"So how does this tie into Katrina?"

"I told this photographer fellow that I was often a little bit lonely."

"You're still technically a married man, Dr McCawley," Crabbie said, utterly appalled by all of this.

"Y-yes, I am. I'm sorry," McCawley said.

"So what was the nature of your relationship with Katrina?" I asked.

"I didn't get to see very much of her. Not as much, well . . . for obvious reasons."

"So what was your relationship?"

"I took her out a few times."

"Where?"

"The cinema mostly. Carol was not a big cinema goer. Katrina and I went a few times."

"Did you have sexual intercourse with her?"

"No. We hadn't built up to that quite yet. I was taking it slowly with her. It wasn't what you think."

"What do we think?"

"She wasn't a prostitute. It wasn't like that. She was an escort. I paid for her time, but it wasn't about sex. She told me about this service she provided. TGE. Do you know what that means?"

"No."

"Total Girlfriend Experience. That was what she offered. She was the best girlfriend in the world, you know? Pretty, charming, funny. Amazing listener. She loved to hear about my books and ideas. It wasn't about sex, although I think eventually it m-m-might have evolved into t-that . . ."

"Did you know how old she was?"

"Yes. I knew. She's only nineteen. And I'm thirty-nine. There's no fool like an old fool I suppose."

"How did you know she was nineteen?"

"She told me."

"In fact, she was fifteen," I said.

"Oh, God!" he said, aghast.

"Are you quite sure you didn't have sexual relations with her?" I pressed.

"No! Not really."

"What does that mean?"

"We kissed at the cinema and sometimes in her car or my car. Sometimes it went a little beyond that."

I tried to wipe that creepy image from my mind.

"Will I get in trouble for that?"

"Possibly, but for the moment, we're interested in finding out about her disappearance. Where were you on the day and night of December thirtieth?"

"I wasn't with Katrina. That's for sure," he said.

"Where were you?"

"I was at Queens. In my office there. P-preparing for this conference."

"From when until when?"

"From morning until about 8.00 p.m."

"And then what?"

"Well then I came home."

"Did anyone see you at the office? A friendly security guard? A friendly CCTV camera?"

"No, uhm, maybe, I don't know. I don't think so. I didn't encounter anyone in the building. The Human Geography Department is on Schooner Street. It's just a row of terraces that the university bought, really."

"So no security guard on patrol or anything like that?"

"No."

"You let yourself out?"

"I let myself out by the front door and my car was parked right outside."

"And after you got in your car, then what?"

"I drove home to the Lodge."

"Anyone see you come in?"

"No."

"Your wife?"

"No. As I said, we sleep in separate rooms. I didn't see her until morning. That would have been about eight or nine the next morning."

"What did you do that night when you got home?"

"I worked on my talk until quite late."

"Your wife claims to have heard you pacing around."

"Well that's possible. I *was* pacing around."

"You didn't go out?"

"No, not at all."

"But she didn't actually see you or interact with you? You met at the bathroom, or had a wee chat or you brought her a cup of hot chocolate to help her sleep?"

"No. Nothing like that."

"And the pacing could have been anything really couldn't it? Boards creaking, the family dog—"

"We don't have a dog."

"The point is, you don't have much of an alibi from 8.00 p.m. on the night of the thirtieth until eight o'clock the next morning. And that's only if there's CCTV around the university. Otherwise you don't have much of alibi for the whole day," I said writing this information in my book.

"No. That evening's when Katrina went missing, is it?" he asked.

"We don't know when she went missing. The last confirmed sighting we have of her was on the morning of the thirtieth."

"And someone killed her?"

"We haven't found a body but we're suspecting foul play. Her car was found driven into the Bann near Ballymoney."

He nodded and shook his head.

"Are we likely to find your DNA or other forensic traces from you in that car?" I asked.

"Yes. I was in her car several times. This is so terrible, the poor girl," he said and stifled a little sob. He eyes were watery and genuinely upset but, of course, he could have been upset for Dr Charles McCawley, not Katrina McAtamney.

"But what possible motive could I have had for killing her?" he asked.

"You're an intelligent man. I'm sure you can think of any number of motives," I said.

"Blackmail?" he suggested. "Because of her age? Is that one of the theories you're working on?"

"It might be."

"Well if it is, you're barking completely up the wrong tree. She wouldn't do anything like that. Blackmail someone? Not her style at all. She was a very good person. Not that kind of girl at all."

I was drifting out now. That bonk on the head.

"I'll change seats with Sergeant Lawson here and he'll ask you some questions," I said.

"I think actually, that's enough questions for today, gentlemen. I was up until three this morning, working, and I don't want to say anything foolish."

"Like what?"

"You can contact my solicitor if you wish to speak with me again. I will cooperate fully. But I did not kill Katrina McAtamney. I had nothing to do with her disappearance. I'm sorry that she's vanished, but it's nothing whatsoever to do with me," he said with finality.

"Well then, thank you for your time, sir. We will be in touch again. When are you returning home?" I asked.

"First thing tomorrow morning."

"I'll contact you tomorrow, then."

"You can contact my solicitors."

"That we will. I'll be especially interested in finding out your exact relationship with Katrina McAtamney, but I think what you've said so far should be enough to prosecute you for sexual assault on a minor which is punishable by up to two years in prison. Think about that before you consider whether you want your solicitors to get high-handed with the RUC."

"I wasn't threatening you or, or, or—"

"Good day, Mr McCawley.

Down the stairs.

Outside to the campus and the blessed relief of fresh air.

"Well, men?"

"Not guilty," Crabbie said. "At least not of murder."

"He did it," Lawson said. "Got so abrupt with us there at the end."

"I'm fifty-fifty on this one. His alibi was the worst of the lot. He admits to driving around Belfast at all hours of the day and night. And then there's motive. Local girl causes scandal—there goes the fucking diamond mine."

We called the airline and found out that we'd missed the last flight home. Lawson got us a hotel in Coventry. It has always been my belief that strange, out-of-the-way hotels in strange, out-of-the-way places are loci of mystery and adventure. That, at any rate, is the theory, but in practice these grim little Holiday Inns on Stabber's Row aren't the sort of adventure you're looking for. The taxi driver dropped us at the back entrance by mistake and the doors were locked. We had to walk around to the front through the enormous car park, in the rain, trailing our bags.

"What's the hold up now, with you lot?" Lawson mocked. "It's not Napoleon's retreat from bloody Moscow, it's a five-minute walk through the car park."

"Too big for his bloody boots, that one," Crabbie muttered.

"Aye and that was another of one my lines he's nicked, wee bastard."

A long bath and some aspirin and the bar downstairs. Get the beers in. Good beers. Marston's Pedigree.

Recapitulating the evidence from today and the case so far.

"Three suspects, none of whom have a bloody decent alibi. What's the world coming to?" I asked rhetorically. "Could be the bloody photographer topped her and we don't even have the time or resources to shake him down."

"We forgot to ask Dr McCawley for a DNA sample," Crabbie said.

"His hair wasn't brown anyway. None of our suspects have brown hair. Hair could be from anybody, anybody that Kat gave a lift to in the last year."

"The Boxer" from *Bridge over Troubled Water* began playing over the trebly hotel speakers.

"This is nice," Lawson said. "What is it?"

Crabbie gave me a look that said: easy Sean, don't go off on one of your rants because he's never heard "The Boxer."

But I was far too exhausted for that tonight.

"I'll lend you the album, bit hit and miss," was all I said.

"Bass harmonica, you don't hear them much," Lawson said. "Sounds awful."

"You think?" I said and, avoiding the bait completely, I finished the last dreary dregs of my pint.

# 15
# SHAKING THE TREE

Back to Ireland, back to Carrick, back to the station.

Sitting there in my office staring out to sea.

Need to think.

Out to the Beemer. Into the wilds of Belfast.

The beautiful cinema of it.

The slick streets. The low winter sun. The high Carol Reed camera angles. Gaping shadows. Glimpses of frightened soldiers on foot patrol. Glimpses of coppers on foot patrol, no less afeared but at least aware of the geography and the specific danger spots.

Wars, rumours of wars, bomb sites, checkpoints, masked men—but also, here and there, new cafes, a McDonald's, a new hotel.

Ulster 1990—on the hinge of history. In one universe the war continues, in another peace shoves green shoots up through the cracks in the concrete.

The Beemer loving the roads.

The Beemer carving them up as it always did.

The A2, the M5, the M2.

Rain on windscreen, rain in the rear view.

Thinking.

Three men. Maybe four men.

Four potential killers.

Duffy's last case.

Four men.

Rain on windscreen, rain in the rear—

Something else in the rear-view.

Was that a brown Mercedes following me?

Change lanes.

Merc still there.

Hmmmm.

Up onto the Antrim Road and down to Mallusk.

Merc still there.

Hmmmm, again.

Red light at the Mallusk turn.

Red light for civilians.

Siren on.

Middle lane.

So long Merc.

Up to the top road.

Check the rear-view.

Yup the bastard, whoever he was, is gone.

Back to the station after that excitement.

Mention it to Crabbie.

"Well the IRA are still trying to kill policemen," he said, which was true, but it didn't have that vibe about it.

"Anything else, Sean?"

"No."

Files.

Papers.

The white board.

No way around it: the case was dying.

Everybody could see that.

We had three suspects but no clear leads.

No new developments anywhere. No forensics, no eyewitnesses, no sudden teary confessions of guilt. No nothing. Cop knowledge is all a posteriori knowledge, gained by the experience of gun fights and riot patrol and interviewing thousands upon thousands of people. It's the latter in particular that clues you in to how society works. Clues you into the ticktock of the human brain. Shrinks talk to maybe seven clients a day. Cops and hacks talk to dozens. Good cops know before they know. Before the pattern reveals itself.

Good cops.

Fuck it, even bad cops.

The guilty spill. Most of them just can't help it. They spill, they want to spill, they're crying out to spill even if they don't even open their mouths.

I knew that I had interviewed the killer. I had talked to him and he had lied to me and to Lawson and McCrabban.

How to bring him in, then? This liar.

Ever been down to Bridewell Garda Station in Dublin? Sure, you have, one too many on a Saturday night after the rugby or the races. *Fiat justitia ruat cælum* it says above the lintel. Next time you're in, stop and read it and have a think.

Let justice be done though the heavens fall.

Damn straight.

You shake things up, you apply the law and you let the chips fall where they may.

Case conference.

"Too many suspects. Three of them. Three of the bastards."

"Four, if you count Mrs McCawley," Lawson said.

"And Mrs Johnny, come to that. And the photog and his boyfriend," Crabbie said.

"I like the jealous wife angle. Jealous wife tops the girlfriend. An old story. Definitely a possibility. Work the men first though, right? In the absence of any forensic evidence or eyewitness testimony, what are our options, Lawson?"

"With no eyewitness testimony? No forensic? All three men say they didn't do it? Uhm . . ."

"Options. Come on, think out loud!"

"We could drop the case? They say they didn't do it and there's nothing to say any of them were in the car that night. In fact, we're not even really sure this is a murder investigation . . ."

"Drop the case? Drop the case, did you say?"

"We've other cases, sir. We've an armed robbery on a post office. I mean that's quite a serious—"

"Drop the case? We're pot committed now. All these fucking man-hours? Me rushing back from me holidays?"

"Come on, Sean, you came back on your regularly scheduled flight, didn't you? You didn't actually—" Crabbie began, but I was on my bloody high horse.

"And the man-hours, Crabbie? All that flying around and nothing to show for any of it!"

"Sir, behavioural economics recognizes that sunk costs often affect decisions due to loss aversion: the price paid becomes a benchmark for the value, whereas the price paid should be irrelevant. This is irrational behaviour, sir, it's called the Sunk Cost Fallacy," Lawson said.

I looked at him.

Blue eyes. Keen as mustard. Wanted the job. Would be good at the job. And behind the jargon, he was right.

But not yet.

"Tell you what we'll do. We'll bring them all in again. One by one. With their solicitors, under caution, formal interviews. Helping with inquiries. Not an arrest. Helping with inquiries. A polite request on the part of us to them."

"If that's what you want," Crabbie said with a sigh.

"It's what I want. And grab that Jordy guy too, the photographer, let's take a look at his alibi for the night of the thirtieth."

INTERVIEW NUMBER ONE: Johnny Dunbar, Alexander Lawson, Sean Duffy, John McCrabban in Interview Room Number One. Mr Dunbar, a walking advert for denim. Shirt, jacket, jeans, probably socks and whips too. Hair freshly dyed and styled. Ciggies, tea, Jacob's biscuits. Acoustic baffle ceiling, fluro light, old-fashioned tape recorder, plastic table, plastic chairs, two-way mirror but nobody on the other side of it. Police and Criminal Evidence Act (NI Order) tape recorder playing and PACE rules mentioned to witness.

SD: Thank you very much for appearing here today, Mr Dunbar.

JD: I'm here under protest. I called my solicitor and he said I should come, otherwise I wouldn't be here. I already told you everything.

SD: And where is your solicitor?

JD: He said it would be fifty pound an hour! I'm not paying that kind of money.

SD: This is a murder investigation. Aren't you worried at all, Mr Dunbar?

JD: No, I am not. I didn't do anything. Took a wee girl to a Status Quo concert and felt her bum. That's all I did.

SD: And you tried to kill those men at the airfield with the guns.

JD: Oh, aye, that? That was the old me. Allegedly. The new me doesn't do stuff like that. I've been going to therapy at the leisure centre. Positive thinking, you know? Don't dwell on the past. Hard to in this town. You should hear our group leader. "Pastor Joe" everybody calls him. "Live in the moment, in the now." What now? This now with you lot? Fucking Carrick? Does it even exist? Nobody lives in this wee shite hole. It's not real Belfast is it? Fake Belfast. And you're fake cops. See what I mean?

SD: Not really.

JM: What?

AL: I think what he's saying—

JD: What I'm saying is, it's the fucking Tories, lad. You're a tool, Duffy. All of youse. You're playing into their hands. They want the working classes at one another's throats because they know that if we're ever going to be united it'll be the fucking Tyburn gibbet for the lot of them. If Kinnock wins, they'll assassinate him. Mark my words.

SD: Mr Dunbar, let's get back to Katrina McAtamney, if we can. You're claiming you never had sex with her?

JD: Never did. And you can't bloody prove I did.

SD: What if I told you there was a condom in her car with your DNA in it.

JD: I'd say you're a fucking liar cos there isn't.

SD: Gimme a timeline for December thirtieth?

JD: Who can even remember now? That was last year.

AL: That was last week.

JD: I don't remember. Home with the missus watching *The Great Escape.* That I do remember. You wanna hear my Bronson? "Willie, since I was a boy, I hate and fear little rooms, closets, caves . . ." Good, eh? Home with the missus and then to bed.

SD: The whole night?

JD: Prove it otherwise.

SD: Perhaps we will find—

JD: You won't.

SD: Well, I'm going to keep at you, Johnny. I know you're lying about something. I'm not buying this political stuff, you—

JD: I'm running for council. Look it up.

SD: I have, but you're a bloody player for one thing—

JD: That's slander unless you can prove that.

SD: You're a player and I'm going to keep at you, pal. If you killed her, you're going down.

JD: That sounds like a threat.

SD: It is a threat.

JD: Aren't you the big eejit with the tape recorder going. My lawyers can subpoena this.

SD: Where did you learn a word like *subpoena*?

JD: You'll find out, Duffy. People in the know *know* that you don't fuck with me. I am someone you don't fuck with. Hear endeth the lesson. See youse later.

INTERVIEW NUMBER TWO: Carol McCawley, Charles McCawley, David Trott, Sean Duffy, Alexander Lawson, John McCrabban in Interview Room Number Two. No ciggies, six strong teas, Jacob's biscuits. Acoustic baffle ceiling, fluro light, old-fashioned tape recorder, plastic table, plastic chairs, two-way mirror but nobody on the other side of it. David Trott, a very well-known solicitor both for his criminal and civil work. Charles McCawley in a nondescript suit. Carol McCawley in a striking red dress. David Trott wearing a black suit with a black-and-white bow tie. Police and Criminal Evidence Act (NI Order) tape recorder playing and PACE rules mentioned to witnesses.

SD: Thank you very much for coming out today. I must say at the outset of this session that we only wanted to talk briefly to Mr McCawley. It wasn't necessary for—

CAROL M: I wanted to come, and Mr Trott here is a friend of the family.

SD: We'll be discussing matters of an intimate personal nature in relation to Mr McCawley. I'm really not sure that it's wise or necessary that you are present for this, Mrs McCawley.

CAROL M: It's fine.

DT: My clients are here voluntarily, and this is the arrangement they are most comfortable with. I believe you have interviewed them both already separately and they are here today to assist the police with their inquiries on an entirely voluntary basis.

SD: Very well . . . Mr McCawley, can you tell us for the record about your relationship with Katrina McAtamney?

CHARLES M: I had a brief nonsexual relationship with Miss McAtamney. I took her out a few times when my marriage was in a troubled area, but I ended that relationship soon thereafter, and thankfully my wife, Carol, has forgiven me for my minor indiscretions and we've put it all behind us.

SD:     Really? I had understood that you were living entirely separate lives at your home, the Lodge, at Castle Hobbs.

CHARLES M: That is an inaccurate characterisation of our life there. We had some difficulties, but since returning to Belfast we've talked those through and we've put those difficulties behind us.

SD:     You weren't sleeping apart?

CHARLES M: I do work at night and I have my own bedroom and study and we do sometimes sleep apart.

DT:     How is this relevant to your investigation, Inspector Duffy?

CAROL M:    This, I think, is well within the bounds of normal behaviour.

SD:     What I'm interested in is whether Mrs McCawley here is able to provide Mr McCawley with an alibi for the night of the thirtieth, and it seems that she is not able to do so. But we'll come to that.

DT:     That's not my reading of the situation.

SD:     Like I say, we'll come to that. Mr McCawley, how would you characterise your sexual relationship with Miss McAtamney?

CHARLES M: As I previously mentioned to you, and which I stress now under oath—

SD:     You are not under oath.

DT:     You are not under oath, Charles.

SD:     Nevertheless, you are under an obligation to tell the truth.

CHARLES M: As I said earlier, I had no sexual relationship at all with Miss McAtamney. I saw her two or three times at a low point in my marriage.

SD:     What did you do those two or three times?

CHARLES M: Dinner and the pictures, I think. That's all. I can barely remember.

SD:     But you did pay her for her company?

CHARLES M: Yes.

SD:     How much?

CHARLES M: I don't recall.

SD: More than a hundred pounds?

CHARLES M: Yes, perhaps just over that.

SD: Just for going to the pictures with you?

CHARLES M: Yes.

SD: If I could bring you to the night of December thirtieth. Actually, I'm glad that you're here, Mrs McCawley. I see in my notes that you said you heard your husband "distinctly" pacing around and working on his speech.

CAROL M: Yes.

SD: But Mr McCawley, you said that you never saw your wife at all that night, never interacted with her in any way until the morning.

CHARLES M: But I did also say, I believe, that she may have heard me pacing around. I was in fact pacing about, muttering lines of my speech to myself.

CAROL M: And I heard him. I may not have seen him, but I heard him.

SD: Are you quite sure about that?

CAROL M: Quite sure.

DT: If I can interject something for the record here . . .

SD: Of course.

DT: As I understand it, Miss McAtamney's body has never been found so no time of death has been determined. All you know is that she was last seen on the morning of the thirtieth and her car was pulled out of the Bann on January second. My client has a full alibi for all of that extensive period."

SD: No, the forensic officers are reasonably convinced from the tyre marks that the vehicle went into the water on the night of December thirtieth and there's an only a slim chance that this happened on December thirty-first. The river was very popular during the day and a car going into the water during daylight hours would have been seen.

DT: It could have gone in the night of December thirty-first when my clients were together at the Lord Mayor's banquet. And if you're sticking to the December thirtieth story, well Mrs McCawley is very clear that her husband was working on his speech until the wee hours of the morning when he went to bed. To me this looks like a pretty tight alibi and certainly not probable cause for any further investigation, never mind charges.

SD: The RUC will have to turn over a report to the DPP. It's not for us to say who gets charged or not.

DT: Indeed. Well, as I can see by my watch, it's four o'clock now, and I told you we only could give you half an hour today. I have another appointment.

SD: That's ok, we can keep interviewing Mr and Mrs—

DT: No, no, no, I won't allow anything like that. You've already had several conversations with my clients without a solicitor being present.

SD: Consensual conversations.

DT: My clients have indeed been very cooperative and have nothing further to add to this tragic case.

INTERVIEW NUMBER THREE: Jordy Hardcastle on the telephone.

JH: I'm not coming in to no cop shop. I don't have the time for this shite. If you want to come and arrest me, go ahead. But you better be ready with a charge sheet cos I'll have my beak with me and I've done nothing wrong. On the thirtieth I had a wee party here until two so, you know, lots of witnesses.

SD: Names of addresses of these witnesses.

JH: I'll have someone bring them over, and I don't expect to hear from you again!

INTERVIEW NUMBER FOUR: Terry Jones, Sean Duffy, Alexander Lawson and John McCrabban in Interview Room Number One. Jones in a white shirt, tweed jacket, brown slacks, black shoes. No ciggies, weak tea, Jacob's biscuits. Acoustic baffle ceiling, fluro light, old-fashioned tape recorder, plastic table, plastic chairs, two-way mirror but nobody on the other side of it. No solicitor with Mr Jones either, which was very surprising, but it probably wasn't best to bring it up in case he suddenly became aware of how surprising it was and stormed out to get one. Police and Criminal Evidence Act (NI Order) tape recorder playing and PACE rules mentioned to witness.

SD:    Thank you for coming in again, Mr Jones. We need to ask you some more questions about your relationship with Katrina McAtamney and the night of December thirtieth.

TJ:    I believe I've answered all those questions.

SD:    I'm afraid we're going to have to keep asking those questions until we're entirely satisfied with the answers.

TJ:    Eventually you'll ask the questions so many times I'll make a mistake and you'll say I'm being inconsistent or a liar.

SD:    Have you been lying to us?

TJ:    No!

SD:    For the record, again, Mr Jones, you say you had a consensual sexual relationship with Katrina McAtamney.

TJ:    Yes.

SD:    You paid her money for personal services, including sex.

TJ:    Yes, but as I attempted to explain, it was more than that. We were, we . . . we understood each other.

AL:    Were you in love with her?

TJ:    (no response)

AL:    Were you in love with her, sir?

TJ:    I don't want to say.

SD:    Why not?

TJ:    I'd rather not answer that question. I don't have to answer every question. I know my rights.

SD: I should tell you, sir, a jury may draw an inference from your silence.

TJ: Let them. I am not going to answer that question.

JM: Sir, on the evening of the thirtieth of December you were doing what exactly?

TJ: I was reading and attempting to translate some poems of Catullus.

JM: All evening?

TJ: Most of the evening.

JM: What did you do for the rest of the night?

TJ: I had a bath and I did the cryptic crossword.

SD: Which paper?

TJ: The *Times*.

SD: How long did that take you? The crossword, I mean.

TJ: About two minutes.

SD: Two minutes? I don't believe it.

TJ: How long does it take you?

SD: Five on a good day.

TJ: Sorry to hear that. But still, that's a good time . . . for a policeman.

JM: I think we're getting a little sidetracked here. You've admitted for the record that you had sexual relations with a fifteen-year-old girl.

TJ: I'm sorry. I didn't know her age. She told me she was eighteen. I saw a driving licence. I had no idea she was so young.

AL: Let's cut to the chase, eh? Why did you do it, Mr Jones?

TJ: Do what?

AL: Kill her.

TJ: I didn't.

SD: Let me posit a scenario: You told her you loved her and she didn't love you back. Something absurd like that? Catullus and Lesbia all over again. It made you furious. You lost your head. You started yelling. She threw something at you. She went for you. You struck her. But you didn't know your own strength. You killed her right there at your house and you didn't know what to do and you had a brain wave—you drove her car to the Bann and pushed her in? Something like that?

TJ:   What utter rot! I didn't do anything like that!

AL:   Just admit it.

TJ:   Admit to something I didn't do?

SD:   You've already confessed to the statutory rape. Why not tell us the whole truth?

TJ:   Which is what?

SD:   You killed her and pushed her car into the Bann and you hoped it would sink forever.

TJ:   No!

SD:   We know you did it and we're going to prove it. I can tell just by looking at you.

TJ:   I didn't do it!

SD:   You did!

JM:   Sean . . .

SD:   I know he did it, Crabbie. He did something. And we're going to get the goods on him.

AL:   Inspector Duffy, I think maybe—

SD:   I'm going to take you down, Mr Jones. You're a self-admitted child rapist. What other secrets are you hiding? I'm going to uncover them all.

TJ:   For a policeman, your behaviour is disgusting.

SD:   Fine talk coming from you.

AL:   Sir, I think we should take a little break.

SD:   What?

JM:   A little break, Sean?

SD:   Oh yeah, maybe you're right.

The office that night. A real feeling of deflation. Rain on the windows, hot whisky in the mugs. "That went well," I said with heavy sarcasm.

I looked at the transcripts of the interviews.

Amateur hour. Clownish.

I was losing my bloody touch. Maybe I had *lost* my bloody touch—
past tense.

"Worse than I was expecting," Crabbie said, reading the same transcripts.

"And you have low expectations, Sergeant McCrabban," Lawson
said.

"That I do, lad, that I do."

# 16

# THE FOLK PARK INCIDENT

No sleep. Bad thoughts: go home to Scotland, Sean, case is dead, finish the bugger, go home and rest, you deserve it, mate. Good thoughts: case is never dead, case has plenty of mileage yet, deep-six the quit idea, deep-six the very thought, deep-six the memory of the thought.

Early morning call to Beth and Emma:

"How's things over there?"

"Lovely. We miss you though, how is everything with you?"

"Good. How's my girl?"

"She's good."

"My cat?"

"He wants out."

"Don't let him out. Remember what the vet said. *Incredible Journey* and all that."

"Are you ok?"

"Yeah."

"What about the case?"

"Great, probably winding it up soon."

"Take care, Sean, I have to dash."

"Love you, babe."

"Love you too."

Early morning call to MI5 to remind them that our boy was getting jumpy about the meet. Told them to do their job and make sure his security was good and you know, maybe, reassure the treasonous bastard, eh?

Early morning call from me da asking how I was doing and whether I'd changed my mind about the genius of Acker Bilk yet.

I hadn't changed my mind about the bowler hat–wearing eejit, but I had one for him that I knew he would like: "Ok, pop, a man walks into a tailor shop in ancient Athens. He tosses a toga on the front desk. The tailor inspects it, finding a big gash on the back. He looks up at the man and asks 'Euripides?' And the man replies, 'Yeah. You mend-a-Dees?'"

"You know togas were a Roman garment, not Greek, so your joke—"

"Goodbye dad, I have to go, case to solve and all that."

Birds singing, blue sky, milkman leaving a pint of gold top on the front doorstep. Quick change into jeans, jumper, Adidas sneakers.

Out to Beemer. Quick shoofty underneath the vehicle for a test-tube full of mercury that was connected to an ignition system which was connected to a couple of kilos of Semtex high explosive.

Nothing like that.

De nada on death notes from the men in masks.

Empty street. Not even the usual wee muckers playing kerby: the Derek Agnews, the Samantha McCombs . . .

Drive into Belfast. So early it was before the rush.

Out along the shore towards Bangor for a wee think about—

And there he was again.

The Merc. The bloody brown Merc.

Who would be following me? Who would want me dead?

Well apart from the IRA, the UVF and Special Branch?

Who?

Find out who.

I pulled into the car park at the Folk Park in Cultra.

Ever been there?

No?

They've rebuilt an entire eighteenth-century Irish village down by the lough shore. It's like a film set, except it's authentic two-hundred-year-old buildings moved and reconstructed there, brick by smoky brick.

Too early for guards or visitors. Too early for everyone.

I hopped the wall and waited for the Merc to pull into the car park.

No Merc.

Ten minutes.

Still no Merc.

Smart, this guy.

Too smart. Who around here is this—

A puff of smoke and a pinging noise from the whitewashed wall of a weaver's cottage.

What the hell was—

A ricochet off the stone work five feet from my head.

Christ! Someone was shooting at me.

The Merc had parked further up the road, the driver had gotten out and come into the village behind me. And now he was up there on the high ground near the mill and I was exposed down here.

Holy shit, this was serious.

I hit the dirt and scanned the buildings, but I had no idea where the sniper was. Another pinging noise from the wall three feet from my head.

Shit again.

No sound of a gun. He was shooting at me with a silenced hunting rifle. That was way more sophisticated than you usually got with the local paras whose idea of finesse was firing an AK into a crowded pub and yelling, "Trick or treat."

No cover anywhere except a bloody well where I would no doubt fall to me death.

Another ping above my head, even closer this time.

Go, Duffy, go, go, go!

I crawled desperately across the open ground towards the well.

Ten feet away.

Five feet away.

Run.

Up over the lip and into the well where I was expecting a fifty-foot plummet into stagnant water.

No plummet. No water. The well head had been moved here and rebuilt but, of course, they hadn't dug down to the water table. Why would they?

I dropped three feet into dirt.

He must have seen me jump into the well, but would he know it was fake or would he assume I'd broken my stupid neck?

Maybe he would come over and throw a hand grenade down the hole just to be on the safe side?

I took out my Glock and waited.

And waited.

But he was a pro.

He knew he had squibbed his chance.

There would be others.

Still I waited.

When the security guards arrived to open shop for the day I climbed out of the fake well and told them to call RUC Forensics.

Forensics came and looked for bullet fragments or shell casings and found nothing.

Chief Inspector Frank Payne asked me if I'd had a late night and one too many to drink. "Drove here drunk? Found a wee cottage to sleep it off?"

"You really think I'd do something like that, Francis? And waste police time into the bargain? Do you think I'm a total fucking moron?"

"You said it, Duffy, not me."

# 17
# THE TIP

Nothing else for it, I drove back to the station and filled in the lads.

At least they believed me.

Crabbie wanted me to go to the hospital but, like Elvis, I was only shook up. Cup of tea, digestive biscuit, another cup of tea.

"Sean, there's a call come through to CT switchboard," Lawson said.

"What sort of a call?"

"The girl. She's been spotted at the old Penny Building in Rathcoole. She's alive!"

"This came through to our switchboard?"

"No. The Confidential Telephone."

"But they say Katrina's alive?"

"Yeah."

"Oh, my God. That's brilliant."

"Message reads: 'Tip for Carrick CID: missing girl Kat McAtamney is in fourth floor squat in Penny Building, Rathcoole.'"

"And this came through this morning?"

"Just now."

"All right. Let's go. She might be in a bad way, so grab a WPC. Also could be a bit of dodgy area. Squat in Rathcoole? After my incident this morning, we should gear up and we'll take an armoured Land Rover."

Land Rover along the seafront up into Rathcoole on what had turned into a rainy, miserable Belfast afternoon. In the Land Rover: Crabbie, me, Lawson and WPC Warren.

Army helicopters up over West Belfast, some kind of riot or bombing incident in South Belfast, but luckily we were in the North.

We pulled up in front of the condemned ten-floor Penny Building. It had been scheduled for demolition years ago, evacuated but then reoccupied by squatters. Some of the local papers said that it was the worst building in the worst estate in the worst town in Ireland. I was a little sceptical, but you'd be hard-pressed to find a place anywhere outside of an actual war zone where the people looked so beaten, dazed and miserable. And certainly the Penny Estate was grim. Sprawled malevolently to the north and west of the city like some hideous concrete sea monster it was your typical 60s Brutalist experiment gone wrong. A Le Corbusier machine for living, which had become a machine for escaping life through solvents, beer, heroin, acid, meth or whatever else you could find.

"This is some place," Lawson said with admiration. Damp, mildew, asbestos, broken windows, big cracks in the flat roof had combined to make the flats completely uninhabitable.

"Where are youse going?" a glue-sniffing yokel asked us as we got out of the Rover. He was twenty going on sixty, this poor eejit.

"Fourth floor," I said.

"Why?" he asked.

"The person we're looking for is on four."

"You'll have to take the stairs."

"I figured."

"You're lucky. The gangs, the neds and the vandals seldom go above the second floor, so the fourth floor should be all right."

We walked into the main entrance foyer. The doors were long gone and inside it stank of nitro-glycerine.

"Smell that?" I asked Crabbie.

"Nitro," he said. "Someone's been shooting small arms."

"Not surprising around here," Lawson said.

But we were to find out the real reason in a couple of minutes: *because a couple of them had been practising.*

Needles and broken glass everywhere.

"Place is full of druggies," Crabbie said. "Fall down in there and you'll catch something chronic, and that's before the roof caves in."

"Don't like the look of this," I said turning on a flashlight. "Maybe we should call in backup."

"Your decision, Sean," Crabbie. "After what happened to you this morning . . ."

"But then again, fine lot of eejits we'll look calling in backup on a routine door-knocking job like this. And just when we're about to solve this bloody case!"

"Sir, if they're on heroin they'll be sleepy junkies," Lawson pointed out. Crabbie nodded. WPC Warren said nothing. Good copper, Warren—didn't really know her but I'd seen her around a few times: smart and she had bottle. Be a fine addition to CID once me and the Crabman were turfed out. Make a note of that.

"But on the other hand, if it's that new crack stuff all the flyers are on about we might be in for a bit more fun and games," I said. "Vests and MP5s, I think, for Crabbie and me, just to be on the safe side. Vests for both of you. Flashlights too. Back to the Rover everyone."

Vests and MP5s.

Just an afterthought, that. CID didn't normally wear bullet proof vests like the uniformed officers.

Really it was just to calm our nerves.

But fifteen minutes later, without those vests and MP5s we probably would have been dead.

We discarded our jackets and put on the body armour which said "Police" on the front and back. The *e* on the front was right over the heart and the rumour was that if you fired at that *e* with a high-velocity round it would go straight through the cheap Kevlar and kill you stone dead.

Comforting.

More than likely though, these junkies and other assorted ne'er-do-wells would give us no trouble at all, which I said aloud to the others.

"Now you've torn it," Lawson said.

"Since when did he get all superstitious?" I asked Crabbie.

"Since his first day on the job, same as everyone else," Crabbie replied.

"Except for you, of course, Crabbie."

"Aye, except for me," he agreed.

"Ok, troops, back inside."

The helpful idiot at the front door had gone now. No people, no rats, just the piles of rubbish everywhere: chip papers, newspapers, shopping trolleys, burst bin bags filled with trash.

In a low voice, I muttered, "I'll go on point and have a wee look through these ground-floor flats just to get a feel for the place. Then we'll go up to the fourth floor. Crabbie, Lawson, blind spots and cover if you please."

There were sixteen ground-floor flats that had all been abandoned years before. The Northern Ireland Housing Executive had evicted the tenants from this floor and presumably the rest of the building prior to demolishing this structure. But it wasn't that easy. They'd gotten the tenants out, boarded up and padlocked all the flats but the demolition order had been halted for fear that dynamiting this property would damage the neighbouring properties. The whole case had gone to court and languished there, and meanwhile, kids, druggies, tinkers and even some of the old tenants had moved back in. That was five years ago and without electricity, water or sewage you can imagine what the place was like now.

"The stink," Lawson said. "What is that?"

"You don't want to know, son," I said.

Lawson optimistically and really quite adorably walked to the lift and pushed the call button.

I nodded at him. "Do you really want him in charge of Carrick CID, Crabbie? Book smarts I'll grant you, but sometimes a bit light in the old hod, if you know what I'm saying."

"It's him or an outsider, Sean."

"Aye."

While Lawson waited for the elevator to appear I walked to one of the nearer flats whose door had been torn off for firewood.

"Hello?" I tried.

"Fuck off," someone grumbled from the shadows.

I shone my flashlight into the room.

We'd been right about the heroin. Three junkies lying on mattresses on the floor surrounded by needles. I lowered the MP5 so as not to freak them out.

"Carrick police," I said shining the torch into their faces.

"What do you want?" a young woman said from the far corner. She was not tripping—or at least, not tripping now.

"I want to fucking nick the lot of you, that's what I want, but I'm not going to if you answer a few questions," I said.

"Is it history?" the girl said. "I'm good at history. I got an A in my O levels." She was a short, blonde-haired little thing, her hair cut into a spikey yellow mess. She was wearing camo pants and a white tank top, and she didn't have the emaciated, scabby look of the long-term H user.

"Aye, she's awful good at knowing stuff," one of the other junkies said. "Ask her any country and she'll tell you the capital. Go on."

"I'm interested in who lives on the fourth floor of this place," I said.

"I know most of the people that live here. They have to come and go right by our door, so they do," the wee girl claimed.

"What's your name?" I asked.

"Leslie."

"Go on, ask her anything. Except Africa, she's not good at Africa," the other one said.

"Do you know someone called Kat McAtamney?" I asked Leslie.

"Tell me what she looks like?" Leslie asked.

"Pretty girl, brown hair, about five foot seven or so. She's a Traveller."

"There's one or two Pavee on the upper floors. They've got a fucking horse up somewhere, so they do. Bloody disgrace if you ask me, keeping a horse in a place like this."

Crabbie poked his head around the door. "Info?" he asked.

"There is a Traveller family on one of the upper floors. They don't know if it's anyone called McAtamney."

"Then we have to go up there, don't we?" Crabbie said. "Due diligence."

"Indeed."

"Thanks, you've been very helpful," I said to Leslie.

"Is it worth a tenner?" Leslie asked.

"It's worth a tenner if you're going to spend it on food, not heroin."

"I might. I just might. I could go a wee pizza," Leslie said.

"All right then," I said. I fished in my trousers and found a ten-pound note and gave it to her.

"Go on, ask her a country, ask her any country," the bloke insisted again.

"Equatorial Guinea," I found myself saying to shut him up.

"Malabo," Leslie said immediately.

"See?" the bloke said with a cackle that became a wicked hacking cough.

I fished out my notebook and wrote down the address of the detox centre. I gave her another couple of tenners and a fifty. "You've got a chance, love. Sort yourself out before it's too late."

We went gingerly up the stairs floor by floor, flashlights on, me on point, Crabbie at the back, guns ready.

There were a few rats, a dog, a couple of feral cats but nothing really bad.

It didn't get bad until we reached the fourth floor.

As soon as we came out of the stairwell and walked about ten feet down the corridor:

*BOOM! BOOM! BOOM! BOOM! BOOM!*

We hit the deck and dived behind a metal builder's skip on wheels that some helpful bastard had left there.

"Back the way we came!" I screamed.

But then we heard gunshots and saw tracer coming up the stairs too. They had followed us into the building and another team had been waiting for us on the fourth floor. We were between two sets of gunmen with no possible way out at all.

# 18
# THE FOURTH FLOOR

Fate, sister's fortune, favours those who keep their nerve, my Uncle Tommy used to say. Something he learned in the war from Blair Mayne. My mother's oldest brother. In '37, he goes to Rome to hand out anti-Mussolini flyers. Arrested, deported. In '38, he goes to Barcelona just as all the sensible people are getting out. In '39, he joins the British Army to continue the struggle against the fascists and ends up as a sapper based in Cairo having, actually, a pretty easy time of it until Blair Mayne arrives one evening and sniffs out a fellow Mick at the bar of the Windsor Hotel. Colonel Mayne needs mechanics more desperately than he needs soldiers, riding those Jeeps day and night over the dunes west of Alamein. Riding those Jeeps into Luftwaffe airfields, pumping Rommel's planes and pilots full of lead. At the age of nearly forty, I still hadn't had half the action to match what Tommy had got up to in his first month with Mayne in the SAS.

"The wrong decision taken immediately is better than the right action in five minutes time."

"Fate, sister's fortune . . ."

"Shoot and move, shoot and move . . ."

Those are three of Tommy's.

"I'll shoot and you move!" I screamed at Crabbie as we sprawled on the floor behind the metal bin. "I'll cover you and you get Warren and Lawson into the nearest flat!"

"What?"

"Crawl for the bloody door! I'll shoot and draw their fire and you crawl for the fucking door and take Lawson and Warren—"

Pause it right there.

Turn the dial back an hour. To uncover my mistake we have to understand why we were put in this position in the first place. Who would want to kill Carrick CID? Who has the most to lose from progress in this case? The three men we'd brought in? The other guy on the phone? At least one of them didn't want to see this case proceed any further. The way normal people make cases go away is by hiring a half-decent lawyer. The lawyer complains about harassment, demands to see our evidence, sees that we have absolutely nothing and tells us to piss off. And if we don't piss off they take out an injunction. But who calls in a hit team?

Not Dr McCawley. He's not hiring a bunch of thugs to ambush me in an abandoned building. Dunbar? Why the hell not? Ex-UVF, probably still UVF even though he is, apparently, running for the council. Jones? Something about him I don't bloody like. All that talk about being lonely and all that "keeps to himself" vibe from the neighbours. Probably half a dozen runaways buried in his back garden. Hardcastle? No, it ain't him. Yeah, he was something of a pimp and in three cases out of five it's the pimp, but it ain't him. Gut says that. That and the fact that his party friends gave him alibis.

Jones or Dunbar.

No time to think about it now. Maybe never time to think about it. But if I lived through this . . .

"Are you ready, Crabman?"

"Aye."

I stood up and fired the MP5 at the muzzle bursts at the ends of the corridor. "Move!" I screamed.

I was shooting short, two-second well-directed bursts but Lawson wasn't moving and Warren wasn't behind him. Lawson wasn't hit, but the noise and the ricochets and the tracer had temporarily put the zap on him. His eyes were a million miles removed from all this madness.

"Crabbie, grab those eejits by their bloody necks and get them to safety. I'll draw the fire!"

"I'll draw the fire, you take them!" he said.

"You bloody idiot. You've been shot before. The bullets love you."

I stood up.

Crabbie grabbed Lawson and Warren by the scruff of their flak jackets and beautifully timed his run as I fired the MP5 and the Glock at the same time, two-handed, like a Goddamned hero.

*BOOM! BOOM! BOOM! Budda-Budda-Budda! BOOM! BOOM! BOOM!*

I'd done the range time and I was on target. The gunmen on the floor ducked behind the corridor wall and the ones at the stairwell kept low. I knew they wouldn't like this one bit. Most gunmen in Northern Ireland were used to dealing with people who didn't shoot back. Unarmed drinkers in pubs, men answering a doorbell in their boxer shorts, someone walking home from the bookies down the shortcut behind the garages.

Crabbie and his charges made it to the first flat and the Crabman kicked the door in. It crumbled like matchwood under his boot and he pushed Warren and Lawson inside.

*BOOM! BOOM! BOOM*! The echoes came back along the concrete as I ran for the flat through the smoke.

A burst of machine-gun fire filled the space between me and the door. *Budda-Budda-Budda-Budda-Budda-Budda . . .*

I leapt into the space.

A bullet struck the shoulder of the flak jacket and spun me around into the hail of fire.

Another pause.

The film jamming in the projector. The film melting. The film distorting on the big screen.

The river under my feet. Cypress trees. Stars. An arrow of cloud intersecting with the moon. Poppies along the granite wall. Wind bringing the scent of fennel, saffron and desert emptiness. Satisfying Zippo clunk. Gasoline smell. Yellow flame on cigarette. Strange earthy tobacco. It was night and everything was pretending to be something else. The stars were camp fires. The cloud, a naked girl. For a city so huge it was remarkably silent. This place belonged to God, not people. Insomniac tourists kept to their hotel rooms, the religious were abed. I smoked Israeli cigarettes and listened to the nothing. My mind wandered in raw time. Don't do well with your own thoughts, do you, Sean? Hence the booze. Hence the drugs. A green phosphorescence played on the tips of the iron railings around the hotel garden. *Hold this moment. Hold it. But you can't hold it.* I coughed, startling a cat walking along the roof tiles, and watched as it jumped from one house to another.

My eyes were heavy.

And I closed them.

Closed them as the second bullet struck me in the back.

A third was heading for my throat.

But Saint Michael, the Patron Saint of Policemen, was watching.

And even better than Saint Michael, the big Ballymena paw of Sergeant "Crabbie" McCrabban was reaching into the death zone and pulling me into the safety of the flat.

I clattered to the floor and sucked air.

Crabbie helped me to my feet.

"You ok?"

"What did you say?"

Ears ringing. Both of us.

"You ok? You hit?"

"Ricochets off my flak jacket. Fine. I think. Yeah. Fine. Sitrep, Crabbie."

"We're ok. Sure you're ok?"

"Copped it on the left shoulder and the back but I'm fine."

"Lemme see," he said, feeling under the shoulder blade. "No blood shoulder. No blood back. Vest saved you."

"You get a chance to count those boys?"

"Aye, I did. Four guns down the corridor. Maybe another two on the stairs, although really, who knows? Machine guns mind. They're serious," Crabbie said, as calm as if he'd been talking about the number of sheep who had strayed into his cow field.

I looked at him. "You're ok, mate?"

"Never better."

I looked back into the corridor. "Do you think they'll come down after us or is that it?"

"What do you mean?"

"Do you think they'll leg it now? All that noise?"

Crabbie shook his head. "No idea, Sean. I suppose we'll find out their intentions soon enough," he said phlegmatically.

He wasn't breathing hard and he didn't even appear to be sweating. He was a lean fellow who was up at the crack to tend his dairy herd which explained the no sweat, but no whiteness in the eyes either? Was he never afeared? "Aren't you the least bit shitting yourself?" I asked him.

"Of what?"

"Death."

He shook his head. "I am confident that the will of the Lord will be manifested one way or the other and if it's in his plan for us to be—"

"You guard the corridor while I check on those two," I said.

He pointed his MP5 at the door jam. I gave his shoulder a squeeze and went over to check on Warren and Lawson who were panting by the broken window.

"Everyone ok?"

Warren nodded.

"Lawson?"

"Fine."

"That's it, keep breathing. Big breaths, breathe it in. Good, fresh Irish air there. Hundred years from now they'll be bottling this stuff and selling it on Mars for a tenner a pint."

Lawson smiled, and Warren looked at me as if I had lost my marbles, which, for your benefit, I will just point out that I had not.

"Are you ok there, Warren? Are you hit?"

"No, I don't think so, no. I scraped my knee. That's it."

"Good on you, lass. Let me see you in the light . . . No you're fine. Skinned your shins, that's all. What about you, son?"

"Nothing . . . so far . . . touch wood."

"Good. Here, drink this," I said, passing them the bottle of water I kept in my trouser pocket. "Holy water from the Jordan Valley, bet you're glad of it now, eh?"

"Yes sir."

I ran back across the derelict flat to Crabbie at the door.

"The kids are all right," I said.

"Good."

"What's your ammo situation like?"

"I thought it was a routine call," he said somewhat defensively.

"So, what then?"

"I'm full on the MP5 but I've only the one clip. You?"

"I'm through on the MP5. Shot the whole load. Full reload clip in the Glock though. That's seventeen, and I've got six in the .38."

"You brought your pistol?"

"Always bring the .38, it's my lucky . . . Wait a minute. Is that a yellow tie under your jumper?" I said.

He looked down at the tie. Crabbie, it had been observed by everyone in the station, had a neo-Calvinist colour palate to his jackets, jumpers and ties. Grey, black, dark grey, dark brown, occasionally the odd very dark blue. But yellow? Yellow on the Crabman? End of the world stuff, that.

"My niece, Sandra, got it for me for my birthday. I've never worn it. Helen kept nagging me about it, so today—"

"So today you break the habit of a lifetime, put on a yellow tie and we're caught in a fucking death trap with no way out. Is that what you were going to say? Well forget it, mate. I'm not buying that. Superstitious mumbo jumbo."

"I wasn't going to say any such—"

"I said forget it, old son. Don't fret yourself. Your bold sartorial choices aren't going to be the death of you or me or Romeo and Juliet over there. We're going to get out of this! I promise you. We've got cover and we have at least some ammo."

"And those two?"

"I'll ask . . . Lawson, Warren, weapons check and tell me your ammo status."

"I fired two rounds, four left," Warren said.

"I fired nothing, six left," Lawson said.

"Spares?"

Both of them shook their heads.

"So between us that makes . . . um . . ."

"Not much," Crabbie said. "But if we ration them out we can keep them at bay, I think."

"Ok, exit strategies and defensive strategies. Crabbie keep an eye on the corridor while we search the room for anything to use or see if there's another way out."

The flat had been stripped by thieves of anything remotely useful. No carpet, no furniture, not even a lamp on the light fixing. There wasn't much graffiti on the walls. This room had been ignored except as a place to do an occasional dump, judging. Escape unconventionally? Well, the walls were solid. The floor was concrete over rebar. Damp had eaten away at some of it, but you'd need a sledgehammer and two days to get through to the floor below and flank the bastards on the stairs, which admittedly would be a lot of fucking fun.

"Can we get out the window?" I asked Lawson.

"Nah," Lawson said peering through the place where a nice plate window once had been. A window which probably only existed in that twenty-four month interval between Sir Basil Spence's firm finishing this block of flats and it going completely *High-Rise* as the lifts broke, the corridors filled with rubbish, drug dealers and vandals smashed all the lights and paramilitary gangs took the building floor by floor.

Lawson winced.

"What's the matter, son?"

"You're not going to be happy, sir."

"Too far for us to jump out and live?"

"Oh, definitely not, but that's not why you're not going to be happy."

"The fuck is it then?"

THE DETECTIVE UP LATE

"They shot out the tyres on the Land Rover just for badness."

They had and of course, because they were sloppy bastards, the spray had gone all over the bonnet and the driver's door too.

"To mess with our wheels like that? Bastards," I said and winked at him. I could tell he was starting to come around. This was not Lawson or Crabbie's first gun battle nor, if their RUC career continued on the standard curve, was it destined to be their last, but WPC Warren? She didn't seem the type who needed a pep talk but I gave them both the boiler plate grin of the happy warrior.

"We're going to be fine, folks, totally fine. Lawson, tighten the Velcro on Warren's vest at the back."

"Sean!" Crabbie was saying—that exclamation mark sufficiently alarming for me to come running.

He was peering down the corridor through the smoke and the darkness.

"What is it?"

"Two of them coming towards us on the right of the hall. And the ones at the top of the stairs are in position now."

"I don't see a bloody thing. Are you sure?"

"Yeah, they're coming. You can see their trainers, look."

"God, you've good eyes, mate. Must be all that early-morning milking. Look at them. Balaclavas, gloves—they're pros, aren't they? You aim at the guy at the front, I'll aim at his mate and then we'll give the top of the stairs crew a burst. Single shot not full auto for you."

"Of course."

"Three, two, one."

*BOOM! BOOM! BOOM! BOOM!*

*BOOM! BOOM! BOOM! BOOM! BOOM! BOOM! BOOM! BOOM!*

Return fire: *Budda-Budda-Budda-Budda-Budda-Budda-Budda-Budda-Budda!*

We ducked back into the flat again as the shooting in the corridor continued.

"You ok, Crabbie?"

"Never better."

"My dream is that the two teams kill each other. Ridiculous to have two of them at either ends of the corridor," I said and went back to Lawson and Warren, who were still getting air at the window. Lawson had fixed Warren's Velcro straps now, and she was ready.

"There are two teams of them. One just to the right by the stairs, another coming down the corridor. They are about thirty from us and moving slowly but moving none the less. We need you two in fire positions. The pair of you will take the team to the right, just shoot at any muzzle flashes, Crabbie and I will shoot the ones on the left. Just a couple of shots each to make them hit the deck. Ration that ammo."

Lawson swallowed hard. I patted the kid on the shoulder. "It'll be all right, son," I said.

"Uhm, Sean," Crabbie said and cleared his throat, which again was about as harsh as he ever got, his version of an army sergeant's: "Enough of the hugging! This isn't the fucking Sacred Band of bloody Thebes! Get over here!"

Back to the door. All four of us.

Lawson was better now.

Warren was solid.

You don't have to ask how Sergeant McCrabban was.

"You two fire right, me and Crabbie will shoot left. On my mark together: three, two, one," I said.

Crabbie and I swung around the door jam and shot to the left; Lawson and Warren shot to the right. We ducked back into the room immediately as automatic rifle fire and tracer rained up and down the corridor through the smoke and dust.

"Everyone ok?"

Everyone was ok.

"You think we hit anyone?"

"No idea. But they won't be able to breathe out there," Crabbie said. "I bet they didn't bring respirators."

"Warren, Lawson, go to the window, get some air and tell me what you see."

"Yes, sir."

Warren and Lawson went back to the window.

"Has all this noise attracted any attention?"

"Two boys, sir!" Warren said.

I ran over. The streets and greenways around the abandoned building were deserted, but there were two wee muckers staring in amazement at our shot-up Land Rover. Both of them were about eleven with crew cuts, Adidas trainers and skinny jeans. They were carrying sticks and they started poking the engine which was an idiotic thing to do if the petrol tank decided to go up. The smaller of the two was wearing a Liverpool top so they couldn't be complete idiots.

"Oi! You two! Up here!" I yelled.

Both of them looked around gormlessly as if this was 1 Samuel 3 and I was the voice of Yahweh.

"Up here!"

The Liverpool-top one looked up at the building.

"Yeah, here! First of all, get away from that car. The petrol tank might explode!"

The older grabbed the younger one by the arm and backed him away from the vehicle.

"Now, listen, I want youse to find a phone box and call 999!" I yelled.

"Are youse police?" the older one shouted.

"Yes!" I replied.

"We're not informers, so we're not!" the older one said.

"Of course not! Don't call police then, call the fire brigade, the building's on fire!"

The older boy led the younger lad away.

"Call the fire brigade!" I shouted after them.

Maybe they'd call it in, maybe they wouldn't.

"Someone will call," I said to Lawson and Warren with a reassuring smile. "Plenty of busybodies around here. That geezer we met at the start. Someone walking their dog. We'll be fine."

"I'm not worried, sir," Warren said.

"Good, good. Ammo?"

"All out, now," Lawson said.

"You Warren?"

"I'm all out too."

"That's ok, Crabbie and I have plenty left."

I went back to the door. "They're all out of ammo and I'm down to three in the Glock and the six in the .38."

"I've nine in the MP5," he said. "One big rush and they'll have us."

"Yeah, but they don't know that. Did we hit any of them?"

"No, doesn't look like it. No moaning anyway. And they didn't kill each other before they stopped firing."

"That's unfortunate."

"Are youse still down there?" a voice yelled down the corridor.

Crabbie looked at me and shrugged. Why not engage in a parley?

"Yeah, we're fine! We're having a wee snack, why don't youse come and join us!" I yelled back.

"Maybe another fucking time, peeler. Why don't youse come down here and join us? We'll give you share of a six-pack. You must be thirsty!"

"No fear, pal. We're just going to sit tight. The boys in the blue and the boys in green will be along presently!"

"Why do you think that?" the voice asked. "No one's called this in, I promise you that."

"Well if we don't check in every twenty minutes, operations assumes that we're out of contact and they do a radio check and if we don't respond to the radio check they raise the alarm!" I said. "So you lads better run if you don't want to be lifted by half the bloody British Army. Or stay if you don't believe me, totally up to you, but don't say I didn't warn you, eh?"

"That's the procedure for patrols but you're detectives on a case. You keep your own hours! Nobody will be missing you lot until the end of the day," the remarkably well-informed voice said.

"We'll see about that. You just wait and see who comes," I yelled.

"We haven't got all day. We're here to parley. Do you wanna listen or not?" the voice said.

"Say what you're going to say."

"Youse can send the woman out if youse want. We're not about killing women today. She can go."

Warren shook her head immediately.

"She wants to stay with us!" I said.

"Did you ask her?"

"She heard you and she shook her head."

"Is she sure about that? Free passage out of here on our word of honour."

Warren shook her head again.

"She's staying with us!"

"Right then. Don't say we didn't give you a fair shake," the voice replied.

I looked at Warren again, but she was solid. Seven out of ten policeman in Northern Ireland are injured in the course of duty every calendar year. They make us tough, so they do. But then again, what other police force in the world would put up with that? There would be a bloody police strike.

"They're coming again," Crabbie said. "To the right."

"Oh, yes, those trainers of theirs, I see them. Let me see if I can kill the bastard in the front."

*BOOM! BOOM! BOOM!*

And then the scream of return fire from the assault rifles.

A hail of white noise and fire and ricochets.

Crabbie and I ducked back into the room.

"I bloody missed them," I said.

"Me too."

"So far nobody's hit anybody today. They're the gang that couldn't shoot straight and we're the Keystone Cops."

"Sir, I think I hear a siren," Warren said.

She was right.

And it was getting closer and closer as the wavelength narrowed.

If the wavelength widened again they would be going past us on the Shore Road to an incident in Belfast . . .

But it didn't narrow. Christian bloody Doppler brought them right to us.

Two big red fire engines parked outside the Penny Building. Lawson and Warren were already screaming at them to call the police and the army.

"Shoot at that bastards, that'll get them panicking," I wanted to say, but I bit my tongue.

I went back to the doorway.

"Looks like you fucked up, lads!" I yelled. "No hard feelings, eh? Why don't youse lay down your weapons and surrender and I'll talk the judge into dropping the attempted murder charges. We'll say it was all youthful high spirits!"

Another burst of gunfire and then silence.

Silence for a full two minutes before another friendly noise was added to the soundtrack.

"Helicopter," Crabbie said definitively.

"Here come the army!" I shouted down the corridor, but I got no response this time.

I did a final check in with Warren, Lawson and McCrabban.

"Anybody hit?"

They all shook their heads.

Amazingly we had got out of this with barely a scratch.

I considered that.

The team that had come to kill us had been tactically astute but very rusty.

It looked like they hadn't shot a gun in years.

What did that mean?

What did it all mean?

The helicopter hovered above the flat roof of the Penny building and a team of soldiers came running down the stairs five minutes later.

"Friendlies. RUC!" I yelled when they appeared on our floor.

"Drop your weapons and show your fucking hands!" they screamed at us from the stairwell in Cockney accents.

We showed our hands and they approached us cautiously. The bullet-proof "Police" vests and the fact that Warren was in uniform convinced them that we weren't the bad guys.

Downstairs into the paradox: glad to be alive but the inevitable de-pression that comes with the adrenaline crash.

Sun setting in the hills to the east of Belfast.

I burbled an incident report to some Chief Super with a moustache.

The whole estate now filled with police Land Rovers and army Land Rovers and ambulances and fire engines.

I got us a lift back to the station.

"Everyone is excused from duty for the rest of the week," I said to Warren, Lawson and McCrabban. "I'll type up the reports. You all go home."

"No, I'll type up the report, you go home," Crabbie said.

"I'm Spartacus," I said. "You go home. I've seen your typing."

Crabbie nodded reluctantly.

"Have a shower and triage yourselves," I said. "And after a good night's sleep I want you to call Dr Havercamp tomorrow to see about counselling."

There were a couple of reservists in the station but no senior officers, so I went to the Chief Inspector's office and found that bottle of 1939 cognac he saved for when the Chief Constable was over.

I poured myself a glass, wiped my prints off the bottle and returned it to his liquor cabinet.

Back to my office. I put my feet up on the desk and looked out the window at the sea. Cargo boats, oil tankers, tug boats, the Belfast pilot.

I sniffed the glass.

Good stuff. Smell of other days. Hayfields, dragonflies, Europe before the fall. Prephylloxera cognac is fundamentally different from the modern product in a way not true of other spirits. The original Cognac vineyards, dating back to Roman times, were chiefly planted with Folle Blanche, a thin-skinned grape variety, prone to mildew and rot, but which produced a brandy of incomparable perfume and character.

The Chief Inspector had a bottle of the old good stuff.

I took a sip and that, my friends, is what we should be drinking when the comet hits the Earth. Actually, if you can get it we should be drinking the 1811 Veuve Clicquot Cuvée de la Comète but that stuff costs more than your house.

I closed my eyes and drifted, but I didn't sleep. I had things to do later. A lot of things to do.

I put music on. Mahler. The number ten. Heartbeat, strings, you know the drill . . .

The sea broke on the shore like curls of burning newspaper. The seagulls hovered on the edge of the strand. A fog began rolling along the bridle path next to the railway lines.

Filaments of blue.

The darkness.

The light.

I put down the Waterford crystal glass, got up and stretched.

"Ok, Duffy, no rest for the wicked, on with the show."

# 19
# THE AK-74S

I went back to Coronation Road, had a sandwich and made calls to check that Crabbie, Warren and Lawson were safely home. "Make sure you avail yourself of the counselling service," I reminded them. Obviously Crabbie was going to be more traumatised by being in a room with a stranger and talking about his feelings than the actual gun battle itself, but I hoped that it would do some good for Lawson and Warren.

Next, I called Beth and Emma just to hear their voices.

Beth had had no more run ins with the neighbours, Emma was definitely reading entire words in books and Beth said they had both made a good job of clearing out some of the weeds in the back garden. The house was looking good and teaching was going great.

She asked me how things were going with ours truly, and I said that everything was chill on the dark side of the moon.

Phone calls made, I poured myself a glass of Bowmore and carried it to the shower. I turned on the hot and scalded myself and then turned the dial all the way to the left for the cold. I towelled, pulled on black jeans, Adidas trainers, a Fairport Convention T-shirt, a black jumper and my old reliable leather jacket. I reloaded my weapons. After an incident involving firearms, you were supposed to turn in your guns, but no one had been killed or even wounded so there would not be a huge spotlight on this one. Not with shit going down all the time all over Ulster.

I checked under the Beemer for bombs, but she was clean.

I drove along the seafront and up to Rathcoole and back at last to the crime scene.

Lot of bloody cops now. Twenty roping off the area, a dozen Forensics officers doing their thing. A small crowd of idiot looky-loos, surprisingly few hacks. I parked the Beemer and dug on the vibe. Spotlights, craic, men in white boiler suits chalking individual shell casings and taking photographs.

I slipped under the police lines and showed my ID to a peeler who asked what the fuck I thought I was doing.

"It's ok, son, I work here."

I found my old sparring partner of earlier in the day, lead forensic boffin DCI Frank Payne, taking a smoke break under a tent the FOs had set up as a kind of canteen. Frank's cheeks were red and what was left of his hair was grey. He was scarfing down a cream bun between puffs of a ciggie.

"Sean Duffy again, as I live and breathe. You're the proverbial bad penny. All you ever do is give me work. But this time you're not making up fairy stories. This time people really were shooting at you, weren't they?" he said and offered me a paw covered with ash and cream. I gave him a friendly dig on the shoulder. "Nice to see you, Francis."

"Seriously, Sean, this time of night, they call us out? You wouldn't believe the backlog we have," he said.

"Sorry mate."

"Three hundred shell casings we've had to log. What did you think you were playing at out here, Sean? Did you think it was the last five minutes of fucking *Zulu* or something?"

"Isn't the last five minutes of *Zulu* a singing contest between the Zulus and the—"

"No. It isn't. That's earlier. Buy you a drink?" he asked fishing in his pocket and handing over a pewter flask.

"What's in it?"

"I'm an honest man."

"So what does that mean?"

"It's whisky."

I sat down next to him on a fold-out chair. I unscrewed the flask cap and took a slug of the bourbon. It was Maker's Mark, which wasn't really my thing, but I took a second drink out of politeness and handed the flask back.

"Thanks. Needed that."

"You're welcome."

"Aye, but for a bit of luck me and my team could have been fucking toast here, mate," I said reflectively.

With uncharacteristic affection Frank leaned forward and patted me on the back. "It's all right, Sean boy. It's all right," he said.

In the haphephobic world of male Protestant Ulster this was quite the gesture and neither of us quite knew what to make of it.

Fortunately, Frank saved the day by clearing his throat and offering me one of his cigarettes. "Fag? I heard you quit. But I'm the devil, so I am."

"Go on then, give us one," I said.

The cigarettes were Camels—one of my favourites, a blend of Virginia and Izmir tobacco, which made them fucking delicious.

"Love these," I said taking a grateful puff. "There's something to being shot at and missed and having a cigarette afterwards."

Frank looked at me, his caterpillar eyebrows raising a fraction. "What are you doing here anyway? This isn't your case. You're the subject of the case but this one will be going to Newtownabbey RUC, right?"

"Yeah, I expect so, which is sort of why I'm here," I said. "Newtownabbey will take a fortnight to boot up their investigation and I bet it'll be six months before there's even a preliminary report to share."

"They are a bit on the deliberate side," Frank agreed.

"And what I want to know is if this is a random hit on an RUC patrol—the sort of thing that happens every day, or if we were specifically targeted."

"Why would you be targeted?"

"Why do they target witnesses and detectives in this country?" I asked with, I hoped, a tone of ineffable, weary sadness in my voice.

"Because it's cheaper and more effective than going to court," Frank said and spat.

"Aye."

We stared at the Penny building and beyond that, the little splatter of blue lough water peaking out between gaps in the trees and buildings. A hawk down from the Knockagh swept to and fro over the crime scene, wondering at all the lights and commotion—perhaps someone had struck a deer or a sheep and there was carrion to be lifted and taken away?

"So, Frank, what I want to know is whether there's anything special or interesting about the forensic data?"

He turned to look at me with his intelligent spaniel eyes that were embedded in a hard-drinking sheet-welder's mug. "You know there won't be any prints, Duffy. You said the men you saw were wearing gloves and they didn't leave anything behind apart from shell casings . . . although . . ."

"Although what?"

He shook his head and finished his ciggie.

"Although what?" I asked again.

"Nah, don't want to lead you off on a wild goose chase. I know what you're like, Duffy. Somebody says one tiny, wee remark and you get a bee in your bonnet and blow it all out of all proportion."

"What about the shell casings, Frank?"

"Ok then. AK-47 casings mostly. Nothing interesting about them. Your standard 1970s Soviet knock-off AK, probably come from one of the shipments Gaddafi sent."

"Ok."

"But there were other casings. None of your team had assault rifles?"

"Nope. Revolvers, semi-automatic pistols, MP5s. Why?"

"Because we also found ammunition that wasn't used in any AK-47. One of the shooters had an M16, an Armalite, which presumably came from our patriotic friends in the USA. The IRA and the Loyalist paramilitaries have access to loads of those. Again, not so special."

"Ok, so?"

"Well there was also one other gun that was present and that's where the story does become much more interesting. So far we've gathered about forty shells that were clearly fired by an AK-74."

"Never heard of it."

"The Kalashnikov's early-1970s replacement. See, your classic AK-47 fires a very distinctive, big 7.62×39 mm cartridge. But your AK-74 fires the 5.45×39 mm cartridge, which is lighter and allows a soldier to carry more ammunition for the same weight. Just as accurate, just as deadly, but a lower bolt thrust and free recoil impulse, ergo increased automatic-fire accuracy."

"I'm not getting your point, Francis."

"Bear with me," he said and heaved himself up. He went into the main forensic tent and came back with a bag full of brass-coloured shell casings. He handed the evidence bag to me. I examined them, but I was no expert. I handed them back.

"My point is this, Sean. There are hardly any AK-74's in Northern Ireland. It never became a popular weapon outside the Soviet Union. It was certainly never sent here in any major arms shipment and I'd never encountered it before tonight."

"How'd you recognise it then?"

"A wily old FO like me has got his files up here," he said, tapping his head.

"What does it mean, Francis?"

"It means quite a lot, Duffy. Another drink?"

"Sure."

Another hit of the whisky.

"I knew you were the right man to come to, Francis," I said, sensing something big happening—tumblers falling into place, phone calls being made late into the night. Men and women who had squibbed a hit shifting into panic mode.

"Aye, I am. So here's the story: right before they called a truce, a very small shipment of guns was sent from the Soviet Union to the Official IRA. There were a dozen AK-74's in that shipment."

"The Official IRA?" I said, amazed.

"Yeah, the Officials."

The Official IRA had been on ceasefire since 1974. They had been replaced everywhere by the Provisional IRA, known these days, simply, as the IRA. The Official IRA were basically defunct as an organisation. They occasionally passed a hat around in a few pubs, but they had no real sources of income and no skin in the game at all. They ran no protection rackets, dealt no drugs, never attacked the police or security forces and the other paramilitary groups left them alone. The Official IRA had sublimed completely into politics, establishing several Marxist or Revolutionary Communist parties that almost never did any business at election time.

"The Officials?" I said, again. "There can't be one of the bastards under sixty . . . Although, now that you mention it . . ."

"What?"

"We had a weird moment in there on the fourth floor."

"Oh yeah? What was that?"

"They saw that we had a WPC with us and they told us we could let her go. That's an old-school move isn't it?"

Frank grinned at me. "What on Earth have you done, Sean Duffy, to bring an Official IRA cell out of retirement after sixteen years?"

What indeed?

I stood. "Gotta fly, mate. Thanks for the info."

Handshake and back down to the station in the Beemer. Skeleton crew. Up to the Incident Room to make some phone calls to the all-night switchboard. Intel req. to Special Branch. Info dump and full background on Johnny Dunbar, Charles McCawley, Terry Jones and Jordy Hardcastle. Everything intel had. High-category request, using my pull as one of the mole team. Pull file too on the Official IRA and what possible connection they might have to a missing tinker girl or any of the above names. Wide sweep, deep sweep. Aye, send me everything you've got. I'll sort through it. I've got the time. And when the fuckers are shooting at you, it gives you the motivation too.

Ticktock.

Ball rolling but the info wouldn't come in till the morning.

What to do until then?

Out to the Beemer.

Trip home on the midnight ferry. Hard to think of Shortbread Land as home but there it is. Familiar diesel smell, familiar biting cold on the car deck, familiar oily tea and cake in the cafeteria. The ferry terminal, Stranraer Town, the countryside, Portpatrick, my street, my parking spot, my front door, my bed. "Sean?"

"It ain't the milkman."

"Oh, that's a shame. You smell of . . . what is that?"

"Nitro. I had a shower, but it lingers."

"Was someone shooting at you?" she asked, alarmed.

"No, no. Nothing like that. Spent some time on the range. Never fret yourself."

"What time is it?"

"Go back to sleep."

"If you're up for it we can do something else first."

The I've-just-cheated-Death fuck—the greatest of all the fucks in the repertoire. "Honey, you're speaking my language," I said.

# 20
# THE MEN WHO BUMP BACK

Morning breakfast with the fam. Coffee. Toast. Marmalade. Radio on. Some cool Scottish radio station whose playlist was more expansive than BBC Radio 1. Bands you never heard on the snot-nosed youth–worshipping Beeb. The Pixies, Dinosaur Junior . . .

Emma drawing pictures of cows with purple crayons.

Beth making notes on a comic book as if it was the first page of a lost novel by Bruno Schulz.

Drizzle outside. Sailboats scudding on a harsh Murmansk convoy sea.

"Whatcha reading?" I asked.

"Don't roll your eyes at me, Sean Duffy. Music snob, book snob. You're all alike, you Catholic schoolboys. If it doesn't have French and Latin in it, it can't be literature."

"Christ on a bike, all I asked was what you were—"

"This is a good line, right here, it's very Sean Duffy," she said. "'There are things that go bump in the night. Make no mistake about that. And we are the ones who bump back.'"

"It is good," I agreed. Very Sean Duffy indeed.

"How's your case?" she asked, to change the subject.

"Three suspects. Three dodgy alibis. Possibly a fourth suspect. But probably only two real contenders. Don't like either of them. We put all of them in the tank and none of them cracked. Two of them came in without lawyers and we tag-teamed them for hours, but they still didn't crack. Not good."

When Emma went to catch the end of her show in the living room, Beth added: "What motivation could there be for killing that poor girl?"

"Blackmail? Or maybe we're dealing with a psycho. They don't vibe psycho, but you never know. The West Yorkshire police interviewed the Yorkshire Ripper nine times and thought he was on the level."

"But you're not the West Yorkshire police."

"No, we are not. Blackmail or worry about blackmail seems the most likely explanation."

And there is that scary terrorist dimension but let's not mention that.

"She was blackmailing one of them and one of them killed her?"

"It's possible but the truth is, I don't like that one either. She seemed like a pretty savvy, intelligent girl and I don't think blackmail sounds likes her style. She seemed to be very choosy about her clients and they all seemed to like her."

"So why kill her then?"

"I don't know. I just don't know."

I looked at my watch. "Better get in gear here. Not even supposed to be out of the country."

"Gear away."

I finished breakfast, walked Emma to playschool, got the 8.00 a.m. SeaCat and was back in the office by 10.00 a.m.

I spotted Crabbie in the Incident Room sorting through intel faxes.

"Oi, mate, I told you not to come in for a few days," I said.

"You're here. I knew you'd be here. And I'm not having you come in and me not," he said with a trace of annoyance.

"All right don't take the huff."

"What's the story with all these faxes from Special Branch? And your phone's been ringing off the hook. What did you do last night, crank call the Chief Constable?"

"I've stirred things up, Crabbie. Called in favours at Special Branch. Deep intel reports on all our suspects: Special Branch, Fraud Squad,

Racket Squad. Had to do it. Gonna bring heat but we have to bring this case to a head."

Crabbie nodded and looked around the cop shop with an elegiac twinkle in his eyes. "Aye, we can't stay here forever, can we?"

"No. We can't. Youth must have its day. The bastards."

And speaking of youth, Lawson came at 11.00. Me and the Crabman were both furious. "What are you doing here?" Crabbie and I asked together.

"Uh, my job," Lawson said.

"Get on home," I said. "You were in a bloody shootout yesterday. What do you think you're playing at?"

"You two are here," Lawson protested.

"Do yourself a favour and get on home, son. Take it easy," Crabbie said.

"Aye, go home or I'll get HR on you," I said.

"If you're coming in to work, I'm coming in to work," Lawson said, defiantly. Before I could think of a response, I noticed a familiar brown-haired bob. "And, holy fuck, is that Warren over there? What's the matter with you kids? Don't you ever listen to your bloody elders about anything? World is going to the dogs, Crabbie."

"Absolutely," he agreed.

Lawson took off his raincoat and draped it over his chair. We weren't going to shift him. And U2 was on his Walkman and his hair was gelled up. "If we were on a ship, this was would be mutiny," I muttered to myself.

Office half an hour later. Rain battering windows. Heater on the blink. Olivier Messiaen's "Quatuor pour la fin du temps" on the record player.

Really, you don't need to do anything. You don't need to go anywhere or do anything. They come to you. They always come to you, these types of men. These men with vague names and vague ranks and vague departments of which you have never heard. Their suits and haircuts are meant to blend in, but like time travellers from the future, everything they do blends them out. They're like characters from *Das Schloss*. They'll come. They'll always come. They're on their way in a brown Mercedes.

Me fielding actually quite an important phone call from John Strong on the scrambler.

"Duffy, are you alone?"

"Yes."

"Look, I'll say it again, I'm very worried about the next meet."

"You're always worried, and you know what, old cock, that's a good thing."

"I think I've said something that has alerted Q. I think he's running a Nutting Squad inquiry on me."

"Has he said anything?"

"No."

"So where's this coming from?"

"It's just a feeling."

"What does Olly say?"

"That's why I'm calling you, Sean. They don't take feelings seriously. I think I should avoid the meet."

"You avoid the meet and that's you over as an agent."

"I think I have to avoid it."

"Olly will send you to prison. There will be a trial, if you're lucky it'll be in camera and if you're not—disgrace, humiliation, loss of pension and twenty years."

A knock at the door. Crabbie's face peaking around the jam. I put my hand over the receiver.

"Couple of blokes here to see you, Sean, Special Branch," Crabbie said.

"Two minutes," I said, and he closed the door behind him. "Listen John, I talked to Olly about this. We're getting no chatter on any of this. It's my feeling that you're fine, but I'll look into it and I'll talk to Olly. If we don't think the meeting's safe, I'll scrub it. And if we do it, I'll be there listening on the wire and at the first hint of trouble, I'll make sure he pulls you out. Ok?"

"Ok," he said reluctantly.

"Ok, I'll have to go. We'll talk again before the meet."

I hung up just as there was a knock at the door. Crabbie led in the goons.

Like I say, two bland looking G-men types. Clean cut, early thirties, sharp suits, one of them wearing bespoke shoes. They didn't look like cops to me. Too thin, too few lines and grey hairs.

They showed me warrant cards before they said anything.

The dark-haired one's ID claimed he was a Chief Superintendent David Armstrong, the blonde's said that he was a Superintendent Philip Hanratty. Hanratty's ID was so shiny and new, my bet was that it was printed and laminated this morning.

"We're from Special Branch. I'm CS Armstrong," Armstrong said, "And this is my partner, Superintendent Hanratty."

"Have a seat," I said.

They took their coats off and hung them on the rack and then they sat down. They had brought combination briefcases with them, but they were waiting for Crabbie to leave the room. They didn't ask him to leave the room they just glared at him until he got the picture.

"I'll go get some tea," he said.

"No, you sit on the sofa there, mate," I insisted, but Crabbie shook his head.

"I'll get us some tea," he said and closed the door after him.

Close-ups a la Leone, nobody saying nothing, but the very un-Leone Olivier Messiaen kept us nicely on edge via the record player.

"Anybody want a drink?" I asked, looking towards the drinks trolley. "I've got some sixteen-year-old—"

"You've started a fire, Duffy, and we're the fucking firemen," Hanratty said in a hard-as-nails North Belfast accent.

I wondered which of my three suspects they had come to get off the hook. Was it McCawley, whose father-in-law had pull with the government? Was it Dunbar, a budding politician, or was it Jones who was well liked by the Secretary of State? Fuck, maybe it was all three of the cunts.

Armstrong opened his briefcase and took out a file in a yellow folder marked MOST SECRET.

The wind and the rain became a howl of Celtic angst outside, and the sea began breaking over the sea wall onto the road. Nice sympathetic fallacy weather.

"Do we have to have the music?" Armstrong asked.

"It's nearly over," I said and took the file.

I opened it and there was the grinning face of Johnny Dunbar. You didn't even have to read the contents. You could guess the rest. There seemed to be only three jobs to be had in Ireland these days: policeman, informer and criminal. Everybody could more or less be fitted into one or other of these categories. Dunbar had been turned as early as 1978. He'd been a paid agent of Special Branch for the last twelve years, all the while rising up the ranks of the UVF and, no doubt, committing many criminal acts while under the full sanction of the RUC's Special Branch.

"I'll need to share this information with my number two and my lead detective. I'm leaving the full-timers in a couple of weeks, they'll be doing the paperwork on this."

Armstrong and Hanratty exchanged a look. Armstrong nodded.

"We researched you and Sergeant McCrabban and Sergeant Lawson. They can see the file, although it is not to be discussed by you or anyone else outside of your department."

Crabbie and Lawson came in and we read about Johnny Dunbar. About how he was a good and faithful agent and a valuable one too. Second in Command of the UVF's East Antrim Brigade, a Capo of their protection and drug racket business, and an influential player in their new political strategy, attempting to get UVF men elected onto councils and into parliament. And all this, while getting five thousand quid a month from the Crown for informing on his friends, family and colleagues.

I got up and poured myself a whisky.

"So you see, Inspector Duffy, we'd appreciate it if you'd let our boy alone from now on. He's a little bit more important than a missing tinker girl that you don't actually even know was murdered," Armstrong said.

"You get our point, don't you, Duffy?" Hanratty said.

"It depends," I said.

"Depends on what?" Hanratty growled.

"Depends where he was on December thirtieth," I said. "If he was drowning Kat McAtamney in the River Bann then your boy is going down for murder."

"No, he isn't," Hanratty said.

"Yes, he is," I said.

"Ever heard of a thing called the chain of command, Duffy? I'm a Superintendent, my gaffer here is a Chief Super, you're a—"

"Man who is getting mighty tired of this shite. I don't care how many murders you've let Dunbar get away with under your watch. I don't care how many terrible things he's done that you have to square with your consciences. That means nothing to me. I've been tasked with finding out what happened to Kat McAtamney, and if he killed her, I'm arresting him, and I'll make it fucking stick one way or another."

"So you admit you're dirty then, Duffy. Why am I not surprised. You should see the file IA has on—"

"Spare me. Getting a morality lesson from you two is like getting sensitivity training from Himmler. Where was 'your boy' on December thirtieth? He's told you and you believe him, otherwise you wouldn't bloody be here," I said, which was perfectly true. If Dunbar had done the murder and Special Branch needed a free pass for him these two clowns weren't ever going to convince me. Surely they knew that? It was going to have to be the Chief Constable himself or the bloody Home Secretary.

"He wasn't at home with the missus, was he?" I said.

"No," Armstrong said.

"Where was he?"

"He was in Lurgan," Hanratty said.

"Doing what?"

Hanratty and Armstrong exchanged another look and said nothing.

"Doing what?" I insisted. "Look gents, I'll bring him in again and ask him in person if you don't tell me."

"Dunbar went down to Lurgan to supervise the kneecapping of a couple of joyriders."

I nodded. "How old were these joyriders?"

"They were both fourteen," Armstrong said.

"What did Dunbar do?"

"It took most of the night. Dunbar and his crew had to find the boys, who weren't at home, then they took them to a local pub, the Harp,

THE DETECTIVE UP LATE

cleared the back room and kneecapped them. Dunbar didn't get home until two thirty in the morning. We know this for certain because another one of our informants was there too," Armstrong said.

"A kneecapping only takes five minutes," Crabbie said.

"No, not this one. The boys had been stealing cars and racing them all over town, so the locals complained to the UVF and the UVF sent Dunbar down to make sure the message went home."

"What did he do?" Lawson asked, aghast.

"Your standard Belfast six pack," Hanratty said.

"With a drill instead of a gun, which is why it took so long," Armstrong added.

"So what you're saying, in effect, is this: Dunbar couldn't have murdered Kat McAtamney because he spent the night of December thirtieth sticking a drill bit into the elbows, knees and ankles of two young boys that a couple of people in the community of Lurgan suspected were stealing cars. Dunbar was too busy torturing two children to have kidnapped and drowned my victim, another child."

Hanratty folded his arms and glared at me. "That about sums it up," he said defiantly.

"I'll need a witness statement from this other informant of yours who said he was there. I'll need to know when Dunbar arrived, when he—"

"Here," Armstrong said handing me over a piece of paper with a signature at the bottom. "We've redacted a few names here and there, but this should satisfy you."

I read the statement from an "Informer C" about what exactly had taken place on the night of the thirtieth. It was very detailed and explicit. One of the boys had a Jamaican father and in amongst the account of drunken torture and mayhem Dunbar had thought to throw in a few racial indeterminacy jokes. I handed the repulsive little document to Crabbie.

"And that's it, is it? I'm supposed to take your word and the word of your creepy informants?"

"We had Dunbar in our interview room twice for several hours and, apparently, he lied to our faces both times?" Crabbie said.

"Christ, you clowns are difficult," Armstrong said, handing me another piece of paper. "Here's the log of Dunbar being stopped at an Army checkpoint in Greenisland on the way back home again at two thirty in the morning. Is that enough proof for you? We can supply you the names and addresses of the two boys who were kneecapped. I'm sure they'll be able to identify Johnny as well. They were not wearing balaclavas."

Hanratty began saying something else now, but I tuned the fucker out. Tuned both of them out. Tuned out their sales pitch and their bullshit. Yeah, I get it. I bloody get it.

Your evil little agent, a UVF man, a drug dealer, an enforcer of protection rackets, a torturer of children and God knows what else was not my killer.

Silent movie now.

They talked, they *showed*, they packed away their supporting materials in their briefcase and stood up.

Hanratty offered me his hand and I shook it. Armstrong offered me his hand and I shook it. Me, the good soldier, who could see the big picture and wouldn't kick up fuss. It would be hypocrisy to kick up a fuss anyway. I was running a man, John Strong, who was, if anything, worse than Dunbar. Ignoring his crimes for the greater good.

Looking into the smug, complacent faces of Hanratty and Armstrong, I saw my own face. My disgust wasn't for them, it was for me.

Lawson saw them to the door while I went to the window and opened it. Drizzle and cold now and the harsh sea breeze.

Crabbie filled my whisky glass and handed it to me.

Waterford crystal, sixteen-year-old Jura whisky, January rain and the grey, bitter Irish Sea—these were good things in life. Why the long face, Sean Duffy?

I sat down at my desk and waited until Lawson came back in.

When he sat down, I poured them both a drink.

Everybody waited until the tears of rage subsided a little.

"So I suppose we're down to two suspects now," Lawson said.

"Yeah. One of whom was home alone reading Latin poetry and the other was home, more or less alone, working on a speech," I said.

"One of them has an alibi. McCawley's wife says she heard him doing his speech," Crabbie said.

"Lucky for him that she did," Lawson muttered.

"What did you make of her, Crabbie? Would she lie for him?"

Crabbie reflected upon it. "I don't know. As I say, forgiving an affair is one thing, covering up for a murderer is quite another."

"Love's a wild card though, and for whatever reason she does seem to love him, doesn't she?" I said. "I don't think we can eliminate McCawley just yet. Walk with me to the Incident Room, gents."

The Incident Room whiteboard had three names on it and a question mark next to Jordy Hardcastle. I nodded at Lawson who took the eraser and removed the name of Johnny Dunbar.

"Kill Hardcastle too. It wasn't that fuck," I said.

"It wasn't him," Crabbie agreed.

"How do you know?" Lawson wondered.

"Get to our age you just bloody know."

"And we called up some of those party alibi guests and they seem pretty believable," Crabbie added.

There were only two names now.

"Which brings us to Mr Jones," I said. "The lonely, sad-sack, nice old gent, Terry Jones."

I took a copy of his two Q&As from the case file and started reading through it for the fifth time. Crabbie lit his pipe and sat down next to me. Lawson sat on the edge of the evidence table and stared at us.

The kid had to learn. Police work in Northern Ireland was 5% what happened yesterday—sudden, dramatic, violence—and 95% this: re-reading old witness statements and interview room Q&As. I looked through the reports on gun use in Northern Ireland and I looked through Jones' personnel file.

Wash and repeat.

Wash and repeat.

Nothing jumped out from the Q&As. McCawley stuck to his story. Jones stuck to his story.

Coffee break. I found Warren in the back room having a smoke.

"You shouldn't be in, today. That was a hell of a thing we all went through yesterday," I said.

She nodded. "You have to get back on the horse don't you, sir? I don't want to be sitting at home brooding about this."

"Have you talked to someone about what happened?"

"No. I was going to tell my mum, but she'd only worry."

"You'll call Dr Havercamp though, won't you? You have to. HR will kick up a fuss if you don't."

"I will, sir," she said. "Did you tell your wife?"

I shook my head. "No."

She nodded.

"Listen, the report on this one is going to take me some time to put in but when I do put it in, you and Lawson are going to come out of it very well. Any mistakes that were made were mine in not sussing out the situation."

"Oh, sir! You can't blame yourself for—"

"That's not my point. My point is, you did very well. And when Lawson takes over this department, he's going to need a lead detective, someone capable and tough and smart. I think you'd be perfect for the job. Think it over, will you?"

"I will," she said. She looked at me with kindness in her eyes. "We're going to miss you," she said.

"I'm not dying. And I'll be skulking around a few days a month, although they'll probably have me down in the basement stamping parking tickets."

"But then retirement," she said happily. "You'll have got out alive."

"Yes," I agreed, hoping she hadn't jinxed it.

"What are you going to do with yourself, sir?"

No one else had asked me that question. "I've been thinking about it, actually. I might write a book."

"About the force?" she asked with mild alarm.

"God, no. Musicology. I've got two ideas: a book on Haydn's Symphonies—a chapter per symphony, never been done before. I'd be the first."

"How many symphonies did he write?"

"104."

"What's the second idea?"

"An analysis of Blondie's *Parallel Lines* album."

"Maybe do the second one," she said.

Lunch break in Ownies bar. Three bowls of Irish Stew. Three pints of Guinness.

"I went back to the flats, last night," I said.

Crabbie raised an eyebrow.

"Don't trust Newtownabbey RUC to get the job done, sir?" Lawson asked.

"No, I don't. I was hoping Frank Payne might be the FO and I got lucky. He was there, large as life and in a chatty mood."

Crabbie took a sip of Guinness and slipped his notebook out of his pocket. He knew this was going to be good.

I told them about the AK-74 ammo and the fact that it hadn't been used anywhere in Northern Ireland in over fifteen years.

"I didn't have much time to do a comprehensive fact check on Frank's claims, but a preliminary scan seems to bear out what he says. The Official IRA got these guns from the Soviets in the early seventies when the Russians thought there was a possibility of fermenting a Communist coup in Ireland, but when that increasingly looked like a pipe dream and the Officials went on ceasefire, the free weapons dried up."

"What about Gaddafi?" Crabbie asked

"I looked into that. Gaddafi sent Semtex, mortars and AK-47s. This AK-74 is a really unusual weapon and it seems to have come in a very small batch for the exclusive use of the Officials."

"If they're on permanent ceasefire, they don't need their guns anymore, so why not give them to the Provisionals?" Crabbie suggested reasonably.

"Have you ever heard of any of the paramilitary groups ever giving up any of their hard-won weapons?"

"No. But it's not impossible, is it?" Crabbie said.

"Or a defector tired of peace and love and international socialism decides to leave the Officials and go to the Provisionals, taking his gun with him," Lawson said.

I took sip of the black stuff. "I've considered that," I said. "But I have a different theory brewing in the back of my head."

"What?"

"Those guys today got me thinking," I said.

"It's definitely not Dunbar, sir. I thought that evidence was pretty overwhelming," Lawson said with the slightest trace of impatience in his voice.

"That's not the angle I'm coming from. Pull the camera back a bit, Lawson. Let's look at the wide shot. Who benefits from assassinating us at the block of flats?"

"The cause? Big propaganda coup if they knock out a bunch of peelers," Lawson said.

"But let's assume that we were specifically targeted. Our team. Who would want to take us out?"

"One of the three suspects," Crabbie said.

"And if it's not Dunbar cos he knows he didn't do it, then it must be McCawley or Jones, right?"

"Yeah."

"Which one of those two men could possibly have any links to an Official IRA cell which has been dormant this last sixteen years?"

Crabbie thought about it and shook his head. Lawson wasn't getting it either.

"Unlikely to be McCawley, I think. He's from Coventry. And his connections to Northern Ireland are through the university and marriage into the upper classes," Crabbie said.

"Which leaves us with Mr Jones. Not the murdering type; quiet man, keeps to himself—which, of course, is what the neighbours always say when they start bringing the body bags out of the back garden."

Crabbie lit his pipe and looked at me keenly. "Why do you think it's him, Sean?"

"All those years in the Soviet Union. I'll bet he was a lonely man in Russia too. A lonely man who doesn't do well at social occasions meets this girl at a party. And the girl's into him. She laughs at his jokes. She is also weirdly obsessed by Roman poets or whatever it was he was into back then. She's a secretary or a translator or a tram conductor. But in reality, she's KGB. They start up a tentative relationship. And you know how the rest goes. They fall in love and they want to get married and she asks him for just one favour and before he quite knows what's happening, he's photographing files and eavesdropping on conversations."

"You think Terry Jones is KGB?" Lawson said, sarcastically.

"No, I don't. I think he's been supplying the Russians with information in his diplomatic postings and I think that since he's moved back here he's been getting access to cabinet papers through the Secretary of State's office and supplying them to the Russians too. Difficult times we live with the Berlin wall coming down, Thatcher on her way out, Bush wanting to show everybody he's as macho as Reagan . . ."

"Gets homesick, comes home, puts his mother in a fold, takes her house, then what?" Crabbie asked.

"He's still a lonely guy. Red Sonia wasn't the lass for him after all, so he starts seeing escorts and he meets this one girl who's very young but very pretty and who laughs at his jokes. And something goes wrong, and they fight, and he kills her. Maybe it's an accident, who knows? And he calls his handler and his handler says sit tight Comrade Jones, we'll take care of the whole thing."

"And then we come a-knocking and we're dragging him in for questioning day after day and Jones contacts his handler and says 'I thought you were going to sort out the whole thing. These cops are going to crack me.' And his handler says, 'Don't worry, we'll deal with them too. We can send a few local guys that we helped out in the past and who owe us a favour . . .'"

Crabbie looked at me with slow-motion-train-crash astonishment. He began furiously puffing his pipe and his eyebrows were going up and down. I'd clearly hit on something that gelled with his instincts.

I liked that.

"When did you think of all this?" he asked.

"Just now over the Guinness."

"You shouldn't be retiring, Sean. You have a knack for this kind of work," he said.

Lawson wasn't having any of it. "So you think Terry Jones did it? Killed the girl, I mean?"

"Aye, maybe."

"But you don't have proof for any of this. It's a, whatchamacallit, a just-so story."

"Sounds good to me," Crabbie said.

Lawson shook his head. "No, he invented all this out of thin air. Just now. That's not police work. Come on, sir. You wouldn't allow me to get away with something like this!"

"You're right, son. We need some proof."

"How are we going to get that? Question him again?"

"A third time? Never. And we can forget about getting a warrant to bug Mr Jones' house. That's not going to happen with zero evidence."

"And I think we can also forget requesting a Special Branch surveillance team to watch him 'round the clock. We're not exactly in their good books, are we?" Crabbie said.

"So what do we do? Surveil him ourselves? The three of us? We try and outwit a KGB-trained agent?" Lawson said.

"Nah, that's not going to work either," I said. "His skills will be far superior to anything we can come up with. The bastard will spot us on Day One."

"So what are we going to do?" Lawson said.

"I have a friend at MI5. I think I'll call him."

# 21
# TERRIBLE TRADECRAFT

Oliver wasn't as sceptical as I'd been expecting. Like all MI5 agents in Ulster, he'd studied Russian history and Slavic languages at university and had been cosmically disappointed when they'd put him in the Belfast station.

"Your theory doesn't sound like total bullshit, Duffy. Senior civil servants to the higher offices of state, of course, get a full vetting by the security services, but as you slip down the chain to Transport, the Environment and Northern Ireland the procedures are a bit more pro forma. I'll look into this character for you and call you right back."

"Thanks, Olly, I appreciate it," I said into the telephone.

"For God's sake, don't breathe a word of this to anyone. You can't go around accusing someone of being a Soviet agent when it's almost certainly not true. Let's keep this between us, ok?"

"I already told McCrabban and Lawson."

"Fuck! Why did you do that?"

"Cos they're my colleagues in a murder investigation."

"All right, Duffy. Don't tell anyone else. Civil servants and indeed everybody can be a bit touchy about being accused of working for the fucking KGB. Leave this with me and I'll get back to you."

"When? Time's a factor here. I'm supposed to turn this department

over to my deputy sooner rather than later. And I can't possibly bring
Terry Jones in a third time. He'll have me done for harassment."

"And someone might stick you with a poisoned umbrella."

"I don't think that's particularly amusing. We were shot at yesterday. Have you been shot at, Oliver?"

"No. I once had a stapler thrown at me by Michael Heseltine but
that's about it."

"Tempus fugit, mate, get on this and call me back today, ok?"

"Ok. No problem."

He hung up.

He didn't, of course, call me back that day. When MI5 makes you
promises, they are like the promises of Lesbia to Catullus and should
be written on the water. Must mention that to Mr Jones.

Crabbie, Lawson and I had a somewhat morose case conference
at five o'clock in the Incident Room. There was really no need for the
downcast expressions. Special Branch had eliminated one of our suspects, cutting our work load down by a third. And yet we were all
depressed.

It was the inevitable endorphin crash after yesterday and the fact
that we still weren't really any closer to finding out who disappeared
Kat McAtamney. We had a nice theory, but it was only a theory. Rain
started dripping from the flat roof onto the grey Incident Room carpet.
I moved a bucket under the drip.

"All right, let's go home."

I drove back to Victoria Estate in the Beemer, got myself a six pack
of Bass from the offy and a fish supper from the Victoria Hot Spot.

Back to Coronation Road. It was drizzling and cold so there weren't
many people around, but I waved hello to Mrs Campbell who was
bringing in her washing from a fruitless afternoon spent on the line.
Troubled times for Mrs C. Her husband had recovered from his many
mysterious disabilities that had kept him from gainful employment and
had run off with a hairdresser from the Beau Monde salon. Run all the
way to Blackpool so there wasn't any realistic chance of getting any of
his dole money or child support. She still had five or possibly six kids

in the house and her only income was a severance pension from ICI, which had closed its factory in Carrickfergus in 1980.

"Evening, Mrs C. I'd stay and chat but me chips are getting cold," I said.

"I understand Mr Duffy. You get in there out of the rain."

"You get out of the rain yourself, Mrs C."

"I will. I'm just bringing in Danny's smalls, so I am."

"Danny? Which one's Danny? You know I lose track, the kids and the cousins."

Mrs Campbell took three steps towards me and looked up and down the street conspiratorially. She was wearing a paisley scarf, hiding most but not all of her gorgeous copper-coloured hair. Damp, rail thin and consumptive she was still a very attractive woman, Mrs C.

"I don't care what they say," she said in a whisper. "A woman has her needs, Mr Duffy. You know."

"Uhm, yeah . . ."

She touched me on the arm and gave it a little squeeze. She regarded me with an odd look in her eye that I couldn't quite decipher. *Un certain sourire*, Françoise Sagan might have said, were poor Françoise to have found herself in the unlikely position of walking down this street. "Timing is all, Mr Duffy. If he'd got off his arse and left me two years ago, things could have been different, couldn't they?"

"Uhm, I'm not sure I quite get—"

"You're happily married and everything's good?"

"Not quite married but everything's—"

"They say Danny's my 'fancy man.' Let them say what they like. He works harder than any of their husbands. Two jobs. At the garage and the joinery works. By the time he's thirty, he'll be running both of those places and then they'll be laughing on the other side of their faces, so they will. You get on in now, Mr Duffy and eat them chips. You can't heat them up again. It never works."

"Uh, ok, see you later, Mrs Campbell."

Inside to a freezing house and cold chips. Sounds fucking bleak doesn't it? Six pack of Bass, cold chips by the two bars of the electric heater in the living room. Sounds like the meal you have before you take an overdose of pain killers in your bedsit in Cumbernauld.

But if you've got a record player and you've got an album by Ella Fitzgerald, you're going to change your mind about topping yourself. At least for fifty minutes or so. I found Ella's album where she sings the Cole Porter songbook, lay down on the rug and just listened.

Phone call in the hall.

"Hello?"

"Holy fuck, Sean. I mean holy fuck. This guy's tradecraft is shocking. You'll get credit, of course. I mean, of course, you will. Your name will get mentioned in dispatches. If you want you can skive off work for a year, but there's not going to be a K in it, or even an MBE, I'm just telling you straight out that he's not exactly Kim fucking Philby."

"What are you talking about, Oliver? Is there a problem with John Strong?"

"Strong? What? No, forget him for a minute. We all know you brought him in. Don't worry, we know. Jesus, Sean, this isn't about bragging rights."

"Oliver can you just calm the fuck down and tell me what you're talking about. Please."

"Your boy. Terry Jones. You asked me to put a team on him. I put a team on him. OK?"

"I didn't ask you to put a . . . Why? What did you turn up?"

"So he was at work today, at Stormont. Briefing the Secretary of State, babbling Peter bloody Brooke. Christ, mate, you know this is going to be a bit of shitstorm too. I mean not just kudos, slaps on the back for catching a fucking Ivan, but also the old, 'How did this dozy bugger slip through the net?' You know? And he's not just a harmless old man is he? He's killing runaways and having his pals in the Official IRA shoot at coppers? I mean that's what you're saying, isn't it Duffy?"

I held the phone away from my ear for a moment to get a break from his blather. When I returned it to my other ear, he was still going on. "Me, you approached me. I'll have to be first responder. Paperwork out the arse, fat chance of overtime. This will be in addition to my other resp—"

"Look, Olly, I'm going down the station. Meet me there in twenty minutes, ok? Carrick police station. Second floor. I'll be in my office."

I hung up and called Crabbie. "How do, John?"

"Not bad," he said suspiciously.

"How's Helen and the boys?"

"Ok, Sean. What's up?"

"I've a contact in MI5 who says Terry Jones is dirty. And by dirty, I mean he's a—excuse my French—fucking traitor. Briefing me down the cop shop in twenty. You wanna be in on it?"

"I'll be there."

"Call Lawson. See you in a bit. Love to the missus."

Seagull's view: Rain. Darkness. Sea spray. Continuous-output xenon arc lamps.

Four men in my office overlooking the black void of Belfast Lough. Introductions. Handshakes. Sixteen-year-old Ardbeg whisky. Serious whisky for serious men and a serious conversation.

Olly chilled right down. Thinking next steps.

"So what happened after I got off the phone with you earlier today?" I asked.

"I have a certain flexibility. A certain discretion," he said.

"What did you do!"

"We looked at his bank accounts and found nothing. Checked his service records and found nothing. Checked Interpol and found nothing. Until you questioned him about this girl we didn't even think he had an overdue library book. And that, my friends, is fucking suspicious, so I sent a team to his house."

"Did you get a warrant?" Lawson asked naively.

"Nah, not necessary if it's national security. Tacit approval from Home Office. Anyway we did a brace and didn't find anything. I bugged his phone and bugged his car and meanwhile looked through his phone records. Started to get depressed now. Thinking the old gut is wrong. Phone records though. Something stood out. All pretty normal except three phone calls from a public call box in Belfast this quarter—two of them in the last two weeks. Two is too many for it to be a random wrong number. Three is just ridiculous. Sent a guy to the phone box and low and fucking behold it's on Talbot Street right 'round the corner from the bloody Russian consulate. Not Terry Jones' fault, that, of course, but still . . . sloppy tradecraft."

"Wait a minute? That's all you've got? A couple of phone calls from a phone box near the Russian Embassy?" Lawson asked. Lawson did not impress Olly. He was wearing his off-duty clothes, which consisted of skinny ripped jeans, Converse sneakers, a thick plaid shirt and a Parka.

"No, that's not all we've got my lad! But that was more than enough for me to institute a little agent provocateuring," Olly explained.

"What did you do?" I asked.

"I drove to Stormont and introduced myself to him and asked him if he could possibly spare some time for a sit-down security briefing in the next couple of weeks. I didn't make it seem urgent or anything because I didn't want him to run but I knew that my MI5 ID would be enough to put the shits up him and institute his emergency protocols."

"And what did he do?"

"Oh, my God. What didn't he do? Sees me at four o'clock. I'm all peaches and cream and 'Would you mind awfully' and 'This is just routine' and he's 'Oh, no problem. I'll check my schedule and get back to you.' And then he goes to his office, tells his secretary he's not feeling well, drives all the way home. Fast. Parks his car. Gets his bicycle. A bright red bicycle mind you. Bicycles down to Carrick Station, gets the train to Belfast with the bicycle in the bike carriage. Gets off at Belfast Central, bicycles to Talbot Street and leaves his bike chained up there by the phone box next to the chemists. Then he goes home again by train where he is right now."

"So what does that all mean, exactly, Olly?"

"Well that's clearly the dead-drop emergency protocol isn't it? The red bike against the phone box. He thinks we're on to him and he's letting his handlers know that his phone might be tapped and they're going to have to meet him at some prearranged spot. Maybe even institute the emergency exfiltration protocols, who knows?"

"This is bloody incredible. Johnny Dunbar is an informer for Special Branch, Terry Jones is a bloody Russian agent, what's Charles McCawley do in his spare time? Recruit for the fucking CIA? Jesus, Kat, did you have any normal clients, love?" I said out loud.

"Grown men who go out with fifteen-year-old girls aren't normal by definition," Crabbie muttered.

"Fair point mate. Right, Olly, so what's the next move? Keep monitoring the phone, 'round the clock surveillance, what?"

"None of that," Olly said. "We have to get him tonight. The torpedoes have hit the *Bismarck* and he's looking for a lifeboat. And we have to be that lifeboat, not the bloody Russkis."

# 22
# THE OLD "DEAD GIRL IN THE ABORTION CLINIC" NUMBER

Black Beemer leading convoy of two other vehicles along the Shore Road in the rain. In the first car there was me, Lawson and McCrabban. In the second car, an Audi, there were four MI5 agents from the base in Cultra: Olly and his mate and two women—all English. In the third car, a Jag, there were four Special Branch officers from the Metropolitan Police. It'll be my collar and I'll get first crack (actually fourth crack) at the interrogation, but MI5 and Special Branch were going to be doing the serious debrief.

Actually, I didn't give two shites about any of that. Unless the KGB had an alibi for him for December thirtieth, none of his fun and games mattered to me.

I was here for the girl.

Close up on the windscreen wipers of the Beemer. Dissolve through the windscreen to an annoyed Sean Duffy wondering how Knocknagallagh BMW could still not have fixed the wiper-streaking issue I'd left it in for. Didn't seem plausible now that they didn't have a replacement wiper. Paddy was pulling a fast one somehow.

I stopped the car outside Terry Jones' house. The other vehicles slid in behind me. My watch said 1.15 a.m.

I got out and walked over to Olly.

"Now?" I asked him.

"As good a time as any," he said.

"I'll need those warrants," I said.

He reached inside his overcoat and handed me an arrest warrant and a search warrant.

I read them to make sure everything was in order.

Everything was in order.

The Special Branch goons and one of the MI5 goons drew their guns.

"I don't think that'll be necessary, do you?" I said to Olly, looking at the weapons.

"Put the guns away, chaps, let's not spook Mr Jones, shall we?"

"If he's here and not on a slow boat to Minsk," I said.

"Geography's not your strong suit, is it, Sean?" Olly said before directing a couple of the coppers around the back to make sure Jonesy didn't make a bolt for it.

I waited until they were in position and rang the doorbell.

The light came on immediately upstairs which meant that he wasn't asleep. He came downstairs in a terrycloth dressing gown in a loser shade of brown. He looked through the frosted glass next to the front door and recognised my ugly mug.

"Inspector Duffy?" he said opening the front door. "Oh, and I see you've brought some friends."

"Apologies for the hour, Mr Jones. We don't normally conduct business at one in the morning if we can help it. But it was impressed upon me that this was a matter of some urgency."

Jones noticed Olly a couple of paces behind and his eyes blinked slowly and sank back in his head. He could see that the game was up, and his body sagged. He wobbled a little and I put my hand out to prevent him falling. After a beat or two he recovered himself and smiled.

"How many are there of you? I'll put the kettle on," he said.

"There's eleven of us all together. I'd like you to read these two warrants before you do anything else, if you don't mind," I said.

He reached in the pocket of his dressing gown and produced a pair of reading glasses. He gave the warrants a cursory look and handed them back to me.

"Am I under arrest then?" he asked.

"I'm placing you under arrest now, Mr Jones. You do not have to say anything, but it may harm your defence if you do not mention, when questioned, something which you later rely on in court. Anything you do say may be given in evidence. You have a right to a solicitor, and a solicitor must be provided to you upon request. I'm arresting you for the murder of Kat McAtamney and for offences committed under Section 1 of the Official Secrets Act 1989. I reserve the right to charge you with kidnapping, false imprisonment and offences under the Police and Criminal Evidence Act 1989 and the Treason Act of 1381."

Jones smiled broadly. "That has to be the first time you've arrested someone under the Treason Act of 1381."

"I don't see the funny side of this, Mr Jones. I'm arresting you for murdering a fifteen-year-old girl."

"Oh, I didn't do that! Never. I'd never harm anyone else!"

"You wouldn't send a group of gunmen to kill me and my colleagues in an abandoned building?"

"No, I would not! That was not my idea! And I'm very sorry that that happened. I'm so relieved that nobody got hurt."

"Whose idea was that?"

"Unless you want to handcuff me and drag me off to the station, let's go into the living room and have a cup of tea. The fire's on. I've kept it stoked all night. I had a feeling something like this, someone like you, might be coming by."

I looked at Olly. He shrugged. Mr Jones' living room, a raging fire and a cup of tea was definitely preferable to Carrick Police Station on the chilly seafront.

"McDermott, you go with Mr Jones to the kitchen and see he doesn't poison us. Right charlies we'd look if he slipped us all a mickey and got clean away."

McDermott went into the kitchen while Olly, Crabbie, Lawson and I sat in the living room. The other MI5 and Special Branch men and women began executing the search warrant. Searching for what I wasn't sure, but they were very professional about their task.

Jones came back with a china tea service, a simply enormous tea pot, twelve china tea cups and shortbread biscuits.

"Shall I be mother?" he said cheerfully. Lawson and Olly looked at him with suspicion, but Crabbie and I exchanged a look and nodded.

Easy to read now. Weight of the world off his shoulders. He was going to spill and spill big. I put my portable tape recorder on the desk. He'd spill again at the police station and for MI5, but the first time was always the best one for catching the emotional nuances.

He gave everyone tea, sat down opposite me and took a sip. I took a sip too—a nice bold Assam that went well with full-cream milk and shortbread.

"What would you like to know, first, Inspector Duffy?"

"Kat McAtamney."

"I have no idea who killed her. It wasn't me. I wouldn't do anything like that."

I put down my tea cup. "Mr Jones, you can't begin like this. It won't wash. You have to tell us the truth. You've wasted a great deal of our time already, not to mention the pain to Mrs—"

"I didn't kill her! I wouldn't. I have an alibi. I obviously couldn't mention it before, but I can now. On December thirtieth I was having dinner at the grill of the Abbey Hotel in Belfast with a . . . well, I don't want to give his name, actually . . ."

"Names if you please, sir," Olly said. "If he's a diplomat, there's nothing we can do to him."

"Oh, yes, of course. Well then, a Mr Andrei Bokorov. We dined until about eleven or so and then we went to Kelly's Cellars for the lock-in and then I had a few drinks at Andrei's house and then I got a taxi home. I got home well after three. Terribly drunk I'm afraid. The taxi driver will remember me. Since it was Andrei's money I gave him a big tip—twenty pounds, I think. He came from Mahoods Taxis. I think his name might have been Ron or Don. That exculpates me for most of that night, doesn't it? And I went into work the next morning."

"Possibly," I said. We didn't have a time of death for Kat or a time for the car going into the water, but it seemed unlikely that he could have killed Kat between three and first light, while drunk.

"Who is Mr Bokorov?"

"He's a cultural attaché, not from the Consulate here, but from the Embassy in Dublin."

"And by 'cultural attaché,' you mean?" Olly asked.

"Oh yes, of course, KGB."

"Is he your handler?" Olly asked.

"No. Not my immediate handler, no."

"Who is your handler?" Olly asked. "I really must insist, Mr Jones. If we're to come to any kind of arrangement."

"I expect you'll find it all out sooner or later anyway. Alexandra Bergen? Sasha, everyone calls her."

Olly shook his head. "I don't recognise that name. Is she with the Embassy?"

"No. Neither Embassy. Not Dublin or London. Came here in the sixties. She runs a ballet school near Stranmillis. Awful cliché, I know, but what can you do?"

"We can get into all that later," I said. "Are you quite sure that you have no idea who killed Kat?"

"None whatsoever. It wasn't me."

"What about your Soviet pals? Could they have abducted her?"

"Oh, good God, no. I couldn't let them know about her. Not after what happened last time."

"What happened last time?" Lawson asked.

He sighed and stared into the fire. "Well, of course, that's how I was recruited in the first place."

"Why don't you tell us exactly how that occurred, Mr Jones?" I said with a look to Crabbie and Lawson.

He nodded eagerly. "Yes, yes, I expect that's a good place to start. I was in Moscow at the British Embassy there. Oh, I should say that I took Russian and Slavonic languages at Cambridge."

"So did we all, mate," Olly said. "And look where we both are now."

"Well anyway, I joined the diplomatic service and eventually I ended up in Moscow. A taxi ran over my foot and I ended up going to the hospital."

"And you met a nurse?" Olly suggested.

"No, I was given a card from a lawyer who offered to sue the taxi company for me. Of course, the Embassy wouldn't allow me to do such a thing but I struck up a friendship with the lawyer and we . . . well at the time I thought we had fallen in love, I suppose . . . She was in her twenties and I was in my mid thirties. She got pregnant and we knew marriage was out of the question, so she asked me for the money for an abortion."

Olly slapped his forehead. "Oh fuck. You fell for the old 'dead girl in the abortion clinic' routine?"

"Uhm . . . yes. I suppose. I was in my flat when the police burst in asking if I knew this girl and showed me a picture of a woman dead, covered in blood. It was Anna, of course, and they told me that she had died during an illegal medical procedure and I was being arrested for murder. They threw me in a cell and explained that I was going to get life in prison. They let me think that for a day or two . . . Anna was dead, I had effectively killed her, I was facing public disgrace, ruin and life in a Russian gulag."

"And a man came to see you who said he could make all the problems go away. A man who, it turned out, worked for the KGB," Olly said.

"Well not exactly," Jones said sadly. "They sent me a friend of mine. Mercado, a diplomat from the Cuban delegation. He told me he could help me. He did help me."

Olly shook his head. "Your 'friend' Mercado was DGI—Cuban secret police—no doubt. They targeted you from the get-go, pal."

"Perhaps. He was a charming fellow. Used to say outrageous things about Castro."

"That's how they win your trust, mate. So what did this Mercado do?"

"He offered to help. He knew some people."

"And these people turned out to be KGB, which you realised far too late," Olly said.

Jones nodded.

"Hack work, and you fell for it," Olly muttered.

"What happened yesterday at the flats?" I asked.

"Oh, that? Well, after you came to see me the first time I had to tell Sasha about it. I'd never told her about Kat before then but now I had to tell her everything. She was furious, of course, that I had exposed myself. And then you just kept after me. After you interrogated me that final time I really thought you were onto me. You promised that you were "going to find out all my secrets". And I told Sasha that and she said that I wasn't to worry, that she would take care of everything."

"She contacted the Official IRA hit team?"

"I have no idea, but I suppose that could have been her idea of taking care of it."

"Did this Sasha kill Kat?"

"Definitely not. When I told her about your inquiry it was the first she'd heard of it."

"And just to be clear—you didn't do it either?" McCrabban asked.

"Absolutely not. I would never have harmed a hair on her head."

"Even if she threated to expose you as a Russian agent?"

"No. I would rather have turned myself in," he said firmly.

I looked him in the eye. What he was saying had the ring of truth about it all. He was unburdening himself with truth.

The tea was cold now.

I asked a few more questions, but I knew it wasn't him. I was wrong. He hadn't killed her. And he hadn't told the KGB about her and they hadn't killed her either.

I did what a good prosecutor does when the tide of the case turns under his feet. I thought it all through, had a mini conference with Olly and sat down in front of Jones again.

"I'm not going to arrest you for murder or kidnapping, Mr Jones. I don't think now that you did any of those things. You are guilty of statutory rape which is a serious offence and can have a penalty of up to five years in prison. However, on advice from the security services, we are going to seal that charge and turn your case over to them. Do you understand what I've said?"

"You're giving me to MI5."

"I should stress again, Mr Jones, that you do not have to say anything to them and anything that you do say may be given in evidence against you. You do still have a right to a lawyer."

"Oh I don't think it will come to that," Olly said. "Mr Jones and I are about to become fast friends."

And with that we left them to it. Jones was going to cooperate. He would either provide evidence against the network or, if he had more moxy than it appeared, they were going to run him as a double agent for a while.

"What now, sir?" Lawson asked as we stepped outside into the rain.

"Bed, I think, now, Lawson," I said with a long deep yawn.

"What now for the case, sir?"

"Nothing else for it, we've got to go see that wanker Charles McCawley again. Process of elimination. As unlikely as it seems, the bland, boring geography professor must have done it."

# 23
# THE DETECTIVE UP LATE

Even with MI5 men outside Mr Jones' house, you never knew, so I looked under the Beemer for bombs, didn't find any and got inside.

"Right, lads, home, you're first, Lawson. You're out in Downshire aren't you?"

"Yes, sir."

We drove to Downshire and I found the house Lawson shared with his dad near the nineteenth-century Gothic-looking Shields Institution.

Lawson opened the front door but didn't get out of the car. He turned to look at me. "What are you going to do after you leave off Sergeant McCrabban, sir?"

"I was going to go home to my bed and finally get some bloody sleep."

"I don't quite believe you, sir."

"Why not, Lawson?

"You've got that glint in your eye, sir. I think you're going out to see Mr McCawley now."

"At this time of night?"

"At this time of night."

Crabbie turned to look at me. "You're right, son. Put your seatbelt back on, lad. We're all going."

Rumbled by the pair of them.

Avoid playing poker with them for a while.

Out to the Lodge of Castle Hobbs.

"How are you going to do it, sir? We don't have any additional information."

"Other than the fact that we know he did it," I said.

"He probably did it," Lawson said. "It could have been another random client whose name wasn't in the book, as you well know, sir."

"That's right, complicate our lives, Lawson, why don't you?"

Doorbell.

Doorbell.

Doorbell.

"In answer to your question, Lawson, I'm going to go through the wife," I said. "I'm going to crack that ludicrous 'I heard him muttering' story of hers. Sensible woman like that protecting her adulterous murderous husband for no good reason at all."

Doorbell.

Doorbell.

Doorbell.

Two very angry faces.

"What is the meaning of this?" Charles McCawley said.

"The meaning? I wish I knew. If I could figure out the meanings of things I'd change my line of work. I'd go into philosophy. Meanings, I don't do. How and when and where and sometimes why is what I do. Can I come in, please?"

"No, you cannot, I'm calling the police," Carol McCawley said.

"We are the police."

"The real police."

"Mr McCawley, this should only take five minutes and after this you'll never hear from me again. I'm retiring tomorrow. You are my very last case."

"Five minutes?"

"Five minutes," I said.

Living room, dying embers in the fire, Mrs McCawley in a dressing gown and pyjamas. Mr McCawley in black jeans and a T-shirt. Working late as usual.

We sat on the sofa. No offer of tea.

"Shall I get right to it?" I asked.

"Please do so," McCawley said.

"We had two suspects in Katrina McAtamney's murder, both of whom have been eliminated in the last twenty-four hours. You're the only one left, Mr McCawley, and you don't have an alibi, so it has to be you."

"I didn't bloody do it! Your logic is faulty because I didn't bloody do it!" he said.

"He didn't do it because he has an alibi," Carol said. "I heard him reciting his speech the whole night. Going over the lines, walking around, I heard him!"

"Why defend him, Mrs McCawley, when you know that's not true? When you know he was having an affair behind your back. God knows how many affairs. With a child!"

"Now, that's not fair, Inspector Duffy, I didn't know she was fifteen. I've told you every single time that I thought she was eighteen."

I ignored him and turned back to his better half. "Mrs McCawley, I think you know more than you're saying. I think you waited for him to come home and he didn't come home. I think you saw his car arrive at three in the morning. I think he was wet and covered with mud and you asked him what had happened, and he said he'd had an accident or the car broke down. And you accepted that. But you knew the truth. You knew what he did. You knew he killed her. You know that you're living with a murderer!"

She shook her head and then stared to tear up. "No, it isn't true! None of that is true!"

"You're living with a murderer, but you don't want to upset your father and get cut out of his will so you're hushing it up. That's what Charles has already told us. You're better than this, Carol. You're an intelligent woman, you've been to university, you're learning to paint. You don't need him, you don't need your father's money. You don't need any of it."

She shook her head. "He didn't do it," she muttered.

"This is appalling behaviour. I'm calling my solicitor! I'm going to get you bloody sacked, mate," Mr McCawley said and went to the sideboard and picked up the telephone.

"He didn't do it, he didn't do it," she kept repeating over and over like a mantra.

I observed. He really didn't deserve her. The good wife, lying for him. Again. Lying for her husband even while their marriage collapsed and he had affairs with much younger women and they slept apart. Lying repeatedly to save her marriage. Look at her. Despite all his fucking bullshit, she still loved him. And what was up with that? Was he so bloody charming? Was he so smart? I didn't get it. Yes, he was handsome, but she could do so much better. Quickie divorce, wash that man right out of her hair, move on to pastures new.

Wait a minute, what was that?

Lying repeatedly to save her marriage . . .

And then, as the man in the circle in the church basement on a wet Thursday night is wont to say: I had a moment of clarity.

She loved him.

She actually loved him.

That was the key to the whole thing.

"Mr McCawley, can you come over here, please," I said. "I want you to read something."

"Fine. I've called my lawyer's office and they are contacting my solicitor right now. He'll be out here in half an hour and when he gets here, your career will be finished."

I took Mr Jones' search warrant from the pocket of my jacket. I showed them the words SEARCH WARRANT on the top of the letter below the seal. The actual address was in small print and I wasn't going to let them read that. It wasn't necessary. I wasn't actually going to do a search.

"Mrs McCawley, as your husband will attest, I have a search warrant for these premises and I'm going to have to go into your quarters," I said while Crabbie and Lawson looked at me in utter bafflement.

"Search away, I've got nothing to hide," she said.

"Oh, I think you do," I continued. I went into her bedroom and came out with a hairbrush sealed in an evidence bag.

"What are you doing with that?" she asked.

"We'll be taking this brush and comparing it to the hair sample we took from Katrina's car. The samples will match, won't they? And what possible explanation could there be for your hair to be in her car?"

Lawson's eyes widened for, in fact, of course, there were dozens of explanations for such an occurrence. Cross contamination from her husband's clothing being the most obvious one and the one any decent barrister would mention in court, but Lawson said nothing because he could see I was on a roll.

"You were in her car that night. You were her passenger. You hijacked her at gunpoint and forced to drive to the River Bann. You told her if she got out of the car you'd shoot her. I'm sure your father has an old Luger or pistol around the main house that you took. *You* did it, didn't you?"

"How dare you, you can't—" Mr McCawley began, but Crabbie put his fingers to his lips and Mr McCawley shut up under the weight of Crabbie's moral authority.

"You forced her to sit there in the driver's seat while you put the clutch in neutral and pushed her car into the water. You did it. And we can prove it. The hair sample and the boot prints in the mud where you pushed the vehicle. You threw away the gun, but you didn't throw away your Wellington boots. I've seen you in those boots, and the prints will match the cast we took from the river. And then there's that taxi ride home from the Bann. Maybe not that night. Maybe you drove your car up there that afternoon and got a taxi back to Carrickfergus. But either way one of the drivers from the taxi companies will remember your photograph. It'll take some legwork, but we'll get there in the end. DNA evidence, forensic boot-print evidence, the lack of an alibi and finally eyewitness testimony from a cabbie. That coupled with motive should be enough to convince a jury that the highborn Lord Lieutenant's daughter murdered a penniless tinker girl."

Charles looked at his wife in astonishment.

He knew too, now, of course. "D-don't say anything darling. You don't have to say anything."

"No, you don't, and anything you do say may be taken down and used against you," I said.

She shook her head. "I'm not going to say anything. I'm no fool."

"Lawson, see if you can find those boots. They should be out in the mud room there."

Lawson came back with a pair of Wellington Boots that looked, in fact, very similar to the size of the ones we needed.

"The DNA on the hairbrush will match the hair we found in the car, won't it?" I said.

"Hmmm," she said.

"The boot prints will match too, won't they?"

She gave a tiny nod of the head and with her lips tightly shut she said another little "hmmmm."

I took my tape recorder out of my pocket, pressed record and put it on the coffee table. I stated my name and gave the date, time and the names of the other people in the room.

"I'm not saying anything!" Carol insisted.

"But you do admit that you were in Kat's car? You admit that much? Maybe you didn't kill her, but you were in her car?"

"Don't say anything until—" Charles attempted, but it was too late.

"All right," she said.

"All right what?"

"I was in her car. That doesn't prove I killed her."

"Did you just want to talk to her?"

Charles got up and began to protest, but I motioned for him to sit down again. Things were delicately balanced now. "Maybe you should go outside and wait for that lawyer," I said.

"No fear, I'm keeping an eye on you, you bloody bounder!" he said.

"Carol, you were in her car, but the talking didn't work, did it? She just wouldn't listen, would she? She wouldn't leave your husband alone. A fifteen-year-old streetwalker talking to you like that?"

Carol's dark eyes flashed. "Exactly! Who did she think she was?"

"When the talking didn't work, you forced her to drive to Bally-money on the Bann on the night of December thirtieth, didn't you? You'd planned it all out, hadn't you? Meticulously. Brilliantly. It was your plan B. If you couldn't convince the little slut, you were going to have to kill her."

"Yes," Carol said.

"It was fool proof wasn't it? You wore gloves the whole time so no prints, you chose where on the river there would be no witnesses and where the car would sink like a stone. You'd stashed your own car nearby so you could get home easily. Such a well-executed plan. One of the best we'd ever seen, isn't that right, Sergeant McCrabban?"

"Oh, yes, one of the best plans I've ever seen," he agreed.

"Me too," Lawson said.

"She just vanishes off the face of the Earth. Charles has no idea you've killed her. She just vanishes and that's the end of that problem, isn't it?"

"Yes," she said.

"Because you really do love him, don't you?"

"I do," she said. "The last man I'll ever love. Did we ever tell you where we met?"

"No. I don't think so."

"We met at the ballroom dancing club at Queens. That was the way shy people could meet other shy people in those days. Damaged people too. You won't believe it, but I've been married before. To an absolute cad who beat me. Dancing! Ha, we were both so useless. I bumped into him on the floor. Knocked him and his partner over. Poor love. The least I could do was agree to go for a cup of tea with him."

"You got a gun, didn't you? Or a replica?" I asked.

"Replica! No! I used a real gun. What if she'd tried to fight me?"

"Would you have shot her?"

"Of course! I didn't need to, but I would have. I knew the river would do the job for me up there. My father used to take me fly fishing on that part of the Bann. He told me about a fisherman who fell in and was carried out to the Atlantic on the flood tide. They found his body on Arran Island in Scotland. It's a pity about the hair and the boot print.

I should have worn a head scarf, but those things have always made me claustrophobic."

It was clear to me that all of this was news to Charles McCawley. He had no idea whatsoever that his wife had done this, and he was horrified. The next step was not so clear. In a normal case when the accused starts to talk, you get them down the station to make a statement. They sign the statement and that's that. They are hamster jam. The best they can do is plead guilty and throw themselves on the mercy of the court. But not with this lady, the daughter of the Lord Lieutenant of County Antrim, probably a distant relative of the bloody Queen of England. How to proceed here? If we got her dressed and took her down the station and she made a full confession I could see a clever lawyer getting the statement thrown out because his client had been railroaded . . .

Hmm, tricky one. I thought about it for a moment or two and made a decision. Make the whole thing seem straightforward and easy.

I got to my feet and forced a grin. I picked up the portable tape recorder and put it in my pocket.

"Well, Mr McCawley, Mrs McCawley, obviously in light of this confession and with our other evidence we're going to want you to come down to the station to make a full statement. I suggest that you bring your solicitor with you. He'll know what to do. Shall we say ten o'clock? Maybe a little later?"

Carol seemed in a daze now. "What?"

"Ten o'clock. Or is that too early?"

"Oh, no, that will be fine. Charles, is that all right?"

"Yes," he said, shell-shocked. "We can manage that."

"We'll make a formal arrest then, and I'm afraid we will have to take you into custody," I continued.

"Oh, no!" Charles said.

"There will be a bail hearing, but I don't think you're a flight risk, are you?"

"No," Carol said.

"So you can tell your solicitor I won't oppose bail. Which means if we can get this over fairly quickly you'll be out by tomorrow afternoon. Does that sound fair enough?"

Carol looked at me gratefully. "Yes, that sounds very fair. Doesn't it, Charles?"

"Indeed."

"We'll cooperate fully. It would be nice to get this over with. I'm seeing Mr Smith for an art lesson at four. Do you think we could get it all done by four o'clock, Mr Duffy?"

"I'm sure we can," I said reassuringly.

I shook Charles' hand and then her hand to add to the chummy atmosphere.

"Remember, ten o'clock then, please."

"Should I pack an overnight bag?" Carol said still somewhat out of it.

"No, like I say, if we continue to get your full assistance we will not oppose bail."

"Thank you very much, inspector," Carol said. "You will get my full assistance. To be honest, I'll be glad to get all of this off my chest. I mean it's a rather beastly thing to do when you think about it, isn't it? Drowning a girl in a river?"

A final round of handshakes with the murderess and her husband and out to the car.

"Wasn't expecting that turn of events," Lawson said in the chilly, damp, January air.

"Nor I when I first got there. Better get a rush on that DNA sample and those boot prints. God knows if they'll match, but hopefully we won't have to use them if she makes a full statement."

"Do you think they'll make a statement?"

"Yeah I do. Either that or fly to South Africa and hide in that bloody diamond mine."

# 24
# CLOSING THE BOOK ON DI DUFFY'S LAST CASE

She made a full statement. Her solicitor was not the competent little local man we had met before, but a bigwig called Ernie Hitchens from the Belfast office of a London commercial firm called Slaughter and May. He was a very experienced solicitor and clearly had done business for the McCawleys for years. A friend of the family he was, however, more of a trusts, contracts and conveyancing guy and it was obvious to us that he hadn't done criminal work in some time. He was quite the wrong person to represent her at the statement stage. Maybe the other guy had been unavailable or wasn't a classy enough dude?

It was a shame.

For them.

A grasping Belfast hack lawyer who represented a lot of Loyalist and Republican terrorists and was used to the police ways would have had her come in and deny, deny, deny. He would have looked at the DNA, eyewitness testimony and forensic evidence and seen it was a crock and he would have dismissed her tape-recording from the night before as the ramblings of a half-awake woman being harassed by the fascist peelers.

Fifty-fifty a jury would have gotten her off and the DPP might have been so worried about an acquittal he'd have offered her manslaughter instead of murder . . .

But that's not what happened.

We were very polite and courteous to the McCawleys and Mr Hitchens, and we stressed to him that if we could get this wrapped up quickly Mrs McCawley could be out by the afternoon, which seemed to be very important to her. Hitchens could see that this was what the McCawleys wanted, so he urged their full cooperation.

She made a detailed statement and a full confession. She talked about stalking Kat's caravan, lying in wait, finding her grandfather's old World War I revolver, formulating the drowning plan and leaving her own car in a lay-by near the river to get her home again after the event. She hadn't, in fact, taken a taxi after she had hidden her car. She had walked to Ballymoney and taken the bus. She waited out near the power station for Kat and when she saw her get in the car, she simply got in beside her and told her to drive. There was little that we hadn't sussed out or guessed at.

We passed the file to the DPP's office, and as it was a murder case, a space was made at the Belfast Central Criminal Court immediately for the preliminary hearing. Mrs McCawley informed the judge that she intended to enter a plea of guilty. I told the judge that the RUC would not oppose bail and the DPP asked for a nominal sum of one hundred pounds.

By the afternoon her guilty plea had been recorded, the bail had been set and paid, Mrs McCawley had been released and for us, the police, the case was over.

We were exhausted.

It had been a hell of a seventy-two hours, and I was desperate to get back to Scotland and the fam.

But not yet. Not quite yet.

I had to babysit John Strong for his meet. When was that? What day was it?

"What day is it?" I asked Crabbie as we drove home from the court.

"It's Wednesday I think," he said.

"Wednesday? Crap on it. I have a job to do tomorrow morning, but Thursday afternoon I'll finish up all paperwork on all the pending cases.

I'll talk to the Chief Inspector and Superintendent Crick on Friday and I guess that's that."

Crabbie nodded. That schedule would work nicely for him too. I turned to Lawson. "What do you say, lad? Do you want to take the weekend off and come on in on Monday morning ready to run Carrick CID?"

Lawson was momentarily stunned. "On Monday? This Monday?"

"Yup."

He gulped. "And you, sir?"

"I'll go to Scotland, join the part-time reserve and come in my seven days a month until I get my bloody pension."

"But, but, I'll see you around the office?" Lawson said.

"Yeah, of course. It'll be *your* office though, son. I can't be a detective anymore, not in the part-timers. You'll have to get yourself a good lead DC. I think Warren shows a lot of promise."

"Warren?"

"Yes, Warren, I like her. Keeps a cool head. Smart," Crabbie agreed.

"And I can consult with both of you if I need to?" Lawson said.

"Of course! Call me day or night, well maybe not night, but call me during the day and I'll always give you my take," I said. "We're not dying and we're not moving to the Costa del Sol. You'll see us both around. We'll be like Banquo's fucking ghost. You'll be desperate to get rid of us."

"I don't think that will ever happen," Lawson said.

"*On verra*, lad. *On verra.*"

Back to the station. Shower. Shave. Change of clothes. Suit, tie, sensible shoes.

"Right boys, the final part of the gig and it's the DPP's responsibility from here on in."

"What's the final part of the gig?" Lawson asked.

"We notify the next of kin that we've got a suspect under arrest. And that's it, we're out."

Lawson looked half dead, but Crabbie seemed up for it.

"You can stay here, Alex. Get a kip on the sofa in my office if you want. Lock the door from the inside so the Chief Inspector doesn't barge in on you."

"Thank you, sir."

"You'll come with me, Crabbie?"

"Of course, Sean."

We drove to the caravan site near the power station. The drizzle had stopped and the field was full of kids playing tag and football and hop-scotch. Men were mending machines and feeding the horses and women were hanging and chatting and keeping an eye on the kids.

Mrs McAtamney was not among the chatting women and she wasn't in when we knocked her caravan door.

"Who is it?" one of her weans asked.

"It's the police," I said.

The door open and a freckle-faced girl about nine years old peeked out. "What do you want?"

"We want to talk to your mother, love," I said.

"She's not here at the moment," the girl said.

"Well can we come in and wait? It's rather important," I said.

"You should let them in. Ma'll be all cross-like if you don't let them in and give them a cup of tea!" a younger voice said from inside the caravan.

"Would you like to come in and have a cup of tea?" the girl asked.

"That would be nice," I said.

We went inside. Mrs McAtamney had made an attempt to tidy the place up since we were last here. A new yellow bedspread on the sofa, a surprisingly expensive-looking Persian rug on the floor, two new post-cards blu-tacked to the tin wall: one of Ballintoy Harbour, the other of Uisneach Hill down in County Westmeath. She had taken the clothes off the floor, scrubbed the stove and aired the place out. She was making an effort, at least, and you couldn't fault her for that.

There were two other girls lying on the fold-out bed playing Op-eration.

"Are youse the peelers again?" one of them asked.

"We are."

"None of them horses are stolen. Just so you know," the little girl said.

"That is good to know," I said.

"When's your mother going to be back?" Crabbie asked.

"She went shopping in Belfast," the stolen-horses girl said.

"When did she leave?" Crabbie asked.

"This morning."

I watched out of the corner of my eye while the first little girl made the tea by putting a tea bag she had fished out of the sink in a mug and filling that mug with hot water, milk and sugar.

I stood up. "You know what, maybe we'll come back another time. I'm going to leave a note for your mother. Make sure she gets it. I'm going to leave my card with my phone number on it. She can call me when she gets home. She can call me there if I'm not in the office."

I scribbled a quick note: "Mrs McAtamney, I just wanted to let you know that we have arrested a suspect in connection with Kat's disappearance. If you wish to discuss this further with me, please don't hesitate to give me a call, anytime."

I drove us back to the station and went to see the Chief Inspector.

"Come in!" he said. "Ah, Sean, rumour has it you've made some progress with Duffy's Last Case?"

Blah, blah, blah. Yeah mate, it's all fine, it's sorted. Wiping the whiteboard, going out on a win.

Barely keeping my eyes open.

Chief Inspector out.

Door knock.

Kenny Dalziel in.

"Duffy, we've had our differences over the years but . . ."

I gave him a hug. "I'll miss you brother, even you," I said.

The hug freaked him out and he skedaddled.

I called home and checked on wife, kid, cat. All three doing well. House cold but fine, neighbours friendly enough. All you have to do is punch one neighbour in the fucking face and the rest will fall in line.

Two more phone calls.

"Duffy you haven't forgotten the meet tomorrow, have you?" It was Olly.

"No, I haven't forgotten."

"Nine o'clock, which means we'll all have to get up about five if we want to get in position before they do! It's absurd. You wouldn't believe the day I had. I'm exhausted."

"You and me both, Olly."

"Ha! I don't believe that for a moment. You probably took a sicky while I spent the night and much of today debriefing you-know-who. All right, well, don't be late. You know the layout and you know how to get there, don't you? Unless you want a lift? Do you want a lift?"

"No. I don't. I'll see you tomorrow."

Second phone call was more unexpected. Janice O'Leary from the DPP's office. Hadn't talked to her for years.

"Hey Jan, what's up?"

"That case you sent over today. Whoa, Sean, you got lucky. A confession. I looked at your evidence, you had nothing."

"Don't I know it."

"Do you know who her father is?"

"I do."

"He's in Australia at the moment. When he gets home, we expect to have the full tidal force of the law turned against us. Whole teams of solicitors and barristers from all over the UK and Ireland."

"Your problem, Janice, not mine. I just deliver them to you, it's your job to get them prosecuted."

"Well, anyway, that's not what I wanted to talk to you about."

"What then?"

"Mrs Carol McCawley, nee Miss Carol Hobbs. I was looking through the sealed records earlier today."

"Yes?"

"Old case you might be interested in."

"Go on."

"1979. Carol's at boarding school in England. She comes home for the Christmas holidays. She and her friend Millie go for a walk in Tollymore Forest. Starts to snow. The friends get lost and separated. Carol gets out, but Millie isn't found until a week later at the bottom of an embankment with her head smashed in. She slipped and fell, say the sealed records. Here's the thing, there were rumours at the time that they both liked the same boy. Poor Millie cops it and Carol marries the boy a year later."

"So now you're thinking Carol's a psychopath?" I said sceptically.

"I didn't say that. The marriage broke up. The boy was allegedly a fortune hunter, but he made some extraordinary claims before the divorce lawyers got him to shut his mouth."

"What sort of claims?"

"Says Carol attacked him with a hammer and a knife and pointed a gun at him twice."

"I don't know, Janice, sounds a bit *Madwoman in the Attic* to me," I said.

"Not to me. Her second marriage ended when she drove her car into her husband's motorcycle. With him on it. Not hurt. Hushed up. But you see what I mean? She has form, Sean, let's hope her dad's fancy lawyers don't get her off again, eh?"

Back to Coronation Road in the rain.

I was beat, but I stayed up until eleven on the off chance that Mrs McAtamney would call.

She didn't and, weary beyond belief, I set the alarm for five in the morning and went to bed.

# 25

# THE MEET

Troubled night's sleep. Worry about the case falling apart. Worry about what was going to happen today and deeper down that intangible nagging little feeling that I'd missed something.

Had I missed something?

Nah, full and complete statement and the lass is a nutter—Janice said so. She did it. She bloody it. And if a card-sharping lawyer gets her off it'll be the DPP's fault, not mine. What more do you want, for heaven's sake? We've got her on tape and her signature at the bottom of a note saying she done it.

Downstairs to the freezing-cold kitchen floor. Kettle on. Stare into the bitter frosty darkness of the back garden.

Coffee, slice of toast, dress in jeans, boots, jumper. Check my guns, put on a woolly hat and a parka. Out to the Beemer. Look under for bombs. Nothing. Nowt. *Aut Caesar aut nihil.*

Key in ignition. Heater on. Radio on.

Radio 3 playing something I didn't know. I mean, obviously it was by Haydn, but exactly what I had no idea. A later concerto.

The mystery kept me going until I lost the Radio 3 signal up near Strabane.

Strabane to the border.

Army squaddies from the parachute regiment manning the checkpoint. Supposed to be on the same side as me, but I could never love a para. Why? My dad and I were in Derry on the night of Bloody Sunday. Is that reason enough for you?

"Where are you going this time of the morning?" the squaddie asked in a flat Lancashire accent.

"That's none of your business," I said and hesitated a beat or two before I showed him my warrant card.

Over the border.

Strabane to Killygordon to Drumkeen through the ever-heavier rain.

I unfolded the map I'd been given and drove to the OP which was a tiny cottage about half a mile from the meet house, an old Manse on the top of the hill. I parked the Beemer and got out. The MI5 team were huddled in the living room attempting to light the peat briquettes with matches.

"Sean! Thank God you're here!" Olly said.

Handshakes all round. Three agents I had never met before. Zoe, Sarah and a skinny bloke named Nate. None of them looked like heavies.

"Where's the SAS?" I asked.

"What SAS?" Olly asked.

"In case we have to get Strong out of there fast," I said.

"We won't. This is a standard meet. There's no problem," Olly said.

"Where is Strong?" I asked.

"I had to send him over. I didn't want anyone to see him coming from here, so I sent him around the long way."

"I thought he wanted to see me."

"I told him you were on the way. He knows you are going to be here, and it made him feel better. Here, have a cup of tea."

I sat down by the fireplace and showed them how to get a peat-log fire lit. Firelighters, kindling, then the peat.

I sat by the window and looked at my watch. Through the binoculars I could see John Strong's car parked outside. That fucking yellow Bentley, of all things.

I looked at my watch again. An hour to go.

"What's he doing over there?" I asked Olly.

"He brought a book to read," Zoe said.

"What book?"

"A book on golf, I think," she said.

I stared through the glass. "We should have a bloody exit team to get him out," I muttered to Olly.

"If it were so easy to assemble these teams of yours, I'd do it every time, Sean," Olly said defensively. "But it's not easy. You have to go through the MOD and it's a real nightmare. They're very protective of their assets. Less than twenty blades at any one time in Northern Ireland. You have to go all the way to the Secretary of State to get 'em."

"Speaking of the Secretary of State. How's our boy? Mr Jones?"

"He's singing like a canary. I love him. I wish they all were like him. We're happy. He's happy. He looks ten years younger."

"Are you going to double him?" I asked.

Olly shrugged. "Not sure. That'll be decided at a higher level. I certainly won't be running him if we do. I've got enough on my plate."

"You'll sort out the angle with my team though, won't you? I don't want any more hassle from those pacifists in the Official IRA."

"You've got your suspect and you've charged her. The KGB and their proxies know you're not pursuing Mr Jones anymore. They won't give a shit about you now."

I sipped the cold tea and stared through the glass. Between us and the Manse was a boggy field, what looked to be a steam and then a little slopey field full of sheep.

I turned to Olly again. "How do you think this is going to go today?"

"Fine."

"Strong's nervous about this one."

"He's paranoid."

"He's right to be paranoid."

"He's right to be cautious, he's wrong to be paranoid."

I yawned and leaned my head against the cold glass window pane.

"You looked tired, Sean," Olly said.

"I feel tired. It's been nonstop."

"Tough week?"

"It's been nonstop since about 1975."

"Vehicle approaching the meet point!" Zoe said. Five sets of binoculars turned to look at the house. There was a tan-coloured Volvo 240 coming from the northwest. Two men inside. One was a little man wearing a big black anorak, so he looked a little like Paul Simon on the cover of the first Paul Simon solo album. The other was a red beardy bloke in a sheepskin jacket.

"Recognise either of these two?" I asked.

Silence.

"Olly?"

"Never seen them before," he said.

"Who is John supposed to be meeting?"

"***** ******," he said.

"Well, that's not him."

"No."

"The one with the sheepskin coat is a Trevor McGurk. He's IRA internal security. Nutting Squad," Zoe said looking up from a ring binder full of names and faces. "Don't know who the other one is."

"Maybe we should get over there," I said.

"And do what? Blow the game? He's on a wire. We'll listen in."

To my left on the table, Nate was listening to a radio connected to a tape recorder on a set of headphones. The men went inside the house.

"Can we hear what they're saying too?" I asked Olly.

"We'll listen on the speakers," Olly said and flipped a switch.

John Strong's voice boomed into life. He sounded scared: "Where are you getting this from?"

"I've been doing a bit of research," McGurk was saying (or so we found out later).

"On your own?"

"On my own. If you've got suspicions you pass them up the chain of command. You know how it works. No lone wolves. But I wanted to talk to you about it first, John. Nice wee chat, eh? Shall I introduce my friend here? This is Charlie Feeney. Wee man. Wee hard man though. He doesn't speak much. He just does. Show him what you do, Charlie."

There was a slap and a yelp.

"Show him again, Charlie."

A punch and a scream.

"Now you're going to talk to me, John. And if I'm satisfied, we'll just forget this ever happened, eh? No need for you to tell ***** or ********. No need for me to bring it up, either."

"You've lost your mind, Trevor. They'll kill you for this. You and your mate," Strong said.

"No, no one's going to be killed. Except maybe you. You'll keep your fucking mouth shut. This is just a wee chat between friends. Savvy?"

Another punch from Charlie, another groan from Strong.

"Ready to talk?" Trevor asked.

"What do you want to know?" Strong asked.

"I want to know what happened at that Courtaulds factory in Carrickfergus that time. I want to know why the nature of the intelligence you've been giving us since then has not been of such high quality despite your fucking promotion to Assistant Chief Constable. What I really want to know is whether you are a fucking double agent or not. And if you are a traitor, I wanna know for how long this has been going on."

"I'm not a traitor. I was recruited by Harry Selden ten years ago and I've been loyal ever since."

"Mad fucking Harry Selden. The late, great, mad fucking Harry Selden. What happened to him at the factory? I want to know that too."

"I don't know what happened to him. He got a bee in his bonnet about a CID team from Carrickfergus and wanted to wipe them out. Nothing to do with me. He squibbed it and got himself killed by the Special Branch."

"Nothing to do with you?"

"Nothing to do with me."

"You weren't there that night?"

"You know I wasn't there. Harry wouldn't be so stupid to jeopardise me and my position in his personnel vendettas. He knew I was a prize asset. Until Harry got himself killed, I used to be treated with a bit more respect around here," John Strong said, getting aggressive now, which I liked. Putting McGurk on the defensive. That was the way to do it. Make McGurk feel that he had fucked up.

"All right. We'll let that one go for now. Now the other thing that's bugging me. You're an Assistant Chief Constable now, John. Assistant Chief Constable! You are privy to information at the highest levels. Where is this fucking highest-level information? You've been giving us nothing but penny-ante shite for the last year."

I turned to Olly. "I keep bloody telling you that, John has to give them more than he's been giving them."

"I agree. It's not me, it's upstairs that authorises that stuff. They're tight with their operational intelligence," Olly protested.

"I'm not privy to every bloody decision the Chief Constable makes. It doesn't work like that. We're all in our own operational commands. I only get access to stuff that comes across my desk," Strong protested.

There was a long silence before McGurk cleared his throat. "No. I don't think so," McGurk said.

"What don't you think?" Strong asked.

"I look in your eyes today and I see someone who is terrified. I think you *were* working for us. But something happened at the factory. After Harry got killed. I think they looked into Harry and you and somebody in MI5 put two and two together and they brought you in for questioning and you fucking cracked and made a deal to keep your sorry arse out of prison. And for the last year, you've been giving us chicken feed and picking up info from ***** and ****** and feeding those scraps back to British Intelligence. That's what I think."

"That's utter bollocks," Strong said.

"We'll see. Maybe I'm wrong and we'll just let bygones be bygones. Charlie, strip and tie him to the chair."

"If he touches me again, I'll report both of you," Strong said.

"Take your shirt off, John," McGurk said.

"No."

"Take it off or I'll blow your fucking head off."

Another long silence and then what sounded like a gasp and the transmission went dead.

"We've lost the connection," Nate said.

I got to my feet. "They've found the wire!" I yelled.

Olly nodded. "Either that or it's shorted out," he said.

"What's the matter with you, Olly? Can't you see everything's gone to shit? They're going to kill the stupid bastard."

"Yes, I think they might. If they've found the wire . . . and there's damn all we can do about it."

There were a lot of reasons not to save John Strong's life. He was a bloody traitor for one. He was responsible for the deaths of God knows how many coppers and other members of the security forces for two. And then there was the fact that he actually wasn't a very nice man.

But he was our asset. And our responsibility. And you don't let one of your assets get tortured to death.

"I'm just a part-timer here, so excuse me for telling you your fucking job, but you don't let one of your assets get killed on your watch, do you? Word gets out and it's bad for fucking morale."

I looked at Sarah and Zoe for support, but they weren't leaping to my defence anytime soon.

"They're going to kill him," I yelled.

Oliver nodded. "This is what happens sometimes."

"And what do we do?"

"Nothing. We'd need specialists to go and do a removal like that. And the nearest specialist unit, I believe, is at Bessbrook. Bessbrook, is that right, Zoe?"

"Bessbrook, yes," she said.

Oliver turned to me. "Blades from D Squadron at this hour of the day. Even if we could round up half a dozen men, it would take them an hour to get their shit together and chopper to Strabane and sneak over the border and by then it'll be too late, won't it?"

"So what do we do?"

"What we're paid to do. Observe, record and report."

"I'm going over there now. Is anyone going to help me?"

Silence.

Fuck.

Olly got to his feet. "I urge you strongly not to go, Sean. We are not authorised to—"

I ran out of the hut onto the bog.

# 26
# A SHORT FILM ABOUT KILLING

Mist in the sloping sheep field somewhere in the Blue Stack Mountains of Southern Donegal. Mist rolling down from the ash, oak and hazel wood. Mist among the cottongrass and in the bog myrtle and in the heather.

Running through the mist, up the hill, to save a man who should not be saved.

Running, breathing hard, in the fog and rain.

Running, as in dreams, with feet barely touching the ground. Noticing everything. The curlew, lapwing, red grouse. The fairy flax, kidney vetch, mouseear, hawkweed, milkwort, harebell.

The last wolves in Ireland ran up these hills towards those mountains. And before them, the last hyenas in Ireland and the last lions too.

Men in those times lived by killing.

As do men today.

Running over the wet bog. Through the sheep shit and the tuft grass and pools of water. The Manse looming larger.

"Breathe, Duffy, breathe."

Fitter than I was last year.

Lungs are stronger.

I remove the Glock from the shoulder holster, the pistol from my pocket. Moving fast now but absolutely still. Low to the ground. Loping like that hyena or like Groucho Marx. The sheeps know only one thing: run from predators. They run. Like silly sentient clouds in the bigger cloud of mist.

Closer.

Closer.

Arm tensed. Safety off. Arse clenched.

Wipe rain from eyes with back of hand.

The house's side door is opening.

Have they seen me?

Shake rain from weapons.

Brace myself for—

*THOCK-THOCK-THOCK-THOCK-THOCK-THOCK-THOCK-THOCK-THOCK-THOCK.*

AK-47 on full auto firing at me.

Am I supposed to be impressed?

Third time this week, lads. And the second was in an enclosed space where the noise could really fucking resonate.

*THOCK-THOCK-THOCK-THOCK-THOCK-THOCK-THOCK-THOCK-THOCK-THOCK.*

A ewe five metres to my right kopping it.

Up the hill.

Zig to the left.

Running sheep, gunfire, yelling.

No gunfire or yelling from me.

Not yet. Not close enough yet.

*THOCK-THOCK-THOCK-THOCK-THOCK-THOCK-THOCK-THOCK-THOCK-THOCK.*

The AK churning up the earth twenty feet in front of me. More carnage among the flock.

Zig to the left again and keep running.

Running as in dreams, over the bog weed and the sheep shit and the bullet divots, over the sinuous grass, over the forgiving curve of planet Earth.

*THOCK-THOCK-THOCK.*

At the low stone wall in front of the Manse now.

Both men have come out to kill me.

Charlie reloading the AK, McGurk shooting at me with a pistol.

I vault the wall, clip the top of it, fall, hit the ground, *hard*, roll, get up and shoot McGurk three times in the chest with the 9 mm. Charlie finishes reloading the AK. I roll again in the beautiful greensward and coolly observe wee Charlie shooting at the position I had been at two seconds earlier.

*THOCK-THOCK-THOCK*, goes the AK on full auto, the weapon rising so high the silly man might have been aiming at the Space Shuttle.

"Drop your gun!" I scream, and he turns and keeps on firing and keeps on firing as the Glock sends death into his throat and left cheek and left temple.

I run into the house and find my agent on the floor, beaten but alive.

I put him in the recovery position and pour myself a glass of water.

I drink it and drink another and take deep breaths and give John Strong a cup of water and untie him from the chair.

"Thank God, Duffy, thank God you—"

I go back outside to check on the two IRA men but they're long dead, absorbed already into the mystery. I close their eyes and mutter a prayer for the pair of them: "*Dimitte nobis debita nostra, libera nos ab igne inferni, conduc in caelum omnes animas, praesertim illas quae maxime indigent misericordia tua.*"

I look at the dead men and sigh.

Forget Duffy the poet, forget Duffy the intellectual, forget Duffy the music lover, none of that is the real me.

The real me is Duffy the thug.

Duffy the killer.

He's good at it.

He enjoys it.

I spit in disgust.

When Olly arrives, I tell him and Strong that I am taking my leave.

"Where are you going?" Olly says.

"Home."

"What about all this?" he asks.

"Do your job, pal. Sort it."

# 27
# THE POSTCARDS

Back to the border, back to Northern Ireland, back to Coronation Road.

A bath and a pint glass vodka gimlet.

I fall asleep in the tub listening to Toru Takemitsu's score for *Ran*.

Ringing phone that I let ring and ring.

Sleep.

Deep, deep down the mine this time.

A hollow where the dreams and the half truths and the forgotten things lay slumbering like old Gods. I drifted idly on the underground inland sea. A sea without edge and smelling of cut grass. Sentient like the sea on Solaris.

The sea washes me up on the Ail na Míreann.

I wake in the cold water.

In Irish mythology, the Ail na Míreann or "stone of divisions" is said to be the omphalos, or mystical spot, at the centre of Ireland, the place that marks the meeting point of the borders of Leinster, Munster, Connacht, Ulster and Meath. The stone of divisions lies on the Uisneach Hill. Bealtaine fires were lit and Druidical ceremonies held on this hill and it is sacred to the Traveller people and the Pavee people.

I get out of the bath, towel, pulled on jeans, a T-shirt, a jumper, DMs and a coat. I get my car keys and money and go out to the Beemer.

I look underneath it for bombs and drive out to the campsite near Kilroot Power Station. I'm lucky, for almost everybody is away at a horse fair on Islandmagee.

I find the McAtamney caravan. Mrs McAtamney isn't home, but there are two girls in there watching TV. Different kids from last time. A little bit younger.

"Who are you?" one of them asks.

I take the two new postcards off the wall and give the kids a five-pound note each.

"Is Kat your sister?" I ask the older girl.

"Her sister, my cousin."

I remember the swim cap in Kat's caravan.

"Here's a weird question for you. You don't happen to know if Kat was a good swimmer, do you? I never thought to ask."

"Kat? You should see her swim, mister. Swims like a fish, she does. She won a competition for it in France. Two years in a row."

"Thanks," I say and put my finger to my lips. "I wasn't here."

I go to the Beemer, look underneath it, get inside and read the postcards.

Funnily enough they say almost exactly what I think they are going to say.

The first, a picture of Ballintoy Harbour is addressed to E. McAtamney, Kilroot Caravan Park, Carrickfergus. It says simply: "Hope you're keeping well down there. All good up here. Sent her on her way," with an amazing number of spelling mistakes in so small an assemblage of words. The postcard is signed: "Uncle Cecil."

The second is a picture of the Stone of Divisions on the Uisneach Hill. It is addressed to the McAtamneys, Kilroot Caravan Park, Carrickfergus.

It says: "I'm ok."

I drive up the A2 coast road to Ballintoy.

Near Cushendun the gorse is on fire from what was said to be a poteen still that had been destroyed by the Excise.

Revenue men. What did they know about police work?

Red sky, blue sea, black smoke.

Ballintoy Harbour is white and crisp and safely huddled under the swell of the Atlantic.

Mr Cecil is sitting outside his caravan in a deck chair. It's freezing, but he doesn't seem to mind. His horses are gone, sold presumably, but there are still the goats, dogs, cars and cats.

I slew the Beemer into the muddy spread in front of his caravan.

I kill the engine and get out.

"Inspector Duffy," he says.

"That's right. You don't seem surprised to see me."

"No, I had a feeling you'd be back at some point."

"Why was that?"

"Oh, no reason, just a feeling."

"I brought you some of that holy water I was talking about."

"Oh?"

There's another deck chair next to his, both chairs bathing in beams of chilly sunlight.

"Mind if I sit?" I ask him.

"Free country," he replies.

"Here's the holy water," I say and gave him the bottle.

"From the River Jordan?" he asks, sceptically.

"Indeed."

I let the silence percolate for a few beats and then a few more beats. The silence is lovely. Sail boats struggle through the deep blue Atlantic at the bottom of the field. A goat nuzzles at my hand.

"So what can I do for you?" Cecil asks.

"You can tell me where your niece is."

"What niece?"

"Your great niece, Katrina McAtamney."

"Niece?"

"Yeah. You forget to tell us that Eileen McAtamney is your niece and that Kat is your great niece."

"Must have slipped my mind."

"Where is she?"

"I have no idea where she is. I thought she was dead. Aren't you conducting a murder inquiry now?" he says coughing.

Coughing is one of his tells. For a tinker, he lies very badly.

I pet the goat. A bee flies across my line of sight. Those scudding sail boats change tack at exactly the same time.

"Beer?" he asks.

"Don't mind if I do."

He goes into the caravan and comes back with a can of Bass.

I pop the lid and drink.

The sky full of gulls and puffins and above us the odd goshawk and grey teal. The sun four fingers above the headland now and night will be here in an hour or less. The sea changing colour. From a crisp Prussian Blue to a warmer indigo and we watch as one of the sailboats glides serenely into the bay.

He turns to look at me. I meet his look. *I know*, and *he knows that I know.*

"Where?" I ask.

"Where what?"

"Where did she go after Carol McCawley tried to murder her?"

"I don't know what you're talking about."

"Sure, you do. She told you everything. Carol McCawley thought her husband was in love with Kat and wanted to kill her. Carol waited by her car and kidnapped her and drove her all the way up near here to the edge of the Bann and made Kat sit in the front while she pushed the car into the water. The car sank, but Kat didn't sink. Kat was a champion swimmer. She learned to swim in France and she was the bloody best in her class."

"Not just her class. Won the French national two-hundred-metre under-twelve freestyle," Cecil says proudly.

I take another gulp of Bass and lean back in the chair. The things I'd been through for this case. Who could have thought one girl could stir up so much shit?

I get to my feet.

"It was the middle of the night and she was drenched, half dead.

She'd walked here from the River Bann and you took her in and told her to call the cops and she said that she didn't want to call the cops because that lady was a crazy fucking lady, but a powerful crazy fucking lady and all she wanted to do was disappear for a while."

Cecil says nothing.

"You saved her life. She could have died of shock or hypothermia. You did well, old-timer," I tell him.

I offer him my hand, and he shakes it.

His eyes narrow and fill with tears.

I let go of his hand, pet the goat and walk to the car.

"Where are you going now?" Cecil asks.

"Up here at the very top of Ireland you can pretty much only go south."

# 28

# THE STONE OF DIVISIONS

The A2 to the M1 to the A4. Through Augher, Clogher and Five-miletown. A change to the little-known, little-used Clones Road. At Clones I stop to get a bite to eat and a pint at a little bar I know called the Mill. From Clones it's a dreary two-hour drive along minor roads through the grim Irish midlands until I get to Mullingar where I stop and buy a local map. From Mullingar it's a five-mile drive west to the hill of the Uisneach. I've been here before on a school trip. There are two sacred hills in Ireland: Tara Hill and this one. This one gets a tenth of the visitors of Tara, but in the olden days this was where the High Kings were crowned under the moonlight.

The old ones know this.

The Travellers know this.

I find the campsite on the north side of the hill just on the edge of the village, near running water and a wood. Two dozen caravans. A big community.

I ask for Bob Patterson but no one appears to understand me.

I ask in Irish and this time there are a few takers. He might be down by the blacksmith's forge.

Down to the forge on the edge of a millstream and under a sycamore tree. Horse shoes are being turned out of the moulds and bent into shape by a pair of smiths who seem to be racing one another to get the job done.

I spy a tall, slender boy with red hair watching the race with obvious excitement. Next to him is the prettiest girl in the village. Probably in the entire county.

I watch them for a while and when they go back up the hill towards the caravans I step in behind them.

"Kat?" I inquire.

She turns. "Yes?"

I show her my warrant card. "Detective Inspector Sean Duffy, Carrick RUC."

Her hand goes to her mouth. "How did you find me?"

"The postcard."

"Oh."

"Is there a problem here?" Robert Patterson asks.

"Not at all," I reply in Irish.

Kat looks at him and looks at me and shakes her head. "I'm going to walk with Inspector Duffy for a bit, you go on now, Robert, and get the supper on."

"Are you sure now?" Robert wonders.

"Absolutely. Would you like to walk in the wood, Inspector Duffy? It's not the time of year for it, but it's been very mild."

We go for a walk in the hazel wood that also has a few big spreading yellow river oaks covered with mistletoe. If you've read *The Golden Bough* you'll understand why the Travellers come here and the priests of Lugh before that.

"How much do you know?" Kat asks.

"Oh, pretty much everything, now," I tell her.

"I'm not coming back to testify. I'm happy here," she says.

"We've charged Carol McCawley with kidnapping and murder."

"Really?"

"Yes. And she's confessed to it all too."

"Good."

"The DPP will, of course, change the murder charge to attempted murder."

"What's the bloody difference? She tried to kill me. It was just luck I got away."

"Luck, yes, and being an excellent swimmer."

"You heard about that? I suppose Uncle Cecil told you."

"Yes."

"That's why I was so calm when I knew what she was going to do. She wasn't going to shoot me and dump my body in the river. She was going to try and drown me and make it look like an accident. If I could get out of the car I knew I'd be ok."

"And were you ok?"

"The current was stronger than I was expecting, and I was pretty disorientated under the water, but I just kept going. It was so dark and so cold but eventually I bumped into the bank."

"You did very well, Kat."

I pick up an oak branch covered with shining mistletoe from top to bottom. I show it to her and she takes it from me.

"You want to know the difference between murder and attempted murder? It's about fifteen years."

"She's a real nutcase," Kat says. "I hope she's in there for a long time."

"Yeah. Nutcase might be the word, but we can't let her go to prison for a murder she didn't commit can we?"

Kat shrugs. "So how long would she get for *attempted* murder?"

"If she sticks with the guilty plea and saves the crown the expense of a trial, I expect they'll run the kidnap and the attempted murder concurrently. Five, maybe seven, years?"

"That's not long enough."

"I quite agree, but the law is the law."

We make our way through the little wood to the Stone of the Divisions—the dead centre, the mystical centre of all of Ireland. I touch the stone and Kat touches the stone and she whispers something in Irish and I whisper something too.

And then we walk back towards the caravan site. Fires have been lit and all the stars are out.

"So, if you hadn't found me they could have put her away for life," she says.

"Maybe if you hadn't sent that postcard."

"A million ifs."

"A million ifs."

We arrive back at the caravan site where wood is being chopped, horses are being shoed, and dinner is being prepared. A five-year-old fiddler is practicing his scales and he isn't bad.

Kat waves to everyone and everyone smiles at the sight of her.

Yes, she's very pretty indeed. It isn't surprising that all those foolish middle-aged men had lost their heads.

It's probably my duty to ask her to come back and testify against the men for statutory rape but I know there was no point. MI5 and Special Branch are protecting Dunbar, and Jones and Charles McCawley have enough shit to deal with.

"So what does this Robert do with himself?" I ask.

She looks at me through those long dark eyelashes.

"He fixes cars. He's learning to fix cars."

"You could do better."

"I could do worse."

"Does he hit you?"

"Never."

"What about your mother?"

"What about her?"

"She misses you."

"She misses having the maid of all work around to do everything for her."

"Well, there's probably that too."

She crosses her arms. "I'm not going back, and you can't force me to go back without dragging in the Irish police, am I right?"

I nod. "If I took you against your will it would be kidnap on my part, but it wouldn't be that difficult to get a local court order and have the Garda grab you and ship you north."

"But you're not going to do any of that are you, Inspector Duffy?"

I smile again. "How did you get to be such a good judge of character?"

"I'm a good judge of men. I know what men are thinking."

It's depressing to realise how she had become such a good judge of men.

We stop at a group of children feeding dock leaves to a big white stallion. I grab a handful of sweet grass and gave it to him and his nostrils flare with delight as he munches it down.

"Give her a call now and again, ok? She's not a bad woman. She's been hard done by life."

"We've all been hard done by life."

"Aye. You'll call her though?"

"I'll call."

I turn to face her. "Well, it's nice to meet you, Katrina. I'm glad I found you. It's very good to see that you're alive."

"It's nice to meet you too, Inspector Duffy."

"I have to be heading back now."

"Will you stop for a cup of tea before you go?"

"No, it's a long drive. I better get going."

"I'll walk you to your car."

She walks me to the Beemer. I offer her my hand, but she kisses me on the cheek instead.

"I will have to tell them you're alive, of course, as I'm an officer of the court, but I don't think they'll need your testimony. If you are alive to tell them everything Carol McCawley did to you, I imagine the defence will just stick to a guilty plea for attempted murder."

"I'm glad to hear that," she said.

"Goodbye, Kat."

"Bye, Inspector Duffy."

I drive east this time.

All the way to the motorway they are building from Dublin to

Drogheda with EU money. I try out this new motorway and it proves good.

Drogheda, Dundalk, Newry, Belfast, Carrickfergus.

I drop by the station. Upstairs to CID. My name is still on my office door. I slide the name plate out. I find Lawson in the Incident Room and walk him down to my office and sat him in my chair in my desk.

"This doesn't feel right," he says.

"You're in charge now."

"It doesn't feel right."

"It's right."

I pour us both a healthy measure of Bowmore. I clink his glass. He looks young and excited and scared and content. Our blue-eyed lad running the station with his gelled hair and his drainpipe trousers and his fucking U2 albums.

"What's the most important thing to remember about being a detective in the RUC?" I ask him.

"Upholding the law. Solving cases. Duty to the—"

"Staying alive, Lawson. Don't get killed on me."

He nods. "I can't believe I'm in charge, Jesus! I keep thinking of that Oscar Wilde quote: 'When the gods wish to punish us they give us what we want.'"

"I counter that with Willy Wonka," I say and take a penultimate swig of whisky.

"What do you mean Willy Wonka?" Lawson said.

"Haven't you seen the film?"

"No."

I shake my head, finish the Bowmore and get to my feet. "I better go lad. I'm getting the midnight ferry across the sheugh."

"Um, yes, of course, sir," he says.

"Oh, and you'll need to talk to Janice O'Leary in the DPP's office in the morning. You'll need to change the charges against Mrs McCawley."

"Why's that?"

"Kat McAtamney is alive and well and living near the Stone of the Divisions on Uisneach Hill in County Westmeath."

"What? Alive! Are you sure?"

"I talked to her this afternoon. So better change those murder charges, eh? Save us all a lot of embarrassment."

I drive the Beemer to the ferry terminal in Belfast. I get onboard and go upstairs for the journey.

"Thus ends Sean Duffy's last case," I say to the seagulls on the lee deck. And thus begins my career as a non detective in the part-time reserve. It will be four years of eating shit and giving out parking tickets until I can collect my pension. But at least I am alive. And that counts for a hell of a lot.

I shiver and go inside to the bar.

"That January air. Gets you every time," the barman says in a Glaswegian burr. "What can I do for you? A wee hot whisky to warm up?"

"Aye, that'll do."

We docked at two in the morning and I'm home by half past the hour.

Pet the cat, kiss the baby, slip in to next the missus.

"Is that you?" she asks.

"*C'est moi.*"

"Did you solve your case?"

"Yeah. Nice one too. I found the murdered girl, alive. That never happens."

"That neighbour across the way left some flowers and an apology note. You see, Sean? Dialogue: it works wonders."

"So it seems."

"Oh, and your replacement called. Sounds like he's in a total panic already. He wants to know the number for the DPP's office."

"I'll give it to him in the morning."

"And he wanted me to get you to tell him the Willy Wonka quote, whatever that means."

"It's just a quote from the film."

"What's the quote?"

"What Wonka says at the end."

"What does he say?"

"'You know what happened to the boy who got everything he wanted?'"

"What?"

"'He lived happily ever after.'"

"God, you're such an old softie, aren't you?"

"Yeah, I think I bloody am," I tell her and turn off the light.